E. H. (Edward Hayes) Plumptre

The Life of Thomas Ken, D.D.

Bishop of Bath and Wells: Vol. II.

E. H. (Edward Hayes) Plumptre

The Life of Thomas Ken, D.D.
Bishop of Bath and Wells: Vol. II.

ISBN/EAN: 9783337095130

Printed in Europe, USA, Canada, Australia, Japan

Cover: Foto ©Raphael Reischuk / pixelio.de

More available books at **www.hansebooks.com**

THE LIFE OF
THOMAS KEN, D.D.

BISHOP OF BATH AND WELLS

By E. H. PLUMPTRE, D.D.

DEAN OF WELLS

WITH ILLUSTRATIONS BY E. WHYMPER

———

"Of whom the world was not worthy."

———

"Isti sunt triumphatores et amici Dei, qui, contemnentes
  jussa principum, meruerunt præmia æterna :
Modò coronantur et accipiunt palmam.

Isti sunt qui venerunt ex magnâ tribulatione et
  laverunt stolas suas in sanguine Agni :
Modò coronantur et accipiunt palmam."

IN TWO VOLUMES

VOL. II.

LONDON

WM. ISBISTER LIMITED

56 LUDGATE HILL

1889

TABLE OF CONTENTS.

VOL. II.

———•———

XVIII.

PAGE

THE TRIAL OF THE SEVEN BISHOPS, A.D. 1688 . . 1

XIX.

THE REVOLUTION OF A.D. 1688 24

XX.

HESITATION — FINAL DECISION — DEPARTURE FROM
WELLS, A.D. 1689—1691 37

Note.—BISHOP KIDDER 60

XXI.

KEN AND THE NON-JURORS TO THE DEATH OF MARY,
A.D. 1689—1694 64

Notes.—1. THE JACOBITE LITURGY AND MODEST ENQUIRY 82

    2. KEN'S LETTER TO ARCHBISHOP TENISON . . 86

XXII.

KEN AND THE NON - JURORS TO THE DEATH OF
WILLIAM III., A.D. 1694—1702 95

Note.—DID KEN WRITE 'THE ROYAL SUFFERER?'. . 115

XXIII.

KEN AND THE NON-JURORS UNDER QUEEN ANNE, A.D.
1702—1705 119

XXIV.

PAGE

EPISODES IN PRIVATE LIFE, A.D. 1695—1710 :

  1. THE "STUDENT-PENITENT" OF 1695 . . . 155

  2. THE TRAGEDY OF STATFOLD 160

  3. LEWIS SOUTHCOMBE, PENITENT . . . 163

  4. THE LADIES OF NAISH COURT . . 167

  5. KEN AND ELIZABETH ROWE 172

  6. KEN'S 'LYRA INNOCENTIUM' . . . 174

XXV.

LITERARY CORRESPONDENCE WITH DR. THOMAS SMITH   179

XXVI.

CLOSING YEARS AND DEATH, A.D. 1709—1711 . . 191

Appendix.—KEN'S WILL 206

XXVII.

KEN'S MORNING, EVENING, AND MIDNIGHT HYMNS . 210

XXVIII.

KEN AS A POET AND THEOLOGIAN 231

XXIX.

ESTIMATES, CONTEMPORARY AND LATER . . 257

APPENDICES.

I. KEN PORTRAITS 291

II. KEN'S BOOKS 294

INDEX   303

KEN'S LETTERS.

VOL. II.

LETTER   PAGE

XXII. To VISCOUNT WEYMOUTH. (Longleat MSS.) 13

XXIII. To LORD DARTMOUTH. (Dartmouth MSS.) 15

XXIV. To ARCHBISHOP SANCROFT. (R., p. 41. A., p. 474) . . 22

XXV. To ARCHBISHOP SANCROFT. (A., p. 489. From Tanner MSS.,
xxviii., p. 299) 28

XXVI. To VISCOUNT WEYMOUTH. (Longleat MSS.) 37

XXVII. To VISCOUNT WEYMOUTH. (Longleat MSS.) 39

XXVIII. To HENRY DODWELL. (Morrison MSS.) 41

XXIX. To HENRY DODWELL. (Morrison MSS.) 42

XXX. To BISHOP BURNET. (R., p. 18. A., p. 530. From Hawkins,
Life) 48

XXXI. To MRS. GRIGGE. (B., ii., p. 192. R., p. 43. A., p. 605,
Malet MSS) 52

XXXII. To THE REV. MR. HARBIN. (B., ii., p. 198. R., p. 44. A.,
p. 370. From Malet MSS) . . . 54

XXXIII. To ARCHBISHOP SANCROFT. (A., p. 564. From Tanner MSS.,
xxvii., p. 155) 66

XXXIV. To BISHOP LLOYD. (R., p. 48. From Williams MSS.) . 78

XXXV. To ROBERT NELSON. (A., p. 671. From Life of Kettlewell,
App., p. lxxxvi.) 102

XXXVI. To VISCOUNT WEYMOUTH. (Longleat MSS.) . . . 106

XXXVII. To DR. THOMAS SMITH. (R., p. 45. From Smith MSS.,
Bodleian Library) 107

XXXVIII. To DEAN HICKES. (R., p. 48. From Bodleian Library) . 108

XXXIX. To DEAN HICKES. (R., p. 50. From Bodleian Library) . 110

XL. To REV. MR. HARBIN. (B., ii., p. 228. R., p. 53. A., p. 682.
From Malet MSS.) 111

XLI. To REV. MR. HARBIN. (B., ii., p. 231. R., p. 54. A., p.
682. From Malet MSS.) . . . 112

XLII. To HENRY DODWELL. (Communicated by Rev. Canon Moor) 113

XLIII. To BISHOP LLOYD. (R., p. 55. A., p. 699. From Williams
MSS.) 120

XLIV. To BISHOP LLOYD. (R., p. 55. A., p. 699. From Williams
MSS.) 122

XLV. To BISHOP LLOYD. (R., p. 54. From Williams MSS.) . 123

LETTER   PAGE
XLVI. To Bishop Lloyd.   (B., ii., 246. R., p. 58. From Williams
                          MSS.)   124
XLVII. To Bishop Lloyd. (R., p. 59. From Williams MSS.)   . 125
XLVIII. To Bishop Lloyd. (R., p. 60. Prom Williams MSS.)   . 126
XLIX. To Bishop Lloyd.   (R., p. 61. A., p. 703. From Williams
                          MSS.)   127
L. To Bishop Lloyd.   (R., p. 62. A., p. 704. From Williams
                          MSS.)   128
LI. To Bishop Lloyd.   (R., p. 63. A., p. 706. From Williams
                          MSS.)   129
LII. To Bishop Lloyd.   (R., p. 64. A., p. 70. From Williams
                          MSS.)   129
LIII. To Bishop Lloyd.   (R., p. 65. A., p. 713. From Williams
                          MSS.)   130
LIV. To Bishop Hooper.   (B., ii., p. 249. R., p. 65. A., p. 712.
                          From Prowse MS.)   131
LV. To Bishop Lloyd.   (B., ii., p. 241. R., p. 66. A., p. 712.
                          From Williams MSS.)   .   .   .   133
LVI. To Bishop Hooper.   (B., ii., p. 250. R., p. 67. A., p. 714.
                          From Prowse MS.)   134
LVII. To Bishop Lloyd.   (R., p. 80. A., p. 715. From Williams
                          MSS.)   138
LVIII. To Bishop Lloyd. (R., p. 81. A., p. 716. From Williams
                          MSS.)   139
LIX. To Bishop Lloyd.   (R., p. 82. From Williams MSS.) .   . 140
LX. To Bishop Lloyd.   (R., p. 68. A., p. 718. From Williams
                          MSS.)   141
LXI. To Bishop Lloyd.   (R., p. 68. A., p. 720. From Williams
                          MSS.)   143
LXII. To Bishop Lloyd.   (B., ii., p. 262. R., p. 74. A., p. 723.
                          From Williams MSS.)   .   .   .   145
LXIII. To Bishop Lloyd. (R., p. 76. A., p. 724. From Williams
                          MSS.)   146
LXIV. To Bishop Lloyd.   (R., p. 78. A., p. 727. From Williams
                          MSS.)   140
LXV. To Bishop Hooper.   (B., ii., p. 252. R., p. 78. A., p. 730.
                          From Prowse MS.)   150
LXVI. To Bishop Lloyd.   (R., p. 60. A., p. 732. From Williams
                          MSS.)   152
LXVII. To Bishop Hooper. (B., ii., p. 253. R., p. 79. A., p. 735.
                          From Prowse MS.)   153
LXVIII. To Mrs. Graham. (From Paget's *Student Penitent*)   . . 158
LXIX. To Viscount Weymouth. (Longleat MSS.)   170
LXX. To Viscount Weymouth. (Longleat MSS.)   171
LXXI. To Dr. Thomas Smith. (R., p. 84. From Smith MSS. in
                          Bodleian Library)   181
LXXII. To Dr. Thomas Smith. (R., p. 85. From Smith MSS., in
                          Bodleian Library) .   .   .   181

LETTER   PAGE

LXXIII. To Dr. Thomas Smith. (R., p. 89. From Smith MSS., in Bodleian Library) 182

LXXIV. To Dr. Thomas Smith. (R., p. 92. From Smith MSS., in Bodleian Library) 184

LXXV. To Dr. Thomas Smith. (R., p. 93. From Smith MSS., in Bodleian Library) 184

LXXVI. To Dr. Thomas Smith. (R., p. 95. From Smith MSS. in Bodleian Library) 185

LXXVII. To Dr. Thomas Smith. (R., p. 98. From Smith MSS. in Bodleian Library) 186

LXXVIII. To Dr. Thomas Smith. (R., p. 161. From Smith MSS., in Bodleian Library) 187

LXXIX. To Dr. Thomas Smith. (R., p. 104. From Smith MSS., in Bodleian Library) 188

LXXX. To Dr. Thomas Smith. (R., p. 108. From Smith MSS. in Bodleian Library) 189

LXXXI. To Henry Dodwell. (From Morrison MSS.) . . . 193

LXXXII. To Robert Nelson. (A., p. 776. From Marshall's *Defence of Constitution*, 1717) 194

LXXXIII. To Henry Dodwell. (Communicated by T. M. Fallow, Esq.) 195

LXXXIV. To Viscount Weymouth. (Longleat MSS.) . . . 196

LXXXV. To Rev. Mr. Cressy. (Sloane MSS., 4,274-15, British Museum) 197

ABBREVIATIONS.

A—Anderdon, *Life of Ken,* by A Layman. Second Edition.
B—Bowles, *Life of Ken.*
R—Round, *Prose Works of Ken.*

LIST OF ILLUSTRATIONS.

VOL. II.

———•———

	PAGE
FAC-SIMILE OF THE DRAFT PETITION OF THE SEVEN BISHOPS (from the Original in Sancroft's Hand, in the Bodleian Library)	*Frontispiece*
MEDALS TO COMMEMORATE ACQUITTAL OF THE SEVEN BISHOPS .	. 9, 36
SANCROFT'S DESIGN FOR MEDAL .	11
LONGLEAT .	57
FAC-SIMILE OF LETTER FROM KEN	. 112
KEN'S PATEN AND CHALICE	. 190
KEN'S TOMB .	. 205
KEN'S COFFEE-POT .	. 230

CHAPTER XVIII.

THE TRIAL OF THE SEVEN BISHOPS.

> " And next I mark, 'twas trial did convey
> Or grief, or pain, or strange eventful day,
> To my tormented soul such larger grace."
>
> *J. H. Newman.*

THE tale of that passage from Whitehall Stairs to the Traitors' Gate, on the evening of that " Black Friday," June 8th, has been told by many masters of narrative. We see the crowds that follow the Bishops to the river's edge, and kneel, asking for their blessing, or rush towards the boats, that they may grasp their hands or touch the hem of their garments. We hear the shouts of the thousands who greeted them as the saviours of their Church and country. Even the soldiers of the Tower by turns fall on their knees before them, and drink their health, in spite of orders to the contrary, with three times three. To one of those who listened to that clamour there must have come, if I mistake not, as there did to William III., when he too was for the moment the idol of the people, the memory of a crowd that once shouted to-day, 'Hosanna,' and to-morrow, ' Crucify.' We at least may remember that, within two years from that day, men were writing pamphlets against Ken and the other non-juring Bishops, and were stirring up the people to that form of 'lynching' which was then known as ' De Witting,' a phrase which to Ken, who had lived in Holland, was only too terribly significant (p. 66).

Men noticed at the time, and doubtless the Bishops themselves felt, that the Second Lesson for that day, as the Calendar then stood (2 Cor. vi.), seemed as if it had a special message to those who, like St. Paul, were called to "approve themselves

as ministers of God, in much patience, in afflictions, in dis-
tresses, in stripes, *in imprisonments*, in tumults, in labours, in
watchings, in fastings." Some of them may have remembered
how the Lesson for the day (Matt. xxvii.) had brought a like
message to Charles I. on the morning of his execution. On
June 10th, Trinity Sunday, the prisoners received the Holy
Communion in the Tower Chapel. The Chaplain had received
special orders from Sunderland to read the Declaration. He
chose rather to suffer affliction with the confessors who were
communicating with him, did not read it, and was dismissed
from his office. The week that followed was one continual
levée. The Bishops were allowed to walk in the precincts of
the Tower, and crowds of all classes, including the very soldiers
on guard, came to ask their blessing. The courtyard was
crowded with the carriages of those of higher rank, among whom
Clarendon was conspicuous. Ten Nonconformists came to express their sympathy and admiration.[1] Evelyn paid a visit on
June 13th, of which Sancroft, Ken, Turner, and Lloyd were
the special objects. We note, with something of the feeling
that " such is life! " that the next entry in his *Diary* records
that he dined on the following day with Jeffreys, and wonder
whether his visit to the Bishops formed a topic of conversation.

One memorable event was brought to the Bishops' knowledge
whilst they were in the Tower. On the morning of Sunday,
June 10th, the long-expected heir to the throne was born at
St. James's Palace, to which the Queen had been carried
after midnight from Whitehall. Sunderland and the Roman
Catholic lords, supported by Jeffreys, urged the King to
signalize the occasion by a general pardon, but in vain.[2] That
birth was destined to play a memorable part in the life of each
of the prisoners, to determine their decisions on great critical
questions this way or that, to advance two to higher positions
in the Church, to consign the other five to an old age of deprivation and poverty. These last, at all events, were not likely
to give credence to the " warming-pan " story, which William
affected to believe, on which Burnet and Lloyd again and
again insisted, but which has now been relegated to the

---

[1] Reresby, p. 396.   [2] Clarendon, ii. 206.

mythical history which is the offspring of popular suspicion. Neither then, nor afterwards, did Ken doubt the legitimacy of the Prince. For him, at least, who believed the father to be incapable of such a fraud, the son was never the Pretender.

Their imprisonment did not last long. Within a week of their committal, on June 15, the Bishops were brought before the Court of King's Bench, and this time, the question having been argued and decided against them, they did not stand on their privilege as peers, and were content to enter into their own recognisances. Had they been required to find sureties, Halifax, or Compton, had arranged to find three peers for each of the seven. It was said that an eminent Nonconformist of the City had "asked for the special honour of being allowed to give surety for Ken."[1] Their progress to and from the Court was attended by the same expressions of enthusiasm as had been shown on their passage to the Tower. When they were seen to leave it, no longer in custody, there were shoutings and ringing of bells. The Abbey struck up a peal, which Sprat, as its Dean, quickly silenced. The prelates made their way to their own houses, or to those of their friends; Ken, probably, to his friend Hooper's Rectory, at Lambeth. Cartwright, the so-called "Papist" Bishop of Chester, one of James's most servile tools, had mingled with the crowd, and was taken by some one, who did not know him, for one of the seven Confessors. The man asked his blessing, and the Bishop gave it. Soon the mistake was discovered, and the suppliant told the "Popish dog" to take his blessing back. The trial was fixed for the 29th of June, and the fortnight that followed the release of the Bishops was spent by them in consultations with counsel, in receiving letters from all parts of the kingdom, even from the Presbyterians of Scotland, of grateful sympathy

---

[1] Macaulay, chap. viii. Mr. Anderdon (p. 432) obtained from Macaulay the information that the Nonconformist was a Quaker. The fact was reported in a dispatch from the Dutch envoy in London. It is, I think, a probable conjecture that the Quaker in question, if not William Penn himself, was one acting under his influence. Penn had been to St. James's on the morning of the previous Sunday, and had urged the King to take the opportunity of the Prince's birth, and to release the Bishops as an act of grace and amnesty. The three peers who were to have answered for Ken were the Earls of Clare, Shrewsbury, and Dorset.—Gutch, *Coll. Curiosa*, i. 356.

and adhesion.   Everywhere the feeling of the people showed
itself in clamorous demonstrations.   The men of Cornwall
revived the burden of an old ballad, and shouted :—

> "And have they fixed the where and when,
>   And must Trelawney die?
> Then thirty thousand Cornish men
>   Will know the reason why." [1]

The memorable 29th at last came, and the lovers of coincidences noted, as doubtless the Bishops themselves felt, that the
services of the day, St. Peter's day, were singularly appropriate.
They told of the Apostle who, because he had said that he must
" obey God rather than man," had been cast into prison, and
had been delivered from it by the ministration of an angel.
The trial, as such, belongs to general history rather than to the
biography of Ken.   It has been told, with more or less fulness,
over and over again, and is probably sufficiently familiar to all
who read these pages.   I must resist the temptation to tell a
twice-told tale yet once more, and will content myself with
what seems to me to fall within my province, by attempting to
enter, more or less conjecturally, of course, into Ken's feelings,
as he watched, in silent expectancy, the proceedings of the trial.
To him, I conceive, the earlier part of those proceedings must
have seemed eminently unsatisfactory.   The counsel for the
defence tried, as they were, of course, bound to do, to win
a verdict for their clients on purely technical grounds.   There
was no sufficient proof that the petition and the signatures were
in the handwriting of the accused.   When that point was settled
by the evidence of Blathwayt, a clerk of the Council, who had
been present when the King interrogated the Bishops on
June 8th, and swore that he had heard the seven prelates own
their signatures, they argued that that confession had been
given under a promise from the King that it should not be
used against them.   When that plea was set aside by the witness swearing that there had been no express promise, they

[1] Macaulay (chap. viii.) quotes the lines with a variation, as if they had been
composed with special reference to the Bishop.   As a matter of fact, however,
they referred to an earlier Trelawney, who had supported Perkin Warbeck against
Henry VII., and was imprisoned at the time in the Tower.—Strickland. *Lives*,
p. 366.   Compare the poem based upon the lines by the Rev. R. S. Hawker, of
Morwenstow.   Another version gives, " Then thirty thousand underground."

started the objection that there was no evidence that the petition
had been written in the county of Middlesex; Sancroft, indeed,
who had written out the petition, had never left Lambeth,
which was not in Middlesex. The Crown lawyers changed
their ground and undertook to prove that the petition, though
not written, had been published, *i.e.* presented to the King, in
that county. But of this there was at first no evidence. No one
had been present when the Bishops presented the petition, and
the King could not be put in the witness-box. Pepys and other
witnesses, including Blathwayt, who had been present at the
Council, while they remembered the Bishops owning their signatures, could not swear that they had admitted the delivery.
That difficulty was got over by sending for Sunderland, just as
the Chief Justice was about to charge the jury, and direct a
verdict of acquittal. He came, and proved that the Bishops had
shown him a petition, and that he admitted them into the royal
closet; and this was held to be sufficient presumptive evidence
of publication, and so that point had to be abandoned. All this, I
imagine, must have seemed to Ken and his fellows wearisome and
unsatisfying. To be set free on such grounds as these would settle
nothing for the future, and would leave the whole battle of the
constitution to be fought over again. It must have been a real
relief to them, when they heard the discussion pass to the graver
questions of the King's dispensing power and of the subject's
right to petition. Their hearts must have burnt within them,
as they listened to that five minutes' speech with which Somers
ended the pleadings on their side, and which established his
fame both as an orator and constitutional lawyer. One by one
he went through every word of the indictment. The petition
was not false, for every fact stated in it could be proved; it was
not malicious, for the Bishops had taken no action till they had
to choose between the King's command and their own conscience; not seditious, for it had not been by them scattered
abroad among the people, but delivered into the King's own
hands; not a libel, because not a single phrase passed the limits
of humble supplication.

After replies from the Attorney- and Solicitor-Generals, the
latter contending that the Bishops had no right to petition
except in Parliament, the judges summed up, each giving his

own view of the case. The Chief Justice was, on the whole, against the prisoners, though he did not go all lengths with the Solicitor-General.[1] Allibone, a Roman Catholic, took the same line. Holloway held, without giving an opinion on the dispensing power, that the petition was such as subjects who think themselves aggrieved had a right to present, and was therefore not a libel. Powell took a bolder tone, treated the Declaration of Indulgence as a nullity, and pronounced against the dispensing power as making an end of parliaments. "That, issue, gentlemen," he said, "I leave to God and your consciences."

It was already dark. The prisoners were allowed, as before, to go to their homes, and the jury were locked up for the night to consider their verdict. One of them, Arnold, the King's brewer, was reported to have said that he would hold out to the last for a verdict of guilty. It was a night of agitated expectancy for all concerned, for the King and his advisers, for the defendants and their friends, for the population of London, for the whole Church and nation. But expectancy at such a time takes different forms, according to the diversity of men's characters. I confine myself to asking how that night was likely to be passed by a man like Ken, feeling, as he did, all the issues for himself and others that hung on the verdict of the morrow. The region to which that inquiry leads us is one on which we may well enter with reverent feet, and our words should be wary and few; but I seem to myself to hear in those midnight hours some such words as these, "Father, forgive them, for they know not what they do;" "If it be possible, let this cup pass from me;" "Lord, lay not this sin to their charge;" perhaps, also, words like those which had passed from the lips of William Tyndale on the scaffold at Vilvorde, "Lord, open the King of England's eyes."

The jury were heard to be in loud debate at midnight, and again at three A.M. It was rumoured once more that Arnold was holding out against the rest. At ten the next morning the court met. The accused were, as before, at the bar. Then came the well-known scene. Sir Roger Langley, the

---

[1] "He behaved with great moderation and civility to the Bishops."—Evelyn, June 29th, 1688.

foreman of the jury, reported, in answer to the questions of the Clerk of Assize, that the jury were agreed, and that their verdict was "Not Guilty."[1] How Halifax waved his hat, and the people shouted by their thousands, first in the court and then in Westminster Hall—a shout, as Reresby describes it, which was a "very rebellion of noise;" how the clamours, as Williams told the Nuncio[2] and Sunderland, were mingled with tears of joy; how loud and long huzzas took up the acclamations in Whitehall, in the Strand, the Temple, and the City; how messengers on horseback carried the tidings far and wide throughout the country; how the news reached James in the camp at Hounslow, and how he said, when he was told that the Bishops were acquitted, *Tant pis pour eux;* how, as soon as his back was turned, the soldiers burst into cheers, which they had repressed while he was still in the camp, and how James asked what the shouts meant, and Feversham told him that it was nothing but the troops huzzaing for the acquittal of the Bishops, and the King said, "Do you call that nothing?" and fell back, as before, on the ill-boding words *Tant pis pour*

[1] The fate of those who serve on a jury in some important crisis of national history has always seemed to me a strange instance of the irony of fortune. For a few hours or days every one watches them, thinks of them, talks of them, and then their names sink into the dim obscure. On the principle of giving honour where honour is due, I print the list of the jury who returned the verdict that determined the course of English history :—

NAMES OF THE JURY ON THE TRIAL OF THE SEVEN BISHOPS.
Sir Roger Langley, of Westminster, Foreman.
Sir William Hill, Teddington.
Robert Jennings, Hayes, Esq.
Thomas Harriot, Islington, Esq.
Jeffrey Nightingale, St. Giles, Cripplegate, Esq.
William Withers, ditto   ditto, Esq.
William Dacres, Enfield, Esq.
Thomas Austin, South Mims, Esq.
Nicolas Grice, Heston, Esq.
Michael Arnold, Westminster, Esq.
Thomas Done, St. Giles-in-the-Fields, Esq.
Richard Shoreditch, Tottenham.

The jury would seem to have been, as was natural in such a case, a special one. Should these pages fall under the notice of any of their descendants I shall be glad if they will favour me with any information as to the life and character of those to whom England owes so much.

[2] Adda says *il Avvocato.* Possibly he may have meant Powys.

eux—of all this we may say, Is it not written in the pages of Macaulay?[1]

It was, perhaps, significant of the prominent position that Ken had occupied throughout, that his name followed Sancroft's in the indictment, and that, when the prelates left the court, he accompanied the Primate in his carriage. Their journey, which was, perhaps, intentionally made in this way, and instead of being by water, took them through the Strand, Fleet Street, Ludgate Hill, Cheapside, across London Bridge, and so on by Southwark to Lambeth, had the character of a triumphal procession. The crowds gathered round the coach, and insisted on both the prelates giving them their blessing. They, of course, complied with the request, and as they did so, repeated, again and again, the counsel, "Keep to your religion."[2]

That 30th of June was, however, memorable, in yet another way, in its bearing on the history of England. It was on that day that Henry Sidney dispatched the famous memorial to William, signed by some of the chief nobles and statesmen of England, begging him to come over and help them, and defend their religion and their liberties. Compton, who had all along been privy to the negotiations, was the only bishop who signed it.

The week that followed was one of rejoicing through the

---

[1] The counsel who defended the Bishops were Sir Robert Sawyer (i. 90, *n.* 3), Pollexfen, Finch, Somers. It may be mentioned that Sawyer and Finch, on one occasion, refused their fees of twenty guineas. The costs were assessed at £240 16s. 6d., and were paid by the Bishops at the rate of six per cent. on the revenues of their sees—Sancroft's being estimated at £4,000, Turner's at £2,000, Ken's at £900. (Dallaway's *Western Sussex*, p. 91; Gutch, *Collect. Curios.*, ii., 368 —360.) The expenses included an express sent by Ken to Oxford, and two to Exeter (*Ibid.* ii. 377). They were probably intended to urge the bishops or deans of those cities to follow the example of the Seven Confessors in refusing to read the Declaration. Trelawney, in a letter to Sancroft, of August 16th, 1688, refers to letters which he and Ken had written to Bishop Lamplugh to that effect. That prelate's motto, however, was, "I will be safe," and he was rewarded for his subservience with the Archbishopric of York. The Dean was faithful to his trust.

[2] Ken was staying with his friend Hooper at Lambeth Rectory (Prowse MS.). The Grenadiers of Lord Lichfield's regiment, who had been posted at Lambeth, received the Archbishop with military honours, made a lane for his passage from the river to the palace, and fell on their knees to ask his blessing.—Ellis, *Corresp.*, i. 350. in Anderdon (p. 433). This, however, was on June 15th, on their release from the Tower.

whole kingdom at the great and unlooked-for deliverance. Portraits of the Bishops were sold by thousands.[1] Not less than eight different medals were issued to commemorate their acquittal, were worn round the neck, treasured up in families, handed down afterwards as heir-looms.[2] The Bishops were

MEDAL TO COMMEMORATE ACQUITTAL OF SEVEN BISHOPS.

[1] The Sutherland Collection in the Bodleian contains a series of seventeen folio and quarto prints of the seven oval portraits, some with the heading, "The Seven Candlesticks," for which the sketches were taken as they sat in court. One of these, Gribelin's, has the device, "Protestant Christianity restored in England."

[2] I reproduce a list of these from Anderdon.

"1. The White Tower of London; in the distance are the Bishops approaching under guard. *Legend.* PROBIS HONORI INFAMLÆQUE MALIS. Honour to the good, infamy to the bad. *Exurge.* ARCHIEPISC. CANTUAR : EPISCOPI· S! ASAPH. BATH. ET WELL. ELY. PETER³ CHICHEST. BRIST. INCARCER. $\frac{8}{18}$ LIBERATI $\frac{15}{25}$ IUNII. 1688.

Reverse. The Sun and Moon equally balanced in scales suspended from the clouds. *Leg.* SIC SOL LUNAQUE IN LIBRA.

2¼ inch diam.

2. Bust of Abp. Sancroft, wearing a cap and robes. *Leg.* GVIL. SANCROFT. ARCHIEPISC. CANTUAR. 1688.

Rev. Busts of the six imprisoned Bishops round that of the Bp. of London. G.B.F. (Geo. Bowers. fecit.)

Edge. SI FRACTUS ILLABATUR ORBIS IMPAVIDOS FERIENT RUINÆ.

2 inch diam.

3. A variety of the preceding, the date in Roman numerals.

4. Bust of Abp. Sancroft, same as No. 2.

Rev. Seven stars in the middle of the starry heavens. *Leg.* QVIS RESTRINGET PLEIADVM DELICIAS. IOB. C. 38. (See p. 36).

2 inch diam.

received on their return to their dioceses with acclamations which reminded students of Church history of those which had greeted Athanasius and Chrysostom on their return from exile.[2] Bonfires and ringing of bells proclaimed, as at Peterborough, the joy of the people, where the thanksgiving service for the birth of the Prince of Wales had been received in sullen silence. In what way Ken's own diocese testified its joy I have not as yet been able to trace, except in the parish of North Curry, where the bells were rung "on the deliverance of the Bishops from the Tower." Letters came from Scotland reporting to Sancroft "the strange news that the Bishops of England are in great veneration among the Presbyterians of Scotland."[2]

Ken remained for some time in town, and was much in San-

5. Bust of Abp. Sancroft, wearing a cap and robes. *Leg.* GVIL SANCROFT ARCHIEP^s CANT.
   Rev. Church founded upon a rock, in the midst of the sea, and assailed by the four winds. *Leg.* IMMOTA TRIUMPHANS.
   1¼ inch diam.
6. A Jesuit and a Monk, with spade and pickaxe, endeavouring to undermine a Church, which is supported by a hand from Heaven. *Leg.* THE GATES OF HELL SHALL NOT PREVAILE. *Matt. xvi.* 18.
   Rev. Seven medallions of the Archbishop and six Bishops, a mitre over each, and name below. *Leg.* WISDOM HATH BUILDED HER HOVS: SHE HATH HEWEN OVT HER 7 PILLERS. *Prov. ix.* 1.
   2¼ inch diam.
7. Same device. *Leg.* THE GATES OF HELL SHALL NOT PREVAILE AGAINST IT.
   Rev. Seven medallions of the Archbishop and Bishops, with their names. Stars interspersed.
   Edge. UPON THIS ROCK HAVE I BUILT MY CHURCH.
   1⅞ inch diam.
8. A Jesuit and a Monk, with spade and pickaxe, endeavouring to undermine a Church, supported by a hand from Heaven; the field chequered. *Leg. incuse.* THE GATES OF HELL SHALL NOT PREVAIL AGAINST IT. A border of large beads.
   Rev. Medallions of the Abp. and Bishops. Legend incuse; the field radiated.
   1½ inch diam."

In addition to these there is the singular design (p. 11) found in Sancroft's papers (*Tanner MSS.*, Bodleian Library), with its Greek inscription. I know nothing of it beyond the fact of its existence, and am in doubt whether it was meant for presentation to the Bishops' counsel, or as a recognition of the work of a higher Advocate.

¹ Overton, *Life in E.C.*, p. 82, with special reference to Lake.
² Gutch, *Collect. Curiosa*, i., 383.

croft's counsels. His hand is to be traced, with a probability little short of certainty, in the *Instructions*[1] which the Primate issued to the Bishops in the course of the following month. The document is a little wordy, and I give extracts that sufficiently indicate its character, instead of quoting it *in extenso*.

The clergy are exhorted to be patterns of all holy conversation ; to be constantly resident ; to catechise the children ; to have daily service even in villages ; to urge frequent commu-

nion. They are, " four times a year at the least," to preach against all usurped and foreign jurisdiction. They are further, "the King's power being in his dominions highest under God," upon all occasions to persuade the people to loyalty and obedience to his Majesty in all things lawful, and to patient submission in the rest; promoting, as far as in them lies, the public peace and quiet of the world.

They are further to " exhort all those of our communion to continue steadfast to the end in their most Holy Faith, . . . to

[2] D'Oyly, *Life of Sancroft*, chap. vii.

take heed of all seducers, especially of Popish emissaries;"
and inasmuch as "those emissaries were commonly most busie
and troublesome to our people at the end of their lives, labour-
ing to proselite and perplex them in time of sickness and in
the hour of death,"[1] the clergy were to be more diligent than
ever in the work of visiting the sick, "watching over every
sheep within their fold . . . lest those *evening* wolves devour
them." In what follows I trace Ken's influence yet more
distinctly. It is entirely on the lines of his own thought and
action, and, though Sancroft had been more lenient to the Dissenters than Sheldon, is in advance of anything he had before
written. The Bishops are to instruct their clergy—

"That they also walk in Wisdom towards those that are not of
our Communion: and if there be in their Parishes any such, that
they neglect not frequently to confer with them in the Spirit of
Meekness, seeking by all good ways and means to gain and win
them over to our Communion: More especially that they have a
very tender Regard to our *Brethren* the *Protestant Dissenters;* that
upon occasion offered, they visit them at their houses, and receive
them kindly at their own, and treat them fairly, wherever they meet
them, discoursing calmly and civilly with them; perswading them (if
it may be) to a full Compliance with our *Church,* or at least, that
' whereto we have already attained, we may all walk by the same
Rule, and mind the same thing.' And in order hereunto that
they take all opportunities of assuring and convincing them, that
the *Bishops* of this Church are really and sincerely irreconcileable
Enemies to the Errors, Superstitions, Idolatries and Tyrannies of
the Church of *Rome;* and that the very unkind Jealousies, which
some have had of us to the contrary, were altogether groundless.
"And in the last place, that they warmly and most affectionately
exhort them, to join with us in daily fervent Prayer to the God of
Peace, for an universal blessed *Union* of all *Reformed Churches,*[2] both

---

[1] Was Ken, or Sancroft, thinking of Charles II. and Huddleston?
[2] The words seem singularly significant, as pointing to the enlargement of
sympathies which followed on the sense of a common danger. The Protestants
of Germany and Sweden, the Reformed Churches of France, Switzerland, and
Holland, were all distinctly recognised as Churches, though they might be wanting in some elements of polity or worship that were necessary for the completeness of a Church. In the idealism of the moment the hope of union included
the Dissenting Communities in England and the Presbyterians in Scotland.
Alas! too soon the dreamers found that neither the hour, nor the man, had come.

at *home* and *abroad*, against our common Enemies; that all they who do confess the holy Name of our dear Lord, and do agree in the Truth of His holy word, may also meet in one holy Communion, and live in perfect Unity and godly Love."[1]

Ken, we may assume, was active in circulating the Instructions among his own clergy, and in exhorting them not to read the King's Declaration. About that time, I think it probable that he returned to Wells, and that the following letter, in which he gives his forecast as to the impending crisis, though bearing no date of place, was written from the palace :—

LETTER XXII.

To VISCOUNT WEYMOUTH.

"All Glory be to God.

"MY VERY GOOD LORD,

"I have a great many acknowledgments to returne to your Lordshippe for the favour of your last visitt, and of your present letter, wch answers those intimations I gave you hence, & wh: I had received when I was last in Towne. I confess I do believe y^t God is doing some great thing for the good of His Church, but, in all probability, some medicinall Chastisement will goe before, to render us the more fitt to receive a blessing. I am further persuaded y^t God will doe ye work Himselfe: so that wee are not to rely on ye arme of flesh; but ye true disposition in wch this Church ought now to be, is most appositely describ'd in ye first Lesson for this day, wch teaches us y^t it is not Ashur y^t shall save us (Hosea xiv. 3), but, that all our hopes of God's Goodnesse to us & of our own prosperity, y^t we shall grow as the Lily, depends on our Returning unto the Lord. I beseech your Lordshippe to present my most humble Service to y^r Good Lady, ye two young Ladys, & to the little Gentileman, & to those Country Confessours who are with you. The blessing of this life & ye next be multiplied on you all. God of His Infinite mercy give us grace to keep ye Word of His Patience, & keep us in the hour of temptation.

"My Good Lord,

"Your Lordshipp's most humble & affect: Servant,

"THO. BATH & WELLS.

"*Sept.* 1st (1688)."

[1] Gutch's *Collectanea Curiosa*, vol. i., p. 386.

[We note the coincidence of thought with that of the last sermon preached at Whitehall. Ken looked forward, as Micah and Jeremiah had done, to the discipline of suffering. The reference to "Ashur" and the "arm of flesh" obviously points to the hopes which some were building on the intervention of the Prince of Orange, but I doubt whether Ken knew of the invitation that had been sent off on the very day of the acquittal of the Bishops, signed by the Earls of Devonshire, Shrewsbury, Danby, by Compton, Bishop of London, William Russell, nephew of the Duke of Bedford, Lord Lumley, and Colonel Churchill, afterwards Duke of Marlborough. The "Country Confessours" are, I imagine, parochial clergy who had refused to read the Declaration of Indulgence. The steps which James had taken, within a fortnight of the trial, in carrying out his threat of *Tant pis pour eux*, ordering the names of all who refused to read the Declaration to be sent by the Chancellors of Dioceses and Archdeacons, and laid before the Court of Ecclesiastical Commission, might well entitle those who followed in the footsteps of the Bishops, to that honourable title. They had the prospect of nothing less than deprivation, fines, imprisonment, if convicted, and of being tried, not by a judge and jury, but by a tribunal over which Jeffreys presided, and which claimed to be above the limitations of other courts, as to evidence and procedure. The threat proved, it is true, a *brutum fulmen*. The Chancellors and Archdeacons made no returns. Sprat, Bishop of Rochester, resigned his seat on the Commission. He had read the Declaration himself in obedience to the King's commands, but he could not condemn the thousands of pious and loyal divines who had taken a different view of their duty. The Court broke up in confusion, and never met again to take any active measures.]

Towards the end of September the King was informed by Louis XIV., on the report of the French ambassador at the Hague, of the expedition which William was preparing, of the invitation which he was reported to have received, of the presence in Holland of English nobles and gentlemen who had gone over to support him.[1]

James was alarmed, and in his distress turned to the very men whom a few weeks before he had sent to the Tower. He clung, we may believe, to the hope that they, at least, were loyal to him. If I am not mistaken, he trusted most of all to Ken's personal affection. The Bishops of London, Winchester, Ely, Bath and Wells, Peterborough, Bristol and Rochester, received a letter from Sunderland informing them that the King

---

[1] At the levee on September 24th, James reported the tidings to those who attended it. "Now," he said, "we shall see what the Church of England men will do." "Your Majesty will see," was Clarendon's answer, "that they will act as honest men, though they have been somewhat ill-used of late." On September 27th Jeffreys, who was getting alarmed, told Clarendon that "some rogues had changed the King's mind, that he would yield in nothing to the Bishops; that the Virgin Mary was to do all."—Clarendon, ii., pp. 221—244.

desired to speak with them, and fixing September 28th, 10 A.M., for their attendance. Ken's answer, addressed to Lord Dartmouth, who apparently had transmitted Sunderland's letter, or communicated a like message, is as follows :

LETTER XXIII.

To LORD DARTMOUTH.

"All Glory be to God.

"MY VERY GOOD LORD,

" The expresse your Lordshippe sent I just now reciev'd, and in obedience to his Majesty's pleasure, by whose command I presume you wrott, I will make what haste I can to the towne, though I am the more unfitt for a journy because I came a tedious one yesterday. I did allwayes thinke that his Majesty could never believe our Church would be disloyall, having given so many undeniable instances to the contrary, and I shall be allwayes ready to serve my Sovereign to the utmost of my power, as far as can be consistent with my superiour duty to God and to that Holy Religion I professe. The declaration you mention is not yett sent downe, which I should have been glad to have seen before I leave this place, which I intend to doe, God willing, earelye to morrowe that I may reach London on Wenesday night if possible, time enough I hope to see you before you goe. My humble service to my good Lady. God, of His Infinite goodnesse, multiply his blessings on you booth, and on your children and keepe you all stedfast in our most Holy faith.

"THO. BATH & WELLS.

" *Sept.* 23 (1688)."

[The letter exhibits the painful conflict in Ken's mind. He is "ready to serve his Sovereign to the utmost of his power," but it must be within the limits of his higher duty. He still cherished the hope, apparently, that James, in summoning the Bishops to advise him, was willing to be guided by their counsels. The declaration referred to was probably that which James issued on September 21st, announcing his resolution to maintain the Church of England. Ken's hopes of being in time to see Lord Dartmouth in London probably refer to that nobleman's appointment as Commander of the Fleet against William. It was on this occasion that the offer of a Chaplaincy, referred to in i. 163, was made to Pechell, Master of Magdalen College, Cambridge.]

Ken accordingly presented himself with five other Bishops— Winchester, Ely, Chichester, Peterborough, and Rochester (Sancroft was unwell), at the appointed day and hour. They found James in one of his fits of oscillation. He would not ask their advice about anything definite, but contented himself with vague professions of goodwill towards the Church of England, and with lecturing them on their duty. Ken, who clearly took the lead in the interview, had to express his own disappointment and that of his brethren, that they had been brought up to London on what was practically a fool's errand. " His Majesty's inclinations towards the Church and their duty to him were sufficiently understood before, and would have been equally so, if they had not stirred one foot out of their dioceses."

Sancroft, on hearing from the Bishops of the result of the conference, went to the King, on September 30th, and asked for another interview. James appointed October 2nd. In the meantime he issued a proclamation in the *London Gazette*, calling on his subjects to rally round him against William's invasion, and recalling the writs which he had issued for a new parliament, on the ground of the confusion into which the country had been thrown by it. On the 3rd of October (James had been engaged on the 2nd) Sancroft, with Ken and the other Bishops, Winchester excepted, who had left London, waited on him, and the Primate, after mildly expressing his regret, in Ken's very words, that the first interview had not advanced matters further than "if the Bishops had not stirred one foot out of their dioceses," presented a Memorial which he and the other Bishops had drawn up, for the King's consideration.[1] It was, beyond all question, a State paper of the first order of importance, a Petition of Rights, in which the *gravamina,* of which the Church and nation complained, were fully and deliberately stated, and, as such, I print it nearly *in extenso.* They recommended him

" 1st. To put the administration of government in the several counties into the hands of such of the nobility and gentry as were *legally qualified* for it.

" 2nd. To annul the Ecclesiastical Commission.

[1] D'Oyly, p. 203. The Memorial was signed by all the Bishops who were present. With the addition, " We do also heartily concur,"

H. LONDON.
P. WINCHESTER.
W. ASAPH.

" 3rd. To withdraw, and in future withhold, all dispensations, under which persons not lawfully qualified had been, or might be, put into offices of trust and preferment in Church or State, or in the Universities, especially such as have cure of souls annexed to them, and particularly to restore the President and Fellows of Magdalen College.

" 4th. To withdraw all licenses for Roman Catholics to teach in public schools.

" 5th. To desist from the dispensing power, until that point had been freely and calmly debated, and settled, in Parliament.

" 6th. To prohibit the four foreign Bishops, who styled themselves Vicars Apostolical, from further invading the ecclesiastical jurisdiction, which is by law vested in the Bishops of the English Church.

" 7th. To fill the vacant Bishoprics, and other ecclesiastical promotions in England and Ireland, and in particular the Archiepiscopal chair of York, which had been so long vacant, and on which a whole Province depended. [1]

" 8th. To restore the ancient Charters of the Corporations, which had been forfeited.

" 9th. To issue writs with all convenient speed, calling a free and regular Parliament, for the purpose of securing the uniformity of the Church of England, due liberty of conscience, and the liberties and properties of the subject, and for establishing, between himself and all his people, a mutual confidence and good understanding.

" 10th. To permit the Bishops to offer to His Majesty such motives and arguments as might, by God's grace, be effectual to persuade him to return to the Communion of the Church of England, into whose most Holy Catholic Faith he had been baptized and educated, to which it was then their earnest prayer to God that he might be reunited.

" These, Sir," concluded the address, " are the humble advices, which, out of conscience of the duty we owe to God, to your Majesty, and our country, we think fit at this time to offer to your Majesty, as suitable to the present state of your affairs, and most conducive to your service; and so we leave them to your Princely consideration," &c.[2]

James thanked them for their advice—there was no " This is the standard of rebellion " now,—and promised to comply with

[1] James acted on the suggestion by appointing Lamplugh Bishop of Exeter, see p. 8, *n.*
[2] Gutch's *Collectanea Curiosa*, vol. i., p. 411.

some of their suggestions. On the point of calling a parliament he could, he said, make no concessions. He summoned the Bishops again for October 8th, directed them to appoint a fast and to compose prayers with reference to the expected invasion, told them he had considered their paper and " seemed sufficiently displeased with it." On the 9th, Turner and Ken held a consultation with Clarendon. On the 10th they presented the prayers they had drawn up to the King. On the 11th they were again summoned to hear that the prayers were approved, and were ordered to be used in all the churches.[1] They then resolved to go to their respective homes, and " feeling no longer bound to secrecy, gave their friends an account of what had passed between the King and them." [2]

That 11th of October was the last day on which James and Ken ever met. The latter, and most of the other Bishops who had taken part in the interviews, left London for their dioceses, and Ken awaited at Wells the issue of events. Meantime those events followed in quick succession. James took a few hasty steps of compliance with the Bishops' memorial. The Charters of the City of London and other corporations were ordered to be restored. The Court of Ecclesiastical Commission was abolished. The Bishop of Winchester (Peter Mews) was ordered, as Visitor of Magdalen College, to restore the President and Fellows, who had been expelled by Cartwright's Commission. On October 16th William started on his expedition. The flag, with his hereditary motto, " *Je maintiendray,*" was hoisted on his frigate, and the sentence was completed by the flag of England, with the words, " The Liberties of England and the Protestant Religion." [3] The fleet made its way, with varying

---

[1] The Form of Prayers was drawn up with singular skill and caution. It consists of three prayers. (1) For Repentance, perfectly general in its confessions of sin. (2) For the King, carefully avoiding all approval of the past, and for the future " Inspire him with wisdom . . . Prosper all his undertakings, for Thy honour and glory." (3) For Peace and Unitie. " Give peace in our days, if it be Thy good will. Prevent the effusion of Christian blood. Reconcile all our dissensions . . . ," and so on. All could join in the prayer, and it committed none to any line of policy.

[2] Clarendon, *Diary,* ii., pp. 72, 73.

[3] It is a curious instance of the ins and outs of the bye-ways of the history of the Revolution that while this was the view popularly accepted then, as it has been since, the Non-juring theory of William's expedition, held by Frampton and the re-

casualties, according as it had a "Protestant wind" with it, or a "Popish wind" against it, and on November the 5th, the memorable anniversary of the overthrow of a former conspiracy against the liberties of England and the Protestant religion, the Prince of Orange landed at Brixham in Torbay.

It is natural to assume that Ken was kept fairly informed of what was passing at such a critical time, both in London and in the West. He would hear how James, startled by the news of the Prince's landing and the statement made in his declaration, that he had been invited by Lords Spiritual as well as Temporal, had first questioned Compton, and on the following day Sancroft and the few other Bishops who were still in town,[1] as to their complicity ; how Compton, in terms

---

fore probably by his friend Ken, was of a very different character. William, as they held, was merely a tool in the Pope's hands. James had refused to enter the continental league against Louis XIV., whom the Pope was bent on humbling, and therefore Innocent XI. was bent on his destruction, and found his tool "in an ambitious son-in-law, and crafty, Jesuitical statesmen." William, accordingly, was sent to possess himself of the Kingdom of England, "with the Pope's Apostolic benediction." The theory was not without, at least, an element of truth. Macaulay exults in the supreme skill with which William made the Pope subservient to his policy, and drew him into the alliance against Louis (chap. ix.) He accepts, that is, the facts, but sees them from a different point of view. Frampton and Ken had both travelled much, the former had been at Rome, the latter both at Rome and the Hague, and they may have understood, better than most of their contemporaries, the inscrutable policy of the Roman *Curia.* To that *Curia* the humiliation of Louis might seem an object of more importance than the re-establishment of Romanism in England, under a Defender of the Faith who, like his "Most Christian" brother of France would, as he said on his accession, be "an upholder of the Royal Supremacy against the Pope in its strongest forms." (Reresby, p. 328.) And so Petre and James's other Jesuit counsellors were only the conscious, or unconscious, instruments by which he was pushed on in the infatuated course that led him to a foredoomed destruction. He was a pawn that was to be sacrificed that the Pope might give checkmate to Louis. If so, it was a case of "Greek meeting Greek" and "diamond cutting diamond." Innocent must have felt, after a time, that William was the better chess-player (Evans, *Frampton,* pp. 179, 180.) Among the strange results of this entanglement of policies we may note that William had 4,000 Papists in his army in London, and James 6,000 Swiss Protestants in that with which he invaded Ireland.—Reresby, pp. 436, 444.

[1] The interviews are reported as follows :—" Oct. 15th, with Sancroft alone ; Nov. 1st, with Compton alone ; Nov. 2nd, with Sancroft, Compton, Crewe, Cartwright, and Watson, of St. David's ; on Nov. 6th, with Sancroft, Compton, Sprat, and White. On Nov. 1st, James questioned Compton as to the share of the Bishops in the invitation addressed to William, and received the answer, ' I am sure my brethren will say that they have taken as little part in

which afterwards proved to be a dishonourable prevarication, and the others in good faith, had denied all knowledge of any such invitation; how they had refused to comply with his demands that they should sign a declaration that they abhorred the Prince's invasion, and had questioned the genuineness of the proclamation, which, it was said, he had issued; how on November 17th the two Archbishops (Lamplugh of Exeter, who had read the Declaration of Indulgence and tried to make his clergy read it, was now Archbishop-elect of York), the Bishops of St. Asaph, Ely, Rochester, Peterborough, and Oxford, and a few peers who were still in town, including Ormond, Clarendon, Rochester, and Dorset, had presented a petition to the King entreating him to call "a Parliament, ready and free in all its circumstances;" and lastly how, on November 20th, James declared that there was nothing he desired so passionately as a Parliament, but that he could not call it while an enemy was in the kingdom and could make a return of nearly a hundred voices. This would bring the London news up to date.[1] From the West there would have come tidings of William's march to Exeter, of the service in the Cathedral there, at which Burnet had preached and had read the Prince's manifesto, of the march eastward in the direction of Honiton and Sherborne, of the appearance of his troops under Kirke's command, probably near Warminster, within ten miles of Wells.

We may venture to ask ourselves with what feelings Ken

it as I have.' On the following day, when the other Bishops gave an explicit denial, Compton contented himself with saying, 'I gave you my answer yesterday.'" It may be noted that Evelyn thought it his duty to write to Sancroft on Oct. 10th, warning him that these invitations to interviews with the King were but a trap cunningly devised in order that they might seem to be identified with his policy, and urgently counselling him to avoid them. He specially urges that the Bishops should always use the word "Protestant" or "Reformed" before the ambiguous formula of "the Church of England as by law established." Watson, of St. David's, whom Burnet describes as "one of the worst men I ever knew in holy orders," took the oaths to William without hesitation, was formally charged with simony in 1699, and deprived, after five years of quibbling and chicane, in 1705, when Bull succeeded him (p. 152).

[1] On November 17th James had set out from London to take the command of his army. He got as far as Salisbury, but on hearing of the growing strength of William's forces, and alarmed by the defection of his own adherents, Cornbury, Prince George of Denmark, Churchill, Ormond, and others, precipitately returned to London on the 26th.

was likely to look on the impending crisis.   Politically, I believe, he had a respect for the part which William had taken in resisting the aggressive ambition of Louis XIV., especially, as he afterwards declared (if the letter to Tenison be authentic), for the heroism with which he had rejected the bribes of wealth and honour with which the French King had, at one time, tempted him.   The Prince had deliberately disclaimed all ambitious projects for himself in his present expedition.   He had simply come, on the invitation of men whom he believed to express the wishes of the English people, to maintain the Protestant religion and the liberties of England. He was content to press for a free Parliament, and to leave the future absolutely in its hands.   Ken, as his after conduct showed, would have acquiesced in the decision of such a Parliament, giving the Prince supreme administrative power.   As a man, I imagine, he could scarcely have felt much affection for him.   He knew that he was as unfaithful to his wife as James was to Mary Beatrice.   He knew that he had treated that wife, as James had not treated his, with boorish rudeness, had sneered at her religion and insulted her chaplains.   If he had broken her in to a complete submission to his will, and that submission was united with affection, it was, in great part, due to Ken's own teaching, when he had impressed on her the wisdom of patience, and had taught her that, subject to the supreme authority of conscience, passive obedience and non-resistance were as much the duty of a wife to her husband as of subjects to their king.   The morals of the Court of Hague were not one whit better than those of the Court of Whitehall under Charles II.   There also was the reign of harlots, and, in the homely language of Dr. Covell, the chaplain who succeeded Ken, " pimps and panders " were the only people who won the Prince's favour.   William had frowned on Ken, had almost dismissed him, because he had prevailed on Zulestein to make to the English lady whom he had wronged the reparation which James, under like circumstances, had made to Clarendon's daughter.   His religion, too, was of the type most alien to Ken's mind.   His Calvinism was not like that of Morley, whom Ken had loved ; nor like that of the Huguenots, whom he honoured and helped ; nor like that of Leighton and Bunyan, one which tends to closer communion with God and greater holiness of life, nor even that of the decrees of Dort, repellent as that form would have been to Ken's more Catholic belief. William's faith in the dogma had more affinity with the belief of the Bonapartes in their star, and may have seemed to Ken simply that kind of fatalism which narcotizes conscience. " What do you think of predestination now, Doctor ? " was the question which he put to Burnet when he landed in Torbay.[1] If that question ever came to Ken's knowledge I imagine it would have reminded him of the title of the treatise by which Sancroft had won his early fame as a controversialist, and that he would have said, when his eyes had been opened to William's schemes, " So then here, at last, is the living *Fur Prædestinatus.*"[2]

As it was he wrote a letter to Sancroft on November 24th, with which I close this chapter :—

LETTER XXIV.

To Archbishop Sancroft.

" All Glory be to God.

" May it please your Grace,

" Before I could return any answer to the letter with which your Grace was pleased to favour me, I received intelligence that the Dutch were just coming to Wells, upon which I immediately lefft the town, and, in obedience to his Majesty's generall commands, took all my coach horses with me, and as many of my saddle horses as I well could, and took shelter in a private village in Wiltshire, intending, if his Ma: had come into my country, to have waited on him, and to have paid him my duty. But this morning wee are told his Ma: is gone back to London, so that I onely wait till the Dutch have passed my diocesse, and then resolve to returne thither againe, that being my proper station. I would not have lefft the diocesse in this juncture, but that the Dutch had seas'd horses within ten miles of Wells before I went, and your Grace knowes, that I, having

[1] Macaulay's explanation that William's question was a gentle hint to Burnet's bustling meddlesomeness, of the *Ne sutor ultra crepidam* kind, seems to me strained and artificial.

[2] Sancroft's book was a somewhat severe exposure of the Antinomian side of Calvinism. It was published in 1651.

been a servant to the Princess, and well acquainted with many of
the Dutch, I could not have staid without giving some occasions of
suspicion, which I thought it most advisable to avoid; resolving by
God's grace to continue in a firm loyalty to the King, whome God
direct and preserve in this time of danger; and I beseech your Grace
to lay my most humble duty at his Majesty's feet, and to acquaint
him with the reason of my retiring, that I may not be misunderstood.   The person your Grace mentions wrote to me to the same
purpose, and I spake with the Archdeacon, who says he demands
nothing but his due, so that the law must decide the controversy.
God of his infinite mercy deliver us from the calamitys which now
threaten us, and from the sinnes which have occasioned them.

> "My very good Lord,
>
> "Your Graces very affect: Servant and B[r],
>
> "THO. BATH & WELLS.

"*Nov. 24th* (1688)."

[The letter has no date of place, but the "private village " was probably Poulshot, near Devizes, where Ken's nephew, Izaak Walton, was rector.   I do not
find any evidence in our city records or elsewhere that the Dutch actually came
nearer Wells than Wincanton.   As Round prints the letter, we read that the
Dutch had "seas'd *houses*," but the context obviously requires "horses."   James
had apparently issued general orders to all his adherents to keep horses and
war provisions generally out of the hands of William's army.   He had been
at Andover, which was within twenty miles of Poulshot.   Burnet, in his
account of the expedition (*O. T.*, B. iv., 1685), specially notes that "being at such
a distance from London, we reckoned that we could provide ourselves with
horses."   A letter in Ellis, 2nd *Ser.*, iv. 156, reports that William had seized all
the horses in Bridgewater and the neighbourhood. (Anderdon, p. 474.) Bentinck
and Zulestein were probably in Ken's mind as among the Dutch to whom he
was known.   The last sentence but one refers apparently to some diocesan
business which I have been unable to trace.]

CHAPTER XIX

THE REVOLUTION OF 1688.

" Read, who the Church would cleanse, and mark
    How stern the warning runs;
    There are two ways to aid her ark,—
    As patrons, and as sons."

J. H. Newman.

WITHIN a few days from the date of that last letter, Ken probably read a document which must at once have astonished and horrified him. A proclamation was circulated throughout the kingdom, purporting to be issued by William at Sherborne Castle on November 28th. It was signed in his usual manner, and countersigned by his secretary, C. Huygens. It gave an entirely new character to the Prince's expedition. It began, as the first manifesto published on his landing had done, with declaring his intention to support the religion and liberties of England, but soon it passed into a very different strain. The Prince expressed his desire to accomplish his purpose "without the effusion of any blood, except of those execrable criminals who have justly forfeited their lives for betraying the Religion, and subverting the Laws, of their native country." This obviously doomed all James's counsellors to the scaffold. But this was not all. "All Papists found in open arms, or with arms in their hands or about their persons, or in any office or employment, civil or military, upon any pretence whatever, contrary to the known Laws of the Land, shall be treated by us and by our Forces, not as Souldiers and Gentlemen, but as Robbers, Freebooters, and Banditti; they shall be incapable of quarter, and intirely given up to the Discretion of our Soldiers."

It is not too much to say that had these orders been acted

on they would have issued in a general massacre of Roman Catholics throughout the kingdom. London would have become an Aceldama. The stain of blood would have cleaved to William's fame, as the slaughter of Drogheda had cleaved to Cromwell's.

Ken may, perhaps, have remembered the proclamation to which, in its "no quarter" severity, this bore a suspicious resemblance, and which Ferguson had drawn up, and Monmouth had signed, as he told James, without reading. He may have doubted, as others doubted then, the authenticity of the document.[1] It would, at all events, have been a relief to

---

[1] The history of the Sherborne proclamation is still an unsolved problem. It appeared in the *Collection of Papers relating to the Present Juncture of Affairs in England*, 1688, in company with other documents, every one of which is received as authentic. Macaulay says that some suspected Ferguson, the 'Plotter,' and some Johnson, the author of *Julian the Apostate*, of being the writer. After the lapse of twenty-seven years the credit of it was claimed by Hugh Speke, a kind of political Barry Lyndon, who boasted that he was the author of well-nigh every act of political scoundrelism that had stained the history of the Revolution. The book bears the title of *A Secret History of the Happy Revolution, by the Principal Transactor in it*. It was published in 1718, dedicated to George I., and presented to him by the Earl of Berkeley. Speke, whose father had been fined, and whose brother had been condemned to death, by Jeffreys, after the Monmouth rebellion, says that he drew up the proclamation as he had drawn a previous *Advice to the Army*, on the same lines; that "it was dispersed over most parts of the kingdom, and believed to be genuine;" that he himself gave it to William at Sherborne Castle (where William halted for two nights, *Somers Tracts*, ix. 280), that "the Prince seemed somewhat surprised at first and openly declared he knew nothing of it," but when "he had read and considered it, his Highness and all that were about him, seemed not at all displeased with the thing ; and they were all sensible, in a very little time, that it did his Highness's interest a great deal of service." Of this passage Macaulay takes no notice, and does not even state that William stopped at Sherborne. Speke's character makes it, perhaps, unsafe to rely on any statement of his, but I do not find that William ever made his disclaimer as public as the proclamation had been. The Prince of Orange was never an Orangeman, but he might have been content, in that inscrutable silence of his, to let the passions, which were afterwards the evil inheritance of the Orangemen of Ireland, do their work. I remember how he pensioned Titus Oates as a man whom he delighted to honour. Ferguson, who had drawn up Monmouth's declaration, and was suspected of complicity with the Sherborne proclamation, received, in the first days of William's reign, a lucrative sinecure place in the Excise. Speke says (p. 65) that after William's accession he "kept up a continual correspondence with King James by his knowledge and direction, and for these and other secret services received from him several sums of money." Letters in the *State Papers* for 1689 and 1704 show that he was always pressing these services upon the government, and claiming compen-

him to hear as the weeks went on that it was not acted on.
James played unconsciously into William's hands. Ken would
hear how he had returned to London ; how, on his arrival on
November 27, he heard that his daughter Anne had fled from
Whitehall with Lady Churchill and the Bishop of London and
Lord Dorset; how, in his despair, he signed writs for a Parlia-
ment, which was to meet on January 13 ; how he published an
amnesty, and removed Sir Edward Hales from his post as
Lieutenant of the Tower ; how, on December 6, he sent
Halifax and Nottingham and Godolphin as commissioners to
treat with William ; how, on December 9, he sent off his
Queen and her infant child to France under the protection of
the Chevalier de Lauzun ; how his negotiations, after all, were
only meant as a blind to put the Prince off his guard ; how on
December 11 he had fled, burning the writs for the new Parliament before he left, and flinging the great seal into the
Thames ; how he had been detected and arrested at Faversham ;
how he had been brought back again to London amid popular
exclamations which led him and others to believe that the people
were still with him, and had resumed his old life at Whitehall [1]
on the 16th; how in the interval the two archbishops, five
bishops (Ken not one of them), and twenty-two peers had
formed themselves into a kind of provisional government at
Guildhall, and had earnestly entreated William to come with
all speed, and avert the anarchy with which London and the

sation for them. I fear we must own that William's Calvinism did not involve
the "clean hand" and the "pure heart," without which the hero statesman is
but as a Machiavelli or a Tiberius. It is perhaps worth noting (1) that a tradition
in the Digby family, then, as now, the owners of Sherborne Castle, runs to the
effect that a printing press was set up in the green drawing-room, and that a
large crack in the hearth-stone remains to testify the fact; and (2) that Speke
boasts (p. 43) of being the contriver of the "Irish scare;" by sending in all
directions letters reporting that the Irish papists were going to rise all over
England and Scotland, and massacre the Protestants. The object in this, as
partly, perhaps, in the Sherborne proclamation, was two-fold: (1) to inflame the
passions of the Protestants, and (2) to drive the Papists, and James and his
adherents generally, who found themselves likely to be the victims of those
passions, to a hasty flight. Speke's chief object was, he says, to get James out of
England, and in that he succeeded. If I mistake not, we shall trace his handiwork again in a memorable incident of Ken's life (p. 85).

[1] Evelyn was present at the supper that evening.—*Diary*, December 17th.

whole country were threatened ;[1] how James had fled again on December 18,[2] and all his evil counsellors, Petre and the rest, had scuttled off in hot haste, with bag and baggage, in all directions ; how Jeffreys[3] had been taken disguised as a sailor, and was now in the Tower; and finally, how William was lodged at St. James's.

[1] On December 11, the mob destroyed Roman Catholic chapels, the King's printing-house, and even attacked the houses of foreign ambassadors, notably Barillon. On the night of the 12th there came the terrible "Irish Scare," of which also Speke claimed to be the contriver.

[2] It is a curious fact that James at one time thought, in those days of confusion, of taking refuge under the wing of Sancroft at Lambeth, or Mews at Winchester.—Reresby, p. 434.

[3] Jeffreys is one of the few characters in history for whom no one has a word to say. Every historian, great or small, thinks it a duty to cast a stone at him. I have no desire to rehabilitate his reputation, but I cannot refrain from giving here what was new to me and may be new to others, the story of his closing days. He was, as I have said, in the Tower. None of his old boon companions, none of those who owed their fortunes to his patronage, came near him. He had, however, one visitor, Robert Frampton, Bishop of Gloucester, one of Ken's dearest friends, who had only escaped through the accidents of travel from being one of the Bishops whom James sent to the Tower, who came to see him. He found him sick, disconsolate, weeping bitterly, with the sorrow which seemed to the Bishop to be the "sorrow of the world that worketh death." He spoke to him as a minister of Christ at such a time ought to speak ; roused his conscience to repentance ; told him to "weep on and spare not." "Those tears of his, if they were the tears of a penitent, would be more precious than diamonds." The Ex-Chancellor was, at all events, not callous. He thanked Frampton for his fatherly advice, recognised the goodness of God in sending him, whom he could least have expected to see, when all others had deserted him, asked his prayers, and entreated that he would give him the comfort of Holy Communion. This the Bishop, believing in his repentance, did when he next came to see him. Jeffreys accordingly received it, with his wife and children, and "in a few days died in peace of mind." (Evans, *Frampton*, p. 197) Frampton had been for many years in the East, as chaplain of the Company of Merchants at Aleppo, and knew Arabic well. I ask myself whether he could have known the Moslem tradition of the Lord Jesus and the dead dog (Trench, *Poems from Eastern Sources*, p. 104). Macaulay (iii., 402) reports like acts on the part of Dean Sharp of Norwich, and Dr. John Scott, author of the *Christian Life*, but apparently with less success than Frampton hoped he had attained. I will venture to add a sentence from a speech of Jeffreys', sitting as judge in a case of high treason, which shows that he was, in one point at least, in advance of his contemporaries : "I think it a hard case that a man should have counsel to defend him for a twopenny trespass, and his witnesses examined upon oath ; but, if he steal, commit murder or felony, ay, high treason, where life, estate, honour and all are concerned, he shall neither have counsel nor his witnesses examined upon oath." (*State Trials*, x. 267, in Lingard x. 95.) It is well sometimes for the historian to turn from Philip drunk to Philip sober, and to remember that even a "dead dog" may have a certain "whiteness of teeth" beyond his fellows.

On that very day Sancroft issued a circular letter to the Bishops requesting them to come up, "with all convenient haste," to London and consult with him on "the perplext state of affairs." To this Ken returned the following answer :—

LETTER XXV.

To Archbishop Sancroft.

"All Glory be to God.

"My very good Lord,

"I received your Grace's letter, which came to my hands late on Thursday night, so that had I had no obligation on me to ordain next Sunday, yett it was impossible for me to have reached the towne before Christmas, but as soone as the weather will permitt, I intend, God willing, to wait on you. God of His infinite goodnesse, send downe a double portion of His Spirit, to rest on your selfe, and on my reverend Brethren, to direct, and support you in this great conjuncture.

"My good Lord,

"Your Grace's very obedient Servant,

"THO. BATH AND WELLS.

"*Dec.* 22, 1688."

When his Ordination and the Christmas services were over Ken accordingly went up to London, and was at Lambeth on January 10th, 1689. A letter from Francis Turner, dated January 11th, shows that he had drawn up a memorial, as the basis of the deliberations of the Bishops, which is probably identical with a paper in Turner's hand among Sancroft's MSS. in the Bodleian Library :—

"*Previous Considerations of what method is left for the Bishops to use, in representing to the Prince of Orange their sense concerning the King and kingdome.*

The earlier part of the paper deals with the question whether the Bishops should unite in addressing the Prince, and decides against it. "It would be premature, before some of us have seen his face, or endeavoured to know what he intends to do." It prefers the plan of publishing three Propositions, "as if they were directed against the bold wild discourse and apparent designes of our commonwealth-men, but without the least reflection on the Prince or his purposes." The Propositions are as follows :—

> " *First—Against deposing the King.*
> " *Secondly—Against electing any other King.*
> " *Thirdly—Against breaking any one link in the royall chaine;* i.e. *any way intercepting the right succession to the imperial crown.*

"These Propositions should, in my judgment, bee drawne and taken from the very words either of our 39 *Articles*, or our *Liturgy*, or our *Rubricks*, or our *Canons*, or our *Homilys*, or our *Acts of Parliament* and *fundamental laws* of the land, or from our *Oaths and Tests* (which indeed are part of our law).

"And this paper of Propositions, with a short preface before it, or something after it, declaring our obligations to maintaine these doctrines, need be directed to no body, though intended, as for our owne vindication, so for every body's satisfaction one day, and for the Prince's presently, and most particularly. This paper should be delivered by one of us to Monsieur Benting, or some chiefe Minister, to be handed by him to his Highness, with as little noise and notice as may bee, and if such a representation dos not putt a stopp (as 'tis to be fear'd it will not), then it will be time enough, *and high time it will bee, for the Lords Spirituall, and those Temporall that will act conjoyntly with us, to oppose the commonwealth-men openly at the Convention.*"

Ken was also of opinion, as Turner's letter shows, that the Bishops should not present themselves at William's court. As Sancroft frankly told William, in the letter which he wrote excusing his absence, while he and his brethren were grateful for "his heroick undertaking upon the reasons exprest in your gratious Declaration, and for the Benefitts that wee enjoy and hope to receive by your means," there were some things "which have bin done since your Highnesse came to Windsor" with which we are "not so far satisfy'd" as to "approve of them or seem to do so."[1] In the meantime William pursued the course of inscrutable silence which might entitle him also to the name of William the Taciturn. On December 4th, Bentinck had told Clarendon at Salisbury that to say that the Prince aspired to the Crown was "the most wicked insinuation that could be invented." On January 5th, Burnet had told Lloyd of St. Asaph that "he would not take the title of King,

---

[1] Tanner MSS., xxviii., p. 319 ; in Anderdon, p. 490.

though it should be offered him." Events, however, were hastening on. William had complied with the request of Sancroft's short provisional Government by summoning a Convention, which was to include the whole House of Lords and all the surviving members of the last House of Commons elected under Charles II. The following extract from Evelyn's *Diary* (Jan. 15, 1689) will show with what views Ken and the other Bishops were prepared to meet the grave questions which the Convention had to settle :—[1]

" I visited the Archbishop on the 15th, where I found the Bishops of St. Asaph (Lloyd), Ely (Turner), Bath and Wells (Ken), Peterborough (White), and Chichester (Lake); the Earls of Ailesbury and Clarendon, Sir George Mackenzie, Lord Advocate of Scotland; and then came in a Scotch bishop, &c. After prayers, and dinner, divers serious matters were discoursed concerning the present state of the public; and sorry I was to find [from them] there was as yet no accord in the judgments of those of the Lords and Commons who were to convene : some would have the Princess [of Orange] made Queen without any more dispute; others were for a Regency : there was a Tory party (then so call'd) who were for inviting His Majesty again upon conditions; and there were Republicarians, who would make the P. of Orange like a Stadtholder. The Romanists were busy among these several parties, to bring them into confusion; most for ambition, or other interest, few for conscience and moderate resolutions. I found nothing of all this in this assembly of Bishops, who were pleas'd to admit me into their discourses; they were all for a Regency, thereby to salve their oaths, and so all public matters to proceed in his Mj$^{ty's}$ name, by that to facilitate the calling of a Parliament, according to the laws in being. Such was the result of this meeting."

It is easy to point out, as Macaulay has done, the inconsistencies and inconveniences to which this theory of a Regency would have led, that it relied on the fiction that the King was insane, that it might have led to the yet further anomaly of a perpetuated Regency in England, governing in the name of a succession of kings in France, who were kept out of their inheritance on the same legal fiction that they were insane, the only proof of their insanity being that they preferred being

---

[1] Evelyn's *Diary* for December 30th notes the significant fact that the prayers for the Prince of Wales were no longer used in Church.

Roman Catholics to joining the Anglican Communion. It is not difficult, however, to see the attractions it may have had for Sancroft and the others, laymen as well as Bishops, who acted with him. As Evelyn says, "it salved their oaths," and, with the natural tendency of the clerical mind, when it deals with legal questions, they became super-subtle in their legalism. It maintained the theory of hereditary right. It met the immediate necessity of providing an executive government, acting in conjunction with Parliament. It left an opening for favourable contingencies, which were, at least, possible. James might be re-converted to the Church of England. There had been instances of such re-conversion before (Chillingworth was a memorable example), as there have been in our own time. The language of the Bishops whom James had consulted in October, of Ken himself, if he was the author of the *Royal Sufferer*, shows that they clung for some years afterwards, hoping against hope, to that possibility.[1] The young Prince of Wales might return to the Church of his fathers. Or he might die, and then the Crown would revert, in succession, to James's daughters, from neither of whom was any danger to be apprehended on the score of religion. On these grounds it may well have seemed to the Bishops, and to men, like Evelyn, more or less of a clerical mind, that this plan would work better than recalling James, with or without conditions, or declaring the Crown forfeited, or falling back on the notion of a Republic, of which their experience of the Long Parliament and of Cromwell had sufficiently sickened the great body of the English people.

On January 22nd, 1689, the Convention met, and the great battle began. Sancroft, whose age and infirmities seem to have led him, with the one exception of the provisional Government at Guildhall, to shrink from publicity, adopted a policy of abstention, and never once appeared in the House of Lords. Ken

---

[1] "Your Royal Father was a Protestant, and liv'd and dy'd in and for that Profession, and I could heartily wish that your Majesty was so too: For then we might quickly hope to see an end of our present miseries in a short time" (p. 1). "If, through the Divine Blessing, they (the arguments against Rome) should be made efficacious to cause your Majesty to return to and embrace the Religion, professed even unto Death by your Royal Father, it would be the Joy and Rejoicing of all your people" (p. 4.)

voted in every division for a Regency, and his friend Turner
was conspicuous as a speaker, on the same side, both in the
debates of the Lords and in their conferences with the Commons. The record of Ken's votes will sufficiently indicate the
line which he took in the great questions which were at issue.
The first act of the Convention was to order a public thanksgiving for the "great deliverance from Popery and arbitrary
power," of which the Prince of Orange had been the "gracious
instrument;" and he, with ten other Bishops, five of whom
were afterwards Non-jurors, accepted the task of drawing up
the form of prayer to be used on that occasion.[1] On the same
day Ken acquiesced in the unanimous address to the Prince,
confirming to him the administration of affairs. On the 28th
the Commons, after a vain attempt on the part of some of the
peers to forestall their action by meeting on the 25th, passed
their memorable resolution, that the King, "having endeavoured to subvert the constitution of the kingdom, by breaking the original contract between King and people, and by the
advice of Jesuits and other wicked persons, having violated
the fundamental laws, and having withdrawn himself out of
the kingdom, had abdicated the government, and that the
throne had thereby become vacant." Macaulay says, with
some severity, that "perhaps, there never was a sentence
written by man which could bear minute and severe criticism
less than this." It assumed, to start with, a theory—that of
the "original contract"—which was historically untenable,

---

[1] The Bishops (I indicate the future Non-jurors by italics), were Compton,
Sprat, *Turner, Lloyd* (of Norwich), *Lake, Frampton, Ken, White,* Barlow, and
Trelawny. It was a curious illustration of the chances and changes of the time
that some of them (Ken being one) had taken part in drawing up the prayers
that James directed to be used at the time of William's so-called invasion. In
this case, as before, the prayers were drawn up with a singular caution and comprehensiveness, avoiding the burning questions of the time, and expressing the
feelings in which all, or nearly all, could concur. Of the Thanksgiving form,
Macaulay says that it was "perfectly free from the adulation and from the
malignity by which such compositions were in that age too often deformed, and
sustains, better, perhaps, than any occasional service which has been framed
during two centuries, a comparison with that great model of chaste, lofty, and
pathetic eloquence, the Book of Common Prayer" (chap. x.). It and the
prayer which was ordered to be used daily for the Prince recognised him as the
divinely sent "Defender of our Laws and Religion," a "mighty deliverer"
from the "intolerable yoke of the Romish Church."

and had never been recognised except by the judges who condemned Charles I. It was less consistent than they had been, in treating the violation of fundamental law and desertion, not as leading to forfeiture, but as an act of abdication, at the very moment when James was asserting his rights to the full. It violated the two principles of English law, that "the King can do no wrong," and that "the King never dies," and by affirming that the throne was vacant, set aside the claims alike of the infant Prince of Wales and of James's two daughters, and substituted an elective monarchy (the words "vacant throne" implied that it was a throne that was to be thus filled up) resting on a Parliamentary vote, alike for the prescriptions of English law and the doctrine of Divine Right. With the exception of that word "throne," it affirmed all that the most zealous Republican could contend for. All that can be said for it is, that it was a compromise, that it was made to catch votes in many different directions, that it caught them, and was thus successful. We may be well content, as I am for one, with the outcome of the whole, but not the less can I sympathise with Ken and others, as they scrutinised the phrases that involved the upturning of all that they had before contended for. On the 29th, Ken joined in the unanimous vote for the declaration, "that it was found by experience to be inconsistent with the safety and welfare of the Protestant religion to be governed by a Popish Prince"—(we note the change from the time when the bishops and clergy had been prominent in opposing the Exclusion Bill of 1678),—the Lords insisting on discussing that question before the resolution of the Commons, but voted in the minority, 51 against 54, as might be expected, for a Regency.[1] Men like Evelyn noted that on the following day, January 30th, the anniversary of Charles I.'s martyrdom, the public offices and pulpit prayers, the collects and litany for the King and Queen were curtailed and mutilated—it does not appear by what authority—to suit the altered conditions of the time.[2] The tone of the sermons on that day must also, one

---

[1] Ken and Turner were the only two Bishops who voted on that side. (Evelyn, January 29th, 1688.) Sancroft, as has been said, never attended the Convention.

[2] Sharp, Dean of Norwich, the Rector of St. Giles'-in-the-Fields, for not suspending whom Compton had been himself suspended, had the courage to read

imagines, have been somewhat different from that with which congregations had been familiar in former years.

On the 31st the Lords discussed the resolution of the Commons, and Ken, as might be expected, voted against the declaration that the throne was " vacant." In this instance he was in a majority of fifty-five to forty-one. William, in the meantime, had allowed Bentinck to say to a meeting of peers " that he would not like to be his wife's gentleman usher," and Mary had written a letter to Danby, confirming a statement which Burnet thought himself justified in making, that if ever she came to the throne, she wished to surrender all her power into her husband's hands; and so the Regency proposal was quashed, and James had addressed a letter to the Convention, as though he was still master of the situation, promising a general pardon, with a few unnamed exceptions. On February 4th Ken voted with the majority who adhered to their objection to the resolution of the Commons. The Commons asked for a conference, which was fixed for February 6th. In the meantime William called together Halifax, Danby, and Shrewsbury, and other political leaders, and at last broke the silence which had till then been so impenetrable. He more than confirmed what Bentinck had hinted. He would not be Regent. He would not even be a King Consort. He would not " submit to be tied to the apron-strings even of the best of wives." He seemed to leave it doubtful, to Burnet's indignation, whether he would allow her to be more than a Queen Consort. " The Convention were free to take their own course. He was free to take his."

There was, after this, no alternative between accepting William's implied demands, swallowing the bitter pill with whatever wryness of face, or the uttermost chaos and confusion. The conference was held, the debates were long. When the Lords returned from the Painted Chamber to their own House it was soon clear that the balance of parties was shifted. Only

the whole service before the House of Commons, at St. Margaret's, Westminster, and preached a sermon in the old tone. He narrowly escaped—on the technical ground that he was bound to ignore the resolution which the Commons had passed the previous day, and of which there had been no official publication—the censure of the House.

three peers voted against the proposition that the King had abdicated. The motion "that the throne was vacant" was carried by sixty-two to forty-seven, Ken being in the minority. The resolution "that William and Mary should be declared King and Queen" was carried without a division, but thirty-seven peers, including twelve bishops, of whom Ken was one, entered their protest against it. Of these only five ultimately refused to take the oaths. On February 9th, 10th, 11th, and 12th, he voted consistently against the measures which followed as natural corollaries from the decision already taken; among others against the new oaths, destined to have so fatal an influence on his own life, and on that of many of his dearest friends, which were to transfer the allegiance, alike of clergy and laymen, to the new sovereigns. On the 12th he left the House of Lords never to enter it again.[1] At some stage in the progress of the Convention he had supported a bill, drawn by Nottingham, for Toleration and Comprehension in matters of doctrine.

On the evening of that 12th of February Whitehall witnessed a scene which, if I mistake not, must have brought a keener pain to Ken's heart, when he heard of it, than even the result of the Convention. Mary arrived at the Palace, and instead of appearing impressed with the solemnity of her position, as others were, acted with a strange and unbecoming levity, came "laughing and jolly, as to a wedding," rose early the next morning, and "in her undress, as was reported," ran from room to room, looking at the furniture, turning up the quilts of the beds with a childish exultation, sitting down within a night or two to play at basset, as her step-mother used to do.[2] Even Burnet was shocked into remonstrating with her, in his character of spiritual director. The explanation which she gave, and which served afterwards as the *apologia* of her champions, was that William, fearful of the inference that

---

[1] Evelyn records (March 29th) that "the Archbishop of Canterbury and foure other Bishops refusing to come to Parliament, it was deliberated whether they should incur Præmunire ; but it was thought fit to let this fall, and bo connived at, for feare of the people, to whom those Prelates were very deare, for the opposition they had given to Popery."

[2] Evelyn (Feb. 13th, 1689) ; Strickland, *Queens*, xi. p. 5.

might be drawn from any appearance of sadness, had told her
that she must look cheerful, and that she, accustomed to im-
plicit obedience, had simply over-acted her part. The break-
ing-in process had succeeded. Never had Petruchio a more
obedient Katherine.

With a sad and sorrowful heart Ken returned to Wells to
wait in patience the course of events which he could no longer
control, in which he could no longer take even a dissentient part.
It lies in the nature of the case that neither he nor Sancroft,
nor the other Bishops who thought with them, attended the
Court of the new King and Queen, in the Banqueting Room at
Whitehall, in which they received, on February 13th, from
both Houses of the Convention, the offer of the crown.

NOTE.—The *Memoirs* of Mary, recently published by Dr. R. Döbner (1886),
give the results of her self-scrutiny during the eventful years 1688—93. They
contain a frank and touching confession, in full accordance with what she told
Burnet. "And here I was guilty of a great sin. I let myself go on too much,
and the devil immediately took his advantage. The world filled my mind, and
left but little room for good thoughts. The next day after I came we were proclaimed, and the government put wholly in the Prince's hands. This pleased me
extremely, but many would not believe it ; so that I was fain to force myself to
more mirth than became me at that time." She adds that she " had been only
for a regency " (p. 11.)

MEDAL TO COMMEMORATE ACQUITTAL OF SEVEN BISHOPS.

CHAPTER XX.

"I step, I mount where He has led;
Then count my haltings o'er;
I know them; yet, though self I dread,
I love His precept more."

J. H. Newman.

IT is not without a sense of relief that I turn from the main stream of English history, in which Ken had been reluctantly compelled to bear a part, to a narrative of more limited scope. I gladly leave the actors in that history—Shrewsbury and Danby, and Churchill and Nottingham, with their rivalries and intrigues, the Scotch, Irish, and foreign policy of William, the Act of Union, the Battle of the Boyne, the massacre of Glencoe—to be with Ken in his retirement. I have had, in justice to him, to tell, as far as he was connected with it, a twice-told tale, in which I expose myself to comparison with the great masters of historical narrative. I now enter on a personal history, within narrower limits, in which, whatever may be my defects, in substance or in style, I shall no longer incur the risk of that comparison.

The two letters that follow, written within a few weeks of Ken's withdrawal from the scene of action, will sufficiently indicate the feelings with which he looked forward to the impending future.

LETTER XXVI.

To VISCOUNT WEYMOUTH.

"All Glory be to God.

"MY VERY GOOD LORD,

"Your Lordship was so well employ'd in a Labour of Love to yᵉ Publick, yᵗ I could not regrate your absence when I came to

Longleat. The trueth is, I fully intended to have wayted on you before, but my Cousin Walton being with me & beinge to returne on Saturday, y⁰ desire I had to accompany him so much on his way determin'd me to y' day. I will take what care I can in the choice of Convocation Men. I thought the two last had been very steddy, but the current of preferment running at present y⁰ other way, t'is hard in so giddy an age as this, to choose those who will row against the Streame, or those who, though they goe well resolved from us, shall not have their braines turned by y⁰ aire of y⁰ Towne. If y⁰ Parlament thinke fitt to give us more time, 'tis all y⁰ kindnesse they can doe us, & that will be a little respite, but not finally prevent y' ruine. God's Holy will be done. I intend, God willing, when the weather grows more temperate, to try my fortune once more ; & I shall not thinke my iourney lost, as long as I find y⁰ good Lady there, & y⁰ young Lady, & Mʳ. Thinne, to whom I beseech your Lordship to present my most Humble Service ; God of His Infinite Goodnesse multiply His blessings on you all.

"Your Lordship's very humble & affectionate Servant,

"THO. BATH & WELLS.

"*March 3rd* (168⅔)."

[The "labour of love" is, I take it, Lord Weymouth's attendance in the Convention Parliament, and his efforts to moderate the rigour of the measures contemplated against those who declined to take the oath to the new sovereign. It is only fair to Burnet to note that he took a prominent part in the debates in the House of Lords in urging, as he himself says, "with vehemence," that the deprived Bishops should be excused from taking the oath, unless tendered by the King in Council. He also proposed and carried a clause in the Act of Parliament (1 William and Mary, c. viii. sec. 17), authorizing the King to allow to twelve of the Non-juring clergy an allowance out of their benefices, not exceeding one-third, during His Majesty's pleasure. It does not appear that the authority was ever acted on, but Ken was probably one of the twelve in whose favour it was proposed. (*Proceedings of Parliament upon the Bill to prevent Occasional Conformity*, 1710.) "My Cousin Walton" is Ken's nephew, Izaak Walton, jun., then Canon of Salisbury, who seems to have been with him at Wells. Convocation had been summoned to meet on November 17th, and Ken was clearly anxious as to the line it might take on Church affairs. The proctors actually chosen were Dr. Busby for the Chapter (see i. 202) and William Clement and Giles Pooley for the diocese. Of the two latter I have not as yet been able to learn anything. The prizes of the Church, as, *e.g.*, a little later in the case of Sherlock, were already beginning to exercise an attractive influence on those who seemed to Ken to be men of mixed motives and unstable characters. The "more time" refers probably to the interval, ultimately fixed as a six months' grace, from suspension on August 1st, 1689, to deprivation on February 1st, 1690, which was to be given to the clergy, in which to make up their minds as to the great question of taking the oaths. He obviously already turns to Longleat as a place where he is sure to find, if not perfect agreement, at all events, a sympathising friendship. The " young lady" and the "Mr. Thinne " are the two children of Lord Weymouth, to whom, in 1685, he had sent copies of his Manual of Divine Love. The form of the oaths was, on the whole, less stringent than that which it replaced. The promissory oath was simply "I, A. B., do sincerely promise and swear that I will be faithful and bear true allegiance to their Majesties King William and Queen Mary." It was followed by that rejecting the " damnable doctrine and position . . . ." with which we are familiar. The scruples of Ken and his brother non-jurors obviously turned entirely on the first of the two.]

LETTER XXVII.

To VISCOUNT WEYMOUTH.

" All Glory be to God.

" MY VERY GOOD LORD,

" It has been a great disappointment to me y^t I could not wait on your Lordship all this while. The trueth is, I had done it, but y^t M^r. Davis assur'd me you would not be at home till ye end of this weeke. On Thursday last I intended to have done it, but was fearefull to loose my labour & so putt it off to this day, wch prov'd so bad I could not stir, and iust now, M^r. Davis sends me word y^t you goe towards London tomorrow, so y^t I now despaire of seeing you before you goe. If your Lordship has leasure to enlighten me in a line or two, who am wholly in the dark, & know nothing, & to give me what advice you think fitt for one who is certainly design'd for ruine, you will doe a great act of Charity, & as soon as ever I have perused your Instructions I promise to burne them. God of His Infinite Goodnesse multiply His blessings on your selfe, your Lady and your family.

" Your Lordship's most humble & affectionate Servant,

" THO. BATH & WELLS.

" *March* 15*th* (168$\frac{8}{9}$)."

[The projected visit to Longleat did not come off. There is something pathetic in Ken's sense of being " wholly in the dark." A few months before the eyes of England had been fixed on him. He was the observed of all observers. James and Sancroft and Clarendon were inviting him to share their counsels. A few weeks before he had been in the "fierce fight " of the Convention, knowing everything, and taking part in the counsels of one of the great parties of the State. Already there presses on him the sense that he is as a man " designed for ruine " by the vindictive policy of the Whigs, who were now dominant in the House of Commons. That text of his, *Et tu quæris tibi grandia ? Noli quærere*, (i. 139), had proved but too prophetic. All that he could now hope for was that, as with him to whom the words were spoken, his " life should be given him for a prey." The promise to burn his correspondent's letters is not without significance as to the temper of men's minds in those dangerous days.]

D 2

During those anxious months the question, which must obviously have been uppermost in Ken's mind, was that which was to determine the whole future of his life. Could he take the new oaths or not? It was, I imagine, not an easy question. He had never, as he himself says, " flown so high " as others had done, into the speculative regions of Filmer's theory of divine hereditary right. He seldom " meddled," in his sermons or otherwise, as he tells Burnet (p. 48), " with the passive obedience " which had been " preached up " by Tillotson, Burnet himself, and others, who were now foremost among the worshippers of the rising sun. He so far accepted the theory of an implied " original contract " between king and people as to maintain that there might be an Act, such, *e.g.*, as James's rumoured transfer of Ireland to Louis XIV.,[1] which, like the sin of unfaithfulness in marriage, would justify a divorce *a vinculo* between the king and the nation. He had voted for the proposition that no Roman Catholic could safely hold the reins of government in England, and so had accepted the principle of the Exclusion Bill, and secured, as it might well seem, the right relations, as far as that point was concerned, between Church and State. He was prepared, as his subsequent conduct shows, to pay obedience to a king *de facto*, and, both on this and the preceding ground, he lived in quiet obedience to the law, and held aloof from all conspiracies for James's restoration. He dreaded above all the perpetuation of the schism in the Church, which was sure to follow on the secession of the non-juring bishops and clergy. It was known among the other non-jurors that he was in doubt. Turner wrote to Sancroft on Ascension Day, 1689, to say that he feared that " this very good man is warping from us and the true interest of the Church, towards a compliance with the new government." He apprehends that " your parson of Lambeth has superfined upon our brother of Bath and Wells." Fitzwilliam wrote to Lady Rachel Russell that he "knew him to be fluctuating," that " the consideration of the peace of the Church " might induce him to comply. Years afterwards, in 1696, Lady Rachel wrote,[2] though in this she, like Burnet, was mistaken, that she knew he had advised others to take the oaths, and had rejoiced that they could take

[1] Macaulay, chap. viii.   [2] *Letters*, 98, 144.

them, though he shrank from doing so himself. Burnet had been told by Dr. Whitby that he had seen a paper, written shortly after Ken's withdrawal from London, which he had prepared, persuading the clergy to take the oaths, and by Ken's chaplain, Dr. Eyre, that "he came with him to London, where at first he owned that he was resolved to go to the House of Lords and take the oaths, but that he was prevailed on to change his mind on the first day after he arrived in town." [1] The author of the *Life of Kettlewell* laments that Turner, dear as he was to Ken, had never been able to "draw him up to the same height as himself in the matter of the oaths."

A correspondence with Henry Dodwell, who now, as throughout his life, assumed what Frampton called the position of the great "lay dictator" of the Church, reminding bishops of their duty, and upbraiding them with their weakness and wickedness when they did not follow his advice, shows at once the imputations to which Ken was exposed and his sensitiveness under them.

Dodwell had written, as we gather from Ken's answer, a strong letter of remonstrance based upon the reports he had heard of his wavering and uncertain counsels. To this Ken replied as follows :—

LETTER XXVIII.

To MR. HENRY DODWELL.

"All Glory be to God.

"SIR,—I was surprised to receive a letter from you, having not had y[t] favour for many yeares, but y[e] letter itselfe did much more surprise me. You are pleased to accuse me of fluctuating, & by y[t] meanes, of being accessory to very many & great sinnes in others, of scandall & perjury & y[e] like, and in a very few lines you inculcate y[e] prevalence of flesh & blood on me, four severall times one after another. I conceive that common kindnesse & equity should have inclined you to have sent to me to know whether y[e] reports you heard of me were true, before you laid so great a load on me. If there had been ground for them, & I had been falling, you should have endeavoured to restore me wth y[e] spirit of meeknesse. If I had actually fallen, I do not apprehend I should have deserved such

[1] Burnet, *O. T.* Book v., 1689.

odious imputations. If I did, I must have condemned a great many wise & good & conscientious men who have allready complyd, wch I dare not doe. So y^t upon the whole, though I perswaded my selfe your letter was well intended, yett it was so worded, y^t it rather causelessly grieved than convinced me. God of his iustice & goodnesse give us grace, in this and all other difficultys, to keepe a conscience void of offence.

" Good S^r,

" Your very affectionate Friend,

" THO. BATH & WELLS.

" *May* 14*th*, 1689."

[The chief points in the letter are—(1) the tone of plaintive protest which runs through it. Ken will not retaliate. He will believe that Dodwell's letter was " well intended," even though it had conveyed " odious imputations " against him. (2) There is the fullest recognition that the question of the oaths was not such plain sailing as it seemed to those who rushed, with a rough-and-ready haste, to extreme conclusions. He, for his part, was not prepared to condemn the " many wise and good and conscientious men " who had already complied.]

Dodwell answered in a letter, too long to be reproduced in full, in much the same spirit as before. He wonders that Ken should have been " surprised " by his former letter. Was he not bound to watch over the interests of the Church, and to warn his friend of the " sin and scandals " to which his example might lead ? And after all his strong language had only been conditional. He had only spoken on the hypothesis of Ken's compliance as to the oaths, and he had not actually gone beyond a remonstrance with him on his doubts and fluctuations. As for the plea that good men had complied, if taking the oath was a crime, the number of criminals could make no difference. It could never be otherwise than wrong to " follow a multitude to do evil." He exhorts Ken finally to follow the examples of Cyprian and Athanasius and Hosius. Probably Ken felt now, as later on, that even the *multitudo peccantium* was a plea for charity (p. 193).

To this letter Ken returned the following answer :—

LETTER XXIX.

To Mr. HENRY DODWELL.

" All Glory be to God.

" S^r,—Your letter followed me into ye country, in wch you expresse so reall a kindnesse & hearty concerne for me, y^t I think my selfe bound to returne you my hearty acknowledgments for them, & I doe withall beg your pardon for my last, wch I had much rather doe than endeavour to justify it. The very trueth is, when your letter came to my hands I was sick, & my indisposition was ye more inflamed by finding my selfe so vehemently assaulted & suspected by boeth sides, & my distemper governed my style. I had given you a full & free account of my selfe before this time; but I could meet with no private hand to conveye it to you, & I thought it not fitt to write by ye post. In short, I am now & allwayes was of your opinion in ye maine, & so I am like to continue, unlesse things change to y^t degree y^t I may lawfully change allso; onely in one thing I cannot goe so far as you seeme to doe, in condemning those who are of another perswasion, because I thinke there are more degrees of excusability in what they have done than perhapps you will admit. God of his infinite goodnesse blesse & prosper all your labours of love for His Church.

"Good S^r,

"Your truely affectionate Friend,

"T. BATH & WELLS.

"*June 12th,* 1689."

[The meek, apologetic tone of the letter is eminently characteristic. It was in Ken's natural man to flash, under the double pressure of bodily infirmities and unjust imputations from "both sides," into a white heat of indignation, but this was, in all cases that we can trace, followed, after no long interval, by repentance and confusion of face and confession of his fault (p. 149). Most of those who have studied the spiritual life will feel, I think, that this implies a measure of saintliness higher even than that of a more uniform, because more natural, equanimity. We note, however, that, even now, he will not go so far as his correspondent. "Things may change" so far that he himself may "fully change" with them. James might so act—he is probably thinking once again of Ireland (pp. 10, 49)—as to justify the renunciation of all allegiance to him. Meanwhile he will not condemn those who are of another persuasion, and recognises, in the temper of a true charity, that there are (it was a favourite phrase of his) different "degrees of excusability" (pp. 93, 110).]

How painful this fluctuation was, how nearly the scales hung balanced equally, was shown in the fact that he went up, probably, as Turner's letter shows, before Ascension Day, 1689, to consult Hooper, who had taken the oaths:

"On parting one night to go to bed, the Bishop seemed so well satisfied with the arguments Dr. Hooper urged to him, that he was inclined to take the oaths." But the next morning he used these expressions to him:—"I question not but that you and several others have taken the oaths with as good a conscience as myself shall refuse them; and sometimes you have almost persuaded me to comply by the arguments you have used; but I beg you to urge them no further; for should I be persuaded to comply, and after see reason to repent, you would make me the most miserable man

in the world." "Upon which the Doctor said he would never
mention the subject any more to him, for God forbid he should
take them."[1]

As we know, he adhered finally to that resolve. As far as I
can judge the workings of his mind, I take it that there were
three dominant elements in his decision. (1) He saw in the
oath of allegiance a personal promise to James. It had been
given unconditionally and in accordance with the laws of England, and, the extremest case, as stated above, excepted, he was
unable to read into it *ex post facto* limitations. He clung to the
theory of a regency, and could not honestly say that James had
abdicated, and therefore, though he might hold that it would
be wrong to entrust him personally with the exercise of
kingly power, and would obey a *de facto* ruler, yet he could
not recognise another king. (2) He could not admit that
Parliament had the dispensing power, against which he had
protested when it had been claimed by James. As he would
not be accessory to James's violations of the law, so neither
could he make himself accessory to the deprivation of his
brother bishops and the clergy by a purely secular authority. That would seem to him simple undiluted Erastianism.
(3) He shrank with, it may be, a morbid sensitiveness from
even appearing to be one of those who changed their voice
according to the time, and abandoned all they had been preaching for years, for the sake of gaining or retaining high places
in the Church. He could not bear to think that men should
speak of him as they already spoke of Tillotson and Burnet,
as they afterwards spoke of Sherlock, when, following the line
of action suggested by Overall's *Convocation Book*, he took the
oaths, and passed from the Mastership of the Temple to the
Deanery of St. Paul's. The temper of his mind inclined in
quite the opposite direction. If he was in doubt it was safer,
in quite another sense than that in which others counted
" safety," to take the losing and not the winning side. The
via crucis, the path of suffering and sacrifice, brought with
it fewer temptations than one of prosperity and ease.[2] And for

[1] Prowse MS. and Hawkins, p. 30.
[2] In 1879, as Canon Jackson informs me, an old playing card, the deuce of
spades, fell out of a volume in Ken's library at Longleat, Priorato's *History of the*

him the sacrifice was great. He had to part not only from the state and income of his episcopate—that for him would have been but a small thing—but from the flock which he loved, dear to him as his own soul. He at last made his choice, and could only say, as he had said to James on that memorable 8th of June, 1688, " God's will be done."

But the very struggles through which he had himself passed gave a very different character to his position from that of most of the other Non-jurors. One of the trials of the years that followed was, indeed, that he found himself in imperfect sympathy with those with whom he was classed, with whom he was compelled to class himself. He shrank from their bitterness and hardness, from their scurrilous libels on men better than themselves, from the anathemas which they dealt out to those from whom they had separated, from the restless conspiracies of some of them, from the tendency of others to take up a position like that of the Donatists and Montanists of old, as though they, and they only, represented the true Church of Christ in England, and all others were renegades and apostates. He foresaw, more clearly than they did, all the evils of a perpetuated schism. If among them there were men like Kettlewell, Fitzwilliam, Nelson, of whom the world was not worthy, whose holiness of life had probably contributed, in no small measure, to influence his decision, there were, on the other side, men of equal holiness, of equal wisdom, of equal loyalty to the principles of the Church of England. He could not and would not blame them. He continued to count Hooper his dearest friend, and he was content to find a home under Lord Weymouth's pro-

---

Wars of Europe, translated by Henry Cary, Earl of Monmouth, in 1648. On the card, which he had apparently used as a book-marker, were two sentences in Ken's writing. The first of these was, " It is better to hazard one's self in war yⁿ to be sure to lose *all* in peace." There is no date, but the maxim may, I think, throw light on Ken's motives in his final decision. He preferred the " hazard " of the conflict which lay before him to the certain " loss " of forfeiting what to him was " all," his self-respect, his conscious integrity, by the ignominious " peace " of surrendering his convictions for the sake of place and power. The other sentence does not connect itself with this or any other special period in Ken's life, but I may as well quote it here: " Yᵉ sun in a direct way enlightens yᵉ object, but confounds the organ." Could this have been suggested by the prayer of Ajax, " ἐν δὲ φάει καὶ ὄλεσσον," and applied to spiritual intuitions ?

tection at Longleat, though both of them had taken the oaths which he felt that he could not take. During the interval that yet remained for the exercise of his episcopal functions, he presented to livings in his gift clergy none of whom were afterwards Non-jurors. With that desire for time which was expressed in Letter XXVI., he waited during the months from February to July without publicly announcing a decision.[1] He waited, it may be, in the hope that a way not yet in view might be opened for him out of his perplexities. At last, on August 1, 1689, the limit fixed by the Act of Parliament came, and not having taken the oaths, he was *ipso facto* suspended from the exercise of his office, but had yet six months' grace before the suspension passed into deprivation. He adopted a course for the administration of his diocese during the interval, which, though it had the precedent of Sancroft's commission to three Bishops to consecrate Burnet, was perhaps scarcely logical, and which, at all events, exposed him to the taunts of inconsistency on the right hand and on the left. Burnet appears to have received a kind of roving commission, or permission, from the Crown to act as Commissary for some at least of the suspended Bishops. We know, for certain, that he acted in that character for Frampton. The following letter to Ken implies, with hardly the shadow of a doubt, that he was acting in a like capacity for the diocese of Bath and Wells. Its importance leads me to depart from my usual rule of giving none but Ken's letters *in extenso* :—

To the Bishop of Bath and Wells.

"My Lord,

"The gentleman who is presented to a living in your lordship's diocese came to me to receive institution, but I have declined the doing of it, and so have sent him over to your lordship that you, being

---

[1] The letter from Turner, quoted above (p. 43), contains another significant passage: "I receiv'd an honest letter from him, and a friendly one, wherein hee argues wrong, to my understanding, but promises and protests hee will keep himself disengaged till he debates things over again with us, and that hee was coming up for that purpose. My Lord Bishop of Norwich has seen such another letter from him to my Lord of Gloucester." Frampton, it will be seen, was more in sympathy with Ken than any other of the Non-juring Bishops.

satisfy'd with relation to him, may order your Chancellor to do it. I was willing to lay hold on this occasion to let your lordship know that I intend to make no other use of the commission that was sent me than to obey any orders that you may send me in such things as my hand and seal may be necessary. I am extremely concerned to see your lordship so unhappily possess'd with that which is likely to prove so fatal to the Church, if we are deprived of one that has served in it with so much honour as you have done, especially at such a time when there are fair hopes of the reforming of several abuses. I am the more amazed to find your lordship so positive ; because some have told myself that you had advised them to take that which you refuse yourself, and others have told me that they read a pastoral letter which you had prepared for your diocese, and were resolved to print it when you went to London. Your lordship, it seems, changed your mind there, which gave great advantages to those who were so severe as to say that there was somewhat else than conscience at the bottom. I take the liberty to write this freely to your lordship, for I do not deny that I am in some pain till I know whether it is true or not. I pray God prevent a new breach in a church which has suffered so severely under the old one.

<blockquote>
"My lord, Your lordship's most faithful
servant and brother,
"Gr. SARUM.
</blockquote>

"Sirum, October 1st" (1689).

[The first sentences refer obviously to some one who had been sent by Ken to Burnet to be instituted under his commission from the Crown. The latter takes the opportunity of twitting Ken with his inconsistency. The rumours to which he refers are those already mentioned (it was even said that Ken had signed the invitation to the Prince of Orange), and the more positive statements came, Burnet says, from Ken's own chaplain, Dr. Eyre (p. 41). We shall by-and-by see Ken's explanation of them. The hint at "somewhat else than conscience" as "at the bottom" of the supposed change, strikes one as un-generous, but it may be pleaded in extenuation that the air was full of rumours of conspiracies, in which some of the Non-juring Bishops, notably Turner of Ely, were, then or later, believed to be implicated. Those who did not understand him might think that Ken also was, after all, playing a waiting game, taking his chance of the return of the King to whom he was now said still to profess his allegiance, perhaps joining with others in treasonable practices to bring about that return.]

To this letter Ken returned an immediate answer, written obviously in much heat of spirit :

To Gilbert Burnet, Bishop of Salisbury.

" All Glory be to God.

"My Lord,

"I am obliged to your lordship, for the continued concern you express for me; and for the kind freedom you are pleased to take with me; and though I have already in public fully declared my mind to my diocese concerning the oath, to prevent my being misunderstood; yet since you seem to expect it of me, I will give such an account, which, if it does not satisfy your Lordship, will at least satisfy myself. I dare assure you, I never advised any one to take the oath; though some, who came to talk insidiously with me, may have raised such a report; so far have I been from it, that I never would administer it to any one person whom I was to collate. And therefore, before the Act took place, I gave a particular commission to my Chancellor, who himself did not scruple it; so that he was authorized, not only to institute, but also to collate in my stead. If any came to discourse with me about taking the oath, I usually told them, I durst not take it myself. I told them my reasons, if they urged me to it, and were of my own diocese : and then remitted them to their study and prayers, for farther directions. It is true, having been scandalized at many persons of our own coat, who for several years together preached up passive obedience to a much greater height than ever I did, it being a subject with which I very rarely meddled, and on a sudden, without the least acknowledgment of their past error, preached and acted the quite contrary, I did prepare a pastoral letter, which, if I had seen reason to alter my judgment, I thought to have published; at least that part of it on which I laid the greatest stress, to justify my conduct to my flock : and before I went to London, I told some of my friends, that if that proved true, which was affirmed to us with all imaginable assurance (and which I think more proper for discourse than a letter) it would be an inducement to me to comply. But when I came to town, I found it was false; and without being influenced by any one, or making any words of it, I burnt my paper, and adhered to my former opinion. If this is to be called change of mind, and a change so criminal, that people who are very discerning, and know my own heart better than myself, have pronounced sentence upon me that there is something else than conscience at the bottom, I am much afraid, that some of those who censure me, may be chargeable with more notorious changes than that; whether more consci-

entious or no, God only is the Judge. If your Lordship gives credit
to the many misrepresentations which are made of me, and which,
I, being so used to, can easily disregard, you may naturally enough
be in pain for me: for to see one of your brethren throwing himself
headlong into a wilful deprivation, not only of honour and of income,
but of a good conscience also, are particulars, out of which may be
framed an idea very deplorable. But though I do daily in many
things betray great infirmity, I thank God, I cannot accuse myself
of any insincerity: so that deprivation will not reach my conscience,
and I am in no pain at all for myself. I perceive, that, after we
have been sufficiently ridiculed, the last mortal stab designed to be
given us, is, to expose us to the world for men of no conscience ;
and if God is pleased to permit it, His most holy will be done ;
though what that particular passion of corrupt nature is, which lies
at the bottom, and which we gratify, in losing all we have, will be
hard to determine. God grant such reproaches as these may not
revert on the authors! I heartily join with your Lordship in your
desire for the peace of this Church ; and I shall conceive great hopes
that God will have compassion on her, if I see that she compassion-
ates and supports her sister of Scotland. I beseech God to make
you an instrument to promote that peace, and that charity ; I myself
can only contribute to both by my prayers, and by my depreca-
tions, against schism, and against sacrilege.

> " My lord, Your Lordship's very faithful
> servant and brother,
> "THO. BATH & WELLS.

" *October 5th* (1689)."

[The declaration of "his mind in public" to his diocese refers, I imagine, to
some sermon or circular letter of which we have no extant record. He had
"never advised any one to take the oath," but he clearly thought that it was
more or less an open question, on which conscientious men might legitimately
differ, and so issued a commission to his Chancellor, authorising him to
administer the oath which he could not administer himself. Macaulay (Ch. xii.)
follows Burnet (*O. T.* Book v., 1689) in charging him and Sancroft with inconsistency. I only find the charity of one who could at once be severe with himself,
and tolerant of a different opinion in others. The reference to his being "scandalized" at the tergiversation of those who had "preached up passive obedience"
to an extent to which he had never preached it, is, I can scarcely doubt, an
allusion to Tillotson and others, Burnet himself included, who changed their
voice according to the time. Ken could not forget the language they had used
to Lord Russell. The hint that he was prepared to take the oath "if that
proved true," which was afterwards found to be false, refers to the report that
James had formally ceded Ireland to Louis XIV.[1] Ken admits that he had

---

[1] See Macaulay (Chap. viii.) for James's probable intentions on this head.

prepared a pastoral letter to his clergy, telling them that this at all events would have been a violation of the original contract, that would have justified the transfer of his allegiance. With a keen irony, which reminds one a little of Cardinal Newman, he admits that it would be an "idea very deplorable" that a man should "throw himself headlong into a wilful deprivation, not only of honour and of income, but of a good conscience." It "will be hard indeed to determine what particular passion of corrupt nature" lies at the bottom of such a choice as that. The allusion to the Church of Scotland refers to the outbursts of mob violence in "rabbling" the Bishops and their clergy, destroying their surplices and their prayer-books, pulling down their manses, and turning them with their wives and families adrift. These outrages were but too sure prognostics of the overthrow of Episcopacy and the establishment of Presbyterianism. Could not Burnet do something to check the one evil and to arrest the other ?—(Macaulay, Ch. xiii.)

Like Sancroft and the other Bishops who were in the same position, Ken not only waited, as we have seen, till the expiration of the six months' grace, but even stayed at Wells for more than a year after February 1, 1690, as Sancroft stayed at Lambeth till his successor was appointed, and there was the risk of a forcible expulsion.[1] Before that 1st of February, efforts were made to avert the threatening danger. In November, 1689, a member of the Lower House of Convocation moved that "something might be done to enable the suspended Bishops" (they were not yet deprived) "to qualify them to sit in Convocation ;" but it came, as might have been expected, to nothing. It was before February 1st that the clergy of Bath and Wells, who had taken the oaths, drew up a petition to the King on behalf of the "prelates under censure." Anderdon (p. 552) gives the petition *in extenso*. It is doubtful whether it was ever presented.[2] The petitioners "passionately entreat" that "the Church might not be wholly deprived of them," nor "they wholly excluded from the comforts of that great deliverance" which they owed to William. They hope, to adopt a briefer phrase than they used, that some *modus vivendi* might even yet be found. When Ken and Frampton went to London, in January, 1690, to visit Turner at Ely House and consult with

[1] Probably during this period he continued to preach, confirm, and exercise other episcopal functions, as in the passage quoted by Anderdon (p. 605, *n.*) from the Lansdowne MSS. in the British Museum, 987.

[2] A form of the Petition, with a blank left for the name of the Diocese, is found in the *Additional MSS.* of the British Museum 13,2095 (403), as if it had been prepared for general use.

Clarendon,[1] it was, probably, with a view to see if any such arrangement were feasible.

No such *modus vivendi* was, however, possible. The patience of the Government was at last exhausted; public feeling had been excited during the spring and summer of 1690, as we shall see in the next chapter, by real or pretended plots, in which some of them were, and others were supposed to be, implicated; and after waiting for more than a year, on or about April 15th, 1691 (Evelyn notes the fact on the 19th), the Nonjuring Bishops were formally deprived, and steps taken for the appointment of their successors.[2] Tillotson was made Archbishop of Canterbury, Patrick was translated to Chichester, Fowler went to Gloucester, Bath and Wells was offered to Beveridge. The choice seems to indicate a desire on Mary's part to send a man who would, in all the great questions of Church doctrine and ritual, be in sympathy with Ken. He, however, though he had no scruple as to the oath, was troubled in mind at the thought of taking a bishopric in the lifetime of a deprived predecessor, and went to Sancroft for advice (Evelyn, May 7th, 1691). The Archbishop advised him strongly to "say *Nolo*, and say it from the heart," but hardly seems to have thought that Beveridge would have acted, as he did, on his counsel.[3] On Beveridge's refusal, after three weeks' deliberation, it was offered to Richard Kidder, then Rector of St. Paul's, Covent Garden, and he accepted it.[4]

---

[1] Clarendon ii. p. 227.

[2] William was in Holland, and the *congés d'élire*, &c., were signed by Mary and sealed with her private seal (Wells, Chapter Acts).

[3] It is a curious illustration of the current belief that Beveridge had accepted, that his name actually appears as Bishop of Bath and Wells, in an almanack published in the spring of 1691. So a French news-letter, dated May 29, 1691, reports that Beveridge, after accepting, had changed his mind, because Ken was reported to be about to take proceedings in the Court of King's Bench against his deprivation, and that he had called his clergy together to support him in that course. The writer, in his next letter, June 5 (May 26), 1691, reports that the affair of the Bishops was not yet finished, and that this was mainly owing to the action of Dr. Ken, who, not content with stirring up the clergy, was also stirring up the Bishops. It was even probable that Tillotson's consecration, fixed for Whit Sunday, might have to be postponed. (Hist. MSS., Comm. *Rep.* vii., 197-8).

[4] See Appendix to this Chapter for Kidder's life.

What Ken thought of his successor is seen in the following letter :—

LETTER XXXI.

To MRS. GRIGGE.

"All Glory be to God.

"GOOD MRS. GRIGGE,

"I hope you received mine by y⁰ post, in answer to your last: one of my neighbours brings this, & I have sent you y⁰ poore woman's paper ; I told you it was for a gentile-woman of my acquaintance. She fancied it was for some great Lady, & brought it me in y⁰ style I now send you, with wch you might despence, unlesse you desire to have it in another, w^{ch}, when I goe next to Winchester, I can easily have done.

"If you heare any thing from my friend, direct your letter not to me, but to Mr. Isaac Walton, Rectour of Polshallt; to be left at y⁰ poste house in y⁰ Devizes, for to his house I am now, God willing, going, for some time, partly for my health, partly to avoid y^t odium under wch I lye, & cheifely from my Brethren ; God foregive them for it, & having done all I can think proper for me to doe, to assert my Character, y⁰ doing of wch has created me many enemies, as I expected it should.

"My B^r of G. is I heare out of harmes way, in Wales at y⁰ present, but I have received nothing from him.

"My best respects to my good mother, & to deare Miss, who, I doubt not, but behaves hereselfe with all y^t Decency, & piety, & humility, as becomes y⁰ daughter not onely of a Bishop, but of a Bishop in affliction.

"Dr Kidder is now said to be my Successour or rather supplanter. He is a person of whom I have no knowledge. God of his Infinite goodnesse Multiply his blessings on your selfe, & on my good friends with you, & enable us to doe, & to suffer His most Holy Will.

"Your very affectionate friend

"THOS. BATH & WELLS.

"*June 7th*, 1691."

[The fact of Ken's writing thus familiarly to a Mrs. Grigge, who does not appear in the main narrative of his life, has perplexed his biographers. Anderdon (p. 605) conjectures that it was a pseudonym for Bishop Lloyd, adopted to evade the opening of the letter by the Post Office. It is clear that the Nonjuring Bishops knew that their correspondence was thus tampered with, and so Ken directs nearly all his letters for the deprived Bishop of Norwich, to "Mrs.

Hannah Lloyd." In this very letter he requests that a letter for him may be directed to Mr. Izaak Walton, and in another instance (p. 124) to Mr. Jones, at Walton's house in Sarum Close. Commonly, perhaps, Ken's correspondence was protected by his residence at Longleat. Miss Strickland (*Seven Bishops*, p. 190) gives a letter from Mrs. Grigge, or Grigg, and says that she was a relation of Francis Turner's, staying at the Palace at Ely. Fox Bourne's *Life of Locke* shows her to have been one of two sisters with whom Locke corresponded on terms of fraternal affection. Her husband, the Rev. Thomas Grigg, of Trinity College, Oxford, was Chaplain to Bishop Henchman, of London, and Rector of St. Andrew Undershaft. He died in 1670. Locke speaks of him as *vir optimus.* In 1680 we find Locke writing to her as travelling with a youth of good family in France. In 1689 he writes to her as "Dear Sister," and after that, she was in the family of Bishop Patrick, of Ely. It is probable enough that she may have been governess to Francis Turner's daughter. Turner mentions her in the "Ascension Day" (1689) letter, already quoted (p. 40), as having received a letter from Ken. She herself had been left, in her widowhood, with one daughter, who by this time must have been over twenty. The internal evidence of the letter is in favour of its being written to some one closely connected with Turner. The ex-Bishop of Ely was in hiding, and it was probably of him that Ken wished to hear news when he asked after "my friends." The "odium," under which he lay, was the report that he was going after all, to take the oaths. The "brethren" who had spread that report were probably Dodwell and Hickes. The "brother of G." is Robert Frampton, Bishop of Gloucester, who also refused to take the oaths, and was suspected, like other Bishops, of being connected with the conspiracy of 1690.[1] The "good mother" is, on this hypothesis, Turner's mother, who kept house for him at Ely after his wife's death, and the "dear Miss," his daughter, then nine years old. The manner in which Ken speaks of his successor, though it does not express more than personal non-acquaintance, implies, I think, something beyond this. He did not know him, and did not wish to know. From first to last the tone in which Ken mentions him (he does not often do so) is that of a thoroughly antipathetic nature. What is said of Kidder in the note to this chapter will show, if I mistake not, that there were reasonable grounds for the antipathy. Anderdon gives only a part of the letter. It is found in full in the British Museum (*Add. MSS.*, 32.095, f. 387). I am indebted to Mr. R. C. Browne for a more accurate transcript than that given by Round.]

Kidder's consecration, and that of three other of the new Bishops, took place at Bow Church, on August 30th, 1691. The manner in which Ken acted on hearing of this decisive step may be best given in his own words, in a letter written by himself some years afterwards :—

---

[1] A letter of Frampton's to Lloyd, of Norwich (February, 169$\frac{8}{9}$), sends a message of respects to our good brother of Ely, our other brother of Bath and Wells, and "Madam Philomela," Turner's daughter, the "little Miss" of Ken s letter.

LETTER XXXII.

To the Rev. Mr. Harbin.

"All Glory be to God.

"Good Mr. Harbin,

"I well remember y* you told me, you were to pay some debts for your mother, but y* sume of £300 I am confident y* you did not mention, & I am unwilling to putt you to any streights. You tell me y* Mr Pitts censures y* deprived Bishopps, for not asserting their Rights, in a publick manner, at their Deprivation. If he putts me among y* Number, he does me wrong, for I, at y* time, in my Cathedrall, wch was y* proper place, from my Pastrall Chaire, publickly asserted my Canonicall Right, professing y* I esteemd my selfe y* Canonicall Pastour (*Bishop ?*) of y* Diocese, & y* I would be ready on all occasions to performe my Pastorall duty : this I did, when all were devoted to y* Revolution. I watched for some expressions, wch they might informe of particularly ; it was then urged y* I said I was y* Lawfull Pastour, Insomuch y* I was faine to appeal to some lesse byassd, whether my word was not Canonicall, wch I usd, as most proper, & as a word y* y* Law was a stranger to, & I professed, y* not being able to make y* Declaration to y* whole Diocese, I made it virtually to all, by making it in y* Mother Church (*Market Square ?*). What others of my Brethren did I knowe not ; but I acted as Uniformly as I could. Pray lett good Mr Jenkins know this, and lett Mr Pitts know it, if you chance to meet him. Probably, I may have y* copy of my Declaration, among my papers at Longleat. I beseech (*pray to*) God to restore my good Lord, I shall be extreamely Glad to hear y* He goes abroad, God keepe us in His Holy fear.

"Your very affec. friend & B^r

"T. B. & W.

"*Dec.* 8*th* (1709 ?)"

[Harbin, to whom Ken writes, was then Chaplain to Lord Weymouth. He was of Cambridge, had been Chaplain to Francis Turner, and was a Non-juror. Curiously enough he had been, in early youth, Kidder's private pupil. Ken was, of course, much associated with him in his retirement at Longleat, and always speaks of him with strong personal affection (see p. 108). The letter was probably written in 1709, in answer to a pamphlet that had appeared, "The Character of a Primitive Bishop, in a Letter to a Non-juror," in which the writer argued that the acquiescence of the deprived Bishops in the appointment of their successors, and their retirement from all Episcopal duties in their several dioceses, virtually amounted to a cession, and that those successors were accordingly not intruders. Possibly, however, it may have been in reply to Burnet himself, who in 1696 had published a *Vindication of Archbishop Tillotson*, and if so, it was written at an earlier date.

I have not been able to ascertain who Mr. Pitts was; probably a Non-juror who felt the force of the "implied cession" argument. Ken says that in his case there had not been the shadow of foundation for such an argument. He had protested; he was ready to perform his pastoral duties. As a matter of fact, it is probable that, like Frampton, he, from time to time, confirmed the children of Non-juring families, catechised or preached in churches, and officiated, as he did (*e.g.*, on Kettlewell's death), at funerals, and other occasional services. Some instances of this will meet us further on. The Government, either, as I think probable, under Mary's influence, who said that "Though Ken and Frampton wished to be martyrs she would do her best to disappoint them," or because it was known that both these prelates held aloof from all political conspiracies, connived in their instance at a greater freedom than was allowed to others. (Evans, pp. 190, 204.) More than a year, as we have seen, had been allowed to intervene between the time when they were legally deprived and their actual expulsion. The distinction between "canonical" and "legal" Bishops seems to me eminently characteristic of one who had been trained in the school of Sanderson. He would not deny the validity of Kidder's acts in the sight of the law of the State; he was bound to maintain that they were not in accordance with the law of the Church. The point had clearly been raised, and he relies on the accuracy of his memory as to having said "canonical." Mr. Jenkins is to me as little known as Mr. Pitts (but see p. 186). The "good Lord" is clearly Lord Weymouth. No copy of Ken's Declaration is, as far as I know, extant. Round and Anderdon make Ken say that he read it also in the "Market Place" of Wells, but I am assured by Mr. R. C. Browne, who has kindly transcribed the original for me, that "Mother Church" is the true reading. It would hardly have been in accordance with Ken's character to appeal to the *demos*. On the other hand, Turner is reported to have read his protest in the Market Place of Ely. (Strickland, *Bishops*, p. 199.) The words in italics represent Round's readings.]

It seems probable that that memorable day on which Ken read his protest from his throne in the Cathedral was his last appearance in the Church which he loved so dearly, until, many years afterwards, he, perhaps, appeared there in another character and with very different feelings (p. 195). It was followed soon afterwards, we must believe, by his departure from his palace. There must have been partings, of which we have no record, from the Cathedral clergy, with whom, though they did not follow his example, he had always been on the friendliest terms; from the poor, who had been his Sunday guests; from the boys, whom he had catechised and confirmed, and to whom he had administered their first Communion. And now all was over. Those six happy years—happy as far as his work in his diocese was concerned—had come to an end, and he left his home, not knowing what the future had in store for him, full of anxious forebodings for himself, for his flock, for the Church at large. Like Turner, when he left Ely, he might have quoted Milton, and said that he "took, *not* through Eden, his solitary way," and had "the world before him, where to choose."[1]

And so the die was cast, and Ken entered by his own choice on the life which, though he never left his native land, was for him practically the life of an exile. And in his case, as in that of other exiles, it is difficult, in the years that followed, to track his wanderings, just as, to speak from my own recent experience, it is difficult to track the wanderings of Dante in his exile. In each case, we know there was a home open for the fugitive. What Can Grande's palace at Verona was for the one, Lord Weymouth's stately mansion at Longleat was for the other. Other houses were also open to him, chiefly, of course, though not exclusively, among the Non-jurors.[2] Poulshot, where Izaak Walton, junior, was Rector; the houses of Mrs. Thynne, at Leweston, near Sherborne; of Colonel Phillips, between Long-leat and Bath; of the Misses Kemeys, of Naish House, near Portishead, Bristol; that of Mr. Cherry, of Shottesbrook; of Thomas Cheyney, his former chaplain, the Head Master of Winchester College from 1700; of Archdeacon Sandys; occasional visits, too, under the constraint of illness, to Bath and the Hot Wells at Clifton. At all these we meet with him from time to time; but dates are so uncertain for the most part that I abandon, at this stage, the attempt to record his wanderings from place to place in strict chronological order, and think it better to treat first, in as clear an order as I can, of the life which was more or less public, and in which he was associated in various ways, if not with the main stream of the nation's life, yet, at all events, with that side-current of Church history in which we follow the windings of the Non-juror movement, and to reserve the treatment of the more private episodes of his fortunes for a distinct chapter.

Anyhow, we have to remember that the life of the exile was one of poverty. He had had to borrow from Morley's nephew the large sum which was required to meet the expenses of entering on his episcopate. His income of £850 scarcely sufficed

---

[1] Strickland, *Bishops*, p 208.   [2] Anderdon, p. 627.

LONGLEAT.

for more than his ordinary
expenses and lavish charities. When the chances of
tenure threw the large sum
of £4,000 into his hands on the renewal of a lease, he treated
it, as we have seen, as strictly a deodand, and gave the greater
part of it to the fund for the relief of the Huguenots. What
he actually started with, as a fund for the chances of the future,
was £700, the proceeds of the sale of his effects at the Palace
at Wells, his library excepted.[1] It was, perhaps, with some
insight into his friend's character, as likely before long to get
rid of his £700, as he used, in old Oxford days, to empty his
pocket of small cash when he went out for a walk (i. 52), that
Lord Weymouth proposed to change the capital in hand into a
life annuity of £80, payable quarterly.[2] He always, he himself

---

[1] I mention, only to reject, the two statements which have here and there
found credence: (1) That Mary allowed him to retain his prebend in Wells
Cathedral, and (2) that Bishop Kidder allowed him one-third of the income of the
see. (Granger, Noble's Continuation, p. 101.) There is not the shadow of
evidence that he ever held a prebend, and Kidder was as little likely to offer, as
Ken to receive, such a pension.

[2] I have seen, through the kindness of Canon J. E. Jackson, one of Ken's
receipts, now at Longleat, given in due business form, for these payments.

says it, refused money which was offered for his own use (p. 122); and though there were legacies left him, as *e.g.* by his friends Dr. Fitzwilliam and the Misses Kemeys,[1] I question whether he allowed himself to think of these as bestowed for any other purpose than that of enabling him to give help to others who needed it, or seemed to him to need it, more than he did. I cannot doubt that he often felt the pinch of poverty. He could not afford a journey to London (p. 437). We get casual glimpses of a "sorry nag" and of a threadbare cassock. The large hospitality of Longleat was, of course, always open to him; and he received it with a deep and sincere thankfulness, and with the warmest admiration for his patron's character. Even here, however, there were drawbacks which he sometimes felt keenly.

Lord Weymouth, though the protector of Non-jurors, was not one himself. The *de facto* rulers were prayed for in his chapel, if not at first, yet after Anne's succession, and Ken, though like Kettlewell and Nelson and Dodwell, he held that private persons might attend the services of the church where such prayers were said, with a mental reservation, or with some manifestation that they were not joining in them, rather than deprive themselves of the means of grace, felt that he as a public person could not so join (p. 121).[2] The presence of such prayers in the Communion Service must have hindered his joining in that act of Christian fellowship, and I incline to think that the small paten and chalice which he left to the church at Frome must have been chiefly used by him in administering that ordinance to the two or three who were like-minded with himself. It was obviously a relief to him at

---

[1] Dr. Fitzwilliam left Ken the interest of £500 for life, with a reversion to Magdalen College, Oxford. Miss Kemeys left £200, suggesting its application to charitable uses (p. 169).

[2] The same reason would obviously keep Ken from Lord Weymouth's parish church of Horningham. Frampton used to preach and read the service in his church at Standish, omitting the names of William and Mary. Unhappily the Prayer Book was not as elastic as the later Jacobite formulary—

"God bless the King, God bless the faith's defender,
"God bless—no harm in blessing—the Pretender;
"Who that Pretender is, and who that King,
"God bless us all, is quite another thing."

times to leave Longleat to join the "ladies at Naish," Mr. Cherry at Shottesbrook, or other Non-juring families, even though he missed not only the magnificence of Longleat, but, what he prized more, the rich stores of his own library and his patron's.

NOTE.—Ken's feelings on leaving Wells are perhaps represented by a Latin inscription written by him in a copy of Diogenes Laertius in the Longleat Library:—

" Si invenero gratiam in oculis Domini, reducet me. Si autem dixerit mihi, ' Non placet ;' præsto sum. Faciat quod bonum est coram se.

"THOMAS KEN."

This inscription is, however, undated, and the form of the signature points to a date before his appointment to his bishopric or after his resignation. The words may possibly have been written when Ken was leaving Winchester for the Hague or Tangier.

[NOTE ON LONGLEAT.—Sir John Thynne purchased, in 1540, the dissolved Priory of Longleat. In 1547 he began building a stately mansion on its site, and, according to an uncertain tradition, employed a John of Padua, who had acted as "Devisor of the King's Buildings to Henry VIII.," as his architect. This house was, however, destroyed by fire in 1568, and Sir John set to work on the construction of another, probably on the same lines but on a yet grander scale. (Canon J. E. Jackson, *John of Padua*, 1886). Thomas Thynne—"Tom of Ten Thousand "—planted the stately avenue which leads from Frome, and under him and Lord Weymouth it became. as Macaulay calls it, "the most magnificent country-house in England." The gardens were laid out in the style of Versailles. Ken's apartments were in the upper part of the house, in what is now the old library, which includes about 1,000 volumes, left by Ken to Lord Weymouth (p. 206). Lord Weymouth was himself a great collector of books, largely of theological works. A point in the grounds, on the way to the parish church of Horningham, is known, from the beauty of its view, as the Gate of Heaven. Ken, as a Non-juror, was not likely to attend the parochial services, but during William's reign Lord Weymouth seems to have had services in his chapel without the "characteristick" prayers (p. 124).]

NOTE TO CHAPTER XX.

BISHOP KIDDER.

It does not fall within the plan of this work to give a full biography of Ken's successor. Some account of Kidder's antecedents may, however, find a fitting place here, if only to explain the tone of dislike, amounting almost to antipathy, with which Ken uniformly speaks of him, and of which the mere fact that he had accepted the bishopric is no adequate explanation. To him he was as a "Latitudinarian traditor" (p. 133), an "hireling" (p. 143); one who "instead of keeping the flock within the fold encouraged them to stray" (p. 148); even "a stranger ravaging the flock" (pp. 132, 141). Even after Kidder's death he was constrained to write—

> "Forc'd from my flock, I daily saw with tears
> A stranger's ravage, two sabbatick years."
> *(Poems, i., Dedication.)*

We have to see how far Kidder's previous career, and his administration of the diocese, justified this language.

As I review that career, I own that Kidder seems to me almost a representative instance of the class of men of whom I have spoken in chapter ii., who pass with a fair reputation, and with no conscious baseness, through many changes of political régime, and who are found "ever strong upon the stronger side," always looked upon as "safe" men for preferment to high places in Church or State. Born in 1633, he was educated at Emmanuel College, Cambridge, was elected Fellow under the Commonwealth, and in 1658 was ordained deacon and priest on the same day by Bishop Brownrigg, of Exeter, at St. Edmundsbury. In 1659 he was appointed Vicar of Stanground, Huntingdonshire, in the gift of his college, but, as he states in the *Autobiography* printed in Cassan's *Lives of the Bishops of Bath and Wells* (p. 113), never took either the "Covenant" or the "Engagement" oaths of the Commonwealth period.[1] It lies, in the nature of the case, however, that he must have used the services of the Westminster Directory, and not those of the Prayer Book. In

---

[1] The more scurrilous Non-jurors used to taunt him with having swallowed every oath that came in his way (*Harl. Miscell.*, v. pp. 263—70 ; in Anderdon, p. 603) ; but the Bishop's word must be allowed to outweigh their assertions.

1662 he was deprived under the Act of Uniformity, because he would not subscribe to the Prayer Book, as restored by it, till he had read and considered it, but he still went to the Church's prayers, and did not set up a Meeting House. For two years he continued without preferment, officiating in churches in London and the country from time to time. At the end of this period he was ready to subscribe, and held in succession the livings of Rayne Parva, near Braintree, Essex (1664), St. Helen's, St. Martin's Outwich, London (1674), and the Preachership of the Rolls Chapel. In the position which he thus gained he soon acquired a reputation as a popular preacher, and Lady Warwick speaks of his sermons in her *Diary* in almost the same terms as of Ken's (i. 88). He must have been looked on as having strong sympathies with the High Church party, for Robert Nelson recommended him to Tillotson, then Dean of St. Paul's, for the living of Barnes, and Sancroft, who, as Dean of St. Paul's, had given him St. Helen's, offered him in 1688 that of Sundridge. More startling still, we find Cartwright, James's Bishop of Chester, the basest of his tools, the man whom he sent to do his dirtiest work at Oxford in the Magdalen Commission, the boon companion of Tyrconnel, who held consultations with Father Petre and Laybourne (Vicar Apostolic) on Sundays at Whitehall, writing to Kidder in 1686, soon after his appointment, and inviting him and his wife and daughter to dinner in 1687.[1] One can scarcely resist the conclusion that he had his eye on Kidder, as a man who, like others, " had his price." When the Revolution came he was again found on the winning side. He was a good preacher and a fair scholar, and his appointment by William and Mary to the Deanery of Peterborough was one thoroughly respectable. His own account[2] of the way in which he was led to accept Ken's bishopric is eminently characteristic. He " waited on their Majesties as chaplain " in the spring of 1691. Tillotson proposed that he should take Peterborough, vacant by White's deprivation. He " refused it absolutely, and gave his reasons." He heard of Beveridge's refusal of Bath and Wells, and hoped that the " reasons " he had given would prevent his being tempted with any like offer. He went back to Norwich, where he held a prebend, and wrote to a friend that he " would not be so stiff as absolutely to refuse a Bishopric, excepting that of Bath and Wells, which I was not willing to take." His friend gave Tillotson the first half of the message (for it was clearly meant to be a message) and suppressed

[1] *Diary*, pp. 9, 13, 67.

[2] *Autobiography*, in Cassan., *Bishops of Bath and Wells*, ii., pp. 142—144.

the second. Kidder knew, indeed, very well that he "should be able to do less good if he came into a Bishopric void by deprivation," but he began to recognise that those who had succeeded the deprived prelates were "men of whom the world was not worthy."

But, alas! messengers "more and more honourable than before" came "with the rewards of divination in their hands" (we seem almost to be reading a chapter in the autobiography of Balaam); and when he was at his deanery, a letter came from Tillotson, who told him that the Queen had nominated him for Bath and Wells, and that the Earl (probably Nottingham), through whose influence he had been made Dean, had said that he must not refuse it. He was in much consternation—"had seldom known anything like it"—(that "seldom" seems to me to imply half-suppressed reminiscences of similar conflicts)—and he was in sore perplexity. If he accepted, there would be "trouble and envy." If he refused, why, he would only be attacked, as Beveridge had been, by Stillingfleet and other pamphleteers: and so he accepted, "not," of course, as he afterwards wrote, "against his conscience," but "if the thing were to do again, he would not do it." He had "often repented of his accepting it, and looked on it as a great infelicity."

The record of trouble and vexation that follows shows that his worst anticipations were fulfilled. He found himself unloved. The Dean and Chapter opposed him because he admitted Nonconformist ministers—as they thought without adequate caution—to holy orders, and would not attend his ordinations. A disreputable physician in Wells, of the name of Morrice, gave him infinite domestic worry by engaging the affections of one of his daughters. In one instance, however, there was something like a worthy "fruit of repentance." He was told in 169?—here again we note what men expected of him—that he must go up to the House of Lords and vote for the bill for Sir John Fenwick's attainder. He said that he must wait to know the merits of the case. The answer was, "Don't you know whose bread you eat?" and at last the better nature of the man broke out, and he replied, "I eat no man's bread but poor Doctor Ken's." On this occasion he adhered to his resolve, and voted, to show his principles, against the bill.

At last the well-known end came, and on the night of the great gale of November 26th, 1703, Kidder and his wife were killed by the fall of a stack of chimneys through the roof into their bed-room. That catastrophe will meet us at a later stage, but I will notice here two local traditions connected with it: (1) It was believed (so Defoe writes in his account of the storm) that the Bishop had said shortly before his death, in a burst of passion, that he would rather "the roof of his house should fall on him" than that he should do so and so.[1] (2) It was reported that, not long before, when one of the guests at a dinner at the Palace remained standing for want of a seat, the Bishop ordered a chair to be brought for him. The guest looked at it and shuddered. "I can't sit on that. It's all covered with blood." On that chair, it was believed in Wells, the corpse of the Bishop was subsequently carried out of his bedroom after his death.[2]

On the other hand, it may be noted, that he enjoyed a considerable reputation as a Hebrew scholar; that he defended Christianity against the Jews, and the Pentateuch against free-thinking critics; that among the scholars of the Continent, Le Clerc and Limborch recognised him as one for whose good opinion they were anxious; that, so far as I know, there is nothing to show that he ever thought of Ken with bitterness or treated him with disrespect. The tradition that he assigned him one-third of the income of the see is, I fear, as I have said elsewhere (p. 57 n.), unsupported. The epitaph on the tomb in Wells Cathedral erected to his memory, at a cost of £300, under the will of his unmarried daughter, who died in 1728, is, I think, singularly touching, as showing the reverence which she felt for the man who had been ousted by her father. The lines referring to him are, I think, worth printing:—

> "DECESSORIS OPTIMI HONORIBUS EXUTI
> HINC MISERATIO, INDE DESIDERIUM,
> HOSTES IMMERENTI SUSCITAVERUNT,
> MITE DIU EXERCITUROS INGENIUM,
> PUBLICISQUE DAMNA CURIS ALLATUROS ;
> MORIBUS TANDEM QUEIS NULLI SANCTIORES
> (RARISSIMA FELICITATE) CONCESSUM
> UT SUA KENNO INCOLUMI FAMA,
> SUA KIDDERO FIRMARETUR DIGNITAS ;
> UT PARTIUM RIXÆ PENITUS SILERENT,
> KENNUSQUE KIDDERUSQUE,
> ILLE PRINCIPI, HIC REIPUBLICÆ,
> OPERÆ FIDELITER NAVATAE
> MUTUIS LAUDIBUS ORNARENTUR."

I should be glad to trace the author of the epitaph, but hitherto I have failed in doing so.

---

[1] Defoe, *Narrative of Storm.*
[2] Letter from the late Rev. W. Dodd to E. H. P.

CHAPTER XXI

" Keep Thou my foot ; I do not ask to see
The distant scene,—one step enough for me."
J. H. Newman.

It was soon to be brought home to Ken's experience that the lot of those on the losing side in a revolution brings with it other and sharper sufferings than the loss of income and home and rank. The beginning of those troubles indeed leads us to go back upon our steps to those early months of 1690, in which we have seen Ken and other bishops coming up to London, to discuss the possibility of a *modus vivendi* with a government to which they, and the clergy who thought with them, could not swear allegiance. Might they be permitted, *e.g.*, to exercise such pastoral functions as did not involve the utterance of prayers for William or Mary ? Might they be allowed to omit names in the State prayers ? Might they, if this were not feasible, have some portion of the incomes of which they were deprived assigned them for a maintenance ?

We who read their letters know what they met to discuss.[1] But to the politicians of the time, these consultations were the starting point of incessant rumours and præternatural suspicions. What secret meetings of aristocrats were to the mob of Paris in the French Revolution, that those gatherings at Lambeth were to the mob of London. Were these Bishops hatching treasonable plots, planning schemes for James's restoration, inviting the French king to invade England ? A state of mind like this, surcharged with electricity, is apt to be

[1] Sancroft's, Turner's, Lloyd's, Ken's, are all extant, and we have also Clarendon's *Diary.*

explosive, and soon there supervened on it that which led naturally to an explosion. The Government had ordered March 12th
to be kept as a fast-day, with special forms of prayer for William's
personal safety and for the success of his campaign in Ireland.
Suddenly, scattered broadcast over England, there appeared
another *Form of Prayer*, which might well seem to be a counter-
demonstration, an intercession for William's failure, and for
James's restoration. No one knew who drew it up or sent it
out; but it was circulated widely and simultaneously by
thousands.[1] Whether it was sent to the Non-juring Bishops
there is no evidence to show. It soon came to be generally
believed that they were its authors. They held their peace, as
far as public action was concerned, and trusted to time to let
the popular agitation calm itself.

On June 30th, however, the day before the battle of the
Boyne, the English and Dutch fleets were defeated by the French
under De Tourville, off Beachy Head. The enemy's ships were
masters of the Channel. They might have done as the Dutch
fleet had done in June, 1667, and sailed into the Thames and
Medway to destroy the ships that were anchored there. The
excitement throughout England, especially, of course, in
London, was immense, and, as one result there came out a
pamphlet, also of unknown authorship, bearing the title, *A
Modest Enquiry into the present Disasters, and who they are that
brought the French fleet into the Channel.*[2] The pamphlet was
sufficiently venomous, more personal, and therefore more
dangerous, even than the Sherborne proclamation. The Non-
juring Bishops were reviled as the "Lambeth Club," the
"Holy Jacobite Club," the "High-flown Passive-Obedience
Men," the "Œcumenic Council of the whole party," and any
number of like epithets. Even the clergy who had taken the
oaths are abused as "cheating the world with ridiculous and
foolish distinctions, playing fast and loose with Almighty God,"
"wretches, great contrivers and managers of cabals." Over and
above the general abuse, some taunts are levelled specially at Ken.

[1] See Note at end of Chapter for a discussion of the authorship of the
Jacobite Liturgy and of the *Modest Enquiry.*

[2] Other pamphlets were published on the same subject, notably one bearing
the title of *Reflections upon a Form of Prayer lately set forth, &c.*

" Amongst the collectors for the *Holy Club*, there must be one
Fellow that ate King William's bread," one of whose arts was
" to persuade silly old women to tell down their dust for
carrying on so pious a work," *i.e.* " to work a mine underground in order to a general assault." Over and above this
onslaught there is the specific charge that they, " our high-
priest and the rest of the gang, " had sent over an address to
Louis XIV., the opening words of which were quoted as if the
writer had it before him, " Great and resplendent Monarch !
The resplendent rays of your Majesty's virtues have rendered
all the world your adorers." . . . . and so on, in a strain of
fulsome adulation. It concluded with a suggestion, in the
usual formula of inciting a mob to acts of outrage, that " it
was a wonder that the English nation," under the affront of
their defeat at sea, " had not in their fury *De-Witted* some of
these men." " The crimes of the two unhappy brothers in
Holland which gave rise to this word, were not fully so great
as some of theirs." [1]

Matters now began to look serious. " The Jacobites all
over England kept out of the way and were afraid of being
fallen upon by the rabble." [2] Bishop Lloyd's London house
in Old Street was attacked by the mob, and he had to take
sanctuary with his wife and child in the Temple for personal
safety.[3] A like fate might have befallen Sancroft at Lambeth
any day, or Turner at Ely House. The accused Bishops
took council as to issuing a disclaimer. Turner drew up a
draft form and submitted it to Sancroft, Lloyd, and Ken. The
last suggested amendments as in the following letter—

LETTER XXXIII.

To Archbishop Sancroft.

" All Glory be to God.

" MAY IT PLEASE YOUR GRACE,

" I have drawne up another forme, which to me seemes more
proper than the other, it being short, therefore lesse liable to cavills,

---

[1] See i. 135. [2] Burnet, *O. T.*, Book v., 1690.
[3] Letter from Bishop Lloyd in Anderdon, p. 563.

and more convenient for dispersing, and I thinke as full as the former; I submit it to your Grace's judgment, and I send it thus early, that you may have the longer time to consider it.

"Your Grace's most obedient Servant and Son,

THOS. B. AND W.

"July 17, 1690."

The form of this Declaration, after much revising, was finally settled as follows :—

"*The* DECLARATION *of William, Lord Archbishop of Canterbury, and of severall of his Suffragans, whose names are underwritten.*

"Whereas in a late pamphlet, entitled, '*A Modest Enquiry into the Causes of the present Disasters, &c.*' we, whose names are hereunto subscribed, are among others represented as the authors and abettors of England's miseries ; and under the abusive names of the *Lambeth-Holy-Club, the Holy-Jacobite-Club, and the Œcumenick Council of the whole Party*, are charged with a *Third Plot*, and with the composing of a *New Liturgy*, and using it in our Cabals ; and whereas the Clergy, such of them as are styled malecontents, are said (together with others) to have presented a Memorial to the King of France, to persuade him to invade England ; and are also affirmed to have kept a constant Correspondence with M. de Croissy in order thereunto :

"We do here solemnly, *as in the presence of God*, protest and declare,

"1. That these accusations cast upon us are all of them malicious calumnies, and diabolical inventions ; that we are innocent of them all ; and we defy the libeller (whoever he be), to produce, if he can, any legal proof of our guiltiness therein.

"2. That we know not who was the author of the *New Liturgy*, as the libel calls it ; that we had no hand in it, either in the *Club*, *Cabal*, or otherwise ; nor was it composed, or published by our order, consent, or privity ; nor hath it been used at any time by us, or any of us.

"3. That neither we, nor any of us, ever held any Correspondence, directly or indirectly, with M. de Croissy, or with any minister or agent of France : *and if any such Memorial, as the libel mentions, was ever really presented to the French King*, we never knew anything of it, nor anything relating thereto.   And we do utterly renounce both that, and all other invitations suggested to be made by us, in order to any invasion of this kingdom by the French.

"4. That we utterly deny, and disavow all Plots charged upon us, or contrived or carried on, in our meetings at Lambeth ; the intent thereof being to advise how, in our present difficulties, we might best keep *consciences void of offence towards God and towards man.*

" 5. That we are so far from being the authors and abettors of England's miseries (whatever the spirit of lying and calumny may vent against us) that we do, and shall to our dying hour, heartily and incessantly pray for the peace, prosperity and glory of England; and shall always, by God's grace, make it our daily practice *to study to be quiet,* to bear our Cross patiently, and to seek the good of our Native Country.

" Who the author of this Libel is we know not: but whoever he is, we desire, as our Lord hath taught us, to return him good for evil: he barbarously endeavours to raise in the whole English nation such a fury, as may end in *De-Witting* us (a bloody word, but too well understood!). But we recommend him to the Divine mercy, humbly beseeching God to forgive him.

" We have all of us, not long since, either actually, or in full preparation of mind,[1] hazarded all we had in the world in opposing Popery and arbitrary power in England: and we shall by God's grace, with greater zeal again sacrifice all we have, and our very lives too, if God shall be pleased to call us thereto, to prevent Popery, and the arbitrary power of France, from coming upon us, and prevailing over us; the persecution of our Protestant brethren there being still fresh in our memories.

" It is our great unhappiness that we have not opportunity to publish full and particular answers to those many libels, which are industriously spread against us. But we hope that our country will never be moved to hate us without a cause, but will be so just and charitable to us, as to believe this solemn protestation of our innocency.

" Signed ; W. Cant.
            W. Norwich.
" Printed in the year 1690.   Fr. Ely.
            Tho. Bath and Wells.
            Tho. Petriburgh.

" *We are well assured of the concurrence of our absent Brother, the Bishop of* Gloucester, *as soon as the copy can be transmitted to him.*"[2]

---

[1] The latter clause is added to include Lloyd and Frampton, who were not actually of the number of the Seven. The allusion to the persecution of the French Protestants seems to me to indicate Ken's handiwork.

[2] The Declaration is printed in the *Life of Kettlewell,* p. 107, in D'Oyly's *Life of Sancroft,* p 269, and is found in two MS. copies in the *Tanner MSS.,* xxvii.,

Strange to say, neither before nor after the Declaration was
signed, could the Bishops obtain a license for its publication.
It can scarcely be said, I think, that there was anything in
the document itself to justify such a refusal, and we are compelled to see in it part of a plan by which the Bishops were to
be held up to public abhorrence, and not allowed to defend
themselves. Sancroft complains bitterly that they were treated
as when "country people get together to despatch a wolf or a
dog." As it was, however, the Bishops printed their vindication without a license. The sympathy of peers and members
of Parliament was enlisted on the side of the accused.[1] Their
assailants had overshot the mark, and there was a reaction in
their favour. Sancroft retired from Lambeth just in time to
avoid ejection, and withdrew, like an ecclesiastical Cincinnatus,
to his paternal acres at Fresingfield, finding himself happier
than he had ever been at Lambeth, except so far as the services
in the chapel there were concerned, seeking to live peaceably
with all men, and above all to keep out of plots. Even the Non-
juring pamphlets which were sent him from London, and which
he read with interest, seemed to him two-edged weapons. While
he welcomed works of learning like Dodwell's, the "wash-balls"
and "razors"[2] (so, to evade the vigilance of the Post-office, he
and Lloyd spoke of the pamphlets) were hazardous. Men might
cut their fingers with the one, and might find the other, to their
own cost—as a Pope, in one memorable instance, he says, had
found a literal wash-ball—somewhat too caustic and excoriating.

Following much the same line as Sancroft, with perhaps more
of the feeling which led Falkland to 'ingeminate peace,' Ken
returned to his palace at Wells, where yet some months were
allowed him before that final departure which I have already
recorded. He and Frampton, the Bishop who of all the six non-
juring prelates[3] was most like-minded with him, seem indeed to

fols. 242 and 245. Another appears in the *Williams MSS.*, in Lloyd's hand.
They present slight variations in the text, as if there had been much revision ;
but it does not seem worth while to note them in detail.

[1] Kettlewell's *Life*, p. 108.

[2] See the correspondence between Sancroft and Lloyd in the *Williams MSS.
passim*.

[3] Cartwright, of course, made a seventh, but as he fled to St. Germain's only to
avoid a worse fate, and was almost, if not altogether, the object of all men's scorn.

have been treated by the Government, under Mary's influence, with special leniency. She was reported to have said that, however much they might wish to be martyrs, she would take care to disappoint them.[1] And so Frampton, when the time came for leaving his palace at Gloucester, and resigning the formal charge of the parish of Standish, which he had held *in commendam*, was yet allowed to reside in his rectory, to catechise, and preach, and visit, and to take such part in the Prayer Book service as did not involve the mention of William's name.[2] The good old man, with the exception of the brief scare which will soon have to be recorded, remained there till his death.

Ken in like manner was allowed, as we have seen in the previous chapter, probably under like conditions, to remain undisturbed at Wells during the autumn and early winter months that followed. Mary perhaps hoped, in his case and Frampton's, not understanding the men and their motives, that moderation would pass into compliance. He had forfeited his see on February 18th, 1690. The bishopric was not offered to Beveridge till May, 1691. The *congé d'élire* for Kidder was not received by the Chapter at Wells till July 8th.

In the opening of 1691, however, the calm was broken by a sudden and unlooked-for storm. The growing discontent and disappointment of many who had first accepted William's government as legitimated by the vote of the Convention led them to combine with others who had from the first refused to acknowledge it. Towards the end of December, 1690, the conspirators met and determined to open communications with the Court of St. Germain's, of which Viscount Preston and John Ashton, who had been Clerk of the Closet to Mary of Modena, with a Jesuit named Elliot, were to be the bearers. They left London on December 31st, 1690. The detectives and *agents provocateurs* of William, however (Speke pro-

he was never counted worthy of belonging to the Company of the Non-juring Confessors. He died in Ireland in April, 1689.

[1] Macaulay attributes the saying to William ; the author of the *Life of Frampton*, to Mary. It may very probably have been said by both, and of different persons.

[2] Once he chanced to find himself alone, and had to take the whole service. He cut the knot by reading the prayers for the King and Queen, omitting their names.

bably among them), had had their eyes on the plot. The envoys were seized off Tilbury, their papers captured and examined. One of them was from the deprived Bishop of Ely. It was addressed obviously to James and his Queen under the pseudonym of Mr. and Mrs. Ridding. It was full of expressions of devotion to their service, and these not in his own name only, but "I say this on behalf of my elder brother, and the rest of my nearest relations, as well as for myself." These mysterious words were naturally interpreted as referring to Sancroft and the other non-juring Bishops. The result was a police surveillance over them more rigorous than ever. A warrant was actually issued for Turner's apprehension, which he escaped by going abroad, " leaping the ditch," as it was called, in disguise.[1] The other Bishops lived for some months in apprehension of a like fate. In the meantime they had to correspond with each other, either by private hand, or, if through the post, under fictitious names.[2] Sancroft's letters to Lloyd[3] show the anxious feelings with which he heard the floating rumours as to his friends. In an undated letter (probably in April or May, 1691) he notices the charge against "our brother of Ely."

"Shall we declare our innocence ? But then nothing is proved against him, and men and angels will hardly be able to prove anything against us." On May 18th, 1691, of someone (probably Turner) he says, " I am sorry that our good brother has got so high up the pinnacle. It was dangerous to fall from thence, could the informers have tript up his heels. 'Tis well we hear nothing of our brother of B. and W. ; in this case no news is good news." On the 30th, " 'Tis a wonder that the same severity goes not on to our poor brother of B. and W., but I am afraid he cannot long escape it." On May 26th,1691, " 'Tis a wonder nothing is yet done against our good brother of B. and W., but I am afraid that at last *Tarditatem supplicii atrocitates ejusdem compensabunt.*" On March 2nd, 1691·2, he prays that he himself may be preserved from the

[1] For Turner's share in the plot see Note at the end of chapter.
[2] Nearly all Ken's letters to the deprived Bishop of Norwich were addressed to Mrs. Hannah Lloyd; letters for him were to be addressed to Mr. Jones.
[3] *Williams MSS.*

threatened visit," and on March 30th rejoices that Lloyd "had avoided the snare set for him."[1] On April 2nd, 1692, he writes that he has "news about Fr. of Ely that makes me tremble."   In July he complains that "all in affairs has been dark to him."   His thoughts have been "taken up by a bloody attempt on my life and the lives of other innocent persons."   It was sought to effect this by "wicked forgery and perjury ;" but "we have escaped out of the snare of the fowler."   He thinks of Lloyd, then in London, as in "a post full of danger, dwelling on the hole of the asp."   His letters are to be thrown into the fire as soon as read.   He signs as "Tito" or "Sempronio."   He does not know how to tell Frampton to direct to him, unless it be as "W. S., labourer."   In view of the helplessness of those who are the victims of popular clamour he quotes the racy but forgotten proverb, "The children of Chepe ring Bow bells as they please."   The rumours that are set floating against them he describes, with a somewhat startling emphasis, as "all of them damned lies."[2]   Of Frampton—to whom indeed the last passage specially refers—he writes that "our good brother of Gloucester is as cheerful under persecution as the birds that sing sweetest in winter," words singularly descriptive of his most loveable character.[3]

Ken himself, partly in consequence of his own wisdom in keeping clear of plots, partly owing to Lord Weymouth's protection, and the Queen's favourable disposition, passed through the fiery trial unscathed, without even the touch of fire upon his garments.   Of all the elements of that trial I fancy that Turner's conduct and its consequences were the most painful to him.   What I have stated in the Note at the end of this chapter is, I believe, a sufficient defence against the charge of perjury, which Macaulay brings against Ken's friend, but it remains true that he fell into the trap that was set for him, and plunged into the life of a conspirator.   He became, as such men tend in the nature of things to become, a wanderer and a fugitive—passing under many names and many disguises.   There is no

---

[1] The extracts of 1692 refer to what is known as Young's plot.

[2] I incline to think, however, that the adjective was not so merely a vulgar expletive as it is now, and that it still had something of a tragic solemnity in it.

[3] The quotations are all from the *Williams MSS.*

trace of any intercourse between him and Ken during this period.
He died November 2nd, 1700, and was buried by the side of
his wife at Therfield, with nothing on his tomb but *Expergiscar*.
Ken, when he writes of him in 1704, speaks of him as " our
brother of Ely, now with God." This was, moreover, but an
example of the opening of a rift, widening rapidly into a chasm,
between the two sections of the Non-juring party. On the one
side were the nobler souls, with hearts enlarged by charity,
and minds capable of combining much practical wisdom with
the theory—to us an untenable theory—for which they suffered.
Among these the most prominent were Ken himself, Frampton,
Kettlewell, and Fitzwilliam. They still clung to the principles
of passive obedience, of the binding force of oaths once taken,
of hereditary right, but they emphasised the *passive*. For
them it was the " doctrine of the cross,"[1] and they were content
to suffer for it, but they would make no self-willed efforts to
assert it. They would wait till this tyranny—so far as
there was a tyranny—was overpast. They would not excom-
municate or condemn those who took the oaths which they
could not take. They could correspond, as Fitzwilliam did with
Lady Rachel Russell, on terms of a deep spiritual affection,
with those who, though like-minded with themselves, did not
think as they did on these questions. They could watch the
progress to place and power of those whom they knew to be
sound in faith and holy in life, as Ken watched Hooper's, with
entire satisfaction. They cherished warm and friendly feelings
even for Dissenters.

And, on the other side, there were those who were restless and
uneasy, who were drawn into plot after plot, were continually
in communication with St. Germain's, and believed that they
could trust its occupant to come back with, or even without, conditions.[2] For them any communion with laity or clergy of the

[1] The title of Kettlewell's work—*Christianity, a Doctrine of the Cross: or Passive Obedience under any pretended Invasion of Legal Rights and Liberties*, shows sufficiently what estimate he took of the theory in question, and is probably referred to in the words of Ken's will, in which he states that he dies " in the Communion of the Church of England . . . . as it adheres to the Doctrine of the Cross." See p. 209.

[2] These two sections of the Jacobite party were distinguished respectively as Compounders and Non-compounders.

Established Church involved the guilt of schism, and so placed the guilty one under a sentence of *ipso facto* excommunication from the true Church of the faithful remnant.   To attend any service of the former in which prayers were offered for William and Mary was a sin (so even Sancroft wrote) that needed absolution at the end of that service as well as at the beginning. It were better for a man never to enter his parish church, or any church at all, than to be a sharer in that guilt.   The men of this class were often, like Hickes and Wagstaffe and Collier and Leslie, men of much learning and considerable brain-power, but they were, for the most part, also men of the narrowing, sectarian temperament, who delighted in drawing hard and fast lines, which excluded others from any hope but that of uncovenanted mercies.   As their after-history showed, they became every year more and more convinced that they were the only pure and Apostolic branch of the Universal Church.   They split once more into two sections on ritual questions, and the minority, the Nonjurors of the separation, claimed to be the true people of God, when Ishmael rather than Israel might have served as their prototype.   In proportion as they dwindled away in numbers and influence, they devised new liturgies, introduced new ritual, signed *concordats*, as representing the Church of England, with Eastern Bishops, and looked on themselves as confessors in whom, and in whom alone, was to be found any hope for the reunion of Christendom.   Booth, the last irregular Non-juring Bishop, died in 1805.[1]   If he inherited the convictions of his predecessors, we can picture him to ourselves, as he drew near the end of his pilgrimage, lamenting that with him there was broken the last link that connected the Church of England with the Church of the Apostles, the last hope of a restored union with Eastern and Latin Christianity.

Others there were, whose line of action must have been yet more distasteful to Ken.   There were Non-juring clergy who practically renounced their orders, and went about, often to escape arrest, in "blue coats" and other lay apparel,[2] who associated in their plots with men of ill repute, who brought

---

[1] Lathbury, p. 412.

[2] This was often the case with Leslie and Turner, and Hearne records his meeting Ken's friend, Harbin, dressed as a layman.   See p. 99.

scandal on the cause of which they professed themselves the adherents, who crept into the houses of the rich and gained influence over weak-minded women. Cibber's transformation of Molière's *Tartuffe* into the "Dr. Wolf" of his once popular comedy, *The Non-juror*, though, doubtless, a libel and a carricature on the class, could scarcely have won the applause of crowded theatres, if it had not been felt that it bore, in some cases, only too close a resemblance to the original.

And as the sections of the clergy were, so were those of the laity. Some there were, of whom Robert Nelson, of the *Fasts and Festivals*, and Mr. Cherry of Shottesbrook, may be taken as types, who sympathised with Ken and Frampton and their fellows. Others, disappointed plotters, like Ferguson and Young, were reckless and unscrupulous. Many of the Jacobite squires throughout the country simply inherited the passions and prepossessions of their cavalier fathers of the Restoration period against Whigs and Dissenters, hated "Dutch William" as a foreigner, while he lived, and toasted the mole which caused Sorrel's fall as the "little gentleman in velvet," when he died.[1] The Squire Western type, roystering and blustering, was, it may be feared, too common among them.

One of these laymen, however, stands apart by himself, and calls for a separate notice. Henry Dodwell, Camden Professor of Ancient History at Oxford, a post which he forfeited by not taking the oaths, was the marvel and prodigy of his time. His reading in classical and patristic literature was immense and omnivorous. He came down on men like Sancroft, himself no mean scholar, with an erudition that overwhelmed them. His pen was looked on as that of the chief apologist of the Non-juring cause; and in him we find an almost representative example of the class of laymen for whom St. Peter's word of *allotrio-episcopos* (1 Pet. iv. 15), a "Bishop in another's diocese," a "busybody in other men's matters," might seem to have been coined. More sacerdotal than any *sacerdos*, he took on himself the functions of an *Episcopus Episcoporum*, rebuked Ken and

---

[1] William, it will be remembered, died from a fall from his horse, which stumbled over a mole-hill. The name Sorrel describes the colour of the horse as a bay or reddish brown. The horse, curiously enough, had belonged to Sir John Fenwick, against whom an Act of Attainder was passed in 1696.

Frampton when he thought them "fluctuating" and weak-kneed, pushed every dogma to its extremest logical conclusion,[1] and absolutely revelled in the thought of his own infallibility. For a time the "extreme right" section of the party looked on him as their leader. Frampton resented the assumption of the "great lay dictator." Ken, as we have seen, answered his expostulations, at first with some natural warmth, then with a characteristically meek apology. After a time Dodwell, too, came round to a better mind, and when Ken sought to terminate the schism, was found one of his heartiest supporters.

For the present the influence of the more vehement spirits told on the somewhat enfeebled mind of Sancroft, and, short of what he calls the *aspera consilia* of plots, he was guided by their counsels. The result appeared in two measures, which boded ill for the Church's peace. On February 9th, 169$\frac{1}{2}$, the Archbishop issued a commission to Lloyd, the deprived Bishop of Norwich, appointing him Vicar-General of the province of Canterbury. He commits to him "my pontificall power, whatever it is, in the Lord," and "approves and confirms" by anticipation whatever his Vicar-General may do. As with a *quasi*-Pauline heat, he substitutes for the formal signature, "Behold! I, William, have writt it with mine own hand; I'll stand to it and confirm it." Against this Ken protested, but, as we see by the correspondence between Lloyd and Sancroft, in vain. The former writes, on May 9th, 1691, that he has been able "to silence the phanci-full objections of my brother, and his half-witted Chancellor," and tells him that he will find in his enclosure (apparently a letter from Ken) "an account of the singular methods which my good Brother lately pursued at Wells."[2] Sancroft says in

---

[1] Macaulay (chap. xiv.) lavishes his scorn on one of Dodwell's speculations, which led him to deny the natural immortality of the soul, and to confine the gift of eternal life to those who derive it from Christ through the ordinances He appointed. He apparently did not know that the same doctrine had been maintained by Locke King (ii. 145-7), and that under the name of "Conditional Immortality," or "Life in Christ," it has commanded the assent of many eminent theologians. I do not hold that doctrine, but I cannot dismiss it, as he does, as a mere eccentricity. For Ken's view see p. 128.

[2] This refers, probably, to the Commission which Ken issued to his Chancellor, empowering him to administer the oaths which he could not take or administer himself, on the institution of presentees to livings in his diocese. (See *Correspondence with Burnet*, p. 46.)

reply, "I am glad if our good Brother is satisfied concerning his former objection against my Commission; but I do not find it in his letter. For his new and singular method it is brave enough, but whether the case makes it necessary, or the event will shew it to be prudent, I must think further before I pronounce." [1]

A little later on, and Sancroft was prevailed on to sanction, though he did not live to take a personal part in it, a yet stronger measure. Taking, with all the Non-juring Bishops, except Ken and Frampton, the view that the whole of the Established Church was in a state of schism, through its acquiescence in the intrusion of new Bishops into the sees of those who had been deprived, he determined on the consecration of two suffragan Bishops, nominally acting in the diocese of Norwich, who should continue the apostolical succession in what they held to be the only true, though suffering, branch of the Church Catholic in England. It seemed to them that they needed for this the sanction of the Prince on whom they still looked as the legitimate King of England, and so Hickes was sent over to St. Germain's with a list of the Non-juring clergy, from which James was to select two. He, after his manner, guided by Melfort, who had been his minister in Scotland, and was himself a convert to Rome, consulted the French Bishops and the Pope, and they very naturally approved a measure which was certain to weaken the position of the Church of England. James left the choice to Sancroft and Lloyd. The former named Hickes for Thetford, the latter Wagstaffe for Ipswich, as their respective sees. They were consecrated (Sancroft having died on November 24th, 1693) by Lloyd, Turner, and White on February 24th, 169¾. The consecration was clandestine. They never claimed any authority or acted pastorally within their nominal dioceses. It was, indeed, specially provided that they should forbear to act till after Lloyd's death, which did not happen for fourteen years. They were obviously consecrated for the sole purpose of perpetuating the Non-juring succession.

Ken and Frampton stood entirely aloof from this action. The former remonstrated earnestly at the time, as we shall see in letters belonging to a later period of his life. He objected

[1] Lloyd and Sancroft correspondence in *Williams MSS.*

to the clandestine character of the act.   He objected yet more strongly to the act itself, as tending to aggravate evils which it was the duty of all men, as far as they had the power, to minimise, and to perpetuate the evil of a causeless schism—causeless as soon as the first uncanonical intruders into the sees of the deprived Bishops had died out—to future generations.   I have thought it desirable to trace Ken's relations to the party with which he was, regretfully and reluctantly, associated, in as continuous a narrative as possible, uninterrupted by letters which are not directly concerned with it.   The consecration of the new Bishops seems a fit halting-point as the close of one stage of those relations and the opening of another.   Of the letters which belong to the period included in this chapter I can find only the following :—

LETTER XXXIV.

For Mistress Lloyd at Hodsden.

"All Glory be to God.

"My good Lord,

"Your Lordship did much cheer me, when you told me that our affaires went on well.   I was in great hopes of seeing you this morning, but you had other avocations: let me know when you can come, and I will be sure to attend you, or when I shall come to you. If anything more occurs, an intimation is enough, and will not take up too much of your time.   D. W. should, I think, be acquainted with our concernes, who is able to advise very well.   My best respects to your good lady.   God of his infinite mercy fitt us for all the trialls He designes us to undergoe.

"Your most affect. friend and Br,

"T. B. & W.

"*Nov. 18th*, 1691."

"My Br has sent you a letter, which I keep till we meet."

[The letter is clearly intended for the deprived Bishop of Norwich; "Mrs. Lloyd" being safer for the Post-office.   Nearly all Ken's letters to the Bishop are so addressed.   It refers probably, in the phrase, "our affairs," to the gradual calming down of the scare created by the *Jacobite Liturgy* and the *Modest Enquiry*. I am unable to identify D.W.   Dean of Worcester or Dr. Wagstaffe suggest themselves, but Ken was not likely, at this period, to attach much weight to their counsels.   The P.S., I am inclined to think, refers to a letter from Frampton, with whom Ken was in frequent intercourse, which was sent through Ken, and was kept by him till he could deliver it personally to Lloyd.   We may surmise that it contained a statement of views in general sympathy with Ken.]

Before the date which I have chosen as the terminus of this chapter, there were two events, both of which must have affected Ken personally, one of which, we find, led on to what with him was rare, the public expression of strong and painful emotions. Archbishop Tillotson died on November 22nd, 1694. Eloquent as a preacher, kindly in character, eminently respectable, Ken could scarcely have admired his teaching or his policy. Under Charles II. he had preached the most naked Erastianism that was ever taught from the pulpits of the Church of England. Hobbes could scarcely have expressed more strongly the position "*cujus est regio ejus quoque religio*" than Tillotson did when he taught that it was a man's duty, unless he could be certain that he had a special revelation to the contrary, to accept whatever religion was established by the civil magistrate.[1] Ken would scarcely sympathise with the easy indifference with which Tillotson wished that "we were well rid" of the Athanasian Creed. He must have remembered how he, who had worried the last hours of Lord Russell with his doctrine of passive obedience, had changed his voice according to the time, and transferred his allegiance without hesitation to William.

Tillotson was succeeded by Tenison, with whom, as Rector of St. Martin's-in-the-Fields, where he had preached one of his most memorable sermons (i. 270), Ken had been more or less intimately acquainted. The choice was probably Mary's rather than William's, and almost the first work of the new Archbishop was to be summoned to the Queen's death-bed— she died of small pox on December 28th, 1694—as her spiritual adviser.[2] He preached her funeral sermon, and, as

---

[1] Birch's *Life of Tillotson*, pp. 62-70. The statement was corrected in a second edition, but without any distinct retractation.

[2] I know few narratives more sad than the account of the way in which Mary passed the first night after she knew the nature of her illness. Shutting herself up in her room at Kensington Palace, she spent the long watches of the night till morning dawned, in burning papers which she did not wish to fall into any one's hands. Then she wrote a letter to Tenison, not to be given him till after her death. It contained another letter to William, reproaching him for his unfaithfulness to her, and entreating him, with a freedom which she had never dared to use before, to amend his life. Tenison delivered the letter and spoke with a boldness which even Ken would have admired. William promised to separate himself from his mistress Elizabeth Villiers, whom he had enriched with the spoils of confiscated estates in Ireland, and kept his promise, alas! for a time only. (i. 143 n.) (Strickland, *Queens*, xi. 306—318.)

might be expected, its tone was one of almost unmixed panegyric. I am not concerned now to pass judgment on Mary's
character. Her life had been but short—she was only thirty-
two at her death—and it could scarcely be said to have been
a happy one. Educated, for reasons of state, in a religion
that was neither her father's nor her mother's; married also, for
reasons of state, to a husband who had no sympathy with her
own form of religion, nor indeed with any, with the possible
exception of the hard Calvinism in which he had been trained;
brought for short periods under teachers who sought to guide her
rightly, and whom she personally esteemed; placed in a position in
which she had to choose between her father and her husband, her
natural and religious affections,—it was not easy for her to walk
warily in those dangerous days. It was to her credit that her
influence should always have been exercised in favour of purity
and devotion and moderate counsels; that she should have given
freely to the poor and the distressed, and have exercised, as far
as she could, a right judgment in ecclesiastical appointments.

It was natural, however, that the Non-juring Bishops should
look on some parts of her conduct as open to censure. They
might pardon her acceptance of the throne, they could not
hear without indignation of her childish exultation when she
took possession of it. Duty might lead her to obey her husband rather than her father; but why did she leave that father
to be dependent on the alms of Louis XIV.? Traces of this
feeling cropped up during her life-time. Sancroft growls at
the "virtuous ladie" into whose privy purse went the revenues of the forfeited bishoprics till they were filled.[1] Frampton,
when Lloyd of St. Asaph, then Bishop of Lichfield, came to visit
him at Standish in 1693, told him that it was his duty as al-
moner, and therefore virtually confessor, to the Queen, to stir
her conscience on this point; and when Lloyd assured him that
Mary never spoke of her father without tears in her eyes, was
rude enough to remark (he had travelled in Egypt) that there
were animals whose tears flowed freely, but not from pity.[2] How

---

[1] Possibly, however, Sancroft's sneer may refer to Elizabeth Villiers, on whom
William lavished much money and many grants of land.

[2] It might not be without interest to inquire when and how that phrase of
"crocodile's tears" first became current in English conversation and literature.
It is found in Shakspeare.

far Ken shared these feelings, we either know more fully than we know the feelings of any other Bishop, or we know absolutely nothing. As before, so here, I will not assume in the body of my history the genuineness of a work which many have thought spurious, and thus " receive " my readers to " doubtful disputations," and so I make the letter to Archbishop Tenison on his funeral sermon the subject of a note. The evidence in its favour seems to me too strong, and its contents too interesting, for me to pass it over, as previous biographers have done, with contemptuous indifference.

NOTE.—I use the vacant space for a few additional facts. (1) Ken's forecast of the future, at this time, is sufficiently suggestive : " Not long after the Revolution, when some of the Non-jurors were very big with great expectations, Bishop Ken was much displeased that any should flatter themselves with vain hopes, and declared to me with great earnestness, as under a sort of divine impulse, that it was then but the beginning of evils, with a pretty deal to that purpose. But notwithstanding that he could not himself comply with what, by the present settlement, was required of him, he had yet a very charitable opinion of many that did, and is known to have been against perpetuating a separation." (See *Life of Kettlewell*, 8vo. p. 427 ; in Anderdon, p. 645.) (2) A letter from Turner to his brother (July 22, 1690), shows that the chronic sufferings of Ken's later years began about this time. " I heartily wish I could give you as comfortable an account of my friend and brother of Bath and Wells as I can of myself. I sent yesterday to see him, but can hear of no amendment. The doctors bleed him often ; my Lord's Grace (Sancroft) apprehends they do it too frequently." (Strickland, *Bishops*, p. 213.) (3) Turner, in another letter (April 20, 1691), names Ken's friend, James Graham (p. 157), and William Penn, as being, like himself, under the suspicions of the government. Warrants were out against all three. (Strickland, *Bishops*, p. 215.)

NOTE I.

THE JACOBITE LITURGY AND MODEST ENQUIRY.

Who wrote the *Jacobite Liturgy* and the *Modest Enquiry* and *Reflections?* Here again, as in the case of the Sherborne proclamation, we find ourselves face to face with one of the unsolved problems of the history of the Revolution period. As Ken and his brother Non-juring Bishops were directly affected by it, it seems to call for a fuller examination than was convenient in the text of my narrative.

The starting-point of the inquiry has been already stated. William III.'s government had ordered a Form of Prayer after the battle, March 12th, 1690, as a day of prayer and humiliation. Shortly before that day came, another Form of Prayer was suddenly circulated by thousands (Macaulay says 10,000) all over England. Its title-page might mislead purchasers. "A Form of Prayer and Humiliation for God's blessing upon his Majesty and his dominions, and for the removing and averting of God's judgment from this Church and State." It contained forms for Morning and Evening Prayer, with proper psalms and lessons. The morning lessons are 1 Kings xvii., or 2 Chron. xiii. 1—21, and Matt. x. Those for the evening, Ezek. xxxiv. or Job i. ii., and 1 Pet. iv. The Epistle in the Communion Service begins with Acts xx. 18. The Gospel with Matt. vi. 24. A prayer is introduced into the Litany "for our enemies, slanderers, and oppressors, especially those that have caused the public distraction ; Lord restrain their malace (*sic*), and open their eyes and hearts." A long prayer, after that for the Church Militant, contains a petition for the nation that it may be delivered from the sin " of rebellion, blood, and perjury, especially that of the careless breach of oaths made to our sovereign," and "for the Church. . . . torn by schism and stripped and spoiled by sacrilege." The strongest passages occur in the evening service—" O Lord, withstand the cruelty of all those which be common enemies, as well to the truth of Thy eternal word as to their own natural prince and country, and manifestly to this crown and realm of England. . . . . Let the wickedness of the wicked come to an end. . . . . To this end take from them all their prejudices and all their passions ; their confident mistakes, their carnal ends. Take away the brow of brass and the whore's forehead." Macaulay (iii. 658) quotes some passages, "Restore unto

us again the publick worship of Thy name, the reverent administration of Thy sacraments. Raise up the former government both
in Church and State, that we may be no longer without king,
without priest, and without God in the world. . . . . Give the
king the necks of his enemies." "Raise him up friends abroad."
"Do some great thing for him, which we in particular know not
how to pray for." In these last three sentences he finds respectively suggestions of a Bloody Circuit, of a French Invasion, of an
Assassination Plot. He asserts that "no more mendacious, more
malignant, or more impious lampoon was ever penned." When he
comes to the declaration of the Bishops that they had no hand in
the new liturgy, that they knew not who had framed it, that they
had never used it, that they were engaged in no plot against the
existing government, that they would willingly shed their blood
rather than see England subjugated by a foreign prince who had
in his own kingdom cruelly persecuted their Protestant brethren,"
he adds that, "most of those who signed this paper did so
doubtless with perfect sincerity; but it soon appeared that one of
them" (he can only mean Ken's friend, Francis Turner, the
deprived Bishop of Ely) "had added to the crime of betraying his
country the crime of calling his God to witness a falsehood." In
support of this last charge Macaulay refers to the intercepted letters
of Turner's, already quoted in p. 71. The words, it is urged, can
be referred only, and this I freely admit, to Sancroft, and some at
least of the rest of the Non-juring Bishops. Some writers have contended (*e.g.* Strickland, *Lives of Bishops*, p. 202), that there is no
evidence that the letters in question were written by Turner, but
Macaulay refers, and, I think, with reason, to a letter from him to
Sancroft, dated January 19th, 1691,[1] in which we find the passage,
"Nothing troubles me so much as that my intercepted letters may
prejudice my brethren. But you must take paines to cleare yourselves and protest your ignorance."

As regards the specific charge of perjury brought against Turner,
I have only to remark (1) that no history gives the date of the
letters, and that the Preston conspiracy with which it was alleged
to be connected had no existence till the close of 1690.[2] It
was perfectly possible that Turner may have signed the declaration of the Bishops in July of that year in as entire good faith
as his brethren. (2) It is perfectly possible also that it might
seem to him that though he had changed his mode of procedure,
the end at which he aimed was not inconsistent with the terms of

---

[1] Printed in Anderdon, p. 575.   [2] Macaulay, chap. xvi.

that declaration. The memorial drawn up by the conspirators in December distinctly disavowed the idea of making England a subject province of France. It could not be governed as a Roman Catholic country. The French force which was to accompany James, was to be only for his personal protection and that of his loving subjects, and was then to be dismissed. The King was to promise to govern according to law, to protect the established religion, to refer all points in dispute between himself and his people to a free Parliament. As far, then, as regards the charge of perjury by Turner, I claim a verdict of Not guilty. I see in his action only the indications of an impulsive, impetuous character; only one more of the examples, of which the history of every revolution is full, of the way in which men are carried by the stream, or rather by the torrent, of events, into measures from which they would but a few months before have shrunk, and which they then had vehemently repudiated.

I return to the more serious question of the "Jacobite Liturgy" and its consequences. And here, my first point in the case for the defence is the character of the accused. I submit that it is absolutely incredible that men, such as they were, should have had part or lot in a document such as that of which I have given an analysis. I submit that it is equally incredible that they, and I include Turner, should have denied all knowledge of it, if they had that knowledge. I submit that the action of William's Government in refusing to allow the declaration to be printed is singularly suspicious, and that it indicates the existence of some slippery and subterraneous policy, which would not allow, in Oates's familiar phrase, the "stifling of the plot." And I think I can show, with a high measure of probability, what that subterraneous policy was.

Macaulay had, in the earlier stages of his *History*, unveiled the secret machinations connected with previous attempts to cause a scare, a panic, and the cruelty that is the child of panic. Aided by the confessions, or rather the boasts, of the man who claimed to be "the chief actor in the Revolution," he has fixed on Hugh Speke, the author of the *Secret History*, the guilt of forging the Sherborne Proclamation and the news-letters, which were the cause of the memorable "Irish Night" in London and the provinces (p. 25).

I find in the publication of the Jacobite Liturgy a strong family likeness to that of the two previous forgeries. In all the three cases there is the same mode of procedure. The forged documents are sent simultaneously by post and by private agents to all parts of the country, a process in which Speke boasts that he excels

all others.[1] They take in a people in a state of excitement
which makes them only too ready to be so taken in. They increase
that excitement to the verge of frenzy. What is Speke's own
account of his action after the Revolution had seated William and
Mary on the throne?

"From the time of King William's accession to the throne to
the Peace of Ryswick, Mr. Speke kept a continual correspondence
with King James by King William's knowledge and direction; for
defraying the charge of which and of *other secret services too tedious
here to mention*" (the italics are mine) "he received several sums of
money from King William. . . . . He had the honour to be
personally known to their Majesties the King and Queen, and to
have private access to them whenever he thought fit to desire it."

It is plain from all this that for some years Speke was content
to play for William the part not only of a spy and detective, but also
—we have had the thing in England and Ireland, but happily,. we
want the word—of an *agent provocateur*. He made the plots which
he detected, and drew unwary men who fell into the trap into a
real or seeming complicity with them. His object was to create a
scare which should sweep Papists and non-juring Bishops alike
into a common destruction. With this in view, as I conjecture, he
compiled, or got some accomplice to compile (Ferguson, who was
then in his sinecure office, and had not yet turned Jacobite, seems to
me likely to have had a hand in it) the Jacobite Liturgy. There is,
I think, internal evidence, especially in the "without a king, without
a priest" passage, that it was largely a compilation from forms of
prayer that had been used by the Royalists under Cromwell.[2] The
device was only too successful. The circumstances of the time, De
Tourville's expedition, and the like, had brought men's minds into a
white heat of excitement. Then, precisely when the combustible elements were ready, there came the *Modest Enquiry* and the *Reflections*
with all their horrible suggestions, (here also I note the resemblance
to the *Sherborne Proclamation*), with all their actual consequences, of
outrage on life and property. And when the Bishops repudiate the

---

[1] *Secret History*, p. 42.

[2] A MS. note of Mr. Anderdon, communicated by his daughter, written after
the publication of the 2nd edition of his *Life of Ken*, shows that he adopted this
view, and he refers to an article by the Rev. T. Lathbury, in the *Literary Gazette*
of July 6th, 1861, as giving proofs of it. Much of the language of the Prayers
on which Macaulay dwells might obviously have been natural after Charles I.'s
execution, and when the Church of England had been overthrown. One such
Liturgy appeared in 1659 under the title of *Prayers for those who mourn in secret
over the public Calamities of the Nation*. Another had been published after the
battle of Worcester. Macaulay inserts the fact in the later editions of his *History*.

charges made against them, they are not allowed to publish their repudiation. The policy of gagging has been a necessary accompaniment, in all times and countries, to that of the *agent provocateur*.

Of all this Macaulay says nothing, though he had Speke's book before him. For him the Jacobite Liturgy was a genuine document. The *Modest Enquiry* was a natural, though over-vehement, ebullition of Whig feeling. He is so far anxious to clear William III. from any share in it, that he records that the Government instituted criminal proceedings against the writer, but he does not record the issue of those proceedings. On the whole, I cannot help feeling that if I may not doubt his good faith, I must, at least, question his skill as an historical detective. An apotheosis of William III. may be a grand and imposing spectacle, but I am not disposed to acquiesce without a protest in the sacrifice of the fair fame of an English bishop on the altar of the new hero-worship.

NOTE II.

KEN'S LETTER TO ARCHBISHOP TENISON.

Did Ken write the Letter to Archbishop Tenison on his Funeral Sermon on Queen Mary?

Here again, as in the case of the *Expostulatoria* (i. 55), I have to deal with one of the Ken *Antilegomena*, as to which I have been led to a different conclusion from that which has hitherto prevailed. Round (p. iv.) rejects it as spurious, without even giving a reason, or any account of it. Anderdon (p. 658) follows him mainly on the ground that the temper of the *Letter* was unlike Ken's, and inclines to think that the pamphlet was written by Hickes. He dwells further on the following facts :—

(1.) In a reprint of the *Letter* in 1782 in the *True Briton*, the correspondent who sends it vouches for its being "indisputably drawn up by the same incomparable hand that so effectually chastised Bishop Burnet at an earlier period." Ken, says Anderdon, never published anything against Burnet.

(2.) In the *Collection of State Tracts published during the Reign of William III.* (ii. 522), there is a defence of the Archbishop's sermon, &c., in which the writer never mentions Ken as the author of the letter, but only says that it is "modester" than another pamphlet which he answers, and adds that "though the voice be Jacob's, the hands are Esau's."

(3.) Anderdon finds conclusive evidence in the language in which Tenison writes to Evelyn (April 20th, 1695) about the letter: "There is come forth an answer to it (the Funeral Sermon), said to be written by Bishop Ken; but I am not sure he is the author: I think he has more wit and less malice."

With his usual thoroughness and fairness, however, Anderdon quotes also from Tindal's *Continuation of Rapin* (i. 264), 1758, in which Ken is mentioned without any reserve as the writer of the *Letter*, and a passage from Hearne's *Diary* in which he records the fact that in 1705 "Bishop Ken's letter to Tenison, and Dodwell's to Tillotson, were printed together."

In answer to these arguments it may, I think, be said, first generally, that as Ken's letter to Burnet (p. 48), and one to Bishop Lloyd (Letter LXIII.), show he could, when roused, write incisively enough. And in this case there was much to rouse him. He had hoped that Mary would have sent some message to her father, asking for his forgiveness, or, at least, for reconciliation; perhaps, also, that she might remember the Chaplain, whom she had at one time loved to honour, and who had helped her in the early trials of her married life. The preacher of her funeral sermon, who had failed to suggest these to her, might well seem to him one who had been unfaithful in his ministry, who had spoken smooth things and prophesied deceits. He may have remembered, perhaps, how Tenison had preached a funeral sermon on Nell Gwyn, who left him £50 on that condition. Under these conditions we can scarcely wonder that he should write with some heat of spirit, even as Cardinal Newman was stirred to write in a like tone of Charles Kingsley and Achilli. This *à priori* ground of rejection seems to me utterly untenable. As regards Anderdon's special heads of evidence I reply as follows :—

(1.) Mr. Anderdon appears to forget Ken's letter to Burnet in 1690, which he himself prints (p. 364), and which was published by Hawkins in 1711.

(2.) The language of the writer of the *Defence*, in the *Collection*, is at the best simply negative. The sentence which Anderdon quotes tells on the other side. He implies, in language which would probably be understood at the time, that two writers had a hand in it. "Jacob" may have been Ken, and "Esau" Hickes. Anyhow he thinks the tone of the letter comparatively "modest."

(3.) The doubtful tone in which Tenison writes to Evelyn is balanced by the fact that in the Tenison MSS. (935), now in the Lambeth Library, there is a MS. endorsed "Dr. Knighton's

Answer to Kenn " (*sic*), and underneath, in Tenison's hand, " I would not have it published. T. C." [1] The letter to Evelyn was written on April 20th, 1695 ; the endorsement on the MS. is dated June 6th. The interval had probably brought a fuller knowledge.

(4.) In the Catalogue of Ken's Library at Longleat, traditionally reported to have been compiled by his friend Harbin, the *Letter to Tenison* appears under Ken's name.

(5.) It is treated as genuine in the *Biographia Britannica*, art. " Ken."

The evidence of (3) and (4) seems to me absolutely decisive, and I have therefore no hesitation in accepting the *Letter* as genuine. But if so, then it is obviously a document of the highest order of interest, if not in its relations to the general history of the time, yet, at least, in its bearing upon Ken's mind and character, and I have therefore thought myself justified in printing it *in extenso*.[2]

"BISHOP KEN'S LETTER TO ARCHBISHOP TENNISON.

" SIR,

" When I heard of the sickness of the late illustrious Princess, whom I had never failed to recommend to God in my daily Prayers, and that yourself was her Confessor, I could not but hope that, at least on her Deathbed, you would have dealt faithfully with her. But when I had read the Sermon you preach'd at her Funerall, I was heartily griev'd to find myself disappointed, and God knows how bitterly I bewail'd in Secret the manner of her Death ; and reflecting again and again on your conduct of her Soul, methought a Spirit of Slumber seem'd to have possess'd you ; otherwise it was impossible for one who so well understood the duty of a Spiritual Guide as yourself, who had such happy opportunities, and such signal encouragements to practise it in her case, should so grosly fail in your performance, as either to overlook or wilfully to omit that, which all the world said besides yourself, and was expected from you, and was of great importance to her Salvation. You are a person of noted abilities, and had a full knowledge of your Duty, you had been many years a Parish Priest, and exercised your function with good repute ; none could be better versed in y[e] office for y[e] Visitation of y[e] Sick than yourself, and the sick person was no stranger to you, and you very well knew her whole Story.

" As you had a full knowledge of y[e] Person and of your Duty, so you had happy opportunities to put that Duty in practice. You had free and frequent access to her, and on Monday, when the flattering disease occasioned some hopes, but especially on y[e] next day, the Festival of Christ's birth, when those hopes were rais'd to a kind of assurance (p. 25), and continued so till night, y[e] peculiar favour of Heaven seemed to have indulg'd you all that inestimable day, on pur-

---

[1] I have read the answer, which is a sufficiently fair and temperate vindication of Tenison's sermon.

[2] I must acknowledge my obligation to a letter by C. E. Doble, in the *Academy* for March 14th, 1885. He comes to the same conclusion as I have done, on Hearne's evidence only.

pose that you might carefully employ it, in clearing her conscience with God and man, and in perfecting her preparations for Eternity ; which, had she recover'd, were so necessary, to render her Life holy and happy as her Death.

" Your Joy enduring but a Day, and that Day being clos'd with a dismal night, you gave her the warning of her approaching Death, which, you say, she receiv'd with a courage agreeable to the strength of her faith (p. 26). You were set a watchman over her, and if you did not give her due warning of her sin also, when you had so proper a time for doing it, and saw her so capable of receiving it, God will require her blood at your hands.

"You had this advantage also, which is often wanting to such persons, y^t in the visits you made her, you did not find her delirious, & the orders she gave for Prayers (p. 29) ; her calling for Prayers a third time, when she feared she had slept the time before ; the many most Christian things she said (p. 26) ; her appointing Psalms, a Chapter concerning trust in God, and a Sermon more than once, to be read to her (p. 29) are signs she was not, or, at least, that she was not so in the intervals wherein you officiated by her. 'Tis true she was often drowzy, but she was so sensible of her drowziness, that she call'd for prayers before the time, for fear that she should not be long composed (p. 28), & whenever you applied yourself to her, she was wakefull enough. You said indeed, (p. 27), That at the receiving of the Holy Eucharist she found herself in a dying condition, and you add, that she presently stirred up her attention, & from thenceforth to the end of the office, had a perfect command of her Understanding, & was intent upon the great work she was going about ; and methinks, Sir, if you had been jealous over her soul with a godly jealousy when you gave her the Viaticum, & saw that she had then a perfect command of her Understanding, & that she was intent, you had another fit season offer'd you by Heaven to have minded her of any but probable defects in her repentance, & to have exhorted her to a short, supplemental Confession. Nay to her very last, she seem'd not wholly incapable of any pious Intimations you might have given her, for her Understanding continued to a degree that nothing of Impertinence, scarce a number of disjointed words, were heard from her, insomuch that she said a devout Amen to that very prayer in which her pious soul was recommended to that God who gave it (p. 49). So that your own Sermon will testifie against you, that you had many happy opportunities of directing her conscience. I must add that you had as signal encouragements also. You had to deal with a Person whose knowledge and wisdom you justly commend (p. 8), and who might easily have been convinc'd of any one instance in which she had mistaken her Duty. You had to deal with one, whose pietie, Charity & humility, you in many places, deservedly magnifie (p. 10). I only wish you had added her Justice also, to have made her character compleat. However, those three Virtues were powerful inducements to have used a conscientious freedom with her. You had, as appears by the Character you gave her, a pious, charitable, humble soul under your care ; a subject most happily dispos'd to work on—who had always been very Reverend and attentive at Sermons (p. 9), who had an averseness to flattery (p. 12), & who would thankfully have receiv'd any Pious or charitable humble admonition you had given her. I now beseech you, Sir, to spend a few thoughtful minutes in comparing your Performance, as yourself represent it in your own Sermon, with your knowledge, with the opportunities & encouragements you had, & with the Rubrick of the Church. You mention a very Religious saying that fell from her, that she had learnt from her youth, a true doctrine, that repentance was not to be put off to a deathbed (p. 26). But it was your duty, considering the deceitfulness of all hearts, and the usual

Infirmities & Forgetfulness and Indisposedness of sick Persons, to have supplied all her oversights and omissions, and to have examin'd the truth of her repentance.

"Whether she truly repented of her sins, and where you knew anything of moment which had escap'd her observation, you ought to have been her Remembrancer. I therefore challenge you to answer before God and the world. Did you know of no weighty matter which ought to have troubled the Princesses conscience, though at present she seem'd not to have felt it, and for which you ought to have mov'd her to a special confession, in order to absolution? Were you satisfied that she was in Charity with all the world? Did you know of no Enmity between her and her father, nor Variance between her and her Sister? Did you know of no Person who ever offended her whom she was to forgive? Did you know of no one Person whom she had offended, and of whom she was to ask forgiveness? Did you know of no one injury or wrong she had done to any man, to whom she was to make amends to the uttermost of her power? Was the whole Revolution manag'd with that purity of intention, that perfect innocence, that exact Justice, that tender Charity, and that irreproachable veracity, that there was nothing amiss in it? No remarkable failings; nothing that might deserve one penitent reflection?

"You cannot, you dare not say it; and if you should, out of your own mouth I can condemn you, for you yourself, in your serious Interval, have pass'd as severe a Censure on the Revolution, as any of those they call Jacobites could do; you have said more than once, that it was all an unrighteous Thing;[1] why did you not then deal sincerely with this dying Princess, and tell her so, when you must needs be sensible that, steering her conscience wrong, you shipwrecked your own? If then, Sir, you consider yᵉ happy opportunities you have lost, yᵉ signal encouragements you have neglected, and yᵉ tremendous Hazard to which you have expos'd the precious soul of the illustrious Princess by your unfaithfulness; if you lay to heart how much you have acted against your own knowledge and convictions, what ill example you have given to the Clergy, what scandal to all good men, what wounds to our most holy religion, and what occasions to the Enemy to blaspheme, what have you to do, but to testifie your repentance before God and the world, and to mourn in sackcloth and ashes all the Remainder of your days?

"What was it, Sir, that moved you to act thus notoriously against your own Conscience? Was it the fear you had of losing the favour of the Court, which made you rather venture the indignation of Heaven? Even that fear was vain, for it had been no offence against yᵉ Government to have persuaded a dying daughter to have bestowed one compassionate prayer on her afflicted father, had he never been so unnatural, tho' the case was quite contrary, for he was one of the tenderest fathers in the world.[2]

"Besides, her illustrious Consort, who manifested so very great and worthy a passion for her, would, I dare say, have had nothing omitted, which might have been thought conducible to her Eternal Happiness; and a conscientious and faithful Confessor, especially on the death-bed, is one of a thousand, who will always be desir'd, and valued, and rever'd. Believe me, Sir, you have given yᵉ world reason to conclude that your own conscience misgave you; being sensible that in reproving her you must have reproach'd yourself.

"You say she was so judicious and devout a saint, the degenerate Church of

---

[1] I have not been able to trace the passages referred to.

[2] Compare Pepys, *Diary*, September 12th, 1664.

Rome can by no means show us (p. 6). But surely it had been prudence in you to have wavi'd that comparison ; for should you chance hereafter to blame that Church for canonizing Thomas à Becket, for which she really is blameworthy, 'tis obvious for her to make this appropriate reply to you, that 'tis as justifiable in her to Saint such a subject as for you to Saint such a Daughter.

"You tell us she was one ' who, I am well assur'd, had all the duty in the world for her other relations, which, after long and laborious consideration, she judged consistent with her obligations to God and to her country' (p. 15).

"The consideration then which she used to reconcile her judgment to the Revolution was, it seems, long and laborious, notwithstanding the assistance of her new Casuists, it being no easie matter to overcome the contrary remonstrances of nature and of her own conscience, and to unlearn those Evangelical maxims which were carefully taught her by the guides of her youth. Others might begin to instil opposite principles in her, but the finishing strokes were reserved for you.

" But what do you mean, Sir, by ' other relations ?' We may guess you mean her royal father, mother-in-law, and brother ; but you are at liberty to say, you mean any other relations, if you please. You give us ambiguous and general words only, when you should have given us most express and particular.

"'All the duty in the world,' is a comprehensive term, but wherein, Sir, did any part of that duty appear? Why are you not so just to her and to yourself as to give us some of those compassionate and melting expressions of filial duty, which flow'd from her on that subject? Why do you not produce some Instances of her mildness and mercifullness to her Enemies ? and whom you know she treated as such (p.16), though their crime was their being her father's friends ; these would have been much for her honour, would have given great satisfaction to all good people, would have convinc'd yᵉ world that the manner of her death had been in all respects truly Christian (p. 28), would have been much for your own reputation and much for the credit of the Revolution, in which you are as great a zealot as a gainer. If you were so well assured of all that duty, what a dreadful negligence were you guilty of in not putting her in mind of it on her Deathbed !

"Methinks, Sir, you are not just to her when you give us Instances of her Charity to several sorts of indigent people and to strangers, which all the world knew, and give us no instances of even her natural affection to her own royal father, of which all the world doubted ; when, had you suggested that duty to her, as you ought to have done, she would have show'd herself a tender-hearted Daughter, and would have been extremely afflicted for having been instrumental to her Father's Calamity. It is far from my intention here, to dispute the Lawfullness of the Revolution ; yet I may say, that I have never yet met any so bigotted to it, who would undertake to justifie all the part, which she, as a daughter, had in it, and I am perswaded that it would mightily puzzle you, to tell us in particular, what those Obligations were, which she had to God and to her Country, which were inconsistent with her Filial Duty. You complain (p. 17), ' Great is our loss of a most pious Queen, in an Atheistical and profane age, in which the Seeds of impiety, which have been sowing for some years, have sprung up in greater plenty than ever ; ' but, Sir, did not your heart smite you, when you utter'd this complaint? for I would fain know whether anything has more contributed to render the age Atheistical, and prophane, or more promoted that fatal plenty, than the prevarication of yourself and your time-serving Brethren ?

" You take notice more than once, of the Shortening the Life of this illustrious

Princess, that She was taken away in the midst of her days (p .18), at thirty-three years old (p. 32), in the flower of her age (p. 33), but you take no notice of that which most probably occasioned it, for the fifth Commandment is not to be Evaded, Honour thy Father and thy Mother (which is the first Commandment with promise), that it may be well with thee, and that thou mayest live long upon the Earth ; and if any, even Princes, for the Commandment makes no exception, do visibly Dishonour Father and Mother, and their lives are cut Short, the very Command of God assigns the Cause of it, and I hope the surviving Princess will consider and take warning and repent, lest God be provoked to cut her life as short as her sister's.

" You say (p. 30), That having, like David, serv'd her own generation, by the Will of God she fell asleep, and if you had been a true Nathan to her, the Similitude had been very proper, but her virtue, having, like David's, suffer'd an eclipse, you took no care that it should break out again, in as conspicuous a repentance. You mention the strong hopes you have of her everlasting felicity, (p. 32), but as you manag'd her conscience, you should rather have call'd them strong presumptions; I have hopes of her everlasting felicity as well as you, though not at all grounded upon your guidance, but on the infinite mercy of God who makes most gracious abatement for all our infirmities, and for all the degrees of excusability we can plead, and when I consider her conjugal love and awe, the horrid misrepresentations made to her of her royal father, the various and studied trains to delude her, the plausible pretences of religion, of Scripture, and of the Glory of God, which she heard daily inculcated, and the unfaithfullness of her guides, who had wholly possess'd her ear, together with her subdued will, her soft tendences and temper, her well mean'd, tho' misguided, zeal, the piety of her inclinations and her ardent desire that her soul might be without spot presented unto God, which she manifested in ordering that Collect to be read twice a day (p. 24), I have hope that God accepted of her general repentance, and by a super-effluence of grace supply'd the defects of it.

" What therefore I have said, is not in the least to derogate from any of her virtues, but to expostulate with you, for being the occasion that they did not shine out in their full lustre, and whether such shepherds may not be said to feed themselves rather than the flock. Whether your behaviour to the dying Princess does not reach those expressions of the prophet, of crying Peace, peace, where there is no peace, and of daubing with untempered mortar; whether it is not treating a spiritual hurt most slightly, let all my reverend Brethren of the Clergy who are untainted with the Latitudinarian leaven, whether they are possess'd of their benefices, or depriv'd, be the judges.

" Before I take my leave, I cannot but remark that Spiteful reflection you bestowed on the poor Sufferers, which you thus express, ' and domestick discontent reigning in those whose resentments are stronger than their reason ' (p. 13). The persons whom you thus characterize will tell you that 'tis much easier for you to revile their reason than to answer them, of which you are so very sensible, that no one labours more industriously than yourself to debarr them the Liberty of the Press.

" As for their resentments, the greatest they have at present, are against yourself, not for your Promotion, wh, I know, none of them envy, but for your misguidance of that illustrious Princess whose everlasting happiness they pray'd for, and whose untimely death they deplore. In the meantime, Sir, none of that dirt, which you cast at the faithful remnant, will stick, but will recoyl on yourself, and I have reason to believe that the Great Prince, whom such as you had rather flatter than imitate, does esteem them at least honest Men, and indeed, in their being tender of their former oaths, they have followed that illustrious example which he himself set them; for there was a time, when he being Prince of Orange, had the Sovereignty of Seven provinces offer'd him, and offer'd him by a Power, which would have put him into possession, and he rejected that tempting offer, with a most Heroic and Christian answer, to this purpose, that he had lately taken an oath to be true to his Country, which he could by no means violate. It was wisdom, not that which is Earthly, but that is from Above, which taught yᵉ Prince of Orange to prefer a good Conscience before a Kingdom, a Blissful and an Eternal Crown before one that was vexatious and transitory; and may the Same divine wisdom in his present circumstances, vouchsafe to be his Counsellor! If then he, when a Prince, was so conscientious in Observing his Oath to the States, can he have an ill opinion of Priests and Bishops who are alike conscientious in Observing their Oaths? 'Tis improbable he should, unless he has such Confessors as yourself who exasperate him against them; but from such Confessors I beseech God to deliver him.

" God of his great mercy grant, that what I have written may awaken you out of your Slumber, and conduce to your repentance, the only Preservative against those woes which are denounc'd against Careless Shepherds !

" Your faithfull
friend in our Common Saviour
" THO: BATH & WELLS.

" March yᵉ 29,
    1695."

I have printed the letter from a MS. copy in the possession of the Rev. H. Tripp. It appears to have been made for the use of a Non-juring family at or about the date which it bears. The printed letter has no signature. The fact that Ken's name is attached to the MS., may fairly, I think, be taken as some additional contemporary evidence as to its authorship.[1] No other name at that time seems to have been connected with it. The letter itself seems sufficiently in harmony with Ken's style when he wrote under the impulse of what he thought a righteous indignation. Two or three special coincidences may be noticed as confirming that conclusion.

(1.) The word "super-effluence" is eminently characteristic of Ken's style, both in prose and verse. See i. 283; ii. 132, 250. The same holds good of "degrees of excusability" (pp. 43, 110).

(2.) The allusion to William III.'s refusal of Louis XIV.'s offers in his early manhood (see i. 135), is precisely what might be expected from one who had lived for nearly two years at the Hague, and who knew the secret history of his early manhood as Prince of Orange. It indicates a desire, eminently characteristic, to recognise, even in those from whom he was most divided in politics or in

---

[1] So in the library of the London Institution there is a printed copy with "Tho. Kenn" added in writing.

religion, whatever elements of a nobler nature he was able to find there.

(3.) The allusion to the part that had been taken by Tenison and others in "debarring" the Non-juring Bishops and Clergy from "the liberty of the press," refers manifestly to the refusal of the Government to license the publication of the Bishops' defence in answer to the charges of the *Modest Enquiry*, as narrated in this chapter, and perhaps also to other refusals of an *imprimatur* to Non-juring publications (p. 69).

(1.) NOTE ON QUEEN MARY.—The *Memoirs* published by Dr. Döbner, and, already referred to in p. 36, exhibit Mary's character, on the whole, in a favourable light. She is full of self-reproaches for many sins and infirmities, but those self-reproaches turn mainly on what to a mind like Ken would seem almost *ficta peccata*, as compared with the alienation of her affections from her father and her sister. As regards the former it is explained by the fact that she had heard in the report of Grandval's trial that "he whom I dare no more name father was consenting to the barbarous murder of my husband" (p. 54). Macaulay (ch. xix.) accepts Grandval's statement that James had encouraged him as conclusive. Mary obviously thought so, but it may be questioned whether the word of an assassin is sufficient evidence. The *Memoirs* show further, as also do Mary's letters to William, the depth of her affection for her husband. She speaks of her disagreement with her sister as "a punishment upon us for the irregularity by us committed upon the Revolution" (p. 45), and incidentally mentions that she had concerned herself in filling up the vacant bishoprics in 1691 (p. 37).

(2.) NOTE ON EDMUND BOHUN.—An incident in Ken's life belonging to this period may rightly find a place here. Bohun, King's printer, published, in 1690, a treatise on the *Doctrine of Non-resistance*, advocating submission to the *de facto* government. In it he stated that Ken had said that, though he could not satisfy his own scruples, yet he thought "the English nation would be fools if they ever suffered King James to return." Ken's friends said that this was a lie, and got the Bishop's certificate to that effect. After this, Bohun met Ken in a bookseller's shop, and fell down on his knees, and asked his blessing. Ken gave it, and as he did so, said, "I forgive the little scribler," or words to that effect. Bohun, *Diary*, pp. 86—90 (privately printed, but in the library of the British Museum).

CHAPTER XXII.

"Brothers! spare reasoning; men have settled long
That ye are out of date, and they are wise."

J. H. Newman.

THE differences in opinion and in action between Ken and the more vehement Non-jurors, which have been traced in the preceding chapter, led naturally to a suspension of intercourse between them. He took his course and they took theirs. They looked on him as weak-kneed, vacillating, halting between two opinions. He thought of them with sorrow, perhaps also with indignation, as rash, self-asserting, wrongly eager to perpetuate a schism, the duration of which it was the duty of every wise churchman to minimise. They carried on their correspondence with St. Germain's, or published scurrilous pamphlets against the powers that be. He sought to live at peace with all men, found a shelter at Longleat, visited at other houses where he was always welcome, acted as a spiritual director to such Non-juring families as chose to consult him,[1] and wrote hymns and poems. But for a time the breach was wide. When Lloyd, the deprived Bishop of Norwich, wrote to him after William's death in 1702, his opening words admit that Ken had, for some years past, withdrawn not only correspondence but the "brotherly affection which you have heretofore vouchsafed me." It is, I think, probable enough that during part of this time Ken corresponded with Frampton (d. 1708), Kettlewell (d. 1695), Fitzwilliam (d. 1699), but, if so, there are unhappily no extant letters.

---

[1] I reserve instances of this for ch. xxiv.

There was, however, one work in which the two sections of the Non-juring party could co-operate, and it is satisfactory to find that, though not initiated, it was warmly supported by Ken. Kettlewell, writing on December 20, 1694, to Lloyd, proposes that a fund should be raised for the relief of the distressed clergy who were suffering for conscience' sake.[1]

"When my L⁴ Bᵖ of B. and Wⁿˢ, in great kindness and charity was pleased last to call here, I was proposing to him the setting up of a Fund of Charity, for regular collection and distribution of the same among the poor suffering clergy."

He assumes as probable that Ken would have conferred with Lloyd on this subject, and discusses the difficulties which had presented themselves to the former.

"Were this a fund for the soldiery, though God knows many of them have need enough, it may be, some might fancy they could with better colour charge it as a listing of men.[2] But being only for the clergye's relief, and their needs being notorious, methinks, let them trouble whom they will, they cannot hurt them, and they may freely own and thanke God they have been employed therein ; and when the truth of all is laid open, all wise men of all partyes must own, that it is an excellent part and proof of pastoral care, and the adversaries can only envy it, not fasten on anything to accuse or punish in it."

He suggests that the Non-juring Bishops might, without prejudice or offence, attach their names and titles to a circular letter inviting contributions to such a fund, adding the epithet, *Suffering, Displaced, Ejected,* or *Deprived,* and says that he is

---

[1] It is interesting to note that one of Kettlewell's most active helpers in this good work was Thomas Firmin, a native of Ipswich, who was active in all philanthropic works, notably in that of helping the French Protestants, and who was reputed to be a Socinian, or, at least, an Arian. He was on intimate terms with Kettlewell, in spite of his heretical opinions. On hearing of the action taken by the Government, he withdrew from active participation. The work was afterwards taken up vigorously by Robert Nelson (*Kettlewell's Works*, i. pp. 163, 169).

[2] The sentence seems to imply that some of the officers in what had been James's army, and was now William's, had thrown up their commissions, and were therefore in distress. To start a public fund for their relief might have seemed not unreasonably to be a "listing of men" to the service of their former master. Ken remembered them also in his will (p. 209).

authorised by a friend (probably, I think, Firmin), to say that he will give £100 and collect as much more as he can.

Kettlewell did not live to see the good work which he thus initiated accomplished, but in the following July the Deprived Bishops issued the following circular :—

" The Charitable Recommendation of the *Deprived Bishops.*"

" *To all Christian people, to whom this Charitable Recommendation shall be presented, Grace be to you, and Peace from God the Father, and from our Lord Jesus Christ.*

" Whereas We, the present *Deprived Bishops* of this Church, have certain information, that many of our *Deprived* Brethren of the Clergy, their wives, children, and families, are reduced to extreme want, and unable to support themselves, and their several charges, without the charitable relief of pious and well disposed Christians ; and being earnestly mov'd by several of them to represent their distressed condition to the mercy and compassion of such tender-hearted persons, as are inclined to commiserate and relieve the Afflicted Servants of God,

" Now We, in compliance with their Intreaty, and with all due regard to their *Suffering* circumstances, have thought it our Duty (as far as in *law* we may) heartily to recommend their necessitous condition to all pious, good people ; hoping and praying that they will take their case into their serious consideration, and putting on the bowels of Charity, extend their Alms to them, and their needy families.

" And we will not cease to pray for a Blessing upon such their Benefactors : and remain in all Christian Offices,

" *Your's*

" William, *Bishop* of Norwich
Robert, *Bishop* of Gloucester
Francis, *Bishop* of Ely } now deprived.
Thomas, *Bishop* of Bath and Wells
Thomas, *Bishop* of Peterborough

" *July 22nd,* 1695."

The limiting clause, " so far as in *law* we may," was possibly inserted at the instance of friendly lawyers who foresaw the risk of a prosecution. For some months no notice was taken of it by others than those for whom it was intended, but the

Assassination Plot, in which Sir John Friend, Sir William Perkins, and others were implicated, and the part taken by Collier and two other Non-juring priests, in publicly absolving the two first-named at their execution on April 3rd, roused the Government to action, and on April 14th, 1696, warrants were issued by the Privy Council for the apprehension of the Bishops who had signed the document, Frampton only excepted, of whom it seems to have been taken for granted that he could not possibly have been implicated in any "treasonable practices," such as the warrants spoke of. Of Ken's appearance before the Council we have a record in his own hand, which it will be well to give *in extenso.* He had to attend—it must have been a strange contrast to his last appearance in the Council Chamber—three times in the outer waiting-room before he was called in and questioned. When the examination was over he was requested to draw up an account of what he had said, and this is the result :—

" *The* Answer *of* THOMAS Bath *and* Wells, *deprived, to certain Interrogatories proposed to him by the Lords of the Privy Council.*

" *April* 28*th*, 1696.

" ALL GLORY BE TO GOD.

" After the favourable hearing, which this day the Lords of the most Honourable Privy-Council gave me, Mr. Bridgman came out to me to tell me, that their Lordships expected a copy of my answers; which, as far as I can recollect, I here humbly offer to your Lordships.

" The printed paper subscrib'd by the depriv'd Bishops, to beg the alms of charitable people, being shew'd me, I was ask'd,

" ' Did you subscribe this paper ? '

" *A*. My Lords, I thank God I did, and it had a very happy effect ; for the will of my blessed Redeemer was fulfill'd by it ; and what we were not able to do our selves, was done by others; the hungry were fed, and the naked were cloath'd ; and to feed the hungry, to cloathe the naked, and to visit those who are sick or in prison, is that plea which all your Lordships, as well as I, as far as you have had opportunities, must make for yourselves at the great day. And that which you must all plead at God's tribunal for your eternal Absolution, shall not, I hope, be made my condemnation here.

"It was then said to this purpose; 'No one here condemns charity, but the way you have taken to procure it: your paper is illegal.'

"*A.* My Lords, I can plead to the evangelical part: I am no lawyer, but shall want lawyers to plead that; and I have been very well assured that it is legal. My Lords, I will sincerely give your Lordships an account of the part I had in it. The first person who proposed it to me, was Mr. Kettlewell, that holy man who is now with God; and after some time it was brought to this form, and I subscribed it, and then went into the countrey to my retirement in an obscure village,[1] where I live above the suspicion of giving any the least umbrage to the Government.

"My Lords, I was not active in making collections in the countrey, where there are but few such objects of charity, but good people of their own accords sent me towards fourscore pounds, of which about one half is still in my hands.

"I beg your Lordships to observe this clause in our paper, 'As far as in Law we may:' and to receive such charity, is, I presume, 'which in Law I may;' and to distribute it, is a thing also, 'which in Law I may.'

"It was objected to this purpose: 'this money has been abus'd and given to very ill and immoral men; and particularly to one who goes in a gown one day, and in a blue silk waistcoat anotner.'[2]

"*A.* My Lords, to give to an ill man may be a mistake, and no crime, unless what was given was given him to an ill purpose; nay, to give to an ill man and knowingly, is our duty, if that ill man wants necessaries of life; for as long as God's patience and forbearance indulges that ill man life to lead him to repentance, we ought to support that life God indulges him, hoping for the happy effect of it.

"My Lords, in King James's time, there were about a thousand or more imprison'd in my Diocese, who were engag'd in the rebellion of the Duke of Monmouth; and many of them were such which I had reason to believe to be ill men, and void of all religion; and yet for all that, I thought it my duty to relieve them. 'Tis well known to the Diocese, that I visited them night and day, and I thank God I supply'd them with necessaries myself, as far as I could, and encouraged others to do the same; and yet King James never found the least fault with me. And if I am now charged with

---

[1] Probably Poulshot.
[2] See p. 74, *n.*, for instances of this lay-apparel.

misapplying what was given, I beg of your Lordships, that St. Paul's Apostolical rule may be observ'd, 'Against an Elder receive not an accusation, but before two or three witnesses;' for I am sure none can testify that against me. What I gave, I gave in the countrey; and I gave to none but those who did both want and deserve it: the last that I gave was to two poor widows of depriv'd clergymen, one whereof was left with six, the other with seven small children.

"It was said to this purpose: 'You are not charg'd your self with giving to ill men, though it has been done by others: but the paper comes out with a pretence of authority, and it is illegal, and in the nature of a brief;[1] and if such practices are permitted, private men may supersede all the briefs granted by the King.'

"*A.* My Lords, I beg your pardon, if I cannot give a full answer to this; I am no lawyer, and am not prepar'd to argue it in law.

"It was further objected to this purpose: 'by sending forth this paper, you have usurp'd Ecclesiastical jurisdiction.'

"*A.* My Lords, I never heard that begging was a part of Ecclesiastical jurisdiction; and in this paper we are only beggars, which privilege I hope may be allow'd us.

"I make no doubt, but your Lordships may have had strange misinformations concerning this paper: but having sincerely told you what part I had in it, I humbly submit myself to your Lordships' justice.

"I presume your Lordships will come to no immediate resolution concerning me; and having voluntarily surrendred my self, and the warrant having never been serv'd on me till I had twice attended here, this being the third time, and my health being infirm, I beg this favour of your Lordships, that I may return to my sister's house, where I have hitherto lodg'd, which is a place the messenger knows well; and that I may be no otherwise confin'd, till I have receiv'd your Lordship's final resolution.

"This favour your Lordships were pleas'd very readily to grant me; for which I return my humble acknowledgments, beseeching God to be gracious to your Lordships.

"THOMAS BATH AND WELLS,
" Depriv'd."[2]

---

[1] The objection seems to imply that collections in churches had been made under the Bishops' paper, but I have been unable to trace them.

[2] Hawkins's *Life of Ken*, pp. 48 to 56. I have given (i. 311) a list of the members of the Privy Council who were present when the Seven Bishops were

On the whole the Bishop seems to have been treated with sufficient fairness. The result of his examination and that of others implicated was that he, Lloyd, White of Peterborough, Wagstaffe, and Spinckes were released from custody by an Order of Council, dated May 23rd, 1696. Turner probably did not surrender, having given other matter of accusation than the circular letter, and thinking it therefore more prudent to keep in hiding.

After this temporary and enforced publicity, Ken retired once more into the obscurity which he loved. He was passing, however, into the period of life when men begin to see the companions of earlier days falling round them, and think with sorrow that they shall see the faces they have loved no more. About a year before the Privy Council examination, Kettlewell had passed away (April 12th, 1695). There were few, if any, among his contemporaries, for whom Ken had a more profound veneration. He looked to him more than to any other as his spiritual director in the confused questions of the time. It was on the strength of his authority that he recommended those in a private station who would otherwise be cut off from Christian communion, to attend the services of the Established Church. In his last will he declared, with manifest allusion to the title of Kettlewell's chief work on the great controversy,[1]

committed to the Tower. It may not be without interest to give a like list of those before whom Ken appeared now.

The Lord Archbishop of Canterbury (Tenison).

Duke of Shrewsbury.	Mr. Vice-Chamberlain.
The Lord Chamberlain.	Mr. Secretary Trumbull.
Lord Godolphin.	Mr. Chancellor of the Exchequer.
Marquis of Winchester.	Lord Chief Justice Holt.
Earl of Bridgwater.	Sir Henry Goodriche.
Earl of Tankerville.	Mr. Russell.
Lord Cornwallis.	Mr. Boscawen.
Lord Coningsby.	• • • •

It will be seen that Godolphin—the indispensable Godolphin—is the only name common to the two lists. He retired from the Treasury in November, 1696, having been accused by Fenwick of being in James's interest. The sister with whom Ken was staying was probably either Martha, who was married to John Beacham, of London, goldsmith; or the widow of Ion Ken, of the death of whose son, in Cyprus, we shall read later on (p. 185).

[1] The *Doctrine of the Cross*, a Treatise on the duty of Passive Obedience on the part of subjects to their rulers. (See p. 209.)

that he adhered to Passive Obedience as the "true doctrine of the Cross." It was the influence, so to speak, of the shadow of Kettlewell during the remainder of his life that led him to take the part he did in minimising, and, so far as in him lay, terminating, the schism which they both lamented.[1] Shortly after his friend's death, Robert Nelson, who knew them both, published a volume of Kettlewell's sermons, sent it to Ken, and received the following letter in return :—

LETTER XXXV.

To Robert Nelson.

"Sir,

"I received the Book which I imagined came from you; and for which I return you many thanks; and since that, your obliging Letter came to my Hands. You have done an Honour to the Memory of our Dead Friend, which we all ought to acknowledge; and I am very glad that his Life is writing by another Hand, as you tell me. *He was certainly as Saintlike a Man as ever I knew; and his Books are Demonstrations of it, which are full of as Solid and Searching a Piety, as ever I read.* God was pleased to take him from the Evil to come, to his own infinite Advantage, but to *our great Loss.* His Blessed Will be done. Since the Date of your Letter, a New Scene has been opened: And if the Act passes which is now on the Anvil, I presume the Prisons will be filled with the Malcontents; and your Friend, though Innocent and Inoffensive, yet apprehends he may share in the Calamity; and foreseeing it, it will be no surprize to him. In respect of that Sort of Men I have been always of the Mind of the Prophet, *that their strength was to sit still.* And so it will be found at the long Run.

---

[1] It may be noted (1) that Bishop Lloyd, of Norwich, administered the Holy Communion to Kettlewell on March 23, 1695, Dr. Thomas Smith (who will meet us soon as a friend and correspondent of Ken's), Thomas Wagstaffe, Nathaniel Spinckes, Thomas Bradley, and Mrs. Kettlewell communicating with him; and (2) that Kettlewell was buried on April 15th, in the Church of All Hallows, Barking, in the same grave with Laud, within the altar-rails; Ken, in his episcopal habit, reading the Burial Office and the whole Evening Service, omitting, we must believe, or altering, the so-called "characteristic" prayers. It will be seen later on that this was not, as stated in Anderdon (p. 672), the "only instance of Ken's public administration of the services of the Church after his deprival." (See p. 163.)

And 'tis the Wisest and most dutiful Way, *to follow, rather than to anticipate, Providence,* etc. I commend you all to God's most gracious Protection.

"Good Sir,
"Your very Affectionate Servant,
"THOS. BATH AND WELLS.

"*March 2nd* (169⅔)."

[The "other hand" who wrote the *Life of Kettlewell* prefixed to the folio edition of his works, Dr. Francis Lee, was probably assisted by Hickes, deprived Dean of Worcester, and Bishop Suffragan of Thetford. The "Act now on the anvil" seems to refer to a Bill talked of in 1696, but not introduced, for the purpose of making the declaration and oaths which were voluntarily taken by the so-called "Association" of loyal subjects, acknowledging William as a lawful king, universal and compulsory. The prospect was a dark one. Ken was prepared to suffer with the others, but in the meantime he would not join the malcontents in any action. He was content to wait. The event showed that this was the "wisest" as well as the "most dutiful" course.]

Another of Ken's friends and associates, Thomas White, the deprived Bishop of Peterborough, died in May, 1698. He had been one of the famous Seven. He had cast in his lot with the five who were faithful to their conscience. Like Ken and Frampton, he led a quiet and peaceful life, chiefly in London, and being unmarried, gave much in charity. His last public act was to attend Sir John Fenwick on the scaffold when he was executed for treason on January 27th, 169⅗.[1] In the same year Ken's early friend, Lord Maynard, passed to his rest, leaving £4,000 to charitable uses, the endowment of a poor living, and the like. The following year witnessed the death (May, 1699) of another old friend, Dr. John Fitzwilliam, whose history has been given in I. 51 *n.* He and Ken had been contemporaries, and probably friends, at Oxford. Fitzwilliam's warm affection had been shown in the way in which he commended Ken's "*seraphic meditations*" to Lady Rachel Russell.[2] He made Ken his executor, and, as has been already stated, left him a life-interest in £500, which was to revert on his death to the Library of Magdalen College, Oxford. Lastly, we note that on November 2nd, 1700, Ken lost his early school friend, Francis Turner, of Ely. Of late years,

[1] White was believed to have drawn up the paper in which Fenwick asserted his loyalty to King James, but repudiated all complicity with the plot for William's assassination in terms full of horror.—Burnet, *O. T.*, Book v., 1696.

[2] Lady Russell's *Letters*, No. xxv.

H 2

from 1691 onwards, there had been the "little rift" of difference of opinion, which had widened into divergence of action.
There had been probably little or no intercourse, either personally or by letter, for some years before Turner's death.   He
was often abroad, often hiding in London and elsewhere, in
disguise, and would naturally shrink from the risk of involving
his friends in his own troubles by corresponding with them.
All the more, we may believe, would the memory of the early
days of their Winchester and Oxford life, when they had
walked in the house of God as friends, come back at such a
time on Ken's mind.   One can think of him as saying, in the
words in which he had been wont to express at once his earthly
affection and his eternal hope, *Requiescat in pace* (i. p. 122).
He speaks of him, as we shall see (p. 107), as our "deare friend,
now with God."

There was yet one other death before the end of the period
embraced in this chapter, of which we may be quite sure that
Ken could not hear without deep emotion.   On September 6th,
1701, James II. closed his strangely chequered life at St. Germain's.   I have shown in Chapter XVI., on what seem to me
sufficient grounds, that Ken's feelings towards the exiled
monarch were something more than those of dutiful obedience
to one on whom he still looked as his rightful King; that with
the loyalty of a subject there mingled the affection of a friend,
the keen watchful anxiety of a lover of souls, who would not
give up the hope that even *there*, in that life so stained by
license, so misguided in judgment, there was a capacity for
better things.   For him he continued to pray when he used
the services of the Church; for him he pleaded in the more
silent sanctuary of the soul.   Was there any further intercourse?   It is clear, beyond the shadow of a doubt, that Ken
took no part in the communications which were opened by the
more violent section of the Non-jurors with the Court of St.
Germain's; that he had no part or lot in the nomination of the
non-juring Bishops, or in the plots which led so many to
imprisonment and exile; that he distrusted the counsels which
emanated from Melfort and others, who were James's chief
advisers.   To answer the question fully, I must enter once more
on the region of questions as to disputed authorship.   If I am

right in the conclusions to which I have been led as to the *Royal Sufferer*, the result is, as before, that we have an addition to the materials hitherto recognised as available for a Life of Ken, of almost priceless value. I write in the full consciousness of the bias which the prospect of that treasure-trove may have given to my judgment. I can but do as I have done in previous instances, relegate the discussion to a note, and leave the decision to the reader. At any rate it is not too much to assume that Ken would hear of the penance and devotion in which James's later years were spent, of his frequent visits to De Rancé at La Trappe, where he shared all the austerities of the discipline of its members; that he would hear some report of the manner of his death,[1] how " he asked pardon of all whom he might have any ways injured. At the same time he forgave all the world, the Emperor,[2] the Prince of Orange, his daughter (sc. the Princess Anne), and every one of his subjects who had designedly contrived, and contributed to, his harms and misfortunes." He would welcome, we may believe, that message as indicating the temper of one who may hope to be forgiven himself, because he forgives others. Of him, too, Ken may have well said, *Requiescat in pace.*

And then, lastly, there was the death which I have taken as the terminus of this section of my history. On March 8th, 170$\frac{1}{2}$, William III. breathed his last. Ken, I imagine, would receive the tidings of his death with the solemn awe which restrains the devout thinker from passing judgment on the character of a fellow-mortal. He knew the vices of his earlier life, his harsh treatment of his wife, his unfaithfulness to one who never, in word or deed or thought, had been unfaithful to him. He saw in him one who had made his way to a crown under false pretences, whose religion had been the hardest and least Christian form of Calvinism, under whose government he and hundreds of his brethren had been driven from their homes into poverty or exile, whose last act had been, when he was too feeble to hold a pen, to affix his stamp to the Abjuration and Attainder

[1] The report is given in Anderdon, p. 693, as from a letter addressed to Lloyd, but with that Bishop, as we have seen, Ken's intercourse was suspended for some years before the death of William III.

[2] It is clear that James felt most keenly his desertion by all the Catholic Powers of Europe except Louis XIV. (Macaulay, ch. xxv.)

Acts, which filled Ken's soul with horror and alarm. And yet there, also, he had recognised at one time the capacity for better things. He respected the patriotism which in early life had stood proof against the bribes of power with which Louis XIV. had tempted him.[1] He saw in him—as when he took part in drawing up the Thanksgiving Service ordered on the first day of the Convention (p. 32)—one who had been "an instrument in the hands of the Providence of God to deliver the Church and nation from Popish tyranny and arbitrary power." He heard that he had met his end[2] as one "who did not fear death;" that he had received the ministrations of his spiritual advisers (Burnet and Tenison, both of whom had, during his life, faithfully rebuked him for his faults) reverently, and had received at their hands the pledges of the Saviour's love; that his death-bed was attended by devoted friends (Bentinck and Albemarle and Auverquerque) who had shared his every danger on the battle-field, or when smitten by foul and contagious sickness, and who loved him steadfastly to the end. With these things in his thoughts, he would at least hold his peace. He would not join in the indecent exultation of the Jacobites, who made merry over the accident that caused William's death. He would not do as Burnet did, and hint at mysterious and secret vices, over and above the failings which were known to all men. Even of him, if I mistake not, he would be disposed to say to those who were loud in their condemnation, "Who art thou that judgest another?" Even for him he would breathe the prayer, *Requiescat in pace.*

I conclude this chapter with some letters which obviously belong to this period. The contents of the letters will furnish the evidence on which I have come to that conclusion.

LETTER XXXVI.

To Viscount Weymouth.

"All Glory be to God.

"My very good Lord,

"Your Lordshippe's letter came to me yesterday, to Bagshott where I have been these ten dayes. I am much troubled for poore

---

[1] See *Letter* to Archbishop Tenison (p. 93).
[2] Macaulay, Ch. xxv.

M^r. King, whom God preserve and restore. I intend, God willing, to wait on you by the ende of next weeke, if my paines, wch still hang about me, permitt me, and I hope, if I can heare of M^r. King, to persuade him to a more consistant temper, and to take a proper medicinall course, though I believe, should he recover his right mind, he would never desire to return to Longleat, upon the account of the memory of his distemper. The Bp. of E. mentions to me one M^r. Harbin, who was his owne Chaplaine heretofore, an excellent Scholar, and as far as I could observe, of a brisk and cheerfull temper. However, I was unwilling to engage your Lordshippe to take him without a previous trial, and I have told ye Bp, y^t your Lordshippe should make experiment of him, for a quarter of a yeare, before he fix'd in your family, and upon that intention, I desir'd him to send him worde that he should meet me at Longleat, ye end of next weeke. I beseech your Lordshippe to present my most humble service to My Lady, and to give my blessing to ye young Gentlemen, and I hope ye country aire will restore your health, wch God grant.

> " My Lord,
>
> " Your Lordshippe's most affectionate and
>
> Obliged Servant,
>
> "T. B & W."

[No date given, but found among Lord Weymouth's Letters of 1699.]

[The visit to Bagshot was probably to Col. James Grahme, who, as Keeper of Windsor Forest, had a house there (p. 160). Mr. King is probably the deprived Rector of Merstham Biggott, who has come before us in earlier letters (i. 254—6). His privations would seem to have led to some mental excitement that had shown itself under Lord Weymouth's roof, in unbecoming words or acts. Possibly he had adopted the scurrilous and abusive tone of the more violent Non-jurors. The letter suggests the inference that he had acted, after his deprivation as chaplain at Longleat. It has the interest of showing that Harbin, with whom Ken corresponded, was recommended by him to Lord Weymouth, with whom he subsequently lived as chaplain and librarian, and that he had previously been chaplain to Francis Turner, who was living when Ken wrote.]

LETTER XXXVII.

To Dr. Thomas Smith.

" All Glory be to God.

" Good Doctor,

" This is onely to wish you a happy new year, having the opportunity of saluting you by Mr. Harbin, who was chaplaine heretofore to our deare friend, the Bishop of Ely, now with God, and is at present in the same station with my Lord Weymouth, who has a great esteeme of him, and that very deservedly; and I entreat you to shew him all the favour you can in his studys. I know my good Lord Weymouth will be very glad to see you, and you will be received by him with great respect, but I would have you dine with him on a day when he shall have least company to interrupt your conversation, and Mr. Harbin can best informe you of that. I beseech God of his infinite goodnesse to make us wise for eternity.

" Your most affect: friend and B^r,

"THO. BATH & WELLS.

" *Jan.* 23 " (170?).

[The date is fixed by the reference to Turner's death (Nov. 2, 1700), as after that event, probably in 170?. It is addressed to Thomas Smith, who seems to have been much in correspondence with Ken in the later years of his life. He had been a Fellow of Magdalen College, Oxford, and was one of the few who acquiesced in James's action in 1687. (For an account of Harbin see p. 54.) It may be inferred, I think, that Lord Weymouth was in London, at his house in Leicester Fields, when Ken wrote, so that Smith might call on him without difficulty. Smith answers the letter on Feb. 25, 170½. He is much pleased with Harbin, who seems to him to have a profound knowledge of Church History, especially of the English Reformation, and hopes he will do something to correct Burnet's blunders and prejudices. He reports that Hooper has been elected Prolocutor to the Lower House of Convocation. " A little time will show whether a license will be given them to enter into a debate" about Church affairs. "Probably not."' And if they should sit, they will probably " quarrell among themselves." Both High Churchmen and sticklers for the Crown's authority "have been wholly silent, not to say consenting, when they saw several righteous Bishops and Priests deprived by a Lay power." Ken, as we shall see, had more hopes, now that Hooper was taking the lead in Church affairs.]

LETTER XXXVIII.

To the Dean of Worcester (George Hickes).

" All Glory be to God.

" My good Friend,

"I wrote to you not long ago, to recommend to your serious consideration, the schism which has so long continued in our Church; and which I have often lamented to my Brother of Ely, now with God, and concerning which, I have many years had ill abodings. I need not tell you what pernicious consequences it may produce, and, I fear, has produced already; what advantage it yields to our enemies, what irreligion the abandoning of the public assemblys may cause in some, and what vexation it creates to tender consciences in the country, where they live banished from the House of God. I know you concur with me in hearty desires for closing the rupture; and methinks this is a happy juncture for it: the

Lower House of Convocation do now worthily affect the rights of the Clergy..and I dare say will gladly embrace a reconciliation; the question is, how it may be conscientiously effected? for which purpose, I wish you would consult with my Brother of Norwich, Dr. Smith, Mr. Wagstafe, and other learned sufferers, who are within your reach. I name not my Brother of Gloucester, partly because of his remoteness, and partly because he never interrupted communion with the jurors, which has been the practice also of our friends at Cambridge; but I cannot forbear to name the excellent Mr. Dodwell, who is near you, and will be ready to contribute his advice to further so charitable a design. If you think fit to discourse this thing among yourselves, when it is done, I could wish, that by the intervention of some friend, a meeting might be contrived, with the worthy prolocutor,[1] and two or three of his brethren. In the mean time, give me leave to suggest my present thoughts. If it is not judged advisable for my Brother of Norwich and myself, to resign up our canonical claims, which would be the shortest way, and which I am ready to do, for the repose of the flock, having long ago maintained it to justify our character; if, I say, this is not thought advisable, then that a circular letter would be pened, and dispersed, which should modestly, and yet resolutely, assert the cause for which we suffer, and declare that our opinion is still the same, in regard to passive obedience, and specify the reasons which induce us to communicate in the publick offices, the chiefest of which is to restore the peace of the Church, which is of that importance, that it ought to supersede all ecclesiastical canons, they being only of human, and not divine, authority. A letter to this purpose would make our presence at some of the prayers rightly understood to be no betraying of our cause; would guard us against any advantage our adversarys may take from our Christian condescension; would relieve fundamental charity, and give a general satisfaction to all well-minded persons. I offer this with submission, and out of a sincere zeal for the good of the Church, and I beseech the Divine goodness to guide both sides into the way of peace, that we may with one mind, and one mouth, glorify God.

"Y' most affect. friend and brother,

"T. B. & W.

"7 *March*, 170?."

[Here also the allusion to Turner's death helps to determine the date of the letter. The deprived Dean of Worcester is George Hickes (for an account of whom see i., p. 226). We note that Ken does not recognise his deprivation, but

---

[1] Hooper, afterwards Ken's successor at Bath and Wells.

writes to him as still Dean. The letter referred to in the opening sentence has not been traced. Apparently it had pressed the risks and evils of perpetuating the schism. He assumes (wrongly, as it turned out) that Hickes would agree with him. Hooper's election as Prolocutor makes him hope that the opportunity has at last come. How can a *modus vivendi* be conscientiously effected? Frampton has never interrupted communion with the Jurors, and has been followed by others at Cambridge (probably the Non-jurors of St. John's). Ken hopes that Lloyd, Smith (to whom the preceding letter was addressed), Wagstaffe (non-juring Bishop of Ipswich), above all, Dodwell, will be ready with conciliatory counsels. After consultation among themselves, they would do well to communicate with Hooper, and two or three leading members of the Lower House of Convocation. The thought of a "cession" on his own part and Lloyd's, already suggests itself to him as desirable. Anyhow there might be a circular sanctioning the attendance of Non-jurors at the services of the Established Church. Hickes, if he answered the letter, would probably throw cold water on the proposals, nor was it likely, as regards the cession, to find favour with Lloyd. Dodwell, as we shall see, came round to Ken's views as to the attendance. See Letters lxxi, lxxxii—lxxxiv.]

LETTER XXXIX.

TO THE DEAN OF WORCESTER (GEORGE HICKES).

"All Glory be to God."

"MY GOOD FRIEND,

"I am still of the opinion that Mr. Cook's aim was extravagant, and was likely to give little assistance to his parents and brothers, and I said enough to convince him of it, when I told him that after his son had served his time, he could be only a journeyman, unless he took the oath, which was at present the case of one whom I knew, and that if he did take it, he could have no seat in the office, unless he could advance about £500 to purchase it. Your concern for the good lady is very kind and just, but if you visit her, and at the same time show an aversion to her husband, it will, I fear, rather afflict than comfort her. The complaisant expressions you censure I never used, and am confident the Coll: will not say I did, so that I look on the imputation as one of those causeless suspicions, under which some of my arbitrary friends are pleased to lay me. In the latter part of your letter you give your own character, on purpose, I perceive, that I should take the reverse of it to myself. And in some respects I am willing to do it, namely, in allowing all degrees of excusability to those who are of a different persuasion, and in the business of clandestine consecrations, against which you know I always declared my judgment; I foresaw it would perpetuate the schism which I daily deplore: and I thought it insidiously procured by Melford for that purpose, who could intend no good to our Church; but I was forced at last to tollerate what I could not approve of. As to the main, I may probably continue as firm as they who keep more bustle ; though I told you long ago I could shew no zeal for it, and then gave you the reason which cooled me, and which I sent to our friends abroad. You have been more than once severe upon me. I leave you at your liberty to dissent from me, and if you will not indulge me the like liberty to dissent from you, I must take it, though without any breach of friendship on my part. God keep us in His most holy fear,

"Your most affectionate friend and B',

"THO: B & W.

"*Octr.* 1, 1701."

[Round prints the letter without a superscription. Internal evidence shows that it was written to Hickes. Mr. Cook was apparently a lay non-juror who had, as was then common, bought a place in a Government office. Hickes, it would seem, had spoken harshly of Cook's action, and was about to condole with his wife on her husband's defection, a procedure from which Ken gently dissuades him. The "complaisant expressions" which Ken repudiates were possibly connected with James II.'s action and proceedings at Magdalen. It is likely that he had been accused of advising a surrender, as his friend Smith had done. Hickes, in his answer, had apparently described himself as firm and 'thorough,' while Ken was, by implication, disposed to weaker and more vacillating counsels. That charge he accepts. He had never disguised his dislike of the "clandestine consecrations." Melford (Melfort), a convert to Rome, and one of James's ministers in Scotland, who had joined him at St. Germain's, was not likely to have the interests of the Church of England very much at heart. Ken, at all events, had stated his objections at the time, both at home and to his "friends abroad," *i.e.* the non-jurors at James's court, when the names of four priests had been sent over for the King to select two of them. A long reply from Hickes is found in the Rawlinson MSS. (Letter 68), in the Bodleian Library. He complains of Ken's conduct at "the Bath," had heard that he had "given leave to people of our Communion to go to Church there," that he had "chid one of them for not going," and expostulated with Mr. Stamp, whom he had not long before "received as a penitent," for "living in the Schism," and had said that he would "resign his Bishopric." Against all this Hickes argues at great length. He writes on November 10th, 1701.]

LETTER XL.

"To Mr. Harbin.[1]

"Good Sir,

"I staid at Sarum longer than I intended, by which means I received your letter, which gave me much satisfaction for the present: but since that, I hear that the *abjuration* goes on, only they have changed voluntary into compulsory. I am *troubled* to see the nation likely to be involved in new UNIVERSAL OATHS, but hope they

[1] Lord Weymouth's chaplain. See pp. 54, 107, 108.

will be *imposed* on none but those who were employed, or promoted, in church and state. I came to Winchester yesterday, where I stay one post more, and then goe either to Sr R. U. (W. ?) or L. Newton, where you shall hear from me. *Little Matthew* is very well, and the schoolmaster, at whose house I lodge, tells me he is very regular, and *minds his book.* My best respects where most due. I beseech God to multiply his blessings on yourselfe and on the family where you are.

"Your truly affectionate friend and brother,

"T. B. & W.

" *Winton, Jan.* 22 (170½)."

[The contents fix the date as being in January, 170½. The voluntary association, for the defence of the King and country, of those who abjured the Prince of Wales, which had been started in 1696 after the discovery of the Assassination Plot, though it had been joined by the municipal corporations all over England, by 37,000 in Westminster, 17,000 in the rural parts of Surrey, 50,000 in Lancashire, and so on in all parts of England,[1] was not thought sufficient, and in the Session of 170½ the Whigs passed a Bill, to which William gave the royal assent in the last hours of his life, making it compulsory. Ken expresses the hope that it would be limited in its operation to those who held office in Church and State. Apparently he had been staying with Canon Walton at Salisbury, and when he wrote, was on a visit to Winchester, with Dr. Cheyney, his former Chaplain, then Head Master of the College. I have been unable to identify " Sir R. U." and " L. Newton." A writer in *Notes and Queries*, 1st S., vii. 526, suggests Sir Richard Worsley, who married a daughter of Lord Weymouth, and thinks that " L. Newton " may be a transcriber's error for Lower Norton or Naunton. Who "little Matthew " was remains equally obscure. The only "Matthew" who appears in the College Register for some years before 1695, and some years after 1703, is a boy named Stent, of the parish of St. Andrew (Holborn ?), in the county of Middlesex. Mr. R. C. Browne informs me that a careful inspection of the original letter shows the true reading to be " little Master," but this does not help us much in identifying him. Probably he was some relation of Harbin's.]

LETTER XLI.

To Mr. Harbin.

"All Glory be to God.

"My good Friend,

"This morning yours came to my hands: yᵉ Recipe I presume was given you by my good Lord, who had it from Lord Godolphin, & it comes seasonably, for I have been in much paine since I came hither. Yᵉ Bill of attainder against a Minor I doe not understand, as for yᵗ of abjeuration, I am more concerned; you will doe me a great kindnesse, to sett me at ease about it, & to lett me know with

[1] Macaulay, Ch. **xxv.**

what penalty it will be enforcd : it is an oath I shall never take ; I will rather leave yᵉ Kingdome, as old, & as infirme as I am, & if it is likely to drive me to yᵗ hardshippe, I would gladly have as much notice, & time to prepare for yᵉ Storme, as possibly may be had. Pray write by Tuesdays post, & direct to W. Jones, at Canon Walton's house in yᵉ Close in Sarum.

"My humble service to yᵉ good Lord, & Lady; God Keepe us iu his Holy feare.

"Yours, good Sʳ, very affectionately,

"T. B & W.

"*Jan.* 10*th* " (170½).

[The date of the letter has no year, but the contents indicate the January of 170½, when the Bill of Attainder against the Pretender was pressed upon Parliament. To give his royal assent to that Bill was, as with the Abjuration Act, one of William's last acts. Ken looked with indignation at the idea of such an Act against a boy of thirteen. Had it accomplished what apparently it was meant to accomplish, Europe might have witnessed the execution of another Conradin, and the house of Stuart might have ended like the house of Hohenstauffen.]

One more letter of this period stands apart by itself, and may be fitly inserted here, though, perhaps, of earlier date than some of the preceding, as preparing the way for our estimate of Ken's conduct after William's death.

LETTER XLII.[1]

"For the worthy Mr. Dodwell, at Shottesbrook, near Maidenhead.

"All glory be to God.

"Sir,

"I return you many thanks for your very kind and Christian letter and for yᵉ enclosed paper, with which I was very pleased, though I was sensible yᵗ it will favour a misrepresentation made of me by one of ō͞r friends, whom I can easily guesse, and w͞h I perceive was suggested to you, that I am about to forsake yᵉ communion of my Brethren, to whom I have adhered as constantly as Himself. It is a great affliction to me yᵗ you lay the schisme so much to heart. It is a thing which has given me trouble for many years, and great vexation to many pious men scattered abroad in the country, and w͞h I once thought would prove fatale to our cause. The shortest way I could think on to extinguish it was yᵉ very same w͞h I find you yourselfe propose, namely to give up

[1] The letter is given in fac-simile by the kind permission of the Rev. Canon Moor, of Truro, to whom I am indebted for my knowledge of it.

my canonicall claim, with a salvo to all ye divine rights of ye order,
& by this means I should first restore peace to my own Diocesse ;
and I shall have this consolation on my death bed, y^t if I did it
not, it was more my Infelicity y^n fault, in regard that my Intruder
betrays so little of a true pastor, y^t I can look for no canonicall
Declaration from him, and I cannot in conscience give up my Flock
to him. I often mentioned my Sentiment to my Brethren, but
found not their approbation, and indeed, when I well considered y^e
case, I saw I could not well expect it, by reason of ye difference
between us, for I had ye like desire with your selfe to put an end
to ye schisme, & they were zealous to transmitt it to succession.
I was for a long time vehemently solicited to lend my hand to
it, but I always remonstrated against it, though I was at last
faine to tolerate what I could not prevent, so y^t ye controversy, wh
you truly say, and I often inculcated, was to end with ye living, is to
be perpetuated, & 'tis my dissent in this instance wh has raised a
prejudice against me. As for my coming to Towne I have told my
friends y^t 'tis neither consistent with my Health, my Purse, or
Inclination, and why is not ye same proposed to my Br of Gl., on
whom ye passion of some friends, misemployed on me, would be
more properly spent ? My best respects to your good wife and to
Mr. Cherry. I beseech God to multiply His blessings on yourself
and family.

"Good Sir,

"Your most affectionate Friend,

"THO. B & W.

"*Nov.* 10, 1701."

[Dodwell, it would seem, had heard from some of his non-juring friends that
Ken was about to leave them, and return to the Established Church. The thoughts
which were afterwards developed in the *Case in View*, which he published in
1705, and which will come before us in a later chapter, were already working in
his mind, as Ken's mention of him in Letter xxxviii. implies, and he was suggesting the resignation of the survivors of the deprived Bishops as the readiest way
of ending the schism, the continuance of which was to him, as well as to Ken,
the occasion of a constant sorrow. As long as Kidder lived, Ken had little
hope that he would, in any way, be party to an arrangement which implied that
his predecessor still stood in any pastoral relation to his flock, such as Ken indi-
cated in his "salvo to all the divine rights of the order." It would appear that he
had already suggested such a step to his brethren, probably Lloyd and Frampton.
On one thing, however, his mind was fixed. The schism was to "end with the living,
and was not to be perpetuated." He, for his part, could not go up to town, to say
nothing of other reasons, to confer with others whose feelings were so different
from his own. Dodwell was living, it may be noted, at Shottesbrook, close to
Cherry's house, and so it was natural to send a greeting to the family of the
latter, whom Ken, from time to time, visited.]

NOTE TO CHAPTER XXII.

DID KEN WRITE "THE ROYAL SUFFERER," *alias* "THE CROWN OF GLORY"?

In 1699 a book was published bearing the title of *The Royal Sufferer : A Manual of Prayers and Devotions, written for the Use of a Royal though afflicted Family. By T. K., D.D.* No publisher's name is given, nor place of publication. Another edition with the same title-page was published in 1701. In 1725 it was republished with a new title, *The Crown of Glory, the Reward of the Righteous: Meditations on the Vicissitudes and Uncertainty of all Sublunary Enjoy. ments. Composed for the Use of a Noble Family. By the Right Reverend Thomas Ken, late Lord Bishop of Bath and Wells. Bettesworth, at the Red Lyon, Paternoster Row.* It has, as a frontispiece, the same engraving (Vertue's) of the Bishop's portrait as we find in Hawkins's edition of his *Sermons and Poems.* The question is, Was this book genuine or spurious? I have not as yet succeeded in finding one jot or tittle of external evidence.

(1) Looking to the probabilities of the case, there is (i.) the question whether it was likely that *The Royal Sufferer*, if spurious, should have been twice published in Ken's lifetime, with initials which must have suggested his name to everybody, without a disclaimer on his part; and (ii.) whether it is likely that it should have been published under another title in 1725, while William Hawkins, the Bishop's great-nephew, who had repudiated the *Expostulatoria* in 1711, and had published the Bishop's Poems in 1721, was living, and might, any day, have repudiated this also. I find no trace of such action in either case.

(2) We may ask whether the contents of the volume are such as Ken might have written. It will be seen, I think, that here, if the book be spurious, the imposture extends beyond the title-page. The writer, if he is not Ken, skilfully assumes his character, and writes of men and things as it might be supposed that he would have written. I give, with some compression, a few of the passages which have this stamp on them.

There is first the dedication "To *****" (James). The Author writes with "no other design, but the supporting you under those calamities which you have borne with so much magnanimity and patience. . . . . I cannot conceive (whatever some may think) that your being of another persuasion than myself can discharge me

from this duty. . . . . And I hope you will not the less regard what
I have written because I profess myself an unworthy Son of the
Church of England . . . . I believe that the next (*i.e.* nearest) way
to Heaven is not Controversy but Conscience." He protests against
the anathemas which the Church of Rome thundered against Protestants. "If I am regenerated by Baptism, believing the Scriptures,
can it, with any colour of reason, be supposed that I shall suffer
damnation for not believing traditions? . . . . As to images, invocation of Saints and Angels, communion in both kinds I
believe the Protestant religion to be the most safe way." The
dedication ends with the hope that, when the time is come, "God
will translate you to a crown of immarcescible glory." It is
signed T. K. in the edition of 1699, "Tho. Kenn"[1] in the *Crown of
Glory* of 1725.

The work itself opens with reflections on the changes and chances
of human life, illustrated by a curious gallery of examples of poor
men who have risen, Peter Comestor, Gratian, Peter Lombard,
Agathocles, Abdalonymus, Iphicrates, Marius, Cosmus de Medicis,
John Hunniades, and Henry III., of Portugal ; and great ones
who have fallen, Agag, Jezebel, Nebuchadnezzar, Bajazet, Vale-
rian, Frederick III., Mauritius, Priam, Palæologus, Edward II.,
Richard II., and Charles I. This is followed by reflections which
must have reminded James of his favourite Nieremberg, *On the
Difference between Things Temporal and Eternal* (see i. 263).

Later on, the writer gives his view of the events through which
he has himself passed. He sees in the calamities of the time
a judgment on national sins, such as the prevalence of "cursing
and swearing and whoredom," especially among the Royalist party,
and the "cruelty and bloodshed " of which the land had been full,
"especially" (he obviously refers to the Bloody Assize) "in the
West, which had been . . . . turned into a slaughter house." He
condemns the "establishment of a new Court" (that of Ecclesiastical Commission), and " the Declaration for liberty of conscience,
though it might, indeed, shew the King's lenity to Dissenters, was
certainly a false step in the advisers, and still more the requiring it
to be read by order of the Bishops. . . . . I am very persuaded of
the King's sincerity, but not so of others. There were servants of

---

[1] The spelling of the name might, at first, seem against the genuineness, but, as
I have said, the two *nn*'s are found in all the Bishop's Registers at Wells, and they
can scarcely be relegated to the character of apocryphal documents. What seems
probable is that, as the name was first given after Ken's death, instead of the
previous initials, T. K., it reproduced not his own signature, but one of the most
common variants.

his who delighted in blood. . . . . I was grieved to see that effusion of Christian blood, and would have prevented it, had I had the power, and, as I had the opportunity, I shewed mercy, and where I could not, I have not been slow to pray that the guilt of that blood might not fall on him, nor on his royal issue, for even then my foreboding soul had great apprehensions that it would call aloud for vengeance." In the violent proceedings against the President and Fellows of Magdalen College he sees a " great piece of injustice." In speaking of the imprisonment of the Seven Bishops, he is careful to add, " not that the Bishops were against indulgence to the Dissenters when it should be proposed in Parliament " (pp. 59—76). As for his own part in those transactions— "What I acted at that time was out of duty to God and the King," and it is not " to be charged with consequences," which no man could then foresee. " If I was at all mistaken, or acted beyond what I ought to have done, I humbly beg pardon both of God and the King."

It will be admitted, I think, that in all this, if the book be spurious, the writer shows an insight into Ken's character and feelings, which can hardly be explained by anything short of thought-reading. I ask myself what motive could any forger have had to publish a work which harmonized so entirely with what Ken thought and felt, and which fell in so little with the passions and prejudices of parties on either side, and the solution of the problem which I offer as, at least, probable, is that Ken, while he found himself precluded, by the line he had taken, from all political communications with the Court of St Germain's, was unwilling that James, for whom he felt both a personal affection and a spiritual interest, should think that he had forgotten him. He heard of the devout, we may add, if we will, the superstitious, asceticism of James's later years, and he sought to guide him into a truer way of penitence than that of the discipline of the scourge. He would not speak smooth things and prophesy deceits, as Tenison, in his judgment, had done to Mary, but when he had placed before him the errors of his past life, would supply him with the Confessions, the Professions of Faith, the Meditations and Prayers, which make up the rest of the small volume, and which were suitable for his spiritual wants. For this purpose he printed the book, mainly for private circulation, and, though he did not expect a large demand for it, allowed it to be sold, that others might see that, though he held aloof from their rash and perilous projects, he was not a less loyal and faithful subject to the exiled King than they were. The beauty of the devotional element of the book told, as might be expected, on the Non-jurors whose minds were attuned to Ken's higher mood, and so there was within two years a demand for another edition. After Ken's death, probably as a consequence of the publication of his poems, there was a yet further demand, and then, as James's death had made the former title of *The Royal Sufferer* obsolete, it was reproduced, with one of more general character, as *The Crown of Glory*.

That is my hypothesis. I leave it to those who think the book apocryphal to suggest another equally fitting in with the phœnomena of the case, and equally probable in itself. If I am right, then I think that Ken may claim some share, as well as De Rancé, whom James often visited at La Trappe[1] (I will add William Penn also, whose wife paid an annual visit to St. Germain's and doubtless brought letters of comfort and counsel), both in the general penitence and devout submission which led Mary Beatrice almost to expect her husband's canonisation, and in the special counsels which the dying King gave to the Prince, whom he was leaving, at the age of thirteen, to the chances of an uncertain and clouded future:

"I am now leaving this world, which has been to me a sea of storms and tempests, it being God Almighty's will to wean me from it by many great afflictions. Serve him with all your power, and never put the Crown of England in competition with your eternal salvation. There is no slavery like sin, nor liberty like His service. If His holy Providence shall think fit to seat you on the throne of your royal ancestors, govern your people with justice and clemency. Remember, kings are not made for themselves, but for the good of the people. Set before their eyes, in your own actions, a pattern of all manner of virtue. Consider them as your children. You are the child of vows and prayers, behave yourself accordingly. Honour your mother that your days may be long ; and be always a kind brother to your dear sister, that you may reap the blessings of concord and unity."—*Somers' Tracts*, xi., p. 342 ; in *Strickland*, ix., p. 345—398.

[1] An interesting account of one of these visits is given in Marsollier's *Life of the Abbot Rancé*, quoted from Twining's *Selections from Papers of the Twining Family*, 1887, pp. 48—55. The Abbé addressed the King, "*Sire ! Dieu nous visite aujourd'hui en la personne de votre Majesté.*" The King attended all the services, rising at 2 A.M., and practised all the austerities of the monastery. It was clearly the established belief that he was too saintly to be the wearer of an earthly crown. [C. J. P.]

CHAPTER XXIII.

KEN AND THE NON-JURORS UNDER ANNE, A.D. 1702—1705.

"This be my comfort, in these days of grief,
  Which is not Christ's, nor forms heroic tale,
  Apart from Him if not a sparrow fail,
May not He pitying view and send relief,
  When foes or friends perplex, and peevish thoughts prevail?"
                                        J. H. Newman.

IT might have seemed as if the death of William and Anne's succession would have been followed, for Ken at least, by a time of tranquillity and peace. Her general sympathies with the High Church party were sufficiently conspicuous. His friend Hooper was rising into royal favour. In an undated letter (i. p. 271),[1] but written after Turner was Bishop of Ely, she had asked him to have places reserved for her and one attendant at the Chapel of Ely House, because she wished to hear "Ken expound." She had heard his memorable sermons at Whitehall, that against the claims of Rome, on March 10, 1687, and again on April 1, 1688, the Babylon and Edom sermon. His friend and patron Lord Weymouth took office under her, and made a suggestion, which the Queen approved, that Kidder should be transferred to Carlisle, vacant by the death of Thomas Smith (1702), and that Ken should return to Bath and Wells, with a prospect of the primacy, should there be a vacancy.[2] He declined the offer, partly as objecting to the oath of abjuration, partly as feeling too old and infirm to resume his episcopal duties.

The period on which we now enter proved, as a matter of

---

[1] Printed in the *Gentleman's Magazine* for March, 1814, and communicated by Richard Fowke, of Elmesthorpe, as then in his possession.

[2] Waylen, *History of Devizes*, p. 330. Lansdown MSS., v. 987, in Anderdon, p. 700.

I 2

fact, quite the opposite of all this. It was, perhaps, the most troubled time of Ken's whole life, in which he felt more than ever that he had fallen on evil tongues and evil days. He had chosen the "golden mean" and, therefore, as in Spenser's Allegory,[1] the "two extremities" combined to banish him. He had taken a *parte per se stesso*, which cut him off from the rash enterprises and violent counsels of his old companions, and he had to pay the penalty of his self-chosen isolation.

Ken, as we have seen, had separated himself from his brother Non-jurors, after what seemed to him the ill-advised step of the consecration of Hickes and Wagstaff as suffragans. He had held aloof from all plots, and even from all direct personal communications, unless the *Royal Sufferer* be an exception, with the Court of St. Germain's. He, Lloyd, and Frampton were now the only survivors of the original Non-juring Bishops. Frampton was looked on as too old, and too persistent in his resolve to lead a quiet and peaceable life, to be invited to any deliberations in the new crisis caused by William's death, but Lloyd[2] felt that he could not well act alone without consulting Ken, and accordingly opened communications with him in a letter dated March 16, 1702, within eight days of the King's decease. In it he expresses his regret that Ken has "withdrawn correspondence with me for some years passed, and also the brotherly affection which you vouchsafed me heretofore," but in view of "the late emergency," *i.e.* the King's death, he begs him, in his own name and that " of such of our brethren as I have seen and conferred with," to " come up to our comfort and assistance."

To this letter Ken returned the following answer :—

LETTER XLIII.

To Mrs. HANNAH LLOYD.

" YOUR's of Mar: 16th, came not to my hands till ye 26th, after the post was gone, so that I was forced to deferre my answer, till this next post day. I have discoursed with the person you mention,

[1] *Faerie Queene*, ii. c. 2.
[2] Lloyd was believed to be one of the thoroughgoing Jacobites who were willing to have invited James to resume the throne without any conditions, and were therefore known as Non-compounders. (Burnet, *O. T.*, Book v., 1696.) On this point Ken had never agreed with him.

and he replied to this purpose. He said that he remembers not that he withdrew correspondence from you designedly, and that you as much withdrew your's from him; or rather it was dropp'd between you both, because there was nothing to maintaine it worth the postage. As for brotherly affection, he denys that it was ever withdrawn on his part. He ownes that he in some things always dissented from his friend, but without breach of friendship. He says he cannot imagine that his counsel and assistance can be worth a London journey, which is consistent neither with his purse, nor convenience, nor health, nor inclination. As to the present emergency, it may, he believes, give a fair occasion to many to alter their conduct; but it does not at all influence him. He has quite given over all thoughts of re-entering the world, and nothing shall tempt him to any oath, onely he heartily wishes that by those who know the towne, some expedient might be found out, to put a period to the schism which is so very vexatious to persons of tender consciences, who live scattered in the country. In any thing of that nature, he would gladly concur: he thinks it had been happy for the Church, had M^r. Kettlewell's state of the case been embraced. In the mean time, he never uses any characterisetick in the prayers, himself, nor is present where any is read, and he has endeavoured to act uniformely to the moderate sentiments which he cannot exceed. He sends his hearty respects to yourself, and family, and to all his, and your friends.

   " Your very affect^{te} friend & brother,

            "T. B. & W.

" *March* 29 " (1702).

[The " person you spoke of " is, of course, Ken himself, the periphrasis being, perhaps, adopted as a precaution against Post-office inspection, or as better suited for the slightly ironical tone of the letter. Lloyd's somewhat offended and condescending tone is naturally met by a slight resentment (I use the word in its older and stricter sense) of wounded feeling on Ken's. What had he done that he should be thus accused of unfriendliness? Why should he spend his money and risk his health where he sees no hope of any good result? He " keeps his old course in a country new;" has said "good-bye" to the world, will not be tempted "to take any oath." He has, of course, the abjuration oath in his thoughts, but the generalising character of his language half suggests the thought that he was coming round to William Penn's view, and saw that all oaths of this nature were a snare to men's consciences. One thing only he desires, and that is to end the schism, as Kettlewell would have ended it, by a declaration allowing Non-jurors generally to communicate in the Established Church. He himself, in this following Frampton, never uses "any characteristicks" in the prayers, *i.e.* had never named either James or William, and being a " public person," as he says elsewhere (pp. 127, 194), had abstained from being present when such prayers were used.]

Lloyd's reply is lost, but it was obviously more friendly than the first letter. We are left to infer its contents from Ken's answer to it.

LETTER XLIV.

To MRS. HANNAH LLOYD.

"I RECEIVED your's, my good friend, and am glad it gave you any satisfaction, which I wrote to you. A friend of late has been much dissatisfied with me, because I will not give up myself to his keeping, which I have no reason to do, and he probably may raise jealousy of me. When I told you that a London journey was not agreeable to my purse, it was no pretence, but a real truth. I am not able to support the expense of it, which all that know my condition will easily believe. I thank God, I have enough to bring the yeare about while I remain in the country, and that is as much as I desire. I have been often offered money for myself, but always refused it, and never take any but for to distribute, and in the country I have nothing now for that good use put into my hands. As for the schism, I believe I can propose a way to end it, but it is not practicable till the Convocation meets, and then if the face of affairs alter not, I make no question but Erastianisme will be condemned, which by some of us has been proposed as a means of reunion. My respects to your fire-side. God keep us in His Holy feare.

"Your's very affectionately.

"T. B. & W.

"*Sarum, Ap :* 7 (1702).

"To-morrow I return, God willing, to Hampshire, for a short time."

[The "dissatisfied friend" (probably Hickes, p. 111) had apparently treated Ken's plea of poverty as an excuse; but his £80 *per annum* was really not enough to allow of spending money in an expedition to London, and his rule was (probably even after Fitzwilliam's legacy) to treat all that came into his hands beyond that as held in trust for those poorer than himself. The hopes with which the letter ends clearly point to Hooper as the Prolocutor and leading mind of the Lower House of Convocation. A declaration on the part of that body condemning Erastianism might, he thinks, open the way to re-union. The journey to Hampshire probably implies a visit to Canon Hawkins or Dr. Cheyney at Winchester. The hint that he sees his way to "end the schism" is noteworthy. See p. 109.]

This letter would seem not to have been answered, and so Ken writes again simply to report his movements.

LETTER XLV.

"FOR MRS. HANNAH LLOYD.

"All Glory be to God.

"MY VERY GOOD LORD,

"This is only to let you know that I go towards Polshot, God willing, to-morrow, and thither, if there is any occasion for it, your Lordshippe may direct to me. I have been more free from my distemper, I thank God, during my stay in this clear air than I have been for many years, and I would gladly seat myself in the down country, but that I must abide not where I would, but where I can; a moist, thick & muddy air does by no means agree with me, though to such a one I am now retiring. My best respects to Mrs. Lloyd, and to your family. God keep us in His holy fear.

"My good Lord,

"Your Lordship's very affect. frᵈ: and Bʳ.

"THOS. B. & W.

"*Apr. 26th*" (1702).

[The living of Polshot, in Wiltshire, was held by Izaak Walton, jun., in conjunction with his canonry at Winchester. One notes the gradual increase of disease and suffering from which the bracing air of the Downs gave him a temporary relief, and the plaintiveness of the remark, not perhaps without its bearing on the report which had spread that his means would allow him to travel freely to London and elsewhere, that he must be content to abide, "not where I would, but where I can." This seems a fitting place to give once for all a medical diagnosis as to the nature of Ken's sufferings, for which I am indebted to Dr. R. Purnell, of Wells, to whom I submitted all the passages in Ken's letters and poems that bear upon the question. "I consider it highly probable that Bishop Ken was the subject of what is commonly spoken of as lithiasis, a condition in which lithic acid is present in the system in excess, giving rise to a long train of morbid symptoms, including those you enumerate. The rheumatic pains would probably be first in order of occurrence, and doubtless were the cause of his being sent either to Bath or the Clifton Hot Wells for the water-cure; whilst the colic, it is more than likely, was of the nephritic variety, resulting from the formation of a small calculus as the disease progressed. The presence of hæmaturia as a later symptom strengthens the diagnosis, as it is of frequent occurrence in these cases. . . . . Opium would have been the only drug available to relieve his severe sufferings." And opium was the one drug which Ken, looking on it as an attempt to evade the discipline of appointed suffering, was unwilling to take. As he wrote—there seems to me something infinitely touching in the words—

"Verse is the only laudanum for my pains."

When the pains of anguish were scarcely endurable he would get up and write hymns. (See p. 199.) In these he found, as Hammond had done, who uses nearly the same words, his true "anodynes." (Fell's *Life*, pp. 228—231.) Hammond's illness seems to have been of the same type as Ken's, in both cases the effect of over-study, under-feeding, and many vigils.]

The next letter seems to have been written spontaneously, the opportunity of conveyance by a private hand having presented itself. This accounts for its being addressed, not like the others to Mrs. Hannah Lloyd, but to the Bishop as such.

LETTER XLVI.

FOR THE BISHOP OF NORWICH.

"All Glory be to God.

"MY VERY GOOD LORD,

" Mr. Jones intending to wait on you, lest the correspondence should quite expire, I took this opportunity of giving you a line or two. I find that I am misinterpreted by some of the brethren, and am charged with giving advices concerning communion, contrary to our Mother, whereas the only advice I have given was to recommend the two last prayers (*sic*, in Round) of good M^r. Kettlewell's book to people's reading. I was always of his opinion, and wished that our brethren had not stated the question on higher terms, and I approved of the book in manuscript. I easily guess from whom the prejudices conceived against me rise, and I had rather be loaded with treble the number, than put myself under his discipline. My best respects to your good wife and to your daughter. I shall spend this summer, God willing, most at Longleat, though I am now very uneasy there; not but that my Lord is extremely kind to me, but because I cannot go to prayers there, by reason of the late alterations, which is no small affliction to me. God keepe us in his holy fear, and make us wise for eternity.

"My good Lord,

"Your Lordship's most affect: friend and B^r,

THOS. B. & W.

" *June* 30 " (1702).

[Mr. Jones is probably the person of that name under cover to whom, as in Letter xli., Ken's correspondents were to address to him at Salisbury. The misinterpretation of which he complains was, I conceive, the report that he had encouraged his brother Non-jurors to communicate with the established clergy, anywhere, and under any conditions. He wishes to defend his position by saying that he agrees with the last section of Kettlewell's book (we should, I believe, read "pages," or probably " chapters,"[as in Letter xlviii.,not " prayers," as printed by Round), which permitted it as a preferable alternative to the entire abandonment of Church ordinances. Kettlewell's book is his *Treatise on Christian Communion*, Pt. III., chaps. vii. and viii. The author of the report in question was probably Hickes, between whom and Ken there seems to have been, at this time, a sense of mutual repulsion. He is inclined to say,

Non tali auxilio, nec defensoribus istis.

I do not feel sure what he refers to as the "late alterations" at Longleat. Probably Lord Weymouth, who may have acquiesced before William's death in the omission of the King's name in the services in his private chapel, may have directed Anne's name to be inserted, and so the prayers contained what were known as "characteristics." Ken felt that while others, who thought as he did as to the Revolution, might rightly attend such prayers and indicate their non-participation by some outward act, he, as a "public person," could not (pp. 121, 194).]

To this Lloyd clearly wrote an answer expressing general agreement, and Ken replied accordingly.

LETTER XLVII.

For Mrs. HANNAH LLOYD.

"MY GOOD LORD AND B',

"I made no sooner a return to your last, because you gave me hopes of hearing from you again, and more at large. It is a great satisfaction to me, that without consulting one another, we were both of the same mind. I confess I never was for extremities, which I soon thought would prove of fatal consequences, but I find that others, who always were, and still are, for them, think but hardly of me, and probably they may think as hardly of your Lordship. As for Mr. Jones, I think him an honest man, but since I conversed with him, and observed him, he is not one whom I would chuse for a governor to a young gentleman. My best respects to your lady, and to your daughter. God keep us in his holy feare.

"My good Lord,

"Your Lordship's most affect: friend & B',

"THO. B. & W.

" *Aug.* 21 " (1702).

[The "extremities" of which Ken speaks, are the denouncing the whole Established Church as involved in the guilt of schism, and refusing all communion with it. Mr. Jones seems to have been seeking a tutorship, for which Ken was not inclined to recommend him. I cannot trace him farther.]

Another letter, in reply to one received from Lloyd, follows before long.

LETTER XLVIII.

For Mrs. Hannah Lloyd.

"All Glory be to God.

" My very good Lord,

" Your's came to my hands, and as to the copy of a letter which
your friend received, I may well doubt of the truth of it, till I see it
confirmed, for certainly had it been true, the powers above must
have had some intimation of it, and as far as I can learn they have
received none. As for the other, I never argued the case with lay-
people, but recommended to them the two last chapters of M^r.
Kettlewell's book, where it is truly and fully stated, to my apprehension, and I am extremely satisfied that your sentiments concur
with mine. Our brother of Ely, now with God, had the like
thoughts, and gave the like advice to a worthy person now near me
in the country, who related it to me, and I always thought and
said, that stricter measures would be of fatal consequence to our
church, for which some of our brethren would never relish me. I
am going to Polsheault tomorrow for a few days, and I have an
invitation to give a visit to our good brother of Gloucester, if the
rheumatic and cholic pains which haunt me permit it. My best
respects to your good Lady and daughter. God of his infinite
goodness make us wise for eternity.

" My good Lord,

" Your Lordship's most affect: B^r,

"THO. B. & W.

" *Sep. 4th* " (1702).

[We are left to conjecture what the opening sentences refer to ; possibly there
were rumours as to action contemplated by the Government against those who
declined to take the oath of abjuration. The "powers above" may be a periphrasis for Lord Weymouth, who took office under Anne, and his friends. They,
Ken knew, had heard nothing of such measures. The rest of the letter deals once
more with the vexed question of attendance at the services in parish churches, and
this time Ken strengthens his position by referring to the authority of Francis
Turner (d. Nov. 2nd, 1700) as agreeing with himself and Kettlewell. Apparently this was a new, and perhaps, looking to the part Turner had taken, an unexpected fact to him, which he had learnt from the unknown "worthy person"
to whom the advice had been given. (But see p. 198.) Frampton, whom he proposes to visit, was then living unmolested at Standish, near Gloucester, preaching, catechising, and sometimes taking part, with necessary omissions of what
were called " characteristics," in the services of the parish church (Evans, *Life
of Frampton*, p. 208.) The wish to confer with him is symptomatic as indicating
general agreement as to what was feasible and desirable under the then existing
circumstances. For this visit, or possibly another at a later date, see Letter lxvi.
We note that Ken's sufferings are increasing in their painfulness.]

LETTER XLIX.

For Mrs. HANNAH LLOYD.

"All Glory be to God.

"MY VERY GOOD LORD,

"Your Lordship's of the 26th, found me at Longleat on the 28th, which I left the next day, my Lord Weymouth removing to the Town, and am now at Polshealt. I am extremely glad that you and the Bishop elect of St. Asaph conversed together. He is one of the best understandings I ever knew, and, if he will exert himself, will do excellent service to this sinking Church. I should think it one of the best excursions I could make to give you both a visit, but besides my aversion to the Town, I am afflicted with such pains, that I am by no means fit for travelling—they are rheumatic, and lie within my joints, and never come to the extreme parts, and at this present, my left arm is in a great measure disabled. I have a great desire to spend Christmas, God willing, with the Kemeyses, but fear I shall not be in a condition to do it. I am much concerned, that the Friend is not yet consecrated, and cannot imagine the reason of the delay. What you write of the Scotch I easily believe, and had thought that their quarrel about Episcopacy had been over. Since that, to my great surprise, passed the Confirmation of Presbytery. It will be a great satisfaction to me, to hear now and then from you. God keep us, in his holy feare.

"My good dear Lord,

"Your Lordps most affectionate Br,

"T. B. & W.

"*Oct. 30th* (1703).

"I shall be glad to see the work you mention."

[A year had passed since the date of the last letter. The date of this is found by the reference to Hooper, who was appointed to St. Asaph in the autumn of 1703. It would seem as if Ken only stayed at Longleat when his host was there, and we find him now once more with Canon Izaak Walton at Poulshot. The Bishop-elect of St. Asaph is Ken's friend, George Hooper, for whom, as always, he expresses the warmest admiration (i. 50). He clearly hopes that Hooper's counsels will strengthen Lloyd against the schemes of the more violent of the Non-jurors. To meet both his friends might almost tempt him to a journey to London, but his ever-increasing sufferings placed it out of his power. The "Kemeyses" are the two devout ladies of Naish Court, Portishead, of whom an account will be given in the next chapter. The friend who is "not yet consecrated" is obviously Hooper. The allusion to Scotland refers to the incipient negotiations for settling the Union which William had urged in his last message to Parliament. English churchmen were, some of them at least, hoping for a restoration of Episcopacy there. The extreme Presbyterians objected to any toleration of it. Ken expresses a natural disappointment at the victory of the latter. The Act of Settlement securing that victory was passed in 1703; the final Act of Union received the royal assent in 1707.]

LETTER I.

For Mrs. Hannah Lloyd.

" All Glory be to God.

" My dear Brother,

"Though I received both your Lordship's, yet having wrote the same post your last came, I forebore to give you a second trouble, having but little matter for a letter in this place where I am. You have a very true apprehension of your brother of S*t*. Asaph. He is of an excellent temper as well as understanding, & a man of sincerity, though he may be of a different judgment; & I much desire that you may often meet, & consult how to moderate things, as much as may be, *salvâ veritate*, for I fear that many of our friends run too high, and that the Church of Rome will reap advantages of excesses in that kind. Your letters are a great consolation to me in this solitude, & therefore I entreat the continuance of them. M*r*. Dodwell's book has been sent me, I presume, by himself. He seems to build high on feeble foundations. I presume he will not have many entire proselytes to all his hypothesies. My respects to the good company with you; God keep us in his holy fear.

" My good Lord, your Lordshipp's

most affect. friend & Brother,

" THO. B. & W.

" *Nov.* 13 " (1703).

[We note the growing affection which characterizes Ken's letters to Lloyd. He finds him, like himself, averse to the falsehood of extremes, and to any course of action which will favour the interests of the Church of Rome. Dodwell's book is, probably, his treatise *On the Immortality of the Soul* (published 1703), in which he taught what has lately been maintained as the Doctrine of Conditional Immortality, *i.e.* that the soul is not, in its own nature, imperishable, but only in virtue of its sharing in the eternal life communicated by participation in the life of Christ, and, as Dodwell held, in that life as imparted through the Sacraments. (Comp. Macaulay, chap. xiv.) Ken did not share that view, and obviously looks on it as a hazardous speculation. A full account of the theory is given by Brokesby in his *Life of Dodwell*, ii., 537—609. See p. 76.]

LETTER LI.

To MRS. HANNAH LLOYD.

"All Glory be to God.

"MY GOOD LORD AND DEAR BROTHER,

"I return you my thanks for both yours. I have no news to return, but that last night there was here the most violent wind that ever I knew; the house shaked all the night. We all rose and called the family to prayers, &, by the goodness of God, we were safe amidst the storm. It has done a great deal of hurt in the neighbourhood, & all about, which we cannot yet hear of; but I fear it has been very terrible at sea, and that we shall hear of many wrecks there. Blessed be God who preserved us. I hope that your Lordship & your family have suffered no harm, & should be glad to hear you are well. I beseech God to keep us in His holy fear,

"Your Lordship's most affect: friend and brother,

"THO. B. & W.

"*Nov.* 27 " (1703).

[The storm of which Ken writes brought, as we shall see, a crisis in his own life, of which he had no anticipation when he wrote to tell his friends of his own providential preservation. In Letter lv. he gives fuller details, hardly known, probably, 't the moment, as to the imminence of the danger and the strangeness of the escape. The storm was one of the most violent ever known in England, and Defoe published a narrative of its devastations (*The Storm,* 1704). Eight thousand lives were said to have been lost in it; twelve ships were wrecked, the Eddystone lighthouse destroyed, four thousand trees blown down in the New Forest, and the amount of the damage estimated at four millions sterling. A public fast was appointed in connexion with it and was devoutly observed throughout the kingdom. Tenison drew up the Form of Prayer, which extorted praise from Whiston as a pattern of what such prayers should be (Whiston's *Memoirs,* p. 132). A memorial of the impression the storm made on men's minds still survives in the form of an annual Commemoration Sermon in the Congregational Chapel in Little Wild Street, Drury Lane, for which an endowment was left at the time.]

LETTER LII.

To MRS. HANNAH LLOYD.

"All Glory be to God.

"MY GOOD LORD & BROTHER.

"I think I told you in my last, that I intended, God willing, to spend the Christmas with the good virgins at Nash; so that after Saturday next, your Lordship must direct nothing hither. The storm on Friday night, which was the most violent, I mentioned in my last, but I then did not know what happened at Wells, which was much shattered, and that part of the palace where Bishop Kidder and his wife lay, was blown down in the night, and they were both killed and buried in the ruins, and dug out towards morning. It happened on the very day of the Cloth fair, when all the country were spectators of the deplorable calamity, and soon spread the sad story. God of his infinite mercy deliver us from such dreadful surprises. I am assured that no one either in the palace, or in the whole town, beside them, had any hurt. God keep us in his holy fear, and our dwellings in safety,

> " My good Lord, your Lordship's
> most affect: friend & B^r,
> "THO. B. & W.

" *Nov.* 29 " (1703).

[The letter is obviously written from Poulshot. The tidings of the catastrophe at Wells had found its way thither shortly after the preceding letter was despatched. Ken probably heard of it with feelings which it is not easy to analyse. There was the natural awe and pity (" *Sunt lachrymæ rerum et mentem mortalia tangunt* ") caused by the suddenness of the blow, felt, it may be, all the more keenly from the recollection of the somewhat harsh way in which he had often spoken of his successor. There was, it may be, mingling with this, the sense of relief, which it was scarcely possible for him not to feel, in the thought that an influence which had worked for evil was removed, that an opening was made for the work of a faithful pastor in his diocese, and for ending a schism over which he had always mourned. Now there would no longer be an obstacle to the resignation which he had contemplated for at least two years (p. 109). Ken would have been almost more than human if he had escaped all touch of that feeling. The mention of the Cloth fair at Wells attests the existence of what was then a flourishing branch of manufacture in that city, of which the only survival at the present time is the existence of a special Almshouse for decayed Clothworkers.]

The letter which follows shows in what direction his thoughts were already drifting (see Letter xliv).

LETTER LIII.

To MRS. HANNAH LLOYD.

" All Glory be to God.

" MY VERY GOOD LORD AND BROTHER,

" Blessed be God who preserved us both in the late great storm ; it is a deliverance not to be forgotten. I hear of several persons who solicit for my Diocese, and whom I know not, and I am informed that it is offered to my old friend, the Bishop of St. Asaph,

and that it is declined by him. For my own part, if times should
have changed, I never intended to return to my burden, but I much
desire to see the flock in good hands, and I know none better to
whom I may entrust it than his; for which reason I write to him
this post, to let him know my desire that he should succeed, with
which I thought good to acquaint your Lordship. I leave this
place, God willing, on Wednesday, hoping to reach Bath, which is
but twelve miles, and to stay a night or two with Colonel Philips.
My best respects to all the good family with you; God keep us in
his Holy feare.

" Your Lordship's most affect. B^r,

"THO. B. & W.

" *Dec.* 6 " (1703).

[As usual in such cases, rumour was busy within a week of Kidder's death
with the appointment of a successor. Who the unnamed applicants were we can
only conjecture. A family tradition among the descendants of Dr. Thomas
Coney, Prebendary of Wells, and at one time Rector of Bath, reports that the
Bishopric was offered to him and refused, but I have been unable to find any
other evidence of the fact. Hooper's daughter, the wife of John Prowse, Esq., of
Axbridge, in her *Memoirs* of her father, says that the Queen sent for him at once
and offered the Bishopric to him, but that he expressed his unwillingness to take
Ken's place, and proposed that he should be restored to his see. " This the Queen
highly approved of, and thanked the Bishop for putting her in mind of it, and
ordered him to propose it to Bishop Ken." The offer mentioned in p. 119,
shows what the Queen felt as to the latter. The letter was probably written from
Poulshot. Bath would lie naturally on his way in the journey to Naish Court
mentioned in Letter lii. Another letter had, as he tells Lloyd, to be written by
the same post. He must not allow Hooper's refusal, generous as was its motive,
to upset the plan on which he had resolved, as best for himself, his diocese, and
the Church at large. I have not succeeded in obtaining any information as to
Col. Philips.]

LETTER LIV.

For the Right Rev. Father in God, George, Lord Bishop of
St. Asaph.

" All Glory be to God.

" My very good Lord,

" I am informed y^t you have had an offer of Bath and Wells, and
y^t you refused it, wch I take very kindly, because I know you did
it on my account; but since I am well assured y^t ye diocese cannot be happy to y^t degree in any other hands than in your owne, I
DESIRE YOU TO ACCEPT OF IT, and I know y^t you have a prevailing
interest to procure it. My nephew and o^r little family, who present your Lordshippe their humble respects, will be overjoyed at

your neighbourhood.   I told you long agoe at Bath how willing I was to surrender my cannonicall claime to a worthy person, but to none *more willingly* than to yourselfe (p. 109).   My distemper disables me from ye pastoral duty, and had I been restored, I declared allways y^t I would shake off ye burthen, and retire.   I am about to leave this place, but if need be, ye archdeacon can tell you how to direct to me.   My best respects to your good family.   God keepe us in his holy feare.

"My good Lord,

" Your Lordshippe's most affectionately,

"T. B. & W.

" *Dec. 6th* " (1703).

[This letter, the first now extant of his correspondence with his old friend, shows how warmly he welcomed his appointment.   He felt sure that the flock for which he cared would be safe in his friend's hands.   His poems show, with more fulness and emotion, what thoughts were working in his mind, as he looked back on the past and forward to the future.   He dedicated his *Hymnarium* to his successor, and this is his retrospect :—

> "Among the herdmen I, a common swain,
> Liv'd, pleas'd with my low cottage on the plain,
> Till up, like Amos, on a sudden caught,
> I to the Past'ral Chair was trembling brought.
> Heaven deem'd that step for me, I fear, too bold,
> And let a stranger climb into my fold.
> I, who the stranger saw my flock invade
> Was forced to fly to unfrequented shade,
> Like captive Judah, by the stream to dwell,
> And with my dropping eye the waters swell.
> ' Ah, my dear Lambs ! ah, my dear Sheep!' I cry'd,
> 'Dear Lambs,' ' dear Sheep,' the neighbouring hills reply'd.
> *   *   *   *   *   *
> But that which most my watery eyelids drained,
> My Lambs, my Sheep, were by this wandering baned ;
> They broke from Catholick and hallowed Bounds,
> And for the wholesome, chose impoisoned, grounds,
> Contracting Latitudinarian taint,
> In Faith, in Morals, suffering no Restraint."

He betakes himself to prayer, and in a strange unlooked-for way his prayer is answered :—

> " And while I mourn'd for the tremendous Stroke
> Which freed them from their uncanonic Yoke,
> Heaven, my Lord, super-effluently kind,
> In you sent a successor to my mind,
> You, in whose care I feel a full Repose,
> As old Valerius,[1] when he Austin chose."

---

[1] Valerius, predecessor of Augustine, in the Bishopric of Hippo.

Of his own willingness to lay down the load of office he writes, in the *Dedication* of vol. i. to Lord Weymouth :—

> "I, crush'd by State decrees and griev'd with pain,
> The past'ral Toil unable to sustain,
> More gladly off the hallowed Burthen shake
> Than I at first the weight could undertake."

It is interesting to note that he reminds Hooper that this resolve of his was no new thing, that he had told him of it " long ago " at Bath, where probably both the friends were staying for the benefit of their health. The hypothetical clause, " had I been restored," refers obviously to the offer made through Lord Weymouth (p. 119). Had it been possible for him to accept that offer, his first act would have been to resign the burden. The " nephew " whom he mentions is Canon Izaak Walton of Poulshot. The " archdeacon " is, probably, Sandys (Archdeacon of Wells), with whom Ken often stayed.]

Hooper's answer obviously conveyed his assent to Ken's proposal, and Ken, full of joy and satisfaction, writes to tell Lloyd that all is settled in accordance with his wishes.

LETTER LV.

For Mrs. Hannah Lloyd.

" All Glory be to God.

" My good L^d and B^r.

" The same post wch brought me your Lordshipp's, brought the news of ye occasionall bills being throwne out by ye lords. I think I omitted to tell you ye full of my deliverance in *ye late storme;* for, the house being searched ye day following, ye workmen found y^t y^e *beame wch supported ye roof over my head was shaken out to y^t degree, y^t it had but halfe an inch hold,* so y^t it was a wonder it could hold together : for wch signall and particular preservation God's holy name be ever praised ! I am sure I ought alwayes thankfully to remember it. I, hearing y^t ye B^p of St. Asaph was offered Bath and Wells, and y^t on my account he *refused* it, wrott to him to accept of it. I did it in charity to ye diocese, y^t they might not have a Latitudinarian Traditour imposed on them, who would betray ye baptismall faith, but one who had ability and zeal to assert it; and the imminent danger in which religion now is, and which dayly increases, ought to supersede all ye antient canons. I am so disabled by rheumatick and colick pains, y^t I cannot in conscience returne to a publick station, were I restored; and I think none ought to censure me, if in such perillous times I desire a coadjutor, for w^h I have good precedents, as well as reasons. It is not yᵉ *first time* I dissented from some of my brethren; and never saw cause to repent of it. The ladys here send you their duty. God keep us in his holy feare.

"Your Lordshipp's most affecᵉ friend and Bʳ,

"T. B. & W.

"*Nash. Dec.* 18" (1703).

[The "occasional bills" were those against "occasional conformity," which had been brought forward by the Tory party in 1703 in order to prevent the evasion of the Test Acts by a single act of communion in the Church of England, while the holder of office continued in all other respects to act as an avowed Nonconformist. Ken, I apprehend, would have been in favour of the Bills as long as the Test Act remained unrepealed. I incline to think, however, that the experience of the working of the Test Act would have made him willing enough to see it repealed. The view of Kidder's character implied in the possibility, if Hooper had not accepted, of another "Latitudinarian Traditour" being imposed on his flock, agrees with what we have already seen more than once (p. 60). One notes the freedom of thought which sees in the urgent necessities of the time a reason for dispensing with "antient canons." He too was learning to say with Tillotson that "Charity was above rubrics," that the *Salus Ecclesiæ* was more authoritative even than her canons. His first thought seems to have been that of accepting Hooper as a "coadjutor," as Valerius had accepted Augustine, without a formal resignation. Already, however, he begins to hear the mutterings of the storm which, before many days, was to burst upon his head. That, however, will not change his purpose, will rather lead to its taking a stronger and more definite form. He looks back on the line that the objectors had taken in other matters, such, *e.g.*, as the consecration of Hickes and Wagstaffe, and has never regretted that he chose another line of action for himself. The "ladys" of the last sentence but one are the Misses Kemeys of Naish Court, with whom he went to spend Christmas (p. 129).]

Two days pass and we have another letter to Hooper.

LETTER LVI.

FOR THE RIGHT REV. FATHER IN GOD, GEORGE, LORD BISHOP OF ST. ASAPH.

"All Glory be to God.

"MY VERY GOOD LORD,

"The last post brought me yᵉ news wᶜʰ I earnestly expected, and wᶜʰ your lordshippe's letter gave me hope of, and I heartily congratulate yᵉ diocese of Bath and Wells of your translation, for it was yᵉ good of yᵉ flock, and not my friendshippe for yourselfe, wᶜʰ made me desire to see you in yᵉ pastorall chaire, where I know you will zealously '*contend for ye faith once delivered to ye saints,*' wᶜʰ in these *latitudinarian times* is in great danger to be lost. I could easily forsee y^t, by my concerne for you, I should incurre ye displeasure of some of my brethren, but this is not ye first instance in wch I have dissented from them, and never had cause to repent of it; and ye good of ye diocese supersedes all other considerations. I have another wish for ye good of ye diocese you are to leave, and it is y^t Dr. Edwards might succeed you there, though he is a person whome I doe not know so much as by sight. My best respects to your good lady, whose paines I can ye more tenderly condole, from what I feele dayly myselfe. God keepe us in his holy feare.

"My good Lord,
"Your Lordshippe's most affectionately,
"T. K.

"*Dec. 20th*" (1703).

[The whole matter now seemed to be settled. The *Congé d'élire*, dated January 7th, did not reach the Chapter of Wells till January 19th, 170$\frac{3}{4}$; but virtually the translation was already accomplished. The storm is still gathering, but the good of the diocese supersedes all other considerations. Of the Dr. Edwards whom Ken wishes to succeed Hooper at St. Asaph's, I am unable to give any certain information. He may have been Jonathan Edwards who wrote against Socinianism, and who was elected Principal of Jesus College, Oxford, in 1686. Another eminent divine of that name was John Edwards, of St. John's College, Cambridge, but as he was an extreme Calvinist, and had not been on good terms with Gunning and Turner, when they were Masters of St. John's, he is not likely to have been within the range of Ken's sympathies. Beveridge was Hooper's actua' successor.]

Three months passed before the next extant letter. In the meantime the storm which we have seen gathering and of which Hickes's letters (pp. 108—111) had given premonitory symptoms, burst in all its violence. The Jacobite section of the Non-Jurors both in Bristol and London, were vehement in their language. To them Ken himself seemed a "Latitudinarian traditour" abandoning the position which was the stronghold of the Non-jurors. A letter printed by Round from the Tanner MSS., undated, and with neither address nor signature, but belonging apparently to this period, is worth printing as showing the kind of language which they used, when they heard of Ken's willingness to accept Hooper as his successor:

"Rev^t. S^r.

"On this day seven-night, I received y^r kind letter, in which the melancholy account of Bp. K. added to the affliction of the day. I had but too great reason to believe all you say of him before y^{rs} came to me, but I was willing (if the History were undoubtedly

K 2

true,) to have it from so good and authentic an hand. When I saw him before Xmas, he gave me great occasion to suspect his declination, for that to my surprise, he told me, he would resign his Bprick to D^r II. for the preservation of the faith, now in danger. I told him practical doctrines were as much in danger as those of our necessary belief, and that however sound Dr H. was in those, (which I thought was very questionable, in relation particularly, at present, to the ninth article of the Creed,) yet his Lordship could not say he was sound as to moral doctrines, and that his very acceptance of the diocess of S^t. Asaph, on the terms of the present gov^{nt}, was an evident proof of it, and that he might as well have resigned before to D^r. K. We had a great deal of discourse, which, with submission, I thought incoherent, and his temper I found, as you well observe, impatient of contradiction ; however with that modesty and deference, which I then owed unto him and his character, I could not forbear replying. The last week I attended the good family, in which Bp. K. used to be when in these parts, and in which he was when I saw him last, I talked with those ladies some time about this unhappy business ; upon reasoning with them, they could not but agree with me, that the Bp. was in the wrong ; but I find them so wedded to an opinion of his great piety and charity, that I fear it will be difficult to dissuade them from communicating with him whilst in the family, wherein he is expected again before Lent. I told them, as soon as I should hear that he was at their house, I would wait on him, and tell him what the world positively affirms of him. If the B^p agree to it, I will modestly beg his reasons for acting thus, and if I can answer them, I will decline his communion, as now himself encouraging and communicating in a schism. I am told that it is verily believed, that after all, he will not communicate with B^p H., which seems to me a greater inconsistency, for it is strange for a B^p to deliver up his flock to another, with whom he thinks it a sin to communicate himself. I am informed likewise, that the B^p of N. hath encouraged, and congratulated B^p K. on his cession to B^p H. and that by a letter sent lately to him. I am fully persuaded it is an arrant calumny, or a mistake. I told the person informing me, that probably the B^p of N. might rejoice, that since a schismatick must be placed at Wells, a person otherwise so acceptable as Dr H. would be the man, but that the B^p of N. sh^d any ways persuade the B^p of B. & W. to concur, in the least, in such an act himself, is past my belief. I thought fit to acquaint you with this story, that justice may be done to that good B^p, and so I submit it to what use you shall please to make of it, begging your direction in this, or any other affair of this nature. I have since a letter from

Bᵖ K. subscribed T. K. I have laboured for some months past to
bring a young lady of quality off from the schismatical churches
entirely. I have talked, and wrote to that purpose, but poor Bᵖ K.
hath undone more in one word, than I was likely to do in ten
thousand, for he allowed that liberty, that strange occasional conformity, and so the Lady is confirmed in her amphibious devotion.
God be merciful to this poor Church. The delusion and infatuation
spreads wider, and wider. This poor gentleman's lapse is occasion
of great lamentation unto us, and laughter to our enemies. It confirms more the otherwise well inclined in their schism, hardening
the obstinate schismatick, and, I fear, gives occasion to the profest
enemies of God to blaspheme more abundantly, and as for my own
part, it is a double affliction to think that I must be necessitated,
to forsake his communion who received me by absolution to the
peace and unity of the Church ; but I must doe it, if that father
hath fallen himself into those errors, out of which (I dayly bless
God) I am retrieved. I congratulate the recovery of yʳ Lady's
health, and so does my spouse. I beg the prayers and continuance
of yʳ friendship, and am,

> "Revᵈ Sir,
>
> " Yʳ most devoted."

[The writer is identified by his reference to Ken's having received him as a
penitent with a Mr. Stamp, mentioned by Hickes in his letter to Ken of November 10th, 1701 (p. 111), who had then reported to him the earlier symptoms of
Ken's falling away. I conjecture that the letter was written to Spinckes (p. 148).
It will be noted that the writer saw Ken before Christmas, at Naish Court, that he
questioned Hooper's orthodoxy, that he found Ken impatient of contradiction, that
Ken had then told him that he meant to resign, that some time after this he went
to Naish Court and tried, but in vain, to persuade the Misses Kemeys to join him
in treating their friend as virtually excommunicated *ipso facto ;* that he makes a
special point of the rumour that Ken did not mean to communicate with his successor. (See p. 195.) He has heard, but cannot believe, that Bishop Lloyd has signified his approval of Ken's action. He dwells on the new signature T. K. (see
Letter lvi. p. 135) as showing that Ken no longer looked on himself as being, either
canonically or legally, Bishop of Bath and Wells. The tone of contemptuous
pity, "the poor gentleman's lapse," and the like, indicates the kind of language
which it was Ken's destiny to bear with whatever patience he could. The Dr.
K. to whom Ken "might as well have resigned," is, of course, Kidder.]

Lloyd had apparently answered Ken's letter of Dec. 20th by
expressing a general satisfaction that such a man as Hooper
had been appointed to succeed Kidder ; and Ken was naturally
glad to find that he had his friend's approval as a set-off against
the reproaches with which the more violent section of the Non-

jurors were assailing him. According to his usual custom at Holy Seasons, he spent his Christmas, as we have seen, with the Kemeys sisters at Naish, and from thence wrote again to Lloyd.

LETTER LVII.

"For Mrs. Hannah Lloyd.

"All Glory be to God.

"My good Lord and B^r,

"I am in debt to you for the last post. It is no small satisfaction to me, that you approve of my choice, in good earnest. I had such experience of one before, who, instead of keeping the flock within the fold, encouraged them to stray—that I was afraid of a traditour, and in such a time as this, thought I could not do a greater kindness to the diocese, than in procuring it one of the most valuable men in the church, and one who was so very able to defend the *depositum*, which seemes to me to be in the utmost danger. The good ladys here present their best respects to your Lordship; and begge your blessing. I beseech God to send you and yours a happy new year, and to keep us in his reverential love.

"Your Lordship's most affect: friend & B^r,

"T. K.

"*Dec.* 27" (1703).

[Here we come across a somewhat definite charge against Kidder's administration of his diocese. He had "encouraged" his flock "to stray," *i.e.* had not only tolerated, but had patronised Dissent. We are left to guess to what special acts Ken refers. Our Chapter Acts show that the Dean and Canons objected to the haste with which he admitted Dissenting ministers to holy orders, and on that ground, for a time, refused to attend his ordinations. The special case on which Kidder dwells in his *Autobiography* was that of a Mr. Malarhé, who had been a schoolmaster in the diocese of Exeter. The Canons (notably Creighton, the son of the Bishop) objected that he was not a graduate, that his testimonials were insufficient, and demanded that he should preach a recantation sermon. He is said to have been a West Indian, with negro blood in him, and that may, perhaps, have told against him (Cassan, *Bishops of Bath and Wells*, ii. pp. 146—153). Another case was possibly in Ken's mind. Janney's *Life of Penn* (p. 398) records an instance in which the great Quaker came to Wells, was mobbed by the populace, and snubbed by the civic authorities, till Kidder intervened and gave him a license for a room, in which he and his followers, then and afterwards, might meet in peace. One notes the anxiety which the letter expresses for the *depositum fidei*, of which the Church was the keeper, with a forecast which was verified by the whole history of the eighteenth century. The mention of the "good ladys" shows that the letter was written at Naish, and though the year, as usual, is not given, its contents shows that it must have been written in December, 1703. It was probably about this time that the irreconcilable Non-juror, whose letter has just been given (p. 135), paid the visit to Naish which he reports.]

About seven weeks later we have another letter in the same tone.

LETTER LVIII.

"For Mrs. HANNAH LLOYD.

"All Glory be to God.

"MY VERY GOOD LORD & BROTHER,

"'Though I have nothing worthy of the postage, yet I thought myself obliged to give your Lordship an account of my motions: I am now at Sarum, where I have been detained by a lame horse, but hope to be gone, God willing, to-morrow, and to be at Nash on Saturday, or Monday, there to spend my Lent. You cannot imagine the universal satisfaction expressed for Dr. Hooper's coming to my See; and I make no doubt but that he will rescue the diocese from the apostacy from ' the faith once delivered to the saints,' which at present threatens us, and from the spirit of latitudinarianism, which is a common sewer of all heresies imaginable, and I am not a little satisfied, that I have made the best provision for the flock, which was possible in our present circumstances. God keep us in His holy fear.

"Your Lordship's most affec^te friend & B^r,

"T. K.

"*Feb.* 21 " (170¾).

[After Christmas tide was over Ken seems to have gone again to Izaak Walton's at Salisbury, but another visit to Naish was in prospect. The "good ladies" had, happily, not been persuaded to renounce his friendship, or to cease to hold communion with him. The tone is as before, one of general content with his own action and its results. Hooper's appointment (he was elected on Jan. 25th, but was not installed till April 3rd) had given "universal satisfaction." As Ken looked back on Kidder's administration it seemed to him to involve something like apostasy from the true faith, leading to the latitudinarian indifference which was, not the "fountain-head," but the "common sewer" of all heresies. One notes how he refers to his own share in Hooper's appointment. He had, in fact, been responsible for that appointment in the act of declining the Queen's offer for himself and asking Hooper to accept the Bishopric. We note once more the signature T. K.]

The journey to Naish was accomplished and Ken writes again.

"To MRS. HANNAH LLOYD.

" All Glory be to God.

" MY GOOD LORD AND DEAR BROTHER,

" I came not to Nash till last night, being detained by the way by a lame horse, and there I met with your letter of Jan^ry 25th, by which I perceive my letter to you, which gave you an account of my motions, miscarried. I read yours with very great commiseration of your condition very painful and afflicting, though thanks be to God, the paroxysm was over before you wrote, and I hope by this time you have recovered your spirits, the sovereign support of which is a good conscience and resignation to the Divine will, of which I assure myself you have a plentiful experience ; my distemper, which is always most domineering at spring and fall, has threatened me with a further assault, but thanks be to God, it soon abated. I presume that my successor has so many avocations, that at present he cannot make so long an excursion as to visit your Lordship, but will do it when he is at liberty. God keep us in his Holy fear, and enable us to improve all the mementoes he is pleased to give us of eternity.

" My good Lord,

" Your Lordship's most affectionate friend & Brother,

" K.

" *Nash, Feb.* 27 (170¾).

" The good Ladys are your servants."

[On the same grounds as before, with the addition of the link with the previous letter, of the " lame horse," I assign the letter to the February of 170¾. Lloyd had apparently been suffering from some acute form of disease, and Ken, himself a sufferer from chronic pains of many kinds, was but too well able to sympathise with him. The latter had hoped, it would seem, that his friend the new Bishop would before this have called on Lloyd and given him whatever assurances were necessary to confirm his feeling of satisfaction that such a man had been appointed. In the absence of any knowledge of the whereabouts of either of the two we cannot tell what was the " long excursion " of which the letter speaks. Possibly Hooper, though not installed till April 3rd, may have already entered on residence at Wells, or he may have been still at St. Asaph, and so was unable to visit Lloyd in London.]

The repose which Ken sought at Naish during the Lent season was unhappily interrupted, as the unknown writer of the letter given in p. 135 had threatened, by more reproaches,

bitter and scornful in their tone, from the more violent Non-
jurors, both at London and Bristol. He turns to Lloyd,
obviously in the full confidence that he will give him his
sympathy and support.

LETTER LX.

" To Mrs. HANNAH LLOYD.

" All Glory be to God.

" MY GOOD LORD AND DEAR B[r],

" Your last came to me yesterday in the morning, blessed be
God, who has given you ease, and sanctified your affliction to you.
All here send most kind remembrances to your Lordshippe, and to
their good friends with you, to which I add my owne. The Jacobites at Bristoll, fomented by those at London, are thoroughly
enraged against me for my Cession to one, whom all mankind, besides themselves, have a high esteem of, and one most able and
willing to preserve the *Depositum, and under whose care I* assure myself that the Diocese will be secured from the Latitudinarian Con-
tagion. Our B[r] of Gl: [Gloucester] is doing the same thing, having
surrendered his cure of souls at Standish to his curate, who, I presume, is by this time possessed of it. *But the same persons, who
inveigh against me, take no notice of him.* I am threatened with something to be printed against me : I believe they had better
let me alone. If I should produce the frequent letters a cer-
taine person wrote to me, for near two yeares together, to impor-
tune me to consent to Clandestine C. [Consecrations] they would
discover the temper of the man, and the zeal he shewed to
make the Schism incurable, which I was always for moderating,
foreseeing how fatal it would prove. *As long as I have your approbation, and the example of our other B[r], I have little regard for the
passion of others ;* I thank God that I have reposed the flock in safe
hands, which is a great ease to me, and I have preserved them from
a wolfe, that might have invaded them. *All who condemn me, owne
that Death legitimates an intruder, and I know no reason, but that voluntary Cession, and that for the apparent preservation of the whole flock, to
one who will not intrude, may be as effectuall as death.*

" God keepe us in His holy feare.

" My good Lord,

" Your Lordshipp's most affect: Friend and B[r],

" T. B. & W.

" *March 7th* " (170⅘).

[It will be seen that now Ken speaks of his "cession" as a thing which, if not formally executed, was virtually a thing accomplished, and separates himself altogether from the "Jacobite" section of the Non-jurors. He strengthens his position by the example of Frampton, who, though he had not resigned his bishopric, had taken that course as regarded his cure of souls at Standish. He looks to Hickes (I take him to be the "certain person") as the chief agent in promoting the attacks to which he had been subject, and looks back with satisfaction to the part he had taken in 1693, in resisting his proposals for the clandestine consecration of two Non-juring Bishops, in order to perpetuate the Episcopal succession in that body as a distinct Church standing apart from the Established Church of England. As yet he feels sure he has Lloyd's approval, and can rest upon Frampton's example, and so he cares little for the opinion of others. He falls back upon the general principle admitted by all canonists, urged afterwards by Dodwell, that "Death legitimates an intruder," and that "voluntary cession" has in such a case, the same effect as death." (See pp. 191—4.) Hickes, in his letter of Nov. 10th, 1701 (pp. 111, 137), had urged that Ken could not canonically resign without the consent of the Primus (*i.e.* Bishop Lloyd), and that if he did so, many Non-jurors would become Papists.]

Lloyd's answer, which, with a view to the correspondence which follows, it will be well to give in full, seems to show that he had listened to the reproaches with which Ken had been assailed, and began to think that he had been acting too precipitately in indicating his approval of Hooper's appointment. If he was satisfied with regard to the man, it did not follow that he approved of Ken's acting as he had done, without consulting those with whom he was associated.

"To Bishop Ken.

"My good Lord and Deare Brother,

" I have your dispatch of the 7th current now before me. I must own the obligations your Lordship and the good ladyes att Nash have layd upon me, for your good wishes to me and my family. I was sensibly grieved, (when I read your letter) for the noyse and outcryes, made both at Bristol, and here above (*also ?*), upon the account of your Cession. How a sudden passion may carry and transport some men at Bristoll I know not; but I am sure I have not heard any of the brethren here, say anything disrespectfull of your person, or your character, unless what amounts to no more than this, viz. that they seemed offended, because your conduct, in and about the Cession, was not managed *communi consensu*. To obviate this objection, I took the freedom to write unto you, and to desire you, not to quit your charge, until we might (for our mutual satisfaction) meet, and consult upon that weighty case, lest we should doe anything that might hurt the Church, or wound the minds of our brethren. To this, you were pleased to inform me, that your Lordship was fully satisfyed in the merits of the person, that was to succeed you, and named the reverend Dr. Hooper. *I was apprised of his piety, learning and good temper, and if my approbation would have signified anything I did then say, and doe now say the same, viz. in my poore opinion you could not have desired, or wished for, a worthier or fitter person for your successor, and thereupon wished that a double portion of his predecessor's spirit might rest on him.* Thus, my Lord, I have plainly laid before your Lordship, all the account I know of, relating to this matter, both to satisfy your Lordship of what I am apprised of, and to prevent (if possible) the groundless surmises of those who are apt to take fire without due materialls. With all respects and service to your Lordship, and to the good ladyes att Nash,

" I remain your Lordship's

" Affectionate Brother, and humble Servant,

" WM. NOR:

" *March* 14*th*, 170¾."

[The chief point in Lloyd's letter is the reference to the fact that in a previous letter he had written in accordance with Hickes's view, as given in the letter of Nov. 10th, 1701 (pp. 111, 137), to desire Ken not to quit his charge till the whole question of what was best to be done, as affairs then stood, had been discussed by the leaders of the party. Against Hooper personally he has not a word to say. No one could be named as fitter for the Episcopate, but he is not prepared at present to commit himself to more.]

To this Ken replies—

LETTER LXI.

" To MRS. HANNAH LLOYD.

" All Glory be to God.

" MY GOOD LORD AND DEAR BROTHER,

" Among other things which are vehemently laid to my charge, one is, that against your advice, and entreaties, I would obstinately go my own way; against this, I owne, that you had wrote to me to deferre my Cession, *but that the nature of the thing would not permit it, and if I had not given my consent that post, I might have had a Hireling and not a Shepherd,* and I wrott to you to that purpose, and that after I had receded, your Lordship approved of what I had done, and that *I had by me your letters, which congratulated my choice, to attest it ;* and that in your last, you seem to lay to heart the danger in which the *Depositum* is, as much as myself, and which was the sole motive which inclined me, and *you expresse your sense of the hardnesse of the Work to stem the strong current which runns against the Church,* in which you have the concurrent testimonies of all sober men. Sure I am, if people will duly weigh all circumstances, no well-minded man can blame me. I am told from London, that 'tis urged that by my action I condemn their conduct, but how I know not :— if any of them had a Cure of Souls, and could transfer it into like hands, as I have done, I should exhort them to recede, as well as myself, for the common good of the flock, without making a bargaine with the successor for a pension, as I fear some have done who blame me. The Ladys here are, God be thanked, very well, and present their respects to yourself and family. God keep us in His Holy feare and prepare us for a happy eternity.

" My dear L^d,

" Your Lordship's most affectionate Brother,

"T. B. & W.

" *March* 20*th,* 170$\frac{3}{4}$."

[Ken seems to feel that there had been a certain amount of trimming on Lloyd's part. It was true that he had urged delay, but after Ken had told him that delay would only lead to the very evil he sought to avoid, he had still written in the language not of remonstrance, but of congratulation. Ken, it will seem, is still with the ladies of Naish. I am unable to identify the persons of whom Ken speaks as having resigned, and made a bargain with their successors for a pension, and who, in spite of this, were found among those who attacked him.]

Two letters were written after this by Lloyd, which are not extant. Their contents may, however, be inferred from the two which Ken wrote in return, and from Lloyd's own subsequent letters. The former began to feel more and more indignant at what seemed to him the inconsistency of Lloyd's more recent language with that which he had used when he first heard of Hooper's appointment. That indignation, combined, we may well believe, with sharp bodily suffering, and with the over-sensitiveness to which the asceticism of a strict Lent not seldom exposes men of weak health and nervous temperament, led him to write strongly, and, as he afterwards felt, to " speak unadvisedly with his lips."

LETTER LXII.

"To Mrs. Hannah Lloyd.

"All Glory be to God.

"My good Lord and Brother,

"I perceive by your two last that your Lordshippe is very shy of owning your approbation of my action, at which I justly wonder, in regard that your expressions signify it very clearly. I have done nothing but what may be justified by primitive precedents, and which is for the preservation of the *Depositum*, which ought chiefly to exhaust a Pastour's zeal, especially when he is, in all respects, *disabled* himselfe for Pastoral care, and that the flock might have a shepherd, and not a *hireling*. As for the clause you mention, I could give some instances, from my own knowledge, but the persons are dead, and I will not name them. If I had been conversant in the towne, I might possibly have heard of more. The truth is, that which provoked me to mention it, was one of our brethren in the Country, who to a friend of mine very much blamed my Cession. My friend who heard him, presently replied to this purpose; that he should rather reflect on himselfe, who had been making a bargain for an acquaintance of his who was deprived, which it seems my friend knew, and he was presently silenced, being told that no such thing was chargeable on me; and this passage coming to my knowledge, occasioned that clause in my letter. I am not surprised at the censures bestowed on me; I foresaw them all; and, to deal freely with your Lordshippe, you are not without your share. 'Tis not long ago that a very sober person expressed some dissatisfaction at your suffering your son to take *all tests;* I reply'd that I never heard you did so; and that it might be a false report; and so the discourse ended. For my own part, I never did anything in my life *more to my satisfaction than my Receding.* It has eased me of a great load which lay on me, and has entirely *loosened me from the world;* so that I have now nothing to doe but to think of eternity, for which God of His infinite mercy prepare us.

"My good Lord,

"Your Lord[ps] very affect: Friend and Brother,

"T. B. & W.

"*April 1st*, 1704."

[The mysterious allusion to those who had "bargained for a pension" had probably been met by Lloyd with some doubt as to the accuracy of the statement. Ken contents himself with saying that he had not spoken without sufficient grounds. There is no evidence to show who were the parties to the conversation of which he gives a summary; nor am I able to confirm or deny the statement that Lloyd had allowed his son to "take *all tests*," including of course the latest test of the Abjuration Oath. The last sentence of the letter, as indicating Ken's desire to give the rest of his life, free from all worldly cares, to preparation for the end, is eminently characteristic. I cannot explain his return to the old form of signature in this and the two previous letters. It may have been simply an instance of the force of habit.]

This was followed up, without waiting for an answer, by yet another, written in still keener language of complaint.

LETTER LXIII.

"To Mrs. HANNAH LLOYD.

"All Glory be to God.

"MY VERY GOOD LORD AND DEAR BROTHER,

"Though I wrote to your Lordship last, yett I am in a manner bound to write again, to let you know that the ferment against me rises higher and higher, insomuch that when the neighbours at Bristol come hither, they manifestly insult me, and though you are pleased to tell me that others kindled this flame, and not yourself, I must take the freedome to tell you that it is yourself have most contributed to it. For 'tis still vehemently urged against me, that I acted quite contrary to your earnest remonstrances, which you know to be false. If I did, I do not remember that I ever put myself into your keeping, and was to do nothing but by your direction; but you yourself can acquit me in that particular, by only relating matter of fact. But I find there is a flat contradiction between them and me; I affirm you approved my action, and they flatly deny it, and affirm the quite contrary, and that increases their zeal: now I calmly appeal to you to let me know the literall importance of this expression, for I will only mention this: '*I heartily congratulate your choice, and wish a double portion of your spirit may rest upon the head and heart of your Successor, for I trust he will act valiantly, and becoming his station.*' If this does not signify an approbation, and more than that, a congratulation, both of my action and the person, to the height, I am much mistaken. Sure you would not have used this language, if you had thought my successour, as you style him, a schismatical Bishop. *No, good Brother, your native thoughts were the same with mine: but when you heard a cry against me, you flew to the distinction of Person and Cession, and 'tis from thence that the fury against me was raised for doing an act which, according to the best of my judgment, appeared truly primitive and charitable, and I may add, neces-*

sary. This is not all; the heat against me is furnished with fresh fuel from the town, and that by your communicating my letters, which I am charged with here. This is hard usage; sure I am, that I have never showed your letters to my angry neighbours, being unwilling to expose private correspondence, which, when exposed, is easily misrepresented, and exaggerated, and if I had done it, I verily believe that the like heat would be raised against yourself. Sure I am, had you acted uniformly to the expressions you used to me, this storm had quite allayed, or at least very much moderated. *Upon the whole matter I,—who desire nothing more than in retreat quietly to serve God, to pray for my brethren, which I daily do, and to mind only my latter end,—seeing my letters do but make more trouble, desire to be excused from writing for the future, for I find it much easier for me silently to endure the passion of others, than to endeavour to mitigate it.* I beseech God to make us wise for eternity.

" Your Lordships very affect: Brother,

"T. B. AND W.

" *April 5th* " (1704).

[Fresh attacks from the Jacobites of Bristol, who came to Naish Court and made free use of Lloyd's name, Stamp, probably, being their leader, roused Ken's spirit once more to a fiery heat of indignation. He was charged with having acted contrary to Lloyd's remonstrances. He falls back on the language of congratulation which Lloyd had used, and which seemed to him to imply approval. He charges Lloyd with recanting that approval under pressure from without. He is hurt that his own letters should have been shown by Lloyd, without his leave, to his opponents, but will not follow his example. As it is he prefers to break off all further correspondence, and to give himself wholly to a life of prayer. He can "endure," even where he fails to "mitigate" the passions of his accusers.]

A letter like this naturally roused Lloyd to a like heat, and he answered in a *verbosa et grandis epistola,* of which, contrary to his usual custom, he kept a copy, which we find accordingly in the Williams' collection of his MSS. It is too long to reproduce in full, but I give some extracts that will sufficiently show its character.

To BISHOP KEN.

" MY GOOD LORD AND DEAR BROTHER,

" I was so amazed at the perusal of your two (one of the 1st and the other of the 5th current), that I could not but wonder that a person of your character and profession could give way to, and be hurried on by, such vehement passion and injurious reflexions. . .

. . You take upon you to charge, censure, and condemn me, without any proof or evidence, nay, without allowing me the liberty to defend myself from those rash and reproachful calumnys laid to my charge. . . . . Wherefore I take the freedom to lay before you the matter of fact as it passed between me and Mr. Stamp. . . . ." Lloyd then complains that "he has been drawn into that unhappy contest wholly against his will." He goes through his correspondence with Ken, including the letters given above, of December 6th and 18th, in which Ken had announced that he had urged Hooper to accept his bishopric and thought of appointing him as his coadjutor, and then refers to his own answers to them, from which he quotes passages to show that he had urged his friend not to "act precipitately" and had never gone beyond an approval of Hooper's personal fitness. So matters rested, he goes on to say, till the beginning of February. Then Mr. Stamp went to Naish Court and was told by Ken that Lloyd approved of his cession. Stamp, as we have seen, doubted the statement, and wrote to his London correspondent (apparently Spinckes) to inquire. Lloyd stated, in answer to the inquiry, that "he had nothing more to say," that he "meddled not with the Cession, that he still congratulated Ken on having such a man as Hooper as his successor." After this Spinckes brought him another letter from Stamp, reporting his contention with Ken, with all the "indecent passions" and "vehement repartees" that had passed between them. He adds that he knew of an earlier correspondence between Ken and Francis Turner, of Ely, in which the former had spoken of Ken's inclination to resign his charge into the hands of the Dean and Chapter of Wells.[1] This led him to warn Ken against precipitate action. After all this, Lloyd says, he did not expect to be so severely handled as he had been in Ken's last letter. He protests against the charge that he has done anything to "kindle a fire" between Ken and his neighbours. He denies that he had ever done more in the way of showing Ken's letters than read one passage of that of December 6th to Spinckes. He repudiates the notion that he ever wished Ken to "put himself into his keeping" (see p. 122), and adds "What stuff is this?" For the future he "will not be further concerned in this business."

The letter is dated April 11th. On May 1st Ken writes his answer. The first vehemence of indignation had calmed down,

[1] The intention thus described rested, probably, on the old idea that the Dean and Chapter were the guardians of the temporalities of a bishopric during the vacancy. Ken would not recognise Kidder as a canonical Bishop, but was willing apparently to let the Dean and Chapter act as they thought fit on receiving his cession. Some curious questions might have arisen had he carried his purpose into action.

and he was ready, as in other like cases, *e.g.* that to Dodwell (p. 42), to confess and ask pardon for his fault.

LETTER LXIV.

" To Mrs. HANNAH LLOYD.

" All Glory be to God.

" MY VERY GOOD LORD AND BROTHER,

" Your Lordship's was sent to me to Poulshot last night.   *I con-fess when I wrote my last I was heated, and provoked to a great degree, and if my provocation transported me to any indecent expressions, I beg your pardon, which you will, I hope, the more readily grant, because you seem to have been in the like passion when you wrote, and because I intend to give you no further trouble.* You must give me leave to be sensible when I am insulted, which I can very easily forgive. Every day encreases the satisfaction I have in providing so well for my flock. God keep us in His holy fear, and make us wise for eternity.

" Your Lordship's very affectionate Friend and B^r,

" T. K.

" *May* 1st (1704)."

[The letter tells its own tale and requires no comment. It has been painful to trace, in its details of mutual reproaches, the sharpness of the contention which divided the two friends, but we may rest in the conviction that, as with the " paroxysm " of a like feeling which parted Paul from Barnabas, so here, the separation was but for a time, though, as yet, the soreness still continued.]

So far Ken's mind was at rest.   It was painful for him to have had to differ from one whose friendship he valued as he valued Lloyd's. The attacks of the more violent and irreconcilable members of the party he was content to bear in silence. He found his consolation in the thought that the flock, for whom he cared so tenderly that he would fain have laid down his life for their sake—we remember the motto, *Pastor bonus dat animam pro ovibus*, which he chose for his episcopal coat of arms—for whom he had actually laid down his office and all that it involved, which was dearer to him than life, were now under the guidance of a faithful and true shepherd.   Compensation of another kind was found in the action of that successor. Hooper, in accepting the Bishopric, had asked the Queen to allow him to retain the Precentorship of Exeter *in commendam* that he might hand over the income (£200 per annum) to Ken.

The Queen was much pleased with the proposal and thanked Hooper for suggesting it. Trelawney, however, who was then Bishop of Exeter, objected to this arrangement. Godolphin, then Lord Treasurer, the husband of the Mrs. Godolphin (Margaret Blagge, whose life was written by Evelyn) interposed with a suggestion which met the difficulty and which the Queen approved, that Hooper should resign the Precentorship, and that Ken should have a pension of £200 from the Treasury. This was accordingly acted on, and Hooper wrote to tell Ken of the Queen's bounty.[1]   Here is the answer to that letter.

LETTER LXV.

To Bishop Hooper.

"All Glory be to God.

"My good Lord,

"Your Lordshippe gave me a wonderfull surprise when you informed me y^t ye Queen had been pleased to settle a very liberal pension on me. I beseech God to accumulate the blessings of both lives on her Majesty for her royal bounty to me, so perfectly free and unexpected; and I beseech God abundantly to reward my Lord Treasurer, who inclined her to be thus gratious to me, and give him a plentiful measure of wisdom from above.

"My Lord, lett it not shock your native modesty, if I make this just acknowledgment, y^t though ye sense of her Majesty's favour in ye pension is deservedly great, yett her choosing you for my successor gave me much more satisfaction; as my concerne for ye eternal welfare of ye flock exceeded all regard for my own temporall advantage, being as truely conscious of my own infirmitys, as I am assured of your excellent abilitys, of wch ye diocese, even at your first appearance, signally reaped ye fruits. God of His infinite goodness keep us in His reverential love, and make us wise for eternity.

"My Lord,

"Your Lordship's most affectionate

"Friend & Brother,

"Tho. Ken.   L. B. & W.

"[Late Bath and Wells.]

"*June 1st, 1704.*"

[It is noticeable that Ken is not deterred by any theories of hereditary rights from acknowledging Anne as a Queen. He had refused the Abjuration Oaths,

[1] *Prowse MS.* in Anderdon, p. 729.

and had expressed a vehement dislike to the Act of Attainder against the Pretender. I do not imagine that he ever shared the doubts that had been raised as to the parentage of that prince. He probably looked on him as James's son and successor, but he had in the Convention voted for the resolution that excluded a Roman Catholic sovereign from the government of England, and his claim was therefore in abeyance, and Anne was accordingly something more, from Ken's point of view, than merely a Queen *de facto*. He was grateful to her for her bounty. He was yet more grateful to her for having followed his counsel when he suggested Hooper as a fit successor.]

The addition of this income to the £80 annuity which Ken received from Lord Weymouth, must have made the last seven years of his life a time of greater comfort than he had known during the fourteen years that had passed since his deprivation. Hooper, with an insight into his friend's character (the same now as it had been when he used to empty his pockets in alms when he went for a walk in his Oxford days—i. 52), insisted that he should consider the additional income as held in trust primarily for himself. He would not allow him " to give it all away, which he was so charitable as to be always doing ; so that his habit was mean, and he had but a poor horse to carry him about, which made Hooper entreat him to lay out something for himself, and from that time he appeared in everything according to his condition."[1]

An anecdote communicated to Mr. Anderdon (p. 734) by Dr. Routh, the President of Magdalen, is interesting as an illustration of the "mean habit " just mentioned.

" Bishop Ken was staying in Gloucestershire, near Badminton, the seat of the Duke of Beaufort, with whom he was acquainted. The Bishop being an early riser, called one morning to pay his respects to the Duke. The Duke was not stirring ; but Ken was received by the Chaplain, who believing him to be a Clergyman from the neighbourhood, invited him to breakfast. Whilst they were so engaged, the Duke entered,—and immediately, on seeing the Bishop, fell on his knees, and asked his blessing. The Chaplain, surprised when he found the distinction of his visitor, began to apologise for the manner in which he had received him ; but was stopped by the Bishop declaring the obligation to be entirely on his side, who had been so hospitably entertained."

The following letter makes it probable that the visit to

[1] *Prowse MS.* in Anderdon, p. 731.

Badminton was in the autumn of 1704, when Ken was in that part of England.

LETTER LXVI.

"For the Bishop of Norwich.

" All Glory be to God.

" My very good Lord,

" I made, as I told you I intended, a visit to our good Brother of Gloucester, who was not a little joyed to see me. He is very cheerful, and being past eighty, does not only daily expect, but, like St. Paul, longs for. his dissolution. He has many infirmities of old age, but his eyes are very good, and he uses no spectacles. With all the tenderness imaginable he remembers your Lordship. Dr. Bull being in my way, I called upon him, which he took the more kindly, because he thought, we had as much abandonned him, as he seems to have abandonned us, and the respect I paid him, I perceive, surprised him, and the rather, because he never has taken any notice of our deprived brethren : but he has reason to value his old friends, for his new have little regarded him. My best respects to your good lady. I beseech God to keep us in His holy fear, and to make us wise for eternity.

" Your Lordship's most affect: Brother,

" THO. B. & W.

" *Sept.* 17*th* " (1704).

[Frampton was, as we have seen, one of Ken's dearest friends, of all the Nonjuring divines the most like-minded with himself. It must have been a refreshment to Ken, after the controversies and strife of tongues of the early months of the year to find himself with one from whom he had never been for a moment divided, either in thought or action, and who was passing the last days of his life, as Ken did, in writing hymns and meditations. Bull, the author of the *Defensio Fidei Nicænæ* and the *Harmonia Evangelica*, appears for the first time as in the circle of Ken's friends, but his two great works were precisely such as Ken would value as a defence of the *depositum fidei*. The latter work, by the way, had been authoritatively condemned by Morley in 1669, but this had not hindered Ken from cultivating Bull's friendship, or from studying and admiring his works. The *Defensio* had indeed received the praises, not only of Anglican divines, but of the great theologians of the Gallican and Latin Churches, notably of Bossuet, to whom it had been sent by Robert Nelson. Bull, like Hooper, had taken the oaths; but Ken, as in Hooper's case, never thought less well of the man, because, in that matter, he had taken another course than he had felt himself constrained to take. Bull at this time was rector of Avening, in Gloucestershire, a living worth £200 per annum, and in private patronage. His "new friends," as Ken remarks, the Government of the day, had not done much for him. It was not till 1705 that he was promoted, at the age of seventy-one, to the see of St. David's, on Bishop Watson's deprivation. He died in 1709. It is, I think, worth noting that Bull was a native of Wells, and had been educated at the Grammar or Blue School there, and that this may have made another link between the two men. The letter is the last extant addressed to Lloyd, and it is a pleasant ending to the correspondence. The bitterness had passed away. The friendship of earlier days returned, and for both there was light at eventide. The letter is given by Round as in the series of letters of 1702, but Anderdon (p. 732) says that it is endorsed by Lloyd with the date given above. See Letter xlviii, p. 126.]

And, as to Hooper, all went as he could wish. Learning, tact, kindness, soundness in the faith endeared him to the diocese as they had endeared him to Ken. The following letter has no public interest, but I print it as throwing light on the relations between the two men. Ken feels that he can write freely to his friend about a sick man's troubles, in the full faith that he will sympathise and help.

LETTER LXVII.

"To Bishop Hooper.

"All Glory be to God.

"My very good Lord,

"I have sent my servant to begge of your Lordshippe two or three bottles of canary for o^r sick friend, wch ye Doctour comends to him. Your Lordshippe gave ye whole family so seasonable and sensible a consolation, y^t it revived ye whole family, and it gave me a very great satisfaction to see my friend doe an act of so great, so free, and so well-timed charity. Y^e good man is full of resignation to ye divine will, and has an humble confidence of a blessed immortality. He has slepped this night as well as could be expected, and is asleepe now, and his pulse, wch for some days was unperceivable, is now become tolerable. He has strength to turne in his bed, as weak as he is, and to expectorate, and is sensibly mended ; and I hope God will restore him, wch will be a blessing next to miraculous. He has his understanding perfectly. My best respects to your good lady, and to ye three young gentlewomen, and to Mr. Guilford. I beseech God to make us wise for eternity.

"My good Lord,

"Your Lordshipp's most affectionate Friend and B^r,

"THO. KEN, L. B. & W.

" *Oct. 6th* " (1704).

[I am unable to identify the "sick friend," on behalf of whom Ken wrote, or Mr. Guilford, to whom he sends greeting. The signature, L. B. & W. (late Bath and Wells), is significant as a practical confirmation of his cession. The "three young gentlewomen" were probably Hooper's daughters, one of whom, Abigail, afterwards Mrs. Prowse, wrote the MS. memoir of her father which has been often referred to.]

The separation from the Non-jurors who were bent on perpetuating the schism was now complete. There was a lull after the storm, and even they ceased from troubling, and the weary soul of the devout Bishop could at last find rest. During the reign of Anne the policy of the party was one of expectation. They hoped that something might be done before her death that would undo the Act of Settlement. They and the statesmen and others, Bolingbroke and Atterbury and their associates who acted with them, worked upon the Queen's affection for her brother, and but for her death on August 1st, 1714, which defeated their plans, he, and not George I., might have been proclaimed as King of England. In the meantime the air was calmer. There were few conspiracies. The excitement of Sacheverell's sermon (1709) and the trial that followed turned the passions of men into another channel. It was not till near the close of Ken's life that he once more decided on a course by which he separated himself more completely than ever from the Non-jurors, and returned into full communion with the Church from which he had been self-excluded. The history of that step will come before us more fully in a later chapter.

CHAPTER XXIV

" The Saint's is not the Hero's praise;
This I have found, and learn
Not to malign Heaven's humblest ways,
Nor its least boon to spurn."

J. H. Newman.

IN the course of the inquiries, the result of which is embodied
in the present volume, I have come across some incidents in
Ken's life which seem to me to have a special interest, as
throwing light both on his own character, and on the relations
in which he stood to the more devout section of the Non-jurors.
It was natural that they should turn to him, as their spiritual
guide, for comfort and counsel. It was natural that he, as a
lover of souls, should sympathise with their sorrows, should
find in his intercourse with them a satisfaction which he could
not find in his intercourse with the more irreconcilable section
of the same party, the writers of scurrilous pamphlets, the
plotters and conspirators against the *de facto* Government, the
men who were bent on perpetuating the schism which he
sought the first opportunity of bringing to an end. To these
episodes of his private life, accordingly, I devote the present
chapter.

I. "THE STUDENT-PENITENT OF 1695."

A small volume bearing this title was published in 1875, by
the late Rev. F. E. Paget, Rector of Elford. It purported
to give letters and other documents of that date, which were
in the possession of the descendants of a Non-juring family.
The Editor stated in his Preface that he had altered names

throughout so as to prevent identification.   The narrative thus introduced had for its hero a Robert, or Robin, the third son of a Cavalier father, Theobald Verdun, of Verdun Court (no county named), who had suffered much, in person and property, in the time of the Rebellion.   Mr. Verdun had also a house in Leicester Fields, London, in which Robin was born in 1678. His mother was of the house of Delamayne, and her brother was a canon of Westminster.   Robin, as a boy, had been brought up devoutly, was frank, open, and affectionate.   At the age of sixteen or seventeen, when the death of his two elder brothers had centred the hopes of his family on him, after being under Busby, or Busby's successor, Knipe, at West-minster, he went to Oxford.   The name of the College is given as All Saints, on the principle of guarding against identifica-tion, and in like manner, his chief Oxford friend is the Rev. Nathaniel Dod, Tutor of St. Peter's.   He finds his way into a somewhat " fast " set, runs up bills for other than necessary expenses, and buys books which include, mingled with classics and divinity, the literature represented by St. Evremond's *Essays*, Ovid's *Epistles*, and *Love Letters* in three volumes.   He makes an attempt to join some comrades in escaping from College, for a cock-fight, by getting out of window on a ladder.   The ladder falls and brings him down with it, and his ribs are fractured.   He has to bear many months of suffering, and at last dies in July, 1696.   The better thoughts of early years come back to him, and he becomes the " Student Penitent " of the title of the book.   He writes affectionate letters to his mother and sisters, and to a college friend who had sought to keep him from evil.   The President of his College and others report that his patience is exemplary and edifying.   He is led to keep a diary, in which he enters his meditations and prayers, and passages from the devotional books of Kettlewell and other writers.   His family, it is said, were intimately connected with the Non-juring clergy.   Among the correspondence which the book reproduces there is a letter, purporting to come from Ken, which is so entirely after his manner that any one familiar with his style would either receive it as genuine, or recognise it as an admirable imitation.   When the book ap-peared, it attracted a fair measure of attention, but some of the reviewers, as *e.g.* in the *Guardian*, hinted a suspicion that it belonged to the category of fiction rather than of fact. The modernised spelling throughout, and a touch of modernism of style as well as spelling here and there in the *Diary*, gave some colour to the suspicion.

I was able, through the kindness of the surviving members of Mr. Paget's family, to ascertain that the book rested on a solid foundation of fact, and ultimately to get at the name of the student. By permission of the late Sir Frederick Graham, Bart., of Netherby, the representative of the family, I am enabled to give the story with more fulness than it has been given before, and to trace the connexion between the "Student Penitent's" family and Bishop Ken.

The father of the Penitent was a Colonel James Graham, or, as the family spelt it, Grahme, whom we meet with, once and again, in Evelyn's *Diary*. On July 8th, 1675, he records the fact that "Mr. James Graham, since Privy Purse to the Duke of York," was "exceedingly in love with Dorothy, daughter of Mrs. Howard, of Berkeley House, one of the Maids of Honour to the Queen, and grand-daughter of the first Earl of Berkshire;" that the mother "not much favouring it," Evelyn's advice was asked, and he "spoke to the advantage of the young gentleman." The marriage took place a few months afterwards. A sister of the lady whom Colonel Graham thus won as a bride was married, on November 11th, 1677, to Sir Gabriel Sylvius, who has met us an English Envoy at the Hague (i. 142), "and the supper," Evelyn adds, "was provided at Mr. Graham's." Evelyn dedicates to her his *Life of Mrs. Godolphin*. In September, 1685, Evelyn, on his way with Pepys to meet the King at Portsmouth, visits the Grahams at their house near Bagshot, and pays another visit to her, in company with Lady Clarendon, on October 22. When the Revolution came, Colonel Graham remained faithful to the fallen house. The family had probably known Ken in earlier days (some such intimacy is implied in the letter to Mr. Graham, given in i. 173), and it was natural that, when the great sorrow of which the narrative tells us fell on them, they should look to him for comfort. The man who had told the tale of Hymnotheo's temptations, who had guided the scholars of Winchester in the paths of peace, was not slow to answer the call.

So it is that in the story of the *Student Penitent* Mr. Dod, the Oxford tutor, writes to Theobald Verdun, *i.e.* to Colonel Graham, suggesting that " my Lord Bishop " should discover the truth to Mrs. Graham, " and at the same time comfort and advise her " (p. 88), and asks him to show the letter to "my Lord," *i.e.* to Ken. On March 14th, 1696, Robin's sister, Lucy, writes to him, and sends (p. 101) a copy of the letter which "my Lord Bishop of B. and W." has written to her mother. It will be admitted, I think, that there is good reason for reproducing it. It is followed by a letter from Kettlewell :—

LETTER LXVIII.

" To Mrs. Graham.

" All Glory be to God.

" My worthy dear Friend,

" I have heard from L^d W(eymouth) of your great trouble, and so hasten to assure you of my continual and hearty prayers. God of His infinite goodness multiply His blessings on you and yours, and enable us all to do and suffer His holy will, and fit us for all He designs us to undergo. Tell your Robin,[1] that I think much of him, and pray God to make all his bed in his sickness. And read to him what follows. ' Be sure, my good youth, that He Who in His wisdom knoweth what is best for thee, hath laid this distemper on thee for thy good, to humble and reform thee. Pray Him, if He will, to divert this sickness from thee, when it has done its sanctifying work : but in this, and all else, pray, that His will, not thine, be done. And therefore, if the sickness grow on thee, try to submit willingly to His afflicting Hand, Who chastiseth those whom He loveth, yet lays no more on them than they are able to bear. It may be that He will yet raise thee up; but prepare thyself lest He should not. And to that end, pray above all things, that He would wean thy affections from earth, and fill thee with ardent desires after heaven ; that He would fit thee for Himself, and then, when He pleaseth, call thee to joys unspeakable, and full of glory, for His Son Jesus' sake. I send you my benediction.'

[1] The " penitent's " real name was Richard.

"Dear Madam, my best respects to your husband and dear miss. God keep us in His reverential love, and mindful of eternity.

"My good Lady,

"Your Ladyship's affectionate friend and brother,

"THOS. B & W.

"From Longleate."

[The "dear miss" is, of course, Robin's sister, who was afterwards Countess of Suffolk and Berkshire. It is undated, but fits in to March, 1696.]

Mr. Dod reports that Lucy's letter and "the messages from my Lord Bishop and good Mr. Kettlewell were a continual feast" to his pupil. And Robin sends, in a letter to his parents, that was not to be opened till after his death, "his humble duty and great gratitude to them." Kettlewell, it would seem, had often been in personal intercourse with the family, and had spoken in Robin's presence of the "heathenishness" of the times. In a letter written shortly before his death Robin speaks of "that day when our dear Lord Bishop (it is obvious that he speaks of Ken) took that long ride over the Downs," on purpose to see his brother, who was then dying from a fall from his horse. He died between July 11th and 13th, 1696. I can scarcely doubt that Ken must have thought over some of the parallelisms which his life presented to that of his own *Hymnotheo*. That "ride over the Downs" (Bagshot Heath?) may have had a far-off parallel in the Apostle's ride over the passes of the Taurus.[1]

---

[1] As these sheets are passing through the press I have been favoured by Mr. Howard Paget, of Elford, near Tamworth, with permission to extract some further particulars from a privately printed volume compiled by his father, the Rev. F. E. Paget, and bearing the title of *Ashstead and its Howard Possessors*. Ashstead is in Surrey, not far from Epsom. It appears that the mother of Mr. Graham's (or Grahme as they spelt the name) wife was the widow of William Howard, grandson of the Earl of Berkshire. Evelyn (June 30th, 1669), relates that he accompanied her on a journey of pleasure with her daughter Dorothy, and Mrs. (*i.e.* Miss), Margaret Blagg, the future Mrs. Godolphin. On June 10, 1673, he receives Dorothy at Sayes Court. In July, 1675, he accompanies them to Oxford, at what would now be called the Commemoration time, and takes them to see the colleges and "all the academic exercises." It is in this journey that James Graham appears as above. The lady whom he loved was "not only a great beauty, but a most virtuous and excellent creature, worthy to have been the wife of the best of men." All Evelyn's sympathies were with the young lovers, and the marriage was mainly brought about through his influence. James Graham was

II. THE TRAGEDY OF STATFOLD.

The village of Statfold, in Staffordshire, is about three miles from Drayton Manor, now the property of Sir Robert Peel, but then belonging to Lord Weymouth, Ken's friend and host, at which, as at Longleat, the Bishop was a welcome visitor. A small church, now in ruins, with a stone altar and an old worm-eaten oak pulpit, was practically the chapel of the squire's house, and the squire of the last ten years of the seventeenth century was a Francis Wolferstan. The family had been settled there for some generations, and a collateral descendant is in possession now. Francis Wolferstan was a strong Jacobite, refused to take the oaths to William and Mary, wrote of the former as " Mynheer with his stolen crown," and, though he kept clear of conspiracies, withdrew from the communion of the Church, in consequence of the "usurpation of the pseudo-Bishop," and the "immorall prayers" in which he could no longer join, was excluded from the bench of Magistrates, and suffered "from the doubling of his poll-tax by the Commissioners," in consequence of his opinions. He dined

a son of Sir George Graham of Netherby. His elder brother, Richard, was created Viscount Preston by James II., was Secretary of State, 1688, attainted and condemned to death, 1690, and pardoned in 1691. James was educated at Westminster, and then at Christ Church. He served in the army, in the war in which Charles II. and Louis XIV. were allied against Holland, under Monmouth and Turenne. In 1679 he and his wife had apartments in St. James's Palace, and in 1685 they had also a country house at Bagshot, where Evelyn (September 15th, 1685), visited them. He was at that time Lieutenant of Windsor Castle and Forest. In all the family troubles, notably in those of the illness and death of their three sons, Ken was their never-failing adviser and consoler. An elder brother, Henry, married the widow of the second Earl of Derwentwater, an illegitimate son of Charles II. by "Moll Davis" the actress, within a year after her husband's execution, and a younger brother, William, Chaplain and Clerk of the Closet to Queen Anne, after holding a 'golden' stall at Durham with the Deanery of Carlisle, succeeded Ralph Bathurst as Dean of Wells in 1704. His grandson assumed the baronetcy, which had been forfeited by Viscount Preston's attainder, in 1738, the Scotch title having expired on the death of the Viscount's grandson in that year. When James II. left London for Rochester, in his flight from Whitehall, the auditor of the Exchequer, Sir. T. Howard, refused to advance any money, and Colonel James Graham lent the king £6,000, which was repaid by a transfer of stock which James had bought, as Duke, in the East India and African Company. This he sold for £10,000, but the Companies afterwards got a decree in the Exchequer, and compelled him to refund. It may be noted as one of the small facts which sometimes refresh us

often with Lord Weymouth.   He was, after the manner of his class, a devout High Churchman, and noted in his Prayer-book the coincidences with events in his own personal life, or in the history of the nation, which had presented themselves in the Psalms of the day.[1] His temper seems to have been hasty; his will strong and inflexible. His eldest son, then twenty-five, appears to have inherited something of his father's temperament. He fell in love with Sarah, the daughter of George Antrobus, the master of the grammar school at Tamworth, also about three miles from Statfold.   The disparity of social position would have been enough to rouse his father's opposi-

as we track the records of revolutions, that James, in his departure, did not forget the domestics whom he left at Whitehall, and that a memorandum in the Levens papers contains a list of gifts, from ten guineas to one, amounting to over a hundred, that were made by James's orders. To Graham James wrote to give the first news of his arrival at Boulogne. He also confided to him his service of plate, the books of devotions and prayers, and the altar plate in his chapel at Whitehall, all which Graham was to receive from the well-known Chiffinch, and, at a later date, his pictures, the latter being received from William III. The fate of the plate has not been traced. The pictures are now at Charlton, near Malmesbury, a seat of the Earl of Berkshire, who married Graham's daughter. Not long after the death of the "Student Penitent" his father seems to have left Bagshot, and to have lived at the family seat of Levens, in Westmoreland. His wife, Dorothy, died in 1700. He married again in 1702, and his second wife died in 1709. He himself survived till 1730. Following in the footsteps of Ken, though a Non-juror, he kept clear of all plots, and was never molested with any charge of treason. He was on terms of intimacy with Lord Weymouth, and the letters of the latter to him always end with messages of warm affection and inquiry from Ken. The "Student Penitent" was matriculated (Oct. 11, 1695), at University College, of which Dr. Charlett, of whom we read much in Hearne, was then Master. His tutor, "Mr. Dod," I identify with Hugh Todd, Fellow of University College, who was Prebendary of Carlisle, and had the living of Penrith given him by Viscount Preston, the "Student Penitent's" uncle. (Hearne ii., 72.) His name does not appear as tutor to any other undergraduate besides Richard Grahme, who is matriculated as under his special care, and probably, therefore, he took charge of him as a friend of the family. Richard Graham, the Penitent, was buried in the chapel of University College. The library at Levens contains many gift books from Kettlewell to Col. Graham. It also contains most of the books charged by the Oxford bookseller, to " Mr. Richard Grahme, Un. Coll., Oxon," above referred to. The whole story, as told by Mr. Paget in the volume from which I have taken this epitome, seems to me a singularly interesting episode in the byways of history.

[1] Some of these are, I think, worth quoting. (1) Ps. xxv: on the Easter Sunday after he was shut out from communion. (2) Ps. lv. 12, 13 : " after the doubling of his tax," the Commissioners, I presume, including some who had been his personal friends, and (3) Ps. lxxix., " when many loyal persons were committed to the Tower and other prisons (1692) for high treason."

tion. It was, as we may well imagine, not diminished by the fact that Sarah Antrobus's father was a Williamite and a Whig. Her sister Ruth married the well-known William Whiston, who had been at Tamworth school. The lovers carried on a clandestine correspondence, in which they poured out their hearts to each other, and which still, as copied into a book by the lover's sister Anne, afterwards Lady Egerton, after all was over, through their discoloured paper and faded ink, breathe words of wild love and passionate complaint. There is, I believe, no reason for thinking that there had been a private marriage, but the lover writes to his beloved as "his own," "his wife," whom he will one day acknowledge. He complains bitterly of his father's harshness. At last, in September, 1698, the climax came. Hot, fierce words passed between the father and the son.[1] The son retired to his room, but when morning came the room was empty. No written words were found to indicate where he had gone, or what was the motive of his departure. No line ever came either to his father or his sister (his mother died in 1673, long before the tragic story began), to tell them where he was, alive or dead. All that is known afterwards is that Shawe's *Staffordshire* records the fact that he died of small pox in London, in 1698 or 99, and was buried, as "unmarried," at St. Giles's in the Fields. The shadow of a lost heir rested on the Statfold home, and his name seldom passed the lips of either father or sister. What became of Sarah I have been unable to trace. At last, when nearly nine years had passed, in May, 1707, below the corner of a mat under which it had been thrust, and which had never since been touched, there was found a letter written to Sarah Antrobus, in bitter heat of spirit, on the morning of the young man's departure. He could bear his father's reproaches no longer. "The horror of present circumstances is not to be conceived, nor can be paralleled, except in Hell. What will be the issue, Heaven only knows, but death is better than damnation."

And across this scene of tragic horrors there flits for a moment the 'calm ghost' of Ken. The father sadly and sternly copies the letter, as closing the whole history, and reviews, at the end of the other letters in his daughter's volume, the

[1] He writes to Sarah on Aug. 5, 1698, that "Hell had broken loose on him."

events which were bringing his grey hairs with sorrow to the grave. He dwells on his son's headlong recklessness. He had been misled by evil advisers, and " knew not what he said or did." He had turned a deaf ear to "the checks of his own conscience, and his father's, and that apostolical Bishop of B. and Wells', warnings and admonitions." A New Testament of 1679, belonging to the sister, with a portrait of Charles II., still remains, with marginal memoranda recording that on October 31, 1697, the good Bishop of Bath and Wells (the Non-juring family, of course, still recognised him in that character) had preached on Matthew xix. 16, 17. Ken, like Frampton, was apparently allowed, without interference from William's Government, to officiate where he could find a church open to him (it is recorded in the letters, on one occasion, that " he gave the sacrament"), and probably, like his brother Bishop, either omitted the State prayers altogether, or left them to be read by the parish clergyman, and preached as he thought best for the edification of his hearers. It is a natural inference from the facts of the case that he was staying at the time at Lord Weymouth's house, Drayton Manor, and that his intervention was sought for by the distressed family at Statfold. It must have been, we may believe, one of the secret sorrows of his life that he could not in this case, as in that of the Student Penitent, see any fruit of his labours. We can picture to ourselves the kind of sermon which he, knowing the sorrows of the house, would preach as he spoke of the young ruler who sought for " eternal life," and boasted that he had kept all the commandments of the second table, the fifth included, from his youth up, and can imagine, without much risk of error, the very different feelings with which father, son, and sister listened to it.[1]

III. Lewis Southcombe, Penitent.

In a small volume of Latin hymns and poems, on sacred subjects, in Ken's Library at Longleat, bearing the title of *Oblectamenta Pia*, the following dedication is found written on the fly-leaf :—

[1] I am indebted for the facts in this section to my friend Miss F. E. Wolferstan.

PRIMÆVÆ SANCTIMONIÆ
PRÆSULI,
CONFESSORI INTEGERRIMO,
GLORIOSISSIMO,
AFFLICTISSIMÆ MATRIS ECCLESIÆ
PATRI, ANIMABUS συμπαθοῦντι,
DOM. JESU στίγμασι ORNATISSIMO,
DOCTORI SERAPHICO ANGELICO,
IN CHRISTO PATRI
THOMÆ
EPISCOPO BATHON. ET WELLEN.
HUNCCE LIBELLULUM
(οὐδὲ κακὸν μέγα)
D. D. D.
EX AMATORIBUS AMANTISSIMUS,
E FILIIS OBSEQUENTISSIMUS,
E CULTORIBUS OFFICIOSISSIMUS,
DEVOTISSIMUS,
AD QUODVIS
AMORIS, OBEDIENTIÆ, HONORIS
MUNUS OBEUNDUM
PARATISSIMUS.

TIMOTHEUS.

It was natural, looking to the warm, devoted affection thus expressed, to inquire whether it were possible to identify the "Timotheus" who thus pours out his heart as ready for any task to which Ken may set him. I was unable to find any one within the horizon of Ken's personal friendships with that Christian name, and was led accordingly to think of it as chosen by the writer to express the relation in which he wished to stand to Ken. He was indebted to him as Timothy was indebted to St. Paul. The choice of the name might obviously be suggested by the "Philotheus" of Ken's *Manual for Winchester Scholars*. He owed his spiritual life to Ken. He desired to be as his true son in the faith, to be likeminded with him in all things. The title-page does not give the author's name, but inquiries led me to identify him[1] with a Lewis Southcombe, who at times Latinised his surname in the form of *de Vallo*

---

[1] See especially Rev. W. Macray, in *Notes and Queries*, 6th S. xi. p. 12.

Australi, and who wrote, as in the work in question, Latin hymns and poems in a spirit in which Ken would find much that was congenial to his own.[1] His history was a somewhat remarkable one. He had, at first, taken his place among the ranks of the Non-jurors, guided, we may well believe, by Ken's example. Like Ken, however, he was able to see both sides of the question. The scholar, like the master, wavered and fluctuated, and at last, like many others,[2] persuaded himself that he might rightly take the oaths which he had at first refused. Before long, however, he went back to his old position, accused himself of having been led by unworthy motives, and sought for re-admission into the communion of the deprived clergy from whom he had thus separated himself. There are, as will appear in the course of this narrative, sufficient grounds for identifying Lewis Southcombe with the "Mr. S.," whose confession and retractation are given in full in Kettlewell's *Life* (pp. 141—149). He had applied to Kettlewell for guidance, and had received an answer which led him to the conclusion that the oath which he had taken was an unlawful one, that the successors of the deprived Bishops were schismatical, and that the prayers for William and Mary were 'immoral.' He addresses his retractation to Lloyd, as Sancroft's Vicar-General (1693), and was received into communion by him. It extends over five folio pages, and covers the whole ground of the disputed positions between the Jurors and the Non-jurors. He relates how he had been halting between two opinions, how he had omitted all names in the "State Prayers" of the Prayer Book, how he had refused to read the Services appointed for Fast-days and Thanksgiving-days by the *de facto* Government, but had asked another clergyman, who could do it with a clear conscience, to take his place. He could not reconcile himself any longer to this evasion of the diffi-

---

[1] The motto on the title-page is sufficiently interesting as reflecting the mind of Ken. I give it from the second edition (1716) : "*Magis spectat Deus quanto quidque amore fiat quam quantum id ipsum sit. Multum facit qui multum diligit.*" The work is described as "*Ab Ecclesiæ Catholicæ sacerdote anachoretâ.*" The preface ends with the following address to the reader: "*Quæso te, mi Frater, memineris mei cum, jejuniis, lachrymis, precibus, rem tuam strenuè apud Deum agis.*"

[2] Compare the case of the other " penitent," probably Stamp, in p. 137.

culty, or to the so-called 'immoral prayers.' He could not hold himself absolved from his allegiance to his lawful sovereign, or from the duty of continuing to pray for him. He asks for a full restitution to the peace and communion of the Church, as represented by Sancroft and the other Non-juring Bishops. The whole document is interesting as showing the difficulties in which men of a sensitive conscience—there is no indication of anything else throughout—were involved in their new position. He states further that he had written to the Lord Bishop of ——, giving him an account of his proceedings. He adds that, by way of atonement for his past errors, he was ready, if called upon by his 'lawful superiors,' to resign his living, and to employ whatever had accrued from it during the time of the compliance which he now held to be unlawful, partly on the poor, and partly in beautifying the chancel of his church at Rose Ash, Devon.[1]

The last fact presents an argument from undesigned coincidences, tending to the identification of Kettlewell's Mr. S—— with the 'Lewis Southcombe, Penitent' (the name appears in Kettlewell's list of Non-juring clergy in this form), who was Ken's "Timotheus." The chancel of the church at Rose Ash was restored by him. He gave the Communion plate now in use. The bells of the church were re-cast in his time, and probably at his expense. A chapel at Honiton, a hamlet near South Molton, was rebuilt. The parish registers contain no record of the events of 1689—91. His signature appears to the entries of burials in every year, from his appointment in 1675 to his death in 1733. He wrote other volumes of Latin verse, chiefly, like the *Oblectamenta*, devotional, and another book under the title of *Œdipus Judaicus*. His son and successor records his death in the register, with the statement that he "had been the most vigilant incumbent of the parish and most faithful instructor of his flock for above fifty-seven years," and that he had been buried in the Honiton Chapel. It may be presumed that he was allowed to continue in his living as having once taken the

---

1 Lathbury (*Non-jurors*, p. 299) gives a history of Thomas Brett, afterwards a Non-juring Bishop, which presents a strong resemblance to Southcombe's. He took the oath under William and Anne, had scruples on the accession of George I., and was received by Hickes as a penitent.

oaths, and that the government did not know, or chose to ignore, his subsequent retractation, and his omission of the names
of William and Mary in the Church Services afterwards. Following in Ken's footsteps he sought only to live in peace and
in works of charity, kept aloof from all conspiracies, or acts
of disobedience to the powers that be, and was therefore left
undisturbed, as Frampton was at Standish. The fact may be
noted as an instance of the general leniency of William's
government. Looking to the warm affection of the language
in which he addressed Ken, it is, I think, natural to infer that
he was the Bishop to whom he says in his *Retractation*, that
he had written a full account of the circumstances of the case,
and by whose advice, as well as Kettlewell's, he had been
guided. It will be admitted, I think, that the relations between
the two men have sufficient interest to deserve being rescued
from oblivion.[1] Lewis Southcombe takes his place side by side
with Ambrose Bonwicke (p. 258), among the young men who
looked to the deprived Bishop with a reverential love.

IV. The Ladies of Naish Court.

It will be remembered that Ken, in the correspondence after
his deprivation, makes frequent mention of his visits to the
"ladies of Naish," the two Misses Kemeys. In one letter of
November 24th, 1707 (Letter lxxvi.), he describes them as "two
good virgins beyond Bristol, where there is a kind of nunnery,
and with whom I usually abide during my Lord's absence."

[1] I am indebted for the information contained in this narrative to the Rev. H.
Granger Southcombe, the present rector of Rose Ash, and a lineal descendant of
the "Penitent." The living has belonged to the family ever since 1655, and
the present incumbent is the seventh rector of the name. An interesting description of the church, with fuller details of the ornamentation of the chancel
than I have space for, may be found in the *Western Antiquary* for April, 1884.
The decorations include scriptural texts (Ps. lxxii. 1, 2; Isa. xlix. 23; 1 Tim.
ii. 1, 2) on the relation of Kings to the Church, and, in sixteen compartments, a
brief history of the Twelve Apostles, and of St. Paul, St. Stephen, St. Mark, and
St. Luke, which is unique in English church decoration. A triangular board
surmounts the chancel screen with the royal arms, including the white horse of
Hanover and G. R. on one side, and on the other a private coat-of-arms with
Q. A. (Queen Anne ?). It would appear from this as if the Penitent, like Ken,
had, after William's death, recognised the *de facto* sovereign.

Dr. Thomas Smith, to whom this letter was addressed, writes in reply as follows :—

"The Christmas festival now approaching, I presume that you have made your retreat from the noise and hurry of a palace, open to all comers of fashion & quality, to the private seat of the good Ladyes, wch has a better pretense to the title of a *Religious House* than those so called in Popish countryes, where superstition, opinion of merit, and forced vowes, take off very much from the pure spirit of devotion, and render their restraint tedious and irkesome. But these good Ladyes are happy under your conduct, and are, by an uninterrupted course of piety, elevated above all the gaudy pompes and vanities of the world, and enjoy all the comforts and satisfactions and serenity of mind to be wished for and attained, on this side of heaven, in their solitudes; and I cannot but looke upon you as another St. Hierome, conversing with the devout Ladies at Bethlehem, instructing and confirming their faith, and directing their consciences in the methods of true spiritual life, and enflaming their souls with seraphic notions of God, and of Christ, and of the other world, and especially by the most convincing evidence & demonstration of example."

I was naturally anxious to learn more than had been given in the scanty notices of previous biographers of the good ladies with whom Ken had been on terms of such affectionate intimacy, and thanks to information supplied by the late Rev. F. Browne and Mr. St. David Kemeys Tynte, a member of the family to which they belonged, I am able to fill up the outlines of their history with somewhat fuller information.

The ladies in question, Mary and Anne Kemeys, were the daughters of Sir Charles Kemeys, of Cefn Mably, Glamorganshire, a distinguished Cavalier, who was knighted at Oxford, June 13, 1643. Their grandfather, Sir Nicholas Kemeys, a gentleman distinguished for his loyalty to Charles I., was created a baronet, May 13, 1642, and was slain in the defence of Chepstow Castle, May 25, 1648. Their mother was Margaret, daughter of Sir George Whitmore, who was Lord Mayor of London in 1631—2. She died July 26, 1683.

After her death the two sisters went to reside at Naish, or Naish Court, in the parish of Clapton-in-Gordano, about a mile from Portishead. The house remains, apparently with little alteration, as it was in their time, and commands a fine view of the Bristol Channel and the Welsh coast. Here they established a kind of nunnery or Anglican sisterhood,[1] of the Little Gidding type, and, on account of their charitable works, were popularly known as the 'good ladies' of Naish. They took charge, besides, of two nieces, Jane and Mary, daughters of their brother, Sir Charles Kemeys, third baronet. The latter seems to have been more or less imbecile, and died single. Jane married Sir John Tynte, of Halswell, Somerset, second baronet of the name, from Naish Court, on December 25, 1704, and Colonel Kemeys Tynte, of Halswell, is the present representative of both families.

Mary died October 5, 1708, leaving all her property to her sister Anne, who died on December 21st of the same year. The will of the latter calls for a fuller notice, and throws light on Ken's relations to both the sisters.

She leaves " to my truly honoured and respected friend, Dr. Ken, the deprived Bishop of Bath and Wells, £100, which I humbly entreat him to accept as a small token of the great duty and affection which my said sister and I bore him." Farther on we have another legacy to Ken of £200, " to be distributed by him among the deprived and Non-jurant clergy, and 5s. to as many poor women as I am years old." Finally, she directs that out of her residuary estate, if any, £100 more should be given to Ken, and £100 amongst the deprived clergy.

A marble tablet to the memory of the two sisters, in the church of Clapton-in-Gordano, bears the following inscription, believed to have been written by Ken. Internal evidence seems to me to confirm the family tradition :—

     "Mary, Anne, Kemeys, sisters, who both chose
      The better part, wise virgins, here repose;

---

[1] I have already noticed (i. 259 n.) the fact that the sisterhood at Naish was probably a reproduction of Pavillon's "Regents," in the diocese of Alet. I find what seems to me an idealised picture of the life of such a sisterhood in Ken's three poems of *Psyche or Magdalum, Sion or Philothea, Urania or the Spouse's Garden.* If I am right, the work of the sisters included the restoration of penitents, as well as other works of love and practices of devotion.

Mary first crowned, Anne languished till possess'd
Of ye same grave, of ye same mansion blest."
"By their Friend."

One thinks that that Christmas of 1708 must have been to
Ken a time of special sadness. The two friends with whom
for many years he had held sweet converse were taken from him.
There was a home the less for him, and that home was one specially adapted to his nature. There, probably, more than in other
places, he could expand freely. He was made much of, and his
infirmities were cared for. He was welcomed as a spiritual
director,[1] and could speak, as a son of consolation, words of
comfort and counsel to those who needed it. He was certain
to find there those who would listen with devout reverence to
his hymns and "seraphic meditations." Happily for him the
separation was not to be long. His store in Paradise was
growing, and he himself was nearing the gates thereof.

Two letters, as usual with no year in the date, may rightly,
I think, be referred to this period, and connected with this
history.

LETTER LXIX.

"To Viscount Weymouth.

"All Glory be to God.

"My very good Lord,

"I fully intended to be at Bath on Saturday, but ye mare your
Lordshippe was pleased to lend me, fell y^t afternoon so very ill, of
what they called ye Gripes, y^t I feard she would have dyed,
and ye next day I sent my Servant to Bath to excuse my
not coming, and he brought me a pacquett from my friends
at Nash, who are so worried by a *Great Man*, y^t they are in great
affliction, and had not one of their horses been lame, they had
certainly come to Bath to meet me, to unload themselves to me,
whome they take to be their friende, though they well know y^t I
never medled with their temporall affaires. I wrott to them, but
on second thoughts, your Lordshippe being to stay at Bath all the
end of ye weeke, I thought it proper for me, if I could, to visitt my

---

[1] On the hypothesis which I have suggested above, Gratian, the spiritual guide
of *Magdalum*, would be an idealised portrait of Ken himself.

friends in affliction, and having *hired a horse*, wch at this Season was a very difficult thing here, I have sent back Leven for fear she would be wanted, and, I hope, perfectly recovered, and I intend, God willing, to give a visit to Nash, and to stay till Mooneday, wch I know will give my friends, who are very worthy persons, a great Satisfaction.

"I beseech God to multiply His blessings on your Selfe and all your good Company at Longleat.

"My Good Lord,

"Your Lordshipp's most affectionate

"Oblig'd Servant,

"T. K.

"*July* 4 " (1701 ?)

[Ken writes, it will be seen, after hearing from his friends at Naish Court. The "great man" by whom they had been "worried" is perhaps the leader of the Bristol section of the Non-jurors, the writer of the unsigned letter in p. 147. It was natural, when they were urged to withdraw from communion with the Bishop to whose spiritual guidance they had looked for many years, that they should wish to open their griefs to him, and seek for further comfort and counsel. Possibly, however, the allusion to "temporal affaires" may imply political trouble of some kind. There is nothing to show where the letter was written. "Leven," as the name of Lord Weymouth's mare, suggests an association with Colonel Grahme, of Levens (p. 161 *n.*)]

LETTER LXX.

"To Viscount Weymouth.

"All Glory be to God.

"My very good Lord,

"Your Lordshippe takes your losse with so much humble Resignation to the Divine Will, y^t I am fully persuaded God will turne it into a Blessing, & make you see by happy experience y^t it was good for you to have been afflicted. I ought to have made my acknowledgment sooner for your most obliging invitation, but till this morning I could not tell how to dispose of myselfe. My friend has left me for herselfe & her sister £200, & £300 for me to distribute among the depriv'd Clergy. Her Trustees and Executours are one M^r· Bastenvil, a worthy Attorney of Bristoll, and M^rs· Matthews, who was some time with M^rs· Portman, & who was kinswoman to my friend, and her Intimate, and lived here with her. I presume that she will not engage in the Trust, but she will stay here some short time, & I, having a most affectionate esteeme for her, have promised not to leave her. The neice who has for many years lost her understanding by convulsive fitts, after having layn a week, speechlesse & senselesse, dyed this morning, and Sir Charles Kemeys, my friend's nephew, will have the Estate.

"I beseech God to send your Lordshippe & my Lady a happy New Year & to keep you in His Reverentiall Love.

"My Good Lord,

"Your Lordshipp's most oblig'd & affectionate Servant

"THO: B. & W.

"*January* 8" (170⁸⁄₉).

[The loss which Lord Weymouth had sustained was the death of his only son, Henry, the husband of Mrs. Thynne, of Leweston, and the father of the two children for whom Ken wrote the poems which are given in this chapter, on Dec. 20, 1708, about a fortnight before the date of the letter. Ken reports, it will be seen, the death of Anne Kemeys, and her testamentary dispositions in his favour. The imbecile niece did not long survive her aunt. I am unable to give any account of the Mrs. Matthews for whom Ken expresses so warm an esteem, beyond the conjecture that she is the "very worthy dear Friend," Mrs. Margaret Matthews, dwelling in Cardiff, to whom he leaves, in his will (p. 209), "My wooden cup lined with gold, and Lord Clarendon's *History*, in six volumes, in red Turkey guilt" (*i.e.* in what we call "red morocco"). The locality, Cardiff, fits in, happily enough, with the Welsh origin of the two ladies of Cefn Mably, in Glamorganshire. I take it that "Mrs." stands, as usual at that date, for our modern "Miss," and that she was an unmarried lady, probably one of the Naish sisterhood. The letter was written apparently at Naish.]

V. KEN AND ELIZABETH ROWE.

Among the minor lights of literature in the eighteenth century a fairly honourable place may be assigned to the lady whose name stands at the head of this section. The relation in which she stood to Ken furnishes another instance of the satisfaction which, like Cowper, he found in the friendship of devout women, all the more interesting because the friend, in this case, belonged to a school of religious thought in many ways far removed from his own, or from that of the "good virgins" of Naish.

Elizabeth Rowe (born 1674) was the daughter of Walter Singer, of Ilchester, where he had been imprisoned for Nonconformity. After his wife's death he removed to Frome, where his family is still worthily represented by the Mr. Singer whose fame is in all the churches as an artist in ecclesiastical metal work, and to whom I am indebted for the drawing of Ken's paten and chalice engraved in this volume. He was known as a man "inflexible in temper and yet of catholic spirit." He was visited and held in much respect by Lord Weymouth.

His daughter Elizabeth began at an early age to give promise of her future excellence. She wrote verses when she was twelve years old ; and Mr. Thynne, Lord Weymouth's son, taught her French and Italian. She corresponded on friendly terms and on literary subjects with Prior, the poet, and published " *Poems on Several Occasions,* by Philomela," in 1696. In 1710 she married Thomas Rowe, the son of a Nonconformist minister, who, after five years of a happy union, died in 1715. She then returned to Frome, published *Friendship in Death, or Letters from the Dead to the Living* (a work which, to some extent, anticipates the *Letters from Hell,* recently edited by Dr. George MacDonald) in 1728 ; *Letters, Moral and Entertaining,* in 1733 ; and a poem on the *History of Joseph,* in 1736. She often visited the Hon. Mrs. Thynne at Leweston and in London, and the Duchess of Somerset (a daughter of the Mr. Thynne who had taught her Italian), and died in February, 1737. Her *Devout Exercises,* and *Miscellaneous Works,* were edited after her death by Dr. Isaac Watts.[1]

It is a pleasant surprise to find a bishop of the high Anglican type, like Ken, on terms of friendly intimacy with the Nonconformist poetess. He visited the Singer family " very frequently, sometimes once a week." She wrote at his suggestion a verse paraphrase of Job xxxviii. It seems probable enough that the Italian lessons were given by Mr. Thynne with his approval, if not at his suggestion. We may enrol her name, I think, with some satisfaction, in the long list of those who owed to him much that was noblest and most precious in their lives. The friendship between the two is, at any rate, worth noting as an instance of Ken's largeness of heart, and of his power to sympathise with all who, however much they might differ from him as to forms of worship or modes of ecclesiastical polity, were, in his judgment, seeking the kingdom of God and His righteousness.

[1] The facts are chiefly taken from Burder's *Memoirs of Pious Women*, 1815.

VI. Ken's "Lyra Innocentium."

Among the documents connected with Ken which have come to light since the publication of Mr. Anderdon's *Life*, few are more interesting than the collection of devout poems written by him, in the form of letters to two granddaughters of Lord Weymouth's—Frances, afterwards Duchess of Somerset, and Mary, afterwards Lady Brooke. They were the daughters of the Mr. Henry Thynne,[1] to whom Ken had sent, in 1685, copies of his Winchester *Manual* and his *Practice of Divine Love* (i. pp. 254, 286), and whom we have recently met as Elizabeth Rowe's tutor in Italian. In reading them we feel, if I mistake not, that Ken in his old age was *qualis ab incepto;* still, as when he wrote the two books just named, and his *Manual* for the boys at Winchester, and his *Directions for Prayers* for the little ones of his diocese, watching with a special interest over the souls of children, finding in their innocency a refuge from the strife of tongues, and leading them in their early years to lisp the praises of the Father. He was to the end faithful to the ideal vocation, which he had sketched out for himself in the character of Hymnotheo.

Looking to the fact that the poems have never before appeared in print, it is, I think, worth while to give them *in extenso :*—

1.

    " *Fan.* Dear Molly, say, what shall we teach
             Our Brother when he aims at speech ?
    Moll. Dear Fan, it must be our first task
             To teach him blessing how to ask.
    Fan. No, Molly, we our Parents dear,
             Next to great God, must still revere.
             God ought to tincture first his thought,
             As we, you know, at first were taught.
    Moll. We'll make it, Fanny, then our care
             To teach him first our Saviour's prayer.

---

[1] Mrs. Henry Thynne (d. 1725) lived after her husband's death at Leweston, near Sherborne, where Ken was often her guest, and where he spent the winter preceding his death. She inherited the estate from her father, Sir George Strode. The house was entirely rebuilt in 1802, but the chapel, now disused, remains in much the same state as in Ken's time. Her chaplain in Ken's time was a Mr. John Martin. (Letter from the Rev. C. H. Mayo to E. H. P.).

Fan. No, Molly, that's too long as yet,
  We'll teach him well by heart to get
  ' Glory to God,' and soon He'll try
  Blessing to ask, like you & I.
Moll. O my dear Fanny, 'tis most true
  God first must have his glory due.
Fan. Moll, first & last to God each day,
  We all our lives must glory pay.

" Remember me to Mr. Martin, Mrs. Rothery & her daughter &
to nurse.[1]

" The Blessing of God rest on you both & on your Brother.

       " TH. B & W."

      2.

" MY DEAR CHICKENS,

Moll. Of children who e'er sucked the breast
  Who think you, Fanny, were most blest ?
Fan. Those, Molly, whom, to Jesus brought,
  Up in His tender arms he caught,
  Laid gracious hands upon each head,
  And Benedictions on them shed.
Moll. In children what did Jesus find
  That he to them should be thus kind ?
Fan. The children who to Jesus came,
  Were taught to praise God's holy name :
  They humble were, & learn'd to pray,
  God & their parents to obey,
  Were inoffensive & sincere,
  And from transgressions wilfull clear.
Moll. If then we live like them, we may
  By God be bless'd as well as they.
Fan. True, Molly, & when old we grow,
  The less the world & sin we know.
  The more like children we remain,
  The greater blessings we shall gain.

" Miss Fanny must teach her sister to say her part.

      "THO. B. & W."

[1] Mr. Martin was, as stated above, chaplain at Leweston. The late Mr. H. C.
Rothery informed me that a branch of his family was settled in Ken's time at Cardiff, and I think it probable, therefore, that Mrs. Rothery may have come from
that neighbourhood, and have been, like Mrs. Matthews, a friend of the ladies
of Naish, another of the "devout women" who were under Ken's guidance.
Comp. i. 4, for Ken's thoughts as to the first steps of religious education.

3.

"All glory be to God.

"My BEST CHICKEN,

Jesus, while He on earth remain'd,
Was by two sisters entertain'd :
Martha & Mary they were named,
Both with the love of God inflamed.
Martha was full of studious care,
A decent dinner to prepare :
Mary sat down at Jesus' feet,
Of heavenly things to hear him treat.
Jesus, of each who saw the heart
Said Mary chose the better part.[1]
Things earthly mod'rate thought require ;
Things heavenly claim our chief desire.
Yet holy souls both sisters join,
Subjecting earthly to divine.

"Your most affectionate friend,

"THO. B. & W.

"My blessing to your brother and sister."

4.

"All glory be to God.
Unbounded is God everywhere,
In heavenly orbes, earth, ocean, air ;
We all day long & all the night
        Are in His sight.
Since then Great God is everywhere,
We to offend our Judge should fear,
To whose just omnipresent eye
        Hearts open lie.

"Dear Miss,

"TH. B. & W."

5.

"All glory be to God.

"My DEAREST CHICKEN,

The Son of God, in flesh debased,[2]
Young children in his arms embraced,
His hands upon their heads he laid,
While for their happiness he prayed.

[1] The poem suggests a comparison with the epitaph on the two ladies of Naish given in p. 169.   [2] "Debased" = humbled.

And now He is enthroned on high,
He keeps good children in His eye.
When'er He sees a virtuous child,
With wilful evil not defiled,
Devout, obedient, humble, meek,
Who no untruth dares ever speak,
Who daily for God's blessings prays,[1]
That child shall here by him be bless'd,
And in His arms in heaven shall rest.
Old saints, now in the heavenly sphere,
Lived all like little children here.

　　　 " The blessing of God rest on you.

　　　　　　　　　 " TH. B. & W.

" My blessing to your brother & sister."

6.

　　　 " All glory be to God.

" MY BEST CHICKEN,

Job naked, with his children dead,
With Satan's boils all overspread,
While on the ashes he reclined,
　　 With will resigned,
More happy was, though left alone,
Than Solomon upon his throne,
Enjoying pleasures of each lust
　　 To feast the gust.
Job had God's love & conscience clear,
Which all afflictions could endear.
Solomon's joys, vexations vain,
　　　 Procured his bane.
Happy is she who, when a child,
By the false world lives unbeguiled,
Whose chiefest care is to fulfill
　　 God's gracious will.

" Give my blessing to your brother & sister.

　　　 " Dear Miss, God bless you,

　　　　　　　 "TH. B. & W."

---

[1] A line seems missing in the copy sent to me.

7.

" DEAR MISS,

    Thrice happy child who, when she's young,
    To sing God's praise employs her tongue,
    Who with truth heavenly stores her thought,
    And keeps in mind the good she's taught.
    Who early learns to do God's will,
    And dreads to think, speak, practice ill;
    Who from the tender duty here
    She renders to her parents' dear,
    Learns that pure reverential love,
    Which she must give to God above.

              " Your affectionate friend,

                             " K."

[The poems, it will be seen, are undated. [I am inclined to refer them to a period shortly before or after the death of their father in December, 1708. At that date Mary, the younger sister, was six years old ; she died in 1720.]

The Poems, which are in Ken's own hand, were purchased for the Bodleian Library, in 1884, from the collection of Thomas Percy, Bishop of Dromore, editor of the well-known *Reliques of Ancient English Poetry.* They are now printed for the first time. How they came into his possession I have not been able to learn. I conjecture that the final signature K. indicates a date after Ken's resignation in 1704, but, as in the letters to Dr. Smith (chap. **xxv.**), the signature "B. and W." seems to have been often used, even to the last.

CHAPTER XXV.

A SERIES of letters passed in the years 1706—1709 between Ken and the Dr. Thomas Smith whom we have met with in an earlier stage of Ken's life (p. 168, i. 282). Smith was born in 1638, and entered Queen's College, Oxford, in 1657. It is probable that Ken's friendship with him began in their under-graduate life. He was elected Fellow of Magdalen, Oxford, in 1666, and spent three years at Constantinople (1668—1671) as Chaplain to the English Ambassador there, Sir Daniel Harvey. He was a man of learning, of the Hearne and Dodwell type, and his name appears frequently in the *Diary* and correspon-dence of the former. His knowledge of Hebrew led to his being popularly known as 'Rabbi' Smith. It was intended, in 1679, that he should edit the Alexandrian Codex, then in the King's Library, and, though that project fell through, he was asked by Bishops Pearson, Fell, and Lloyd (of St. Asaph) to visit the monastery at Mount Athos, and other places in the East, with a view to collecting MSS. of the Greek Fathers. He did not accept the offer, and remained in England, pub-lishing Latin works on the *Manners, Religion, and Government of the Turks*, in 1678 ; an *Account of the Greek Church*, and *Lives* of Camden, Usher, Cosin, Patrick Young, Dr. John Dee, and others. In 1688 he was conspicuous as the only Fellow of Mag-dalen who was in favour of submission to James II.'s action (p. 108). Even he, however, felt that he must draw the line somewhere, and he refused to acknowledge Giffard, the Roman Catholic President whom James appointed on Parker's death, and who was one of the four Bishops *in partibus* that were named by the King as Vicars Apostolic, and the Fellows of the same communion who came in with him. He was accordingly deprived in August, 1688, but was restored in the October of the same year, when James sought to avert the coming crisis by some hasty steps of amendment. On William and Mary's accession he refused to take the oaths, and was accordingly again deprived. He seems, like Ken and Fitz-william, to have led as quiet a life as it was possible for a Non-juror to lead, avoiding conspiracies, and occupying himself with his literary tasks. He died May 11, 1710.[1]

The letters have, it will be seen, the interest of presenting Ken's character under an aspect, of which hitherto we have seen but little, as a man of general reading and culture. They bring out, as it seems to me, with peculiar vividness, the refine-ment and gentlemanliness of his character. For this reason I reproduce the correspondence here. I give Ken's letters in full, but the exigencies of space compel me to epitomise Smith's. The correspondence opens with a letter from the latter

To Bishop Ken.

Smith sends a volume lately printed in Holland, probably the " *Vitæ quorundam eruditissimorum et illustrium virorum* " (1707), men-tioned above. He complains that the Dutch editor "has mangled his 'copy,' "[2] on pretence that they contained reflections on the transactions of the late times; in particular that they had cancelled a passage in which he had spoken of Sancroft as " *invictum Ecclesiæ Anglicanæ confessorem*, of his own deprivation *in nupera fatali ista rerum apud nos catastrophe*, and the like; "which would not pass muster among the Dutch Dominees and the Huguenots." He speaks of having sought, in the *Lives* of Usher and Cosin, to "do right to the memory of the blessed Saint and Martyr, King Charles I.," and of having done some service to religion in that of John Dee, in ex-posing "magic, witchcraft, and other works of the devil." Dated December 19, 1706.

---

[1] For an earlier letter of Ken's to Smith, see p. 107.

[2] So in a letter to Hearne (November 9, 1706) Smith states that he is dissatisfied with the Dutch printers, chiefly for their "mangling and leaving out" para-graphs distasteful to the Dutch and French Presbyterians in Holland. (Hearne, i. 307). I find the volume among Ken's books at Wells.

LETTER LXXI.

To Dr. Smith.

" All Glory be to God.

" My worthy good Friend,

" I should sooner have returned you my thanks for the excellent present you designed for me, and withall should have condoled with you for the injurious treatment, which your book has met with, but that it is not yet come to my hands. This night I expect it, or, at the farthest, to-morrow morning. I am of opinion that the Dominees are not to be blamed ; they are too Calvinisticall to be in league with those who oppose you. There is a remarkable scripturient person, who keeps correspondence with your adversaries here, as appears by what is published, who to gratify his paymasters, might easily do you the unkindnesse, but this is onely my conjecture at a distance. I wish that you had sent your copy to Dr. Cockbourne ; I believe that he would have done you right, and he may yet print a sheet, to be bound up with the book, which may supply what is omitted, and might rectify the wilfull mistakes they have made who printed. Mr. Harbin corresponds with him. I most heartily wish you a new yeare, & beseech God to keep us in his reverentiall love.

" Your truely affect: friend & B^r,

" THO. B. & W.

" *Dec. 30th* " (1706).

[Ken seems to exonerate the " Dominees," or Dutch divines from Smith's censures. His opponents were of another school, probably, Ken means, of that of the English latitudinarian Whigs. I fail to identify the " scripturient person." The Dr. Cockbourne I conjecture to be a Scotch Episcopal divine of that name who took a D.D. at Oxford, May 25, 1709. He had been pastor of an English church at Amsterdam since 1688, and Ken naturally wishes that Smith had entrusted his " copy," in the printer's sense, to his care. (Hearne i., p. 202). He was a friend of Harbin's, and would have done his work faithfully. Queen Anne presented him to an English living, and this was the occasion of the Oxford D.D.]

LETTER LXXII.

To Dr. Smith.

" All Glory be to God.

" My worthy dear Friend,

" I returne you many thanks for your last very valuable present. I remember that when I read the first edition of the lamentable persecution of the great good man to whom you have worthily done

justice, it made me sad, and the second reading revived the same
sad thoughts, but the afflicted Patriarch is happy in this, that God
has moved you to embalme his memory. Living so long and so
much in the country, I have no charitable contributions put into my
hands, but of my owne I can spare you the contents of the following
note, which, you would oblige me by accepting. I beseech God to
keep us in his reverential love, and mindfull of eternity.

"Your most affect. friend and B^r,

"THO. B. & W.

"*May 24th*" (1707).

[The context suggests that the valuable present was a copy of a second edition
of Smith's book. The "Patriarch" is, of course, Sancroft. One can picture to
one's self the feelings with which Ken would read that history of a past that had
faded into the dim distance. The "note" enclosed (amount not stated), not from
funds given to him specially for distribution, but from his own money, indicates
what use Ken made of the comparative opulence of his £200 per annum pension.]

To Bishop Ken.

Smith thanks Ken for his gift. Twelve years ago he had contemplated a life of Mary, Queen of Scots, vindicating her memory
against those "furious incendiaries" who attacked it, and had
collected materials, but was deterred from finishing it by the cost.
It is too late to return to it now, and the work has been undertaken
by Mr. Crawford, Her Majesty's historiographer to the Kingdom of
Scotland, "of which title he is since deprived," but he cannot judge
how far he is competent for the task. At all events he is "of
good principles, and a great enemy of the covenanting Lords Kirk-
men of that age." He (Smith) is now arranging his correspondence and collections of materials supplied by deceased friends.
Dated, June 7th, 1707.

LETTER LXXIII.

To Dr. Smith.

"All Glory be to God.

"My worthy dear Friend,

"Your letter was sent beyond Bristol, where I had been, when I
was come away, so that I had it not till some time after I returned
to Longleat. I give you thanks for your kind acceptance of the
little I could doe for you. If you want me at any time, I entreat
you to let me know it. I discours'd with my Lord concerning you.
He has a just value for you, and has sent you a token. If you will
call on Mr. Brome the bookseller, he has ten pounds for you, for

which, by this good Lord's order, I sent him a note. As for your
design in writing the life of the Q. of Sc. I am not sorry for your
disappointment, for you would have been engaged to have made
some severe reflections, though just, on Q. Eliz. which would have
given offence, she being the darling of the people, and I had rather
that the odium should fall on another than on yourself. Mr. Harbin
has papers by him which will give great light into the history, and
a letter of Q. E. herself, to excite her keeper to assassinate her, of
which he will give you an account, if need be, and which ought to
be published by the writer whome you mention, and who, with your
directions, may be enabled to perfect his designe. I perceive that
we are much of an age, for next month I shall be in my seventieth
year. I beseech God to keep us in his reverential love, and mindfull of eternity.

" Your's very affectionately,

"THO. B. & W.

" June 28 " (1707).

[Ken was obviously not an admirer of Elizabeth. Harbin had apparently
found the letter which suggested assassination, among the Longleat papers,
but Ken is not sorry that the odium of publishing should not rest on his
correspondent. Brome was the publisher of Ken's *Manual.* Smith had asked,
in his previous letter, that Harbin would send him Mr. Burkin's unpublished
MSS. at Longleat, which Lord Weymouth had promised him. Letter xxxvii.
shows that Ken had introduced Harbin to Smith as one likely to be a friend of
congenial temperament, engaged in like studies.]

To Bishop Ken.

Smith thanks the Bishop for his good offices with Lord Weymouth. He would fain have written to that " good Lord," but
thought it might be "more offensive than agreeable." He had not
intended, when he spoke of his money troubles, to suggest that he
needed help, but he is very glad to receive it. He had purposed in
his history to expose the schismatical and seditious principles of the
Scotch Presbyterians, but would have had "a tender regard to the
fame of Elizabeth." "*Ragion di Stato,* and the incessant, importunate,
and united addresses of Parliament and people, and opinions of
judges and lawyers will, I feare, be no good plea at the barre of
God's tribunal, but we may charitably hope that some graines of
allowance may be put in the other scale, to take off from the weight
of her scarce justifiable severity." He knows her letter to Sir
Amias Paulet, "which choques me more than all the imputations"
of the Papists. "It is a curious fact that the register of the commission by which Queen Mary was tried, placed in the Exchequer

N 2

Office by Lord Burghley in 1595, was withdrawn by order of King James in 1603, and never restored, though demanded." The King apparently took care that the record should "never appear in after-times to the infamy of his mother." Dated, July 5th, 1707.

LETTER LXXIV.

TO DR. SMITH.

" All Glory be to God.

" MY WORTHY GOOD FRIEND,

" You need not write to this good Lord, lest your acknowledgments shock his modesty, as his present did yours, and I dare say that he has so great an esteem of you, that he would on all occasions generously assist you.   He tells me that he has papers which will justify all the severe reflections which can be made on Q. E., of which I presume that Mr. Harbin has given you an account, or will do it whenever you shall desire it, though considering how much an impartial relation will disgust the prevailing many, I wish it rather published by another than by yourselfe, she is so much the Heroine of the Multitude.   I doubt not but that she had many and great provocations, but the way she took to free herself will not appear excusable.   I entreat you to let me know with the freedom of a friend, when you are in any streight, or want supplys, to carry on your labours of love for the publick.   God keep us in his reverential love, and mindful of eternity.

" Your truely affect: friend and B^r,

" THO. B. & W.

July 12th " (1707).

[Ken's judgment, based on what he is told of the Longleat documents, is still strongly adverse to Elizabeth ; but he cannot desire that his friend should incur the odium of exposing her. " No scandal against Queen Elizabeth " seemed to him a safe rule of action in the then state of public feeling.   The *animus* of one who always held it more blessed to give than to receive, appears strongly in the penultimate sentence.]

LETTER LXXV.

TO THE SAME.

" All Glory be to God.

" MY WORTHY GOOD FRIEND,

" My poor sister Ken is now in great affliction for the loss of her onely son, who dyed at Cyprus, & I entreat your charity, which I

know is truly evangelicall, to visit her, & to apply such ghostly
lenitives to her sorrow, as may set her at ease, or, at least, very
much moderate her passion. When my Lord comes to town, you
will be a welcome visitant to him, he having a just value for you.
God keep us in his Holy fear, & wise for eternity.

"Your truely affect: friend and B',

"THO. B. & W.

"*Oct. 25*" (1707).

[The nephew who died in Cyprus was the only son of Ion Ken, the Bishop's
brother, who was treasurer of the East India Company. Letter viii. suggests that
the latter had died in 1684. The *Athenæum* of March 24th, 1879, contains a
review of Thomson's "*Through Cyprus with the Camera*" (1878), and quotes a
passage describing the church of St. Lazarus, at Larnaca, in which there is a
memorial of John Ken, of London, merchant, born February 6, 1672, died
July 12, 1707, in excellent preservation. The other monuments of the church
are chiefly Venetian.]

To BISHOP KEN.

Smith lost no time in visiting the bereaved mother whom Ken
had commended to him. Her religion and piety have taught her to
submit with all Christian patience to these sad inflictions of Providence. When Lord Weymouth next comes to town he will call
on him. Things in London appear of a "sickly and frightful com-
plexion." The "hand of God is punishing us for our horrible
wickedness." Others may dream "of triumph in the next campaign," but we are plunging deeper into guilt and labour under a
judicial infatuation. The year 1707, it may be noted, had been full
of failures and disasters, crowned by the wreck of Sir Cloudesley
Shovel's fleet off the Scilly Isles, on October 22nd. Smith was
not likely to look on the passing of the 'Union with Scotland' Act,
May 1st, as a set-off against these. Dated, November, 1707.

LETTER LXXVI.

To DR. SMITH.

"All Glory be to God.

"MY WORTHY DEAR FRIEND,

"I beseech God to reward you for your charitable visitts to my
sister, who, I hope, by this time, has overcome her passion. I deferred
writing to you till the family removed, intending to send by good
Mr. Jenkins, from whom you will receive five pounds, as a token of
the real respect I have for you. I can, thanks be to God, very well

spare it, and I entreat you to oblige me by accepting it. I intend, God willing, to spend the winter with two good virgins beyond Bristol, where there is a kind of nunnery, and with whome I usually abide in my Lord's absense. God keep us in his reverential love, and make us wise for eternity.

" Your most affect: friend and Bᵣ,

"THO. B. & W.

"*Nov. 24th*" (1707).

[The letter tells its own tale and needs no explanation, but we may note the fact that Ken usually stayed with the ladies of Naish whenever Lord Weymouth was not at Longleat. Mr. Jenkins remains unidentified, but the name appears as one of the witnesses to Ken's will (p. 209). The vicar of Frome of that date bore the name of Jenkyns. He was a lineal ancestor of Richard Jenkyns, Master of Balliol, and Dean of Wells (1845—54). Comp. Lett. lxxviii.]

To BISHOP KEN.

Smith begins with the passage quoted in page 168, on the life of the "Religious House" at Naish. He is confounded, " *stupito e stordito*," at Ken's fresh act of bounty to him. He thinks himself bound to tell him, though he will not refuse his gift, that he has been for nineteen years, since his deprivation, supported by a brother with whom he lives, and that his literary labours and the gifts of friends put him beyond the reach of poverty. He mentions, in a P.S., that he had seen Lord Weymouth, and had been much impressed with the goodness of his character, as one who had learnt fully the lesson that " it was more blessed to give than to receive," and would scarcely suffer himself to be thanked for his liberality. Dated, December 20th, 1707.

LETTER LXXVII.

To DR. SMITH.

" All Glory be to God.

"MY WORTHY DEAR FRIEND,

"Till I was settled with the good virgins, of whom you have such respectful thoughts, and whose habitation I reach'd not till last night, I deferred to send you my acknowledgments for your obliging acceptance of the little present which I sent you. I am very glad that you were with yᵉ good lord; he does really conduct his life by the divine maxim recorded by St. Paul, & he is truly rich in good works, & indeed, so are his near relations; munificence seems to be the family virtue, & traduced to their posterity. I know

that you are so fully employed, & so rich in good works of another
nature, which yet are a charity to the publick, y⁴ I make a scruple
of giving you any long diversion from your studies.   I beseech
God to send you a happy new year, & to prosper your labours of
love, in which, I know, you spend your time.

" Good sᵣ,

" Your most affect: friend and Bᵣ,

" THO. B. & W.

" Dec. 28th " (1707).

[The "good virgins" are, of course, the Naish ladies.   Ken, like Lord
Weymouth, thinks that he has to thank his friend for accepting his gifts.   The
"near relations" of the "good lord," are, probably, Mr. and Mrs. Thynne, of
Leweston, near Sherborne, with whom Ken often stayed.   One notes his use of
"traduced," as often also in his poems, in its strict etymological sense.]

To BISHOP KEN.

Smith has been reluctant to trouble Ken with letters during his
season of retirement. He did not wish to interrupt his intercessions
for the " poore harassed and afflicted clergy," who had " kept themselves clear from the pollutions of false and wicked oaths, and
other gnostic practices." Yet, after all, " their sufferings were light
as compared with those of their predecessors, between 1641 and
1660." He thanks God, that in spite of his infirmities and his
anxieties for his country, he can still " do some service to learning
and the concerns of our common Christianity." He would gladly
take any opportunity of seeing Ken, should anything bring him
within reach.   Dated, April, 1708.

LETTER LXXVIII.

To DR. SMITH.

" All Glory be to God.

" MY WORTHY DEAR FRIEND,

" I should be ashamed to lett your letter lye so long without
thankful acknowledgment, but that I received it not till Friday
evening yᵉ 14th, from good Mr. Jenkins. I not coming to Longleate
till then, by reason of the illness of my horse. I could not, without
great fraternall sympathy, hear of your late troubles, but I make
no doubt, but that they were sent you from the benigne direction
of providence, to quicken those graces, which otherwise might have
layn dormant, and I am confident that you have experimented y⁴ it
was good for you to have been in trouble, and I hope that our

brethren will copy the example you have given them. I have no
inclination to the Towne; it neither agrees with my healthe nor
temper, but if anything should draw me up, my good friend shall
be sure to be one of the first, to whom I would pay my respects. I
thank God, that I am unmolested in the country, & I hope I shall
continue so, and one would think that our yeares & our profession,
and course of life, would give no occasion for the least suspition.
I beseech God to prosper your labours of love for the publick, and
to keep us both mindful of eternity.

" Good Dr.

" Your most affectionate friend & B\^{r\},

"THO. B. & W.

"*May* 16*th*" (1708).

[The hope that "our brethren" will follow Smith's example, *i.e.* will give
themselves to useful studies instead of plunging into plots or publishing railing
accusations, strikes one as eminently characteristic. So also is the continued
dislike to the idea of visiting London (see pp. 121, 122). As far as I can gather, Ken
never went there, except for Kettlewell's funeral, in 1695, after his deprivation.
He seems to have been unlucky in his horses. See Letters lviii., lix.]

To the Bishop of Bath and Wells.

Smith has left with Brome, Ken's publisher, a copy of his
edition of the Epistles of Ignatius, which he offers as a "sincere,
but poor, acknowledgment" of his many obligations. He refers to a
recent gift which he had received from Ken, looking to his "narrow
circumstances," and his own sufficiency, "with great reluctance."
He recommends to his charity "Lady D. and her two daughters,"[1]
left very destitute by the death of that loyal gentleman, Sir R. D."
He hopes Ken will represent their case to Lord Weymouth. He is
suffering "great uneasiness both in mind and body." Dated,
February, 170⅞.

LETTER LXXIX.

To Dr. Smith.

" All Glory be to God.

"My worthy dear Friend,

"I return you many thanks for the most valuable present you
sent me, and I entreat you to permit me to send you, now and then,
some testimony of my esteem, which I can well spare, and indeed

[1] Ken's next letter gives the name as Dutton. I find a Sir Ralph Dutton,
Baronet, of Sherborne, Gloucestershire, but he died in 1721.

considering your labours of love & learning, all your friends can
give to you is given to the publick. I cannot tell whether I should
condole. or congratulate, your goutish distemper, for some are of
opinion that it prolongs life, & for that reason, wish for it, & your
friends will be glad for anything which will prolong a life so very
useful. I am sorry for good Lady Dutton and her daughters: I
beseech God to support them. If, when you go into the city, you
call on Brome the bookseller, he will pay you fifty shillings, which
I design for them, though I desire you to make no mention from
whom it came. I intend to mention you to my Lord when I have a
fair opportunity. God keep us in his reverential love, resigned to
his will, and mindful of eternity.

"Dear S^r,

"Your very affectionate Friend & B^r,

"THO. B. & W.

"*Feb. 21st*" (170$\frac{8}{9}$).

[The letter requires no comment, save that it may be almost taken as a
model of refinement and delicacy in the art of giving.]

To the Bishop of Bath and Wells.

Smith has seen Lord Weymouth, but had not the courage to
name Lady Dutton to him, yet he is a hundred times more concerned
for them than for himself, and will ask Ken therefore to name them
to his host. He is gratified with Ken's acceptance of his Ignatius.
It counterbalances the fact that he has no expectation of any money
profit from it. The University has only given him forty copies in
quires, and after a sale of about one hundred in Oxford, has sold
the remainder to a bookseller. Dated, May, 1709.

LETTER LXXX.

For Dr. Smith.

"All Glory be to God.

"My worthy dear Friend,

"I have already putt his Lordshippe in mind of your distressed
Lady, & her two daughters; but in regard the Legacy will not be
suddenly raised, I could not further presse their relief at present.
I am sorry that the university made you not a more respectfull
return. I heartily congratulate you in the happinesse you enjoy
in a good conscience, which is an anticipation of heaven, & am

scrupulous of taking up too much of your time, which you so bene-
ficially employ for the public, & for the future generation, to whom
you will make your memory pretious.   God keep us in his reverential love, resigned to his will, and mindfull of eternity.

"Good Dr Smith,

" Yours very affectionately,

"THO. B. & W.

"*May 23*" (1709).

[There is, perhaps, a touch of the weariness of age and pain in the brevity of
Ken's answer to Smith's long letter, and in the hint, courteous, yet significant,
that he is scrupulous as to taking up too much of his time.   It was the kind of
letter that would naturally terminate, or at least, suspend, the correspondence.
And as a matter of fact it is the last letter extant.   Smith died May 11, 1710.

KEN'S PATEN AND CHALICE.

From a drawing by Mr. W. Singer (see p. 209).

THE years that followed the embittered controversy which was roused by Ken's resignation of his bishopric were, as I have said, a time of comparative calm. But they brought with them, as was natural at his age, the loss of not a few friends, which must have made him feel his loneliness more and more. The two ladies of Naish died in 1708 ; Frampton, of all the Bishops of the time the one most like-minded with himself, and whom, as we have seen, he visited in his old age, in the same year ; Smith, in May, 1710. On January 1st of that last-named year, William Lloyd, the deprived Bishop of Norwich, was called to his rest, and his death left Ken as the last survivor of the deprived Bishops. That event brought about a new crisis in his relations with the Non-jurors. He had, at the time of Kidder's death, declared his conviction that the death, or cession, of a deprived bishop gave a legitimate character to the ministrations of his successor, and cleared him from the guilt of schism. He had acted on that principle himself. He had looked on its recognition by others as the right way to terminate the unhappy divisions by which the Church was rent asunder. He had been supported in that view, shortly after his resignation in Hooper's favour, by Dodwell, who in 1705 published a book, the title of which is, for our present purpose, a sufficient epitome of its contents :—[1]

"*A Case in View Considered :* in a Discourse proving that (in case our present invalidly deprived Fathers shall leave all their Sees vacant, either by Death or Resignation) we shall not then be

[1] See generally for the history and correspondence connected with this chapter, Lathbury's *Non-jurors,* chap. vi.

obliged to keep up our Separation from those Bishops, who are as yet involved in the Guilt of the present unhappy schism."

His principle, to put the matter in its briefest form, was that the intruded Bishops were *nulli* because they were *secundi;* when they ceased to be *secundi,* their nullity also came, *ipso facto,* to an end. He was supported by Nelson, Brokesby, and others, while, on the other hand, Hickes, Wagstaffe, and Collier, held that the schism, of which the new Bishops had been guilty in entering on their sees, was not purged by the death or resignation of those who had been ejected to make room for them. They must acknowledge their guilt, and be restored by consent of the Church, before they could be accepted as canonically in charge of their respective Dioceses. The controversy waxed hot, after the fashion of such disputes. Dodwell, in 1707, published "*A Farther Prospect of the Case in View, with Answers to Objections.*" He turned the tables, in this again following Ken, upon Hickes and Wagstaffe, and denied the validity of their clandestine consecration. They did not even pretend to any diocesan authority, though they claimed to perpetuate the spiritual succession, and maintained that they and the faithful remnant that followed them, were the only successors "in the royal priesthood, even to the end of the world."

Within ten days after Lloyd's death Dodwell wrote to Ken, as he tells Nelson in a letter dated January 11th, $170\frac{6}{10}$, asking him, " as the only survivor of the invalidly deprived Bishops, and as thereby having it in his power now to free, *not only his private diocese, but the whole National Church* from the schism introduced by filling the sees, whether he insisted on his rights as diocesan." " If," he adds in his letter to Nelson, " my Lord of Bath and Wells declare that he will not so far insist on his right as to justifie our separate communions on his account, we must then enquire whether any claim appear, derived from his deceased Brethren, for keeping any one See full which had been otherwise vacant by their death ; and what evidence appears for supporting that claim, and whether that evidence be satisfactory." In answer to Dodwell's inquiry, Ken wrote as follows :—

LETTER LXXXI.

To HENRY DODWELL.

"All glory be to God.

"GOOD MR. DODWELL,

"Where your letter of Jan. 10th stopped by the way I know not, but it came not to me till the last post February 9th, and in that you are pleased to ask me whether I insist on my Episcopal claim, and my answer is that I do not, and that I have no reason to insist on it, in regard that I made a cession to my present most worthy successor, who came into the field by my free consent and approbation. As for any clandestine claim, my judgment was always against it, and I never had nothing to do with it, foreseeing that it would perpetuate a schism which I found very afflicting to good people scattered in the country, where they could have no divine office performed. I was always tender of the peace of the Church, especially in this age of irreligion; I always thought the *Multitudo Peccantium* might justify some relaxations of canonical strictures. I beseech you to present my hearty respects to good Mrs. Dodwell. You both, and your family, have all along had my daily prayers. God keep us in his reverential love, and mindful of eternity. Your very affectionate friend,

"THO. B. & W.

"*Feb.* 11" (170$\frac{8}{10}$).

[The letter was obviously written with a full knowledge of Dodwell's reasoning in the *Case in View*, and was intended to confirm it in the strongest possible manner. It is a striking illustration of the charity of Ken's temper, that while the more violent Non-jurors, including even Dodwell himself at an earlier stage of the controversy (p. 42), were never weary of quoting the text against "following a multitude to do evil," he sees, even in the *multitudo peccantium*, a ground for relaxation of ecclesiastical rules, and this, specially with a view to the "many good people" who, without such relaxation, would be deprived of the privilege of attending divine offices. Ken's letter, as usual, gives no year, but I cannot doubt that I have given the right date.]

This answer Dodwell reports to a friend on March 2nd, and says that he has seen a letter from Ken to another person, probably Nelson, on the same subject. That letter we have, in substance, in one from Nelson to a friend, and as the greater part of it is in Ken's words, I number it as one of his :—

LETTER LXXXII.

To HENRY DODWELL.

" SIR,

" In order to satisfie your enquiry, I can acquaint you that I have received a letter from Bishop Ken, who assures me;

'That he was always against that practice which he foresaw would perpetuate the Schism, and declared against it, and that he had acted accordingly, and would not have it laid at his door, having made a recess (as he says) for a much more worthy person; and he apprehends it was always the judgement of his Brethren, that the death of the Canonical Bishops would render the Invaders Canonical, in regard the Schism is not to last always.'

" Afterwards his Lordship adds this;

'I presume Mr. Dodwell, and others with him, go to Church, tho' I myself do not, being a publick person; but to communicate with my Successor, in that part of the Office which is unexceptionable, I should make no difficulty.'

" This letter I communicated to Mr. Dodwell, when in town, which he thought clear enough for closing the Schism, and I suppose in a short time he may have one to the same purpose.

    *   *   *   *   *   *

" Your faithful humble Servant,

"ROB. NELSON.

" *Feb.* 21 " (170$\frac{6}{9}$).

[The letter has the advantage of adding a new fact to the grounds of Ken's decision. His brethren, the other deprived Bishops, had always held the same judgment that he did as to the effect of their death in giving canonical validity to the acts of the " Invaders." His own position, he thinks, is, in one respect, different from that of laymen. He still holds that James II.'s son is the rightful King of England, and, therefore, being a " public person," does not think it right to give an apparent sanction to the State Prayers in Matins, Evensong, or Litany, by going to church as he advised others to do. But he did not hold that the acknowledgment of the *de facto* sovereign was a sufficient ground for withdrawing from communion with the Established Church, and therefore proposed to communicate with his successor " in that part of the office " (he meant, I presume, the part that follows the Prayer for the Church Militant) at some convenient opportunity. See p. 195.]

The advice thus given decided the action of the two friends at Shottesbrook. On the first Sunday in Lent, Cherry and Dodwell went to their parish church with their families for the

first time since their secession.[1]   Archbishop Sharp, who had
taken a leading part in bringing about the healing of the schism,
administered the communion to Nelson on Easter Day.   The
bells rang out their peal of joy for the termination of the
schism, which had vexed the parish, as it had vexed the nation.
Their example was followed by Nelson, and by other conspicuous
laymen in London and the country.   Virtually that Sunday was
memorable as the " beginning of the end " of the Non-juring
schism, and that beginning, as we have seen, was due to Ken's
influence.

A few weeks later, and Ken, at least, continued steadfast in
his purpose thus announced :—

LETTER LXXXIII.

To HENRY DODWELL.

" All glory be to God.

" MY VERY WORTHY FRIEND,

" I returne you many thanks, for ye Caution you give me, y^t my
Example should not be mistooke, lest it have an ill influence on
others, wch is very far from my intention, & as soone as I am fitt for
travelling, I shall, God willing, goe to ye Cathedrall on purpose, to
communicate with my Successour; That being ye most conspicuous
place, and ye Communion office has nothing exceptionable.   At present I am stopp'd at Long-leat, by " [he names a new symptom of his
disease,] " for wch distemper I am to goe to Bristoll, to drink ye water
there, wch I hope will relieve me.   I beseech God to multiply His
blessings on your selfe, and good Mrs. Dodwell, and on your
children.

" Your very affectionate friend,

"THO. B. & W.

" *Ap. 21st* " (1710).

[It is open to question whether the scruples which, in Ken's previous letter,
limited his presence at the Communion Service to that part of it which was " unexceptionable," in which, *e.g.*, the name of the ruling sovereign did not occur,

---

[1] Brokesby's account is worth quoting, " We are here satisfied that the schism
is at an end, when there is no altar against altar, nor any other bishops but
suffragans to require our subjection.   And, therefore, we all go to church."
—Lathbury, ch. x., p. 203.

were now removed, or whether the wider language of the present letter is to be interpreted by the former limitation. The symptom which Ken describes is that which physicians know as *hæmaturia*.]

I have not been able to ascertain whether the intention thus expressed passed into an act. If it did, I can imagine few scenes in his life, or in that of any man, more striking and pathetic. When he was last present in the cathedral at Wells, he had sat in the episcopal throne, and had there read his public protest against his deprivation. Now he enters it, a feeble old man, bowed with years and sufferings, to receive the sacred pledges of communion with his Lord and with his brethren, from the same paten and chalice in which he used to administer them, and at the hands of the friend whom he himself had virtually chosen as his successor, and to whom he had, in spite of obloquy and opposition, resigned his pastoral office. One would like to know, if it were possible, with whom he stayed at Wells, whether he were the honoured guest of the Palace, or was received by Dean or Canon (the Dean of his time was William Graham, who had been chaplain to the Queen when she was Princess, and was the younger brother of his friend, James Graham, and therefore uncle of the " Student Penitent "), or took up his abode, in the humility of his nature, at some humble hostelry, but this of course we can only conjecture.[1]

Two letters, which Ken leaves, as was his wont, without the date of year, seem to me probably to belong to this period of his life :—

LETTER LXXXIV.

To Viscount Weymouth.

"All glory be to God.

"My very Good Lord,

"I am afresh oblig'd to your Lordshippe for your Charitable Concerne for me. I was seas'd in Easter weeke with a very severe

---

[1] I doubt, however, whether the Dean was a man with whom Ken would be much in sympathy. Unlike his brothers, James, Fergus, and Viscount Preston, he had chosen the winning side, had held a ' golden stall ' at Durham, with the Deaneries of Carlisle and Wells in succession, and still thought his claims to preferment neglected. (Paget's *Ashstead*, pp. 87, 88.) On the whole I incline to the Palace, where Hooper's daughter, Mrs. Prowse, says that he often stayed.

fitt of y⁰ Rheumatisme. It came on me three weeks before, but
never was at y⁰ night till here, and in four and twenty hours, it
weak'ned me to yᵗ degree yᵗ my legge sunk under me, and I fell
down severall times, though I had a stick to support me. I thank
God y⁰ Violence is over, and I recover my strength, but my paine
still continues and is most raging when I am in bed. I am sorry
that my little friend does not mind his businesse, and I believe
the Idle fitt came on him since I was there, for then Mr. Usher
assured me to y⁰ contrary. I would by no means trouble Mr. Oord
to come hither, and I have sent to Langford y⁰ bookseller to receive
y⁰ mony for me, and he, being to come this way, will, I presume
bring it. I heartily congratulate my Lord. Abingdon's new post,
and look on it as a Good Omen. I am extreamely glad yᵗ your
Lordshippe enjoys so good health. God be praised for it, but I
fear you will hardly see Longleat till Whitsontide. I beseech God
to multiply His blessings on your selfe, and on my Lady, and on
your family.
> "My Good Lord
> "Your Lordshipp's most affect: Servant,
> > "T. B. and W.

"*May* 5" (1710 ?).

[The illness to which Ken had referred in Letter lxxxiii. had apparently increased
in violence, and it is possible that it may have hindered the visit to Wells which
he contemplated when he wrote to Dodwell. The description which he gives of
his sufferings agrees with what we find in the poems which probably belong
to this period, as will be seen in p. 199: I take the "little friend" to be
a grandson of Lord Weymouth's, son of Henry Thynne, of Leweston, and
brother of the two children for whom Ken wrote the poems given in the
preceding chapter, the "Mr. Usher" being his tutor. "Lord Abingdon" was
the second Earl. In 1702 he had been made Privy Councillor and Constable of
the Tower. This post he lost in 1705, but in 1710 he was appointed Chief
Justice, and Justice in Eyre of the Royal Forests South of the Trent.]

LETTER LXXXV.

To Mr. Cressy.

"All Glory be to God.

"Sʳ,—I receivd your letter, from worthy Mr. Nelson, & I returne
you y⁰ enclosed, wᶜʰ was written to you by my deare Friend, & Bʳ,
now with God. You have in towne so many very able persons to
consult, yᵗ I wonder you should send to me, when you must needs
be sensible yᵗ you may much sooner have satisfaction by word of
mouth than 'tis possible for you to have by letter, wᶜʰ often is liable

to be misunderstood, & to raise more scruples than it solves. Besides, you are a stranger to me, and though I think extreamely well of you, from ye piety of your expressions, yett, living retired from ye world, I have no reason to engage in a correspondence, especially in so nice a point, w^{ch}, when once begun, I may perhaps see no end of. I shall therefore commend you to ye serious perusall of ye two last chapters, in good Mr. Kettlewell's book of Communion, & by y^t you will know my mind. I wonder y^t ye turne, wch ye clergy generally made at ye Revolution, should give any considering person an inclination towards Rome, when ye Romanists have made as many such Turnes as there have been usurpations in o^r Monarchy, wch have not been few.

"I beseech God to guide you, & to multiply His blessings on your selfe, wife & children.

                    "Your affect: Freind & B^r,
                                    "THO. B. & W."

(1710 ?)

[I have been unable to learn anything about the Mr. Cressy to whom the letter is addressed. In the Sloane MSS. in the British Museum (4,274) there is a letter from Francis Turner apparently addressed to him (there is no superscription, but Mrs. Cressy is named in the letter), dated June 27th, 1700. This was probably the very letter that Ken returned. He seems from this to have been a Non-juror, a friend of Lord Preston's, who consulted Turner then on the same point as that on which he now consults Ken. Turner gives advice of an opposite character to that which Ken states in a previous letter (p. 126) that he had given. Cressy was then living at York, and in need of relief from the fund entrusted to Turner for distribution. Ken's letter to him has no date. I have assigned it to this period as thinking it likely to have been occasioned by Dodwell's *Case in View*, *now a Case in Fact*. Cressy had apparently applied; through Nelson, for Ken's guidance, probably, as the reference to the two last chapters of Kettlewell's *Book of Communion* shows, as to whether he would be acting rightly in attending the services of the Established Church. The title of the book is *Of Christian Communion to be kept in the Unity of Christ's Church*, and the headings of the two chapters referred to are, Ch. VII. "*Of the Excusableness of the People receiving Ministerial Offices from Men in a Schism, rather than live without any at all*," and Ch. VIII. "*Of Communicating in like Necessity, where there are some Prayers sinful in the Matter of them*." They were published in 1695, just before Kettlewell's death, and Ken, as we have seen more than once already (pp. 124—126), took them as giving the principles which had guided his own course of thought and action. The letter shows the natural reluctance of an old and suffering man to enter into a correspondence with a stranger, which might become interminable, and in the course of which his letters might be put to some use more or less objectionable. Cressy was apparently taunted by his Romish friends with the part taken by the English clergy at the Revolution, and Ken had, as might be expected, his *tu quoque* ready. One wonders whether his correspondent was in any way connected with the Hugh Serenus de Cressy who has met us at an earlier stage. See i. 24.]

The letter just printed is the last now extant.   It is possible, indeed, that both it and its immediate predecessor may belong to an earlier date.   On this hypothesis there would be a singular fitness in the fact that the last letter known to exist (Letter lxxxii.) should record the act, or at least the intention of the act, which brought the singularly varied changes and chances of Ken's life, to an almost dramatic ending.   That communion in Wells Cathedral would have been a fit close to the " strange eventful history."

Anyhow, that brings to a conclusion all that we know of the activities of Ken's life.   The eleven months that followed were passed under the discipline of acute suffering.   All the worst symptoms hinted at in the letters to Dodwell and Lord Weymouth, and described in the Note, p. 123, came back in an aggravated form.   The series of poems under the head of *Anodynes* belong probably to this period, and were the last fruit of the tree which had borne the Morning, Evening, and Midnight Hymns as its *primitiæ.*   They tell their tale of constant pain and utter sleeplessness—

> " I feel my watch, I tell the clock,
>   I hear each crowing of the cock."

He feels as if he had " red-hot needles in his breast."   "Nerves, tendons, pores, arterys, veins," are all racked with "disseminated pains."   There are traces of delirious and horrible visions.   He has tried opium, but it only beguiles him with its stupefaction, and he will have no more of it.   He leaves the ' dull narcotic, numbing pain ' to those who seek to silence their conscience, and chooses rather, like the great Pattern Sufferer, to put aside the ' spiced bowl,' which those who were crucified with Him, it may be, took freely, and to trust in the angelic sympathy and help, of the nearness of which he was conscious in his inmost spirit.   He tried other " anodynes " of a different kind.   He sought to find refuge in books—

> " But soon as I begin to read,
>   I scarce one line can heed."

Friends came to visit him, but—

"While my anguish they deplore,
They only irritate the sore."

He tried meditation, but pain distracted him—

"And while I feel these fiery darts,
I cannot pray, unless by starts."

At last he fell back, in the spirit of his *Hymnotheo*, and after the pattern of the Psalmist sufferer—

"I some remission of my woes
Feel, while I hymns compose.
    *   *   *   *
And when my pains begin to rage,
I them with hymn assuage."

And in the series of poems which he groups together under the title of *Anodynes, or Alleviations of Pain,* and which fill some eighty-six pages of the third volume of his Poems, we have the fruit of those months of discipline.

In April, 1710, he was, we have seen (Letter lxxxiii.), intending to go to the Hot Wells at Bristol. There he stayed till the following November. There is, I think, good ground for inferring that whatever powers of mental activity he retained were given to the work of putting in order the MSS. of his poems. It was by these that he wished to be remembered and to testify the feelings of gratitude which he felt for Lord Weymouth, under whose roof most of them had been written, and for his friend Hooper. In his "Address to the Reader" he states that he at first thought of burning them, lest they should bring more censure than praise on his memory ; but he had changed his mind, had learnt to be indifferent to censure, and to hope that they might do some good, but he would at all events defer their publication till after his decease. After his earlier manner, he describes himself as "Philhymno," who amidst "State earthquakes" had sought a refuge in "a vale which shady woods surround." (*Works,* i. 1—3). With a prophetic forecast which was fulfilled in one sense within narrower limits, and, in another, to a yet wider extent, than he had dreamt of, he found comfort in this thought—

" 'Twill heighten ev'n the joys of Heaven to know,
  That in my Verse the Saints hymn God below."

[i. 200.]

William Hawkins, his great-nephew and executor, and the
editor of his *Poems*, asserts that Ken had given him at Leweston
(presumably in the last months of his stay there) a full verbal
authority for their publication, and the MSS., from the general
accuracy of the text, must have been fair copied by the author
and systematically arranged, as the legacy which he wished to
leave to devout souls in the Church of a future generation. In
November, as I have said, Ken went to Lëweston, the seat of the
Hon. Mrs. Thynne, the widow of Lord Weymouth's eldest son,
Henry, where he was always a welcome guest. There, early in
the year 1711, he was seized with paralysis, which affected the
whole of one side of his body. At the beginning of March he resolved to go to Bath, in hope to find relief from the waters there
for that malady, and for the dropsy which accompanied it. Mrs.
Thynne tried to dissuade him from taking a journey for which
she saw that he had no sufficient strength, but he persisted in his
purpose, and she sent him in her carriage to Longleat.

I conjecture that his wish to travel thither was in part connected with the desire to ' set his house in order' before the final
summons. He reached Longleat on Saturday, March 10th, and
spent that evening in "adjusting his papers." We may infer
from the fact that the MSS. at Longleat, while they include the
letters to Lord Weymouth which are printed in this volume,
contain none of the letters which his numerous correspondents
must have written to Ken, no sermons or sermon-notes, or other
papers, that that adjustment must have been with him, as it was
with Bishop Butler when he destroyed his sermons and other
MSS. shortly before his death, as it had been with Queen
Mary on the first night of her fatal illness, chiefly, if not altogether, a work of destruction. Like most wise and good men, Ken
was unwilling to transmit to posterity documents which were
connected with the bitterness of the past, and the publication of
which might be painful to the writers or their representatives.

On Sunday he was confined to his room, and on Monday he
took to his bed. On the 16th physicians were sent for—Dr.
Merewether of Devizes, whose daughter was married to William

Hawkins, and Dr. Bevison of Bath—and the former came again on the 18th, and for the last time on Monday, the 19th. It was probably at the first consultation that Ken asked how long he was likely to live, and desired his physicians, as he had "no reason to be afraid of dying," to speak plainly; and when they said "about two or three days," replied, in his favourite phrase (we remember it, when he and the other Bishops presented their petition to King James), "God's will be done" (i. 308), and begged that they would let nature take her course, and use no applications which could only make him "linger in pain." He mentioned Hooper's name, and sought to send a message to him, which was too inarticulate to be understood. We do not know whether his friend Harbin (still chaplain at Longleat) was with him, or administered the Holy Eucharist to him, in his last hours. At last the end came, and Dr. Merewether enters in his Diary, perhaps as recording the dying man's last words,[1] perhaps as remembering that Ken had used those words in every letter he wrote :—

"*March* 19*th.*—*All glory be to God.* Between five and six in yᵉ morning, Thomas, late Bishop of Bath and Wells, died at Longleat." "He dozed much the day or two before he died; and what little he spake was sometimes not coherent; which, having been plied with opiates" (his power of resisting their administration had, one may assume, passed away), "seem'd to be rather the effect of dream than of distemper."

For that end, which had probably, for many months, if not years, past, never been absent from his thoughts, Ken had made two very characteristic preparations. For many years previous he had always travelled about (we are reminded, as I have said in Chapter II., of Donne's more eccentric action, of which this may have been a reminiscence) with his shroud in his portmanteau. With a sensitive delicacy of feeling, which led him to shrink from the thought of exposure to the touch of hireling hands, as they did their usual offices for a corpse, he put it on, on the very evening of his arrival at Longleat, and on the day before he died, gave notice that he had done so.[2] He had thus provided for his death. He had also pro-

---

[1] See Note, p. 205.   [2] Hawkins, pp. 43—45.

vided for his burial. He had desired that, wherever he might
die, he should be buried "in the Churchyard of the nearest
parish within his Diocese, under the East Window of the
Chancel, just at sunrising, without any manner of pomp or
ceremony besides that of the Order for Burial in the Liturgy
of the Church of England."[1] He had also prepared his epitaph,
which Bowles has reproduced in fac-simile, as in Ken's own
hand.[2] The writing is not unlike that of the will and of some
of the inscriptions in Ken's books, as *e.g.* in the *Et tu quæris
tibi grandia* and others, but differs from that of Ken's letters
in later years, and it is open to conjecture whether he
habitually used two hands for different purposes, or whether
the will and the epitaph, if in his, belong to an earlier period of
his life. The way in which the name is spelt in the latter, however ("Kenn," whereas the Bishop had always signed "Ken"),
leads me to suggest as probable, that both the documents were
written by the notary or lawyer who prepared the will. The
first of the two runs as follows:—

"The inscription order'd by Bishop Kenn for his tombe."[3]

"May the here interred Thomas, late Bp. of Bath and Wells, &
uncanonically Deprived for not transferring his Allegiance, have a
perfect consummation of Blisse, both in body and soul, at the great
Day, of which God keep me always mindfull."[4]

I incline to the conclusion that the inscription must have
been written before Kidder's death, and that this explains the
touch of bitterness in the "uncanonically deprived." He would
hardly, I think, have written thus after his resignation, or have
omitted all mention of his satisfaction, as he thought of the
character of the friend in whose favour he had resigned. For
some reason or other, perhaps for this, the inscription was not
placed over his grave, nor indeed was there any tombstone
erected to his memory. His grave was simply enclosed with an

[1] Nichol's *Literary Anecdotes,* v. 128, in Anderdon.
[2] *Life,* ii. 34.
[3] The opening phrase, as well as the spelling of the name, seems to me to
indicate the hand of a professional scribe.
[4] We have found *Requiescat in pace* in Ken's earliest extant letter (i. 124).
We note that he asks like prayers for himself at the end of his life.

iron grating, coffin-shaped, surmounted by a mitre and pastoral staff, which was placed there by Lord Weymouth.

I print the will as an Appendix to this chapter.

In accordance with his wishes, the Bishop was buried in the parish churchyard of Frome Selwood, the nearest parish of his diocese to Longleat, at sunrise, a little after five A.M., on the morning of March 21st, 1711. His funeral was attended by Lord Weymouth's steward from Longleat. The coffin was borne by twelve poor men, who carried it in turn, in relays of six. It was covered not by the " pall " of more lordly funerals, but " by a few yards of black cloth, and that given to the minister."[1] The Parish Register of Burials gives the entry, " 21 (March, 1711). Thomas, late L[d] Bishop of Bath and Wells. Deprived." [2]

One can scarcely picture a scene more touching and solemn in its simplicity, more entirely in accordance with Ken's character as one who died as he had lived, "a plaine humble man." Twelve poor men had been his favourite and honoured guests at Wells. From twelve poor men he received the last earthly ministrations to his remains. One may wish, but one can scarcely hope, that they had sung his Morning Hymn as the sun rose over his grave. I reserve all that I have to say as to the character of the life which thus reached its close for a later page.

NOTE.—KEN'S LAST WORDS.—I find in Anderdon (p. 300) the following paragraph :—

" But it was decreed he should not die anywhere but at Longleat, which is hallowed by his name, and the near neighbourhood of his grave. What place so fitting as the well-known, much-loved refuge of his last twenty years ? It was the best return he could make for all the benefits he had received from his faithful, enduring friend, Lord Weymouth : ' I can but give you my all—myself— my poor heart, and my last blessing.' " The first impression suggested by the inverted commas is that they indicate that the words which they enclose are an

---

[1] See *Athenæum* of July 25, 1874, in review of Hearne's *Correspondence*, privately printed by Frederick Ouvry. The Vicar of Frome at the time was a Mr. Jenkyns (see p. 186).

[2] Compare Mayor's *Life of Ambrose Bonwicke.*

actual quotation of words written or spoken by Ken shortly before his death, and Bishop Alexander has so taken them in his sermon (p. 286). No traces of them, however, are to be found in any contemporary record of Ken's death, and I am obliged to rest in the belief that the words in question were simply what Anderdon thought he ought to have said, what seemed to him implied in his wish to end his days at Longleat.

BISHOP KEN'S TOMB.

APPENDIX.

WILL OF BISHOP KEN.

" *In the Name of the* FATHER, SON, *and* HOLY GHOST, ONE GOD,
Blessed for ever. Amen.

"I Thomas, late Bishop of Bath and Wells, unworthy, being at
present, thankes be to God, in perfect health, both of body and
mind, doe make and appoint this my Last Will and Testament, in
manner and form following;

"I commend my Spirit into the Hands of my Heavenly Father
and my body to the Earth, in certain hope, through Jesus, my Redeemer, of a happy Resurrection.

"As to my worldly goods, I desire my debts, if I leave any, may
be first paid, and that done,

"I leave and bequeath to the Right Honourable Thomas Lord
Viscount Weymouth, in case he outlives me, all my Books, of which
his Lordship has not the Duplicates, as a memoriall of my gratitude
for his signall and continued favours.

"I leave and bequeath to the Library of the Cathedrall at Wells
all my Books of which my Lord Weymouth has the Duplicates, and
of which the Library there has nòt: or, in case I outlive my Lord,
I leave to the Library aforesaid to make choice of all of which they
have not Duplicates; and the remainder of my Books not chosen
for the Library, I leave to be divided between my two Nephews,
Isaac Walton, and John Beacham, excepting those Books which I
shall dispose of to others.[1]

---

[1] It is rather a curious circumstance, that of all these books, there are only
two or three which have Ken's name in his own hand. One is in the Library at
Longleat,—a copy of DIOGENES LAERTIUS,—on the Fly-leaf of which is this
memorandum, in Ken's handwriting, written, apparently, shortly after his
deprivation—

"*Si invenero Gratiam in oculis Domini, reducet me. Si autem dixerit mihi,
Non placet, præsto sum, faciat quod bonum est coram se.*   "THO. KEN."

Bowles mentions à small Greek Testament, "*Amstellodami, apud Gulielmum
Blaeu,* 1633," on the Blank-leaf of which the following notices are written:
"Guil. Coker, ex dono clarissimi viri Thomæ Ken."
"Char. Coker."
"Ex dono Car. Sutton Coker."
"Ad Episcopatum Bath et Wellen; A.D. 1685, cvecti; ab eodem, anno 1690, .
ejecti. J. Beavor."

"I give and bequeath to my Sister Ken the sum of Ten pounds. To my niece Krienberg the sum of Fifty pounds.[1]

"I give and bequeath to my Nephew, John Beacham, the sum of Fifty pounds, and to my Nephew, William Beacham, the sum of Forty pounds.[2]

"I give and bequeath to my Nephew, Isaac Walton, the sum of Ten pounds, and to my Niece Hawkins, his sister, the sum of Ten pounds, and to her daughter, Ann Hawkins, the sum of Fifty pounds, and to her son, William Hawkins, the sum of Fifty pounds, and to my Niece, Elizabeth Hawkins, the sum of Twenty pounds,

"This book, from its having been the Manual of that great and good man, Bishop Ken, is invaluable. G. H. Bath and Wells.—Wells, 1829."

Thus, the book appears to have been given by Ken, to Dr. William Coker, a Physician in Winchester;—to have passed out of that family to Dr. Beavor, Rector of Trent, in Somersetshire, Fellow of Corpus Christi College, Oxford, and from his possession into that of the late Bishop of Bath and Wells, Dr. George Henry Law. Bowles, who had seen the book, says, "So familiar was Ken with the sublime chapter on the Resurrection, that at this present day—so many years since—the small volume opens generally of its own accord at the 15th chapter of the Epistle to the Corinthians." Bowles's *Life of Ken*, vol. ii. p. 93. I am able to carry the succession two stages further, and to state that this Greek Testament was given by the late Dean Law, of Gloucester, son of Bishop Law, of Bath and Wells, to Bishop Ellicott, and is now in his possession.

Several years ago, Mr. Thomas Kerslake, of Bristol, bought at a miscellaneous furniture auction, at Cricklade, another "Pocket Greek Testament," which had belonged to Ken, and which he thus entered in his Book Catalogue for the year 1849:

"5384. *Bp. KEN'S POCKET GREEK TESTAMENT:*—Novum Testamentum Gr. Curcellæi, *Amst.*, *Elzevir*, 1658, 18mo., *in the old black fish-skin, with silver corners, with a most interesting autograph of that eminent Christian Soldier*, 7l. 7s.

" *On one of the fly leaves is written :*—'T. K.——Tu Grande illud q^d in terris Quæsivi——Et inveni——Phar: Fiennes.' Pharamond Fiennes was a Fellow of New College. He died young. I conjecture that Ken gave him the book, and wrote the inscription for his guidance.

" *On the opposite leaf :*—'Et tu Quæris tibi Grandia? Noli Quærere.—— Tho: Ken.'—*under which, in Greek*,—1 Tim. iv. 15. *and* 1 Cor. iv. 6."

This interesting volume is in the possession of the Rev. A. Wyndham, of North Bradley, Trowbridge. I have already referred (i. 139) to the same inscription in another book.

[1] "Sister Ken" was the widow of Ion Ken, daughter of Sir Thomas Vernon, mother of the Ken who died in Cyprus (see i. p. 90). "Niece Krienberg" was Martha, daughter of this sister, and married to Christopher Fred. Krienberg, Resident in London of his Electoral Highness of Hanover, afterwards George I. Ken's family clearly did not follow him into the ranks of the Non-jurors.

[2] The two Beachams were sons of Ken's sister, Martha, and James Beacham, of London, goldsmith. John was Fellow of Trinity College, Oxford; William of New College. The latter died within a year of the Bishop (see i. p. 12).

to be paid to her on the day of marriage, or when my executor shall see it most for her advantage.[1]

"I give and bequeath to the English Deprived Clergy the sum of Fifty pounds; to the Deprived Officers the sum of Forty pounds, and to the Deprived Scotch Clergy the sum of Fifty pounds.[2]

"To the poor of the parish where I am buried the sum of Five pounds, and to my servant who shall be with me at my death the sum of Ten pounds.[3]

"I bequeath to the Library at Bath all my French, Italian, and Spanish Books.[4]

[1] Isaac Walton has met us frequently (pp. 123, 152), as Canon of Salisbury and Rector of Poulshot, Wilts, at both of which places Ken often stayed with him after his deprivation. He died unmarried in 1719. His sister, Anne, was the widow of William Hawkins, Prebendary of Winchester, and Rector of Droxford, Hants, who died 1691. Their son, William Hawkins, barrister-at-law, was Ken's executor and biographer, published his three sermons in 1711, and in 1721 edited his *Poems* in four volumes 8vo. He married Jane, daughter of John Merewether, M.D., who attended Ken in his last illness. I conjecture that Ken's coffee-pot, of which an engraving is given in this volume (p. 230) and which is in our Cathedral Library, with other Ken relics, came to her as well as the £50. She resided with her brother till his death, and remained at Salisbury afterwards. The coffee-pot bears the Hawkins arms, passed through Ann Hawkins, daughter of William, to her husband, the Rev. John Hawes, Rector of Wilton, then to his son, the Rev. Herbert Hawes, Rector of Bemerton (George Herbert's parish), and was in his possession when Bowles wrote his *Life of Ken* (1830). Mr. Hawes left it to Mr. William Hayter, who left instructions that, after his wife's decease, it should go to the Rev. R. W. Barnes, of Probus, Cornwall, and Prebendary of Exeter. Shortly before his death Mr. Barnes, in 1884, hearing of the Ken Memorial Window, which was about to be placed in Wells Cathedral, sent it me on the condition that it should be kept in the custody of the Dean of Wells for the time being, as a memorial of the Bishop. What one may call the pedigree of the coffee-pot is thus well established, and Bowles (i. p. 7), who dedicated the second volume of his *Life* to Herbert Hawes, speaks of it as "the companion of all Ken's vicissitudes." Coffee-houses, we may note, are reported by Ant. à Wood to have been first opened at Oxford in 1650, during Ken's time there (p. 253 *n*). His use of that liquid may have dated from his earlier years. I find no trace of the niece Elizabeth. Bowles (*l. c.*) mentions a watch, which was also in the possession of Herbert Hawes, the history of which I have not been able to trace.

[2] The legacy indicates the same charitable interest in the deprived Clergy which we have seen in pp. 98, 171. A like interest in the Non-juring officers who had lost their commissions appears indirectly in the explanation given in p. 96 for their not being included in the scheme which brought Ken and the other Bishops before the Privy Council. The deprived Episcopal Clergy of Scotland were obviously as near his heart as when he wrote his letter to Burnet (p. 49).

[3] The £5 went, of course, to the poor of Frome. Of Ken's personal servant I have not been able to learn anything.

[4] I have, in i. 94, 251, 259, referred to some of these books.

"I leave and bequeath to my very worthy dear Friend, Mrs. Margaret Mathew, dwelling in Caerdiff, my woodden Cup lined with gold, and Lord Clarendon's History, in six volumes in red Turkey guilt.[1]

"I bequeath my little Patin and Chalice guilt, to the Parish, where I am buried, for the use of sick persons who desire the Holy Sacrament.[2]

"As for my Religion, I die in the Holy Catholick and Apostolick Faith, professed by the whole Church, before the disunion of East and West: more particularly I dye in the *COMMUNION OF THE CHURCH OF ENGLAND*, as it stands distinguished from all Papall and Puritan Innovations, and as it adheres to the doctrine of the Cross.[3]

"I beg pardon of all whom I have any way offended: and I entirely forgive all those who have any ways offended me. I acknowledge myself a very great and miserable Sinner; but dye in humble confidence, that, on my repentance, I shall be accepted in the Beloved.

"I appoint my Nephew, William Hawkins, to be my sole Executor of this my last Will and Testament, who, I know, will observe the directions punctually, which I leave for my Buriell.

"Witness my hand and Seal,

"THOMAS BATH & WELLS, Depr.

"Signed and delivered in the presence of

"FRA. GREEN = JO. JENKINS."[4]

---

[1] I have succeeded in identifying Mrs. Mathew with an intimate friend of the Misses Kemeys of Naish Court (p. 175).

[2] The "Patin and Chalice" have remained as sacred heirlooms, attached to the Church of St. John the Baptist, Frome. I am indebted to Mr. William Singer for the drawing from which the engraving on p. 190 is taken. The late Vicar of Frome, the Rev. W. J. E. Bennett, told me, about three years ago, that he was often specially asked, as a favour, by the older parishioners, that they might receive their last Communion from it. There is no Hall mark or date, but both the vessels have the initials "R. P.," probably those of the silversmith who made them. The present Vicar, the Hon. and Rev. A. Hanbury Tracy, informs me that a small gold crucifix, which Mr. Bennett fixed to the Cross on the altar table, is traditionally believed to have belonged to Ken, but I have no further evidence of the fact.

[3] The declaration of Ken's faith may be compared with that of Izaak Walton given in i. 24. The "doctrine of the Cross," as I have shown in p. 73, is that of passive obedience and non-resistance.

[4] The Will was proved by William Hawkins, April 24th, 1711.

CHAPTER XXVII.

AMONG the subjects which present themselves for examination after the actual narrative of Ken's life has been completed, the Hymns on which his world-wide fame rests, and with which his name is inseparably associated, seem to have a preferential claim. They present not a few points, both difficult and interesting, for inquiry.

For the most part so little is known of them beyond the five or six verses that have found their way into hymn-books, that it will be well to begin by giving the three Hymns in full from the edition of the Winchester *Manual* of 1697, noting in italics the various readings of that of 1712.

A MORNING HYMN.

AWAKE my Soul, and with the Sun,
Thy daily stage of Duty run;
Shake off dull Sloth, and early [*joyful*] rise,
To pay thy Morning Sacrifice.

Redeem thy mispent time that's past,
Live this day, as if 'twere thy last:
T'improve thy Talent take due care,
Gainst the great Day thy self prepare.
[*Thy precious Time mis-spent, redeem;
Each present Day thy last esteem;
Improve thy Talent with due care,
For the Great Day thy self prepare.*]

Let all thy Converse [*In Conversation*] be sincere,
Thy [*Keep*] Conscience as the Noon-day [*Noon-tide*] clear;
Think how all-seeing God thy ways,
And all thy secret Thoughts surveys.

Influenc'd by [*By influence of*] the Light Divine,
Let thy own Light in good Works [*to others*] shine:
Reflect all Heaven's propitious ways [*Rays*],
In ardent Love, and chearful Praise.

Wake and lift up thyself, my Heart,
And with the Angels bear thy part,
Who all night long unwearied sing,
Glory [*High Praise*] to the Eternal King.

Awake, awake, [*I wake, I wake*],[1] ye Heavenly Choire,
May your Devotion me inspire,
That I, like you, my Age may spend,
Like you, may on my God attend.

May I, like you, in God delight,
Have all day long my God in sight,
Perform, like you, my Maker's Will;
O may I never more do ill!

Had I your Wings, to Heaven I'd flie,
But God shall that defect supply,
And my Soul wing'd with warm desire,
Shall all day long to Heav'n aspire.

Glory [*All Praise*] to Thee who safe hast kept,
And hast refresht me whilst I slept.
Grant, Lord, when I from death shall wake,
I may of endless Light partake.

I would not wake, nor rise again,
Ev'n Heav'n itself I would disdain,
Wert not Thou there to be enjoy'd,
And I in Hymns to be imploy'd.

Heav'n is, dear Lord, wheree'r Thou art,
O never then from me depart;
For to my Soul 'tis Hell to be,
But for one moment without [*void of*] Thee.

Lord, I my vows to Thee renew,
Scatter my sins as Morning dew,
Guard my first springs of Thought, and Will,
And with Thy self my Spirit fill.

1 This is a later variation.

Direct, controul, suggest this day,
All I design, or do, or say ;
That all my Powers, with all their might,
In Thy sole Glory may unite.

Praise God, from whom all blessings flow,
Praise Him, all Creatures here below,
Praise Him above, y' Angelick [*ye Heavenly*] Host,
Praise Father, Son, and Holy Ghost.

AN EVENING HYMN.

GLORY [*All Praise*] to Thee, my God, this night,
For all the Blessings of the Light ;
Keep me, O keep me, King of Kings,
Under [*Beneath*] Thy own Almighty Wings.

Forgive me, Lord, for Thy dear Son,
The ill that I this day have done,
That with the World, my self, and Thee,
I, ere I sleep, at peace may be.

Teach me to live, that I may dread
The Grave as little as my Bed ;
Teach me to die, that so I may
Triumphing rise at the last day.
[*To die, that this vile Body may
Rise glorious at the Awful Day.*]

O may my Soul on Thee repose,
And with sweet sleep mine [*my*] Eye-lids close ;
Sleep that may me more vig'rous make,
To serve my God when I awake !

When in the night I sleepless lie,
My Soul with Heavenly Thoughts supply ;
Let no ill Dreams disturb my Rest,
No powers of darkness me molest.

Dull sleep of Sense me to deprive,
I am but half my days alive ;
Thy faithful Lovers, Lord, are griev'd
To lie so long of Thee bereav'd.

But [*Yet*] though sleep o'r my frailty reigns,
Let it not hold me long in chains,
And now and then let loose my Heart,
Till it an Hallelujah dart.

The faster sleep the sense doth bind, [*the senses binds,*]
The more unfetter'd is the Mind ; [*are our Minds ;*]
O may my Soul from matter free,
Thy unvail'd Goodness waking see !
[*Thy Loveliness unclouded see.*]

O, when shall I, in endless day,
For ever chase dark sleep away,
And endless praise with th' Heavenly Choir
[*And Hymns with the Supernal Choir*]
Incessant sing, and never tire ?

You, my blest Guardian, [*O may my Guardian,*] whilst
I sleep,
Close to my Bed your [*his*] Vigils keep,
Divine Love into me [*His Love angelical*] instil,
Stop all the avenues of ill ;

Thought to thought with my Soul converse,
Celestial joys to me rehearse,
[*May he Celestial joy rehearse,*
And thought to thought with me converse.]
And [*Or*] in my stead all the night long,
Sing to my God a grateful Song.

Praise God from whom all Blessings flow,
Praise Him all Creatures here below,
Praise Him above y' Angelick [*ye Heavenly*] Host,
Praise Father, Son, and Holy Ghost.

A MIDNIGHT HYMN.

LORD, now my Sleep does me forsake,
[*My God, now I from Sleep awake,*]
The sole possession of me take ;
Let no vain fancy me illude,
No one impure desire intrude.
[*From midnight Terrors me secure,*
And guard my Heart from Thoughts impure.]

Blest Angels! while we silent lie,
Your Hallelujahs sing on high,
You, ever wakeful near the Throne,
Prostrate, adore the Three in One.
[*You joyful hymn the ever Bless'd,*
Before the Throne, and never rest.]

I now, awake, do with you joyn,
To praise our God in Hymns Divine:
[*I with yon Choir celestial join*
In offering up a Hymn divine.]
With you in Heav'n I hope to dwell,
And bid the Night and World farewell.

My Soul, when I shake off this dust,
Lord, in Thy Arms I will entrust;
O make me Thy peculiar care,
Some heav'nly Mansion me [*Some Mansion for my Soul*]
    prepare.

Give me a place at Thy Saints' feet,
Or some fall'n Angel's vacant seat;
I'll strive to sing as loud as they,
Who sit above in brighter day.

O may I always ready stand,
With my Lamp burning in my hand;
May I in sight of Heav'n rejoyce,
Whene'er I hear the Bridegroom's voice!

Glory [*All Praise*] to Thee in light arraid,
Who light Thy dwelling place hast made,
An immense [*A boundless*] Ocean of bright beams,
From Thy All-glorious Godhead streams.

The Sun, in its Meridian height,
Is very darkness in Thy sight:
My Soul, O lighten, and enflame,
With Thought and Love of Thy great name.

Blest Jesu, Thou, on Heav'n intent,
Whole Nights hast in Devotion spent,
But I, frail Creature, soon am tir'd,
And all my Zeal is soon expir'd.

My Soul, how canst thou weary grow
Of ante-dating Heav'n [*Bliss*] below,
In sacred Hymns, and Divine [*Heavenly*] Love,
Which will Eternal be above?

Shine on me, Lord, new life impart,
Fresh ardours kindle in my Heart;
One ray of Thy All-quick'ning light
Dispels the sloth and clouds of night.

Lord, lest the Tempter me surprize,
Watch over Thine own Sacrifice,
All loose, all idle Thoughts cast out,
And make my very Dreams devout.

Praise God, from whom all Blessings flow,
Praise Him all Creatures here below,
Praise Him above y' Angelick [*ye Heavenly*] Host,
Praise Father, Son, and Holy Ghost.

I. We naturally ask, when and where did Ken write the Hymns, with what circumstances were they connected, of what inner experience were they the outcome. The answers to these questions are various and perplexing. The honour of having witnessed their birth is claimed by nearly as many places as the cities of Greece which boasted of having given birth to Homer. Winchester finds it hard to separate them from the *Manual* for his scholars, in which they first appeared in their completeness. Brightstone believes that they were the fruit of Ken's meditative hours, as he walked to and fro, along the yew-tree hedge in the Rectory garden. We, at Wells, are wont to point to the Terrace overlooking the moat, on the south of the Palace Garden, as the place where Ken composed them. Naish Court is not altogether willing to surrender the thought that the Hymns were written for, and sung by, the sisters of the "good virgins' nunnery." "*We* do think," said a farmer from near Longleat to me once, "that he wrote those hymns in the big house there."

To ascertain the date of the Hymns may be of some help towards deciding these rival claims.

The *Manual for Winchester Scholars* was first printed

anonymously in 1674. It passed through five editions[1] before the sixth appeared with Ken's name, as Bishop, in 1687. The earliest edition which contains the Hymns is the eighth, that of 1695, after his deprivation.[2] This, of course, fixes a *terminus ad quem*, but the *terminus a quo* is still to seek.

At this stage of the inquiry a new fact presents itself which has not, so far as I know, come under the notice of any of Ken's previous editors or biographers, and for which I am indebted to Mr. A. Clarke, of Bristol.

In 1693 a curious little volume, two inches square, was published with the following title-page:

" *Verbum Sempiternum.* The Third Edition, with Amendments. London. Printed for Tho. James, and are to be sold at the Printing Press in Mincing Lane, and most Booksellers in London or Westminster." [3]

It has the *imprimatur* of "G. Lancaster, Oct. 6, 1693." The fly-leaf has the shorter title of "The Bible." A portrait of "His Illustrious Highness, the Duke of Gloucester," the son of the then Princess Anne, to whom there is a dedication as follows, faces the title-page:

"THE EPISTLE.

"Most Hopeful Prince, into Your hands I give,
     The sum of that which makes us ever live,
And tho' the Volume and the Work be small,
     Yet it contains the sum of All in All;
And therefore crave, Your Highness would accept
     This pledge of my great duty and respect."

There is next an Address to the Reader in the same metre, signed "J. Taylor." The book itself consists of an

[1] See the complete list of Editions by the late G. W. Napier, of Alderley Edge, in *Notes and Queries*, 5th Series, vol. v., 416.

[2] Anderdon, not knowing of the editions of 1695 and 1697, gives 1700 as the date of the earliest publication of the Hymns. In the title-page of that edition they are said to be added, "not in the former edition by the same author," but this was apparently a publisher's "puff," as they are found in the copy of that of 1695 in the Bodleian Library.

[3] The *Verbum Sempiternum* was republished from this edition by Longman & Co. in 1849.

epitome of the Bible in the same style, at about the rate of a verse *per* book. When we come to the New Testament there is a fresh title-page, in which *Salvator Mundi* takes the place of *Verbum Sempiternum*, the rest continuing as before. Here also there is an Address to the Reader with the signature of J. Taylor.

Mr. G. K. Fortescue, of the British Museum Library, informs me that the *Verbum Sempiternum* is one of the numerous works of John Taylor, known as the " Water Poet," and appears in the folio edition of those works in 1630, dedicated to Charles I. Taylor died in 1654. An edition of this work, now in the British Museum Library, was published in 1693—the same year as that of the volume I am now speaking of—dedicated to Queen Mary. The dedication in all three editions is identical, with the variation of " Most mightie Soveraigne," in 1630, and " Most mighty Princess," in that dedicated to Mary. The volume which I have described—and this is the reason why I have described it thus fully—ends with the following verses :

A PRAYER FOR THE MORNING.

Glory to Thee, my God : who safe hast kept,
  And me refresh'd, while I securely slept ;
Lord, this day guard me, lest I may transgress,
  And all my undertakings guide and bless.

And since to thee my vows I now renew,
  Scatter my by-past sins as Morning Dew,
That so Thy Glory may shine clear this day,
  In all I either think, or do, or say.

ANOTHER, FOR THE EVENING.

Forgive me, dearest Lord, for thy dear Son,
  The many ills that I this day have done,
That with the world, my self, and then with thee,
  I, ere I sleep, at perfect peace may be.

Teach me to live that I may ever dread
  The Grave, as little as I do my Bed ;
Keep me this night, O keep me, King of Kings,
  Secure under thine own Almighty Wings.

It will be admitted that the resemblance between these prayers and the corresponding verses in Ken's Hymns is too close to be accidental, and the question presents itself how we can account for that resemblance, seeing that the Hymns did not appear in the *Manual* till two years later. Critics might seem to have plausible grounds for suggesting that Ken found the language of the "Prayers" suitable for his purpose, and incorporated them, without acknowledgment, in the Hymns he was then about to publish, altering their metre, accordingly, from lines of ten syllables to lines of eight. I do not adopt that theory, and I suggest another as equally solving the problem, and more in harmony with Ken's character. My conjecture is that though Ken's Hymns were not published in the *Manual* till 1695, they were previously accessible in some other form, probably in that of leaflets, with, or less probably, without, music. That conjecture seems to me to receive some confirmation from the following facts—

(1.) In the earlier editions of the *Manual* (1675, 1677, 1681, 1692), at the beginning of the work, there are some "*Directions in General*," addressed to Ken's ideal scholar, the young Philotheus. Among those "directions" we find this: "Be sure to sing the Morning and Evening Hymn in your chamber devoutly." Unless we assume that the words refer to the "*Jam lucis orto sidere*" in common use at Winchester (see i. 34), and to some corresponding Latin evening hymn, say that for daily use at Compline in the Roman Breviary, "*Te lucis ante terminum*," which is scarcely, I think, probable, it seems natural to think of them as indicating some English hymns with which the young scholar was familiar, and as natural to assume that these were Ken's.[1]

(2.) Playford's *Harmonia Sacra* (Part II.), published in 1693, and dedicated to Ken, contains his Evening Hymn with music by Jeremiah Clark, and this seems distinct evidence of the existence of that hymn, and presumably therefore of the

---

[1] It is possible, however, that Ken's directions may refer to the compilation from the Psalms of the Vulgate which were to be used by the Scholars of Winchester "*in cubiculo*" (i. 104). It is noticeable that in the directions for Midnight in the *Manual* (Round, p. 376), he gives four distinct ejaculations for his *Philotheus* to use, but makes no allusion to the Midnight Hymn.

Morning Hymn also, prior to the publication of the *Verbum Sempiternum* in the same year.

(3.) I am informed by a correspondent that the *Catalogue* of the Society for Promoting Christian Knowledge for 1707, contains, in addition to Ken's *Exposition of the Church Catechism* and his *Directions for Prayer*, " *Three Hymns*, viz. for Morning, Evening, and Midnight. By the Author of the *Manual of Prayers for Winchester College*. (C. Brome). Price 2d., or 10s. per hundred." The date of the catalogue is, of course, too late to allow it to decide the question, but it seems to make it probable that the hymns had previously been printed in the same separate form.[1]

On the whole, therefore, I incline to the conclusion that the hymns were written prior to the first edition of the *Manual*, and that they belong, therefore, to the earlier Winchester period of Ken's life (1666—1674), and about seven years after his election as a Fellow of the College. If I am right, even Wells must resign the honour of having heard the Hymns when they were sung for the first time, and Winchester may cherish the thought that they came from Ken's pen and lips there, and were accompanied by him on his lute, or on the organ which was the cherished treasure of his chamber in the College.

II. Side by side with this question as to the date of composition is another, of much less importance, as to the reading of the first and most familiar lines in that for the Evening. We have the two forms—

" Glory to Thee, my God, this night,"

and

" All praise to Thee, my God, this night."

The latter has the merit of being metrically more accurate, and therefore better fitted for music. The former has the interest of presenting a closer parallelism to that " All glory be to God " which was the superscription of every letter that Ken

---

[1] The growing popularity of the hymns is shown by their appearance in a devotional book with the title, *A New Year's Gift. Prayers, &c.*, which, having reached a fourth edition in 1685, appeared in 1709 with " Morning and Evening Hymns," by Thomas, late Bishop of Bath and Wells.

wrote. The question which of the two readings was the original, and whether the alteration was sanctioned by Ken himself, has been discussed with an almost exhaustive fulness by Lord Selborne, Mr. Anderdon, and others. I will endeavour to state the facts as briefly as I can. Some of them are stated for the first time.

(1.) The first line of the Morning Hymn in the *Verbum Sempiternum* (1693)—

"Glory to Thee, my God, who safe hast kept,"

is strongly in favour of that having been the original reading of the Hymns before they were incorporated with the *Manual*.

(2.) The contemporary text of the Evening Hymn, set in a *cantata solo*, in Playford's *Harmonia Sacra* (Book II.), on the other hand, gives "All praise to Thee." As Book I. is dedicated to Ken, it is probable that he sanctioned the variation. I am inclined to think, from the facts that follow, that Ken preferred the "Glory," but yielded to the wishes of a musical expert.

(3.) The "Glory" appears in the 1695 edition of the *Manual*, when the Hymns were first published, and holds its ground through all the five editions between that and 1712. In that of 1705, Brome, the registered proprietor of the copyright of the *Manual* since 1680, in an "Advertisement," states that Ken "absolutely disowns" and repudiates every text of the Hymns (notably that published in a *Conference between the Soul and the Body*, with a commendatory preface by Dodwell) as "very false and incorrect" but that which he then published. The text in the *Conference* gives "All praise" and many other alterations, with two new stanzas at the end of the Evening Hymn. Another book, called *New Year's Gift*, appeared in 1709, giving the hymns as printed in the *Conference* and was met by Brome in the same way. So far, the case for "Glory" is strengthened, up to the year of Ken's death.

(4.) In 1712, however, the year after Ken's death, Brome published an edition of the *Manual* in which "All praise" takes the place of "Glory," and that text continued to be reproduced in later editions, and found its way into general use.

Lord Selborne[1] assumes that this alteration must have had Ken's sanction in a revision of the text shortly before his death, and therefore adopted it in his *Book of Praise.* To me it seems more probable that Brome, or the editor he employed, adopted the "All praise," partly on the strength of the text in Playford's *Harmonia,* partly as being, what it obviously is, the more singable of the two ; possibly, I will admit, with the same measure of approval from Ken himself, and on the same grounds, in the last months of his life, as he had given to Playford's text. In yet two other points Playford's text differs from that which appeared in the *Manual* from 1695 to 1709. Where, in the Evening Hymn, the latter gives—

> " Dull sleep of sense me to deprive,
>   I am but half my time alive ;
>   Thy faithful Lovers, Lord, are grieved,
>   To lie so long of Thee bereaved,"

the former has—

> " My dearest Love, how am I grieved
>   To lie so long of Thee bereaved ;
>   Dull sense of sleep me to deprive ;
>   I am but half my time alive."

Again, where the *Manual* of 1695 gives—

> " You, my best Guardians, whilst I sleep
>   Close to my Bed your vigils keep,
>   Divine Love into me instil,
>   Stop all the avenues of ill.
>
> " Thought to thought with my soul converse,
>   Celestial joys to me rehearse ;
>   And in my stead, all the night long,
>   Sing to my God a grateful song,"

Playford's text, on the other hand, gives one verse only, as follows :

[1] In a letter published with the three Hymns, by Daniel Sedgwick, 1864. Lord Selborne even conjectures that the author of the *Conference* may have seen, in Dodwell's hands, or at Winchester, copies with MS. corrections in the Bishop's hand, which he accordingly reproduced.

> " You, my best Guardians, whilst I sleep,
>   Around my bed your vigils keep,
>   And, in my stead, all the night long
>   Sing to my God a grateful song."

The transposition in the first case, and the expansion of one verse into two in the second, are changes which we may legitimately regard as the result of Ken's own revision subsequent to 1693, the date of Playford's text.

In the edition of 1712 we find the two verses again altered, and apparently for the same reason, as Lord Selborne points out, as that which Ken gives (see i. 101) for a corresponding change, substituting an optative form for a direct invocation, in the prose devotional exercises of the *Manual*—

> " [*O may my Guardian*], while I sleep,
>   Close to my bed [*his*] vigils keep ;
>   [*His love angelical instil*],
>   Stop all the avenues of ill !

> " [*May he*] celestial joy rehearse,
>   And thought to thought with me converse ;
>   Or in my stead all the night long,
>   Sing to my God a grateful song ! "

III. Ken has been supposed by some writers to have borrowed, in greater or less measure, from hymns by Sir Thomas Browne in his *Religio Medici*, and by Flatman, who published a volume of *Poems and Hymns* in 1674, and it seems, therefore, desirable to give the passages to which he is supposed to be indebted.

SIR THOMAS BROWNE.

> " The night is come, like to the Day ;
>   Depart not thou, Great God, away.
>   Let not my sins, black as the Night,
>   Eclipse the Lustre of thy Light.

> " Keep still in my Horizon, for to me
>   The Sun makes not the Day, but thee.
>   Thou, whose Nature cannot sleep,
>   On my Temples Sentry keep.

" Guard me 'gainst those watchful Foes,
  Whose Eyes are open while mine close ;
  Let no Dreams my Head infest,
  But such as Jacob's temples blest.

" While I do rest, my Soul advance,
  Make my Sleep a holy Trance,
  That I may, my Rest being wrought,
  Awake into some holy Thought,
  And with as active Vigour run
  My Course, as doth the nimble Sun.

" Sleep is a Death ; Oh make me try
  By sleeping what it is to die,
  And as gently lay my Head
  On my grave, as now my Bed.

" Howe'er I rest, great God, let me
  Awake again at last with thee ;
  And thus assur'd, behold I lie
  Securely, or to wake or die.

" These are my drowsy Days,—in vain
  I do now wake to sleep again ;
  O come that Hour when I shall never
  Sleep again, but wake for ever ! "

FLATMAN.

" Awake my soul, awake mine eyes,
  Awake my drowsy faculties,
  Look up and see the unwearied sun
  Already has his race begun.

  Arise my soul, and thou, my voice,
  In songs of praise early rejoice.
  O great Creator, heavenly King,
  Thy praises let me ever sing.
  Thy power has made, thy goodness kept,
  My fenceless body while I slept,
  Let one day more be given me,
  From all the powers of darkness free.
  O keep my heart from sin secure,
  My life unblameable and pure,
  That when the last of all my days is come,
  Cheerful and fearless I may wait my doom."

I confess that I do not find in the passages quoted any evidence of indebtedness having the character of conscious reproduction. Ken may have read them, and they may have been floating in his mind, but the parallelisms are not more than we might expect to find in devout poems written with a like spirit and for a like occasion. If I were to think of any sources from which Ken drew—but even here I am disposed to think that the derivation was unconscious—I should look rather to the Hymns for Matins and Lauds, for Vespers and Compline, in the Roman Breviary, notably to the *Jam lucis orto sidere* and the *Te lucis ante terminum*, but I do not find, even in these, any instances of direct parallelism (see i. p. 34).

IV. *The wider use of Ken's Hymns.*—It would be an interesting element of the religious history of the eighteenth century to ascertain when and how Ken's Morning and Evening Hymns found their way into general congregational use. I cannot pretend to have made an exhaustive study of the question, but it may be worth while to put together such facts as I have met with in the course of my inquiries. I shall welcome any additions or corrections.[1] The Hymns do not appear together in the *Supplement* to Tate and Brady's version of the Psalms, published in 1699, nor in any subsequent editions, till we find the Morning Hymn in one published by J. Harrison for the Company of Stationers in 1789, and the Evening Hymn in an Oxford edition of 1801. The Morning Hymn appears with it shortly afterwards (I cannot say in what year), and both have kept their place in all editions of the *Supplement* since printed. In the meantime, however, both the Hymns had appeared in some of the earlier collections of Hymns for congregational use by English clergymen between 1750—60. It will be noted that this coincides roughly with the influence of the early Methodist revival, under the influence of the two Wesleys.

Since the publication of the *Supplement*, subsequent to 1801, it would require a wider knowledge of Hymnology than that to which I can lay claim, to say in what English-speaking community they have not been used, the Society of Friends excepted, whose congregational worship excludes all hymns. Notably they have found their way into the hymn-

[1] I am mainly indebted, for the facts that follow, to Mr. William S. Brodie.

books published within the last few years by the three great sections of Scotch Presbyterians, the Established Church, the Free Church, and the United Presbyterians.   Here and there, as is the fate of all hymns, they have been subject to alterations at the caprice of compilers,[1] and no collection, as far as I know, has printed more than from four to ten verses, selected at discretion.   They have probably been translated into many languages, in connexion with the work of the Society for the Propagation of the Gospel and the Church Missionary Society, and in other fields of Mission labour; but my direct knowledge does not go beyond a Telugu version, published by the C.M.S. for their Masulipatam Mission, a Maori version for New Zealand, one in Dutch for South Africa, used both in Church of England and in Wesleyan Missions, and one in Kafirland. Among translations, not for congregational use, by scholars for scholars, I may note one into Greek verse by the Rev. R. Greswell (Oxford, 1851), and into Latin by Dr. Charles Wordsworth, Bishop of St. Andrews.[2]

If one were to pass from the public to the private use of these hymns, a long list might be made out of those who have found their lives strengthened, or their deathbeds cheered, by the words with which Ken cheered and strengthened his own soul.   Foremost and nearest of these comes the name of Robert Nelson, of whom Samuel Wesley, the father of John and Charles—himself, like both his sons, a writer of hymns, among others of one of singular beauty, under the name of " Eupolis "[3] —records, from personal knowledge, that he was in the habit of singing Ken's hymns.[4]   Of Colonel Gardiner, Doddridge reports that the Midnight Hymn was often on his lips.

[1] Of fifty editions, says Anderdon (p. 114), not one follows Ken's own version.

[2] *The College of S. Mary Winton.* Oxford, 1848. Printed also in *Anni Christiani,* &c. Edinburgh, 1880.

[3] The name has led to the appearance of the hymn in some collections of British Poets as " From the Greek of Eupolis." The only known Greek author of that name did not write hymns.

[4] Nelson appended the three hymns to his *Practice of True Devotion,* and adds (I take the quotation from the edition of 1708, p. 28), " The daily repeating of them will make you perfect in them, and the good fruit of them will abide with you all your days."—Abbey, on *Robert Nelson and his Friends,* in *English Church in the Eighteenth Century,* Ch. ii.

The last book that was in the hands of John Keble, of all
Anglican divines the likest to Ken "in look and tone," was
Lord Selborne's *Book of Praise*, which he sent for that
it might help him to say all the verses of the Evening
Hymn,[1] which he failed to remember, but which were read
to him at his desire.   Were my knowledge of the deathbeds
of devout Christians wider than it is, I doubt not that the
time would fail me to tell of the thousands of those whose
spiritual life was linked with Ken's hymns, which they learnt
in their childhood, which nourished and sustained them in the
changes and chances of their lives, and which seemed to them,
as they stood on the verge of the unseen, anticipations of the
songs of Heaven.

Yes, Ken's ideal of Hymnotheo was realised for him, but not
as he expected.   He dwelt, in the last years of his life, on the
fairly copied MSS. which he left behind him, and, it may be,
seemed to hear the praises of a distant age.   The four octavo
volumes appeared in 1721, were little noticed, if at all, at the
time, and were soon forgotten.   Epics, Anodynes, Pastorals,
Hymns on the Festivals, anticipating the *Christian Year*—
these have all vanished from men's knowledge.   Few of my
readers will have heard, till they read this volume, of *Edmund*
or *Hymnotheo*, fewer still of *Damoret and Dorilla*.   And
yet his fame has been wider than he dreamt of, and those
primitiæ of his earlier years (I have all but proved, I think,
that the Hymns were written in 1674) have spread far and
wide, to continents and islands of which he had never heard,
have been sung wherever the English tongue is spoken, and have
passed into the languages alike of ancient civilisation and bar-
baric rudeness.   If we may think of the souls of the departed as
knowing aught of what passes on earth, we may rightly deem
that it is one of the minstrel's joys in Paradise to feel that his
words mingle, with ever-increasing frequency, and in many
tongues, with the minstrelsy of the angelic choir, of which, even
in this life, he felt himself a member.

V. *Music of Ken's Hymns.*—My want of musical knowledge
prevents my writing on this subject in the character of an
expert, and I must content myself with reproducing what

[1] Miss Yonge, *Musings on the Christian Year*, p. 162.

I have learnt from others. Hawkins (p. 5) relates that Ken was used to "sing his Morning Hymn, to his lute, daily, before he put on his clothes," and Bowles infers, naturally enough, the three Hymns being all in the same metre, that the same tune served for all of them.[1] Anderdon (p. 122) reports a tradition in the Fenwick family, of Hallaton, in Leicestershire, that there also he "used to sing his Hymns to the accompaniment of a spinet." We know, also, that he had an organ in his chambers at Winchester. If I am right in my conclusions as to the date and history of the Hymns, this was probably the tune to which the *Philotheus* of the *Manual* was directed to sing his Morning Hymn. What this tune was there is, I believe, no direct evidence, but Bowles (ii. 17) supplies a chain of tradition which makes it probable that it was an adaptation of an ancient melody by Tallis, "the Chaucer of the English Cathedral Quires," who was organist of the Chapel Royal under Henry VIII., Edward VI., Mary, and Elizabeth. This Bowles reproduces, set by the composer to a "Hymn beginning 'Praise ye the Lord, ye Gentiles all,' to be sung before Morning Prayer," as from an "old collection of the sixteenth century." Bowles's maternal grandfather, Dr. Gray, author of *Memoria Technica*, was, he says, chaplain to Bishop Crewe of Durham, an Oxford contemporary of Ken's, whom Anthony à Wood names as a member of the same musical society there (i. 52). Gray's daughter, Bowles's mother, taught him to sing Ken's Hymns to the same tune as her father had taught her, and he had probably learnt that tune in his earliest days, while Ken was still living. Gray was born in 1693, and Crewe died in 1722.

Anderdon (pp. 119—121), who was assisted in this part of his work by the Rev. T. H. Helmore, gives the score of Tallis's tune from Archbishop Parker's *Psalter*, as the "original form of the music of Ken's Evening Hymn," headed as "the Eighth Tone," as being "in the eighth of the Ecclesiastical, or

---

[1] Another passage in Hawkins (p. 15) might almost suggest that Ken composed the tune as well as words of his hymns. "He had an excellent genius for, and skill in, musick, and whenever he had convenient opportunities for it, he performed some of his devotional part of praise with his own compositions, which were grave and solemn."

Gregorian, Modes," but the hymn there connected with it begins with "God grant with grace, He us embrace." Apparently, therefore, we have two tunes by Tallis, each adapted for the metre of Ken's Hymns. He reports further that "some have thought that the original melody may have been still earlier than Tallis, and might be found in the collection of Luther, or Clement Marot," but adds, on the authority of the Rev. W. H. Havergal, as a musical expert, that it is not found among Luther's hymn tunes, or in the early French collections of Guillaume Franc or Claude le Jeune. I am not aware that the tune by Jeremiah Clark, in Playford's *Harmonia Sacra*, has ever found its way into general use. Ken may have learnt Tallis's tune, assuming it to be that to which he sang his hymns, from *The Whole Booke of Psalms, with the Hymns Evangelical*, by Thomas Ravenscroft, 1633, in which he gives it (p. 260) as " an Hymn by Tho. Tallis, for four voices in A." Bowles (though he speaks of a Collection of the *sixteenth* century) is believed to have transcribed it from Ravenscroft.[1] Anyhow, this tune of Tallis's has remained, with few exceptions, associated with Ken's Hymns. Anderdon speaks of it as commonly used for the Evening Hymn, " though distorted from its ancient simplicity," and of the tune " in present use " for the Morning Hymn, as being "a corrupt version of a tune by Barthelemon, a violinist of the last century." *Hymns Ancient and Modern*, under the musical editorship of Mr. W. H. Monk, gives Tallis's tune for the Evening, and one by " I. Baptista " for the Morning.[2]

I am enabled to add one more fact to this history, by giving yet another tune, which may possibly represent a Ken tradition. In 1885, the late Rev. J. J. Moss sent me a tune published for Ken's Hymns, about 1750, to be sung to the lute-harp, an

---

[1] Havergal reports that Ravenscroft's tune is a version, altered for the worse, of the 'eighth tone' in Archbishop Parker's Psalter, printed by John Daye, without date, and referred to above.

[2] F. H. Barthelemon (1741—1801) appears in Sir George Grove's *Dictionary of Music and Musicians* as having composed the "well-known tune " for the Morning Hymn, about 1780. His other musical works were chiefly operatic. Of Baptista I find nothing in the *Dictionary*, but Baptiste Anet is named as a violinist and a pupil of Corelli, who died in 1713. Possibly " Joannes Baptista " may have been the name of the tune, not of the composer.

BISHOP KEN'S EVENING HYMN.

Glo - ry to Thee, my God, this night, For all the bles - sings of the light;

Keep me, O keep me, King of Kings, Be-neath Thine own Al - might - y wings.

Praise God from whom all bles - sings flow, Praise Him all crea - tures here be - low,

Praise Him a - bove, An - ge - lic Host, Praise Fa-ther, Son, and Ho - ly Ghost.

instrument which was then popular.[1] This I append.[2] I
may add that it was used with Ken's Morning Hymn on the
occasion of the Memorial Festival held in Wells Cathedral on
June 29th, 1885, the Bicentenary year of his Consecration,
and the Anniversary of the Trial of the Seven Bishops. On
that occasion the window to his memory, in the north aisle of
the choir, was seen by the public for the first time.

[1] The volume containing the tune is in the possession of Mrs. Yorke, of
Erddig, Wrexham. Ken, it will be remembered, sang his hymns to the lute.
[2] I am indebted to Mr. C. W. Lavington, organist and choirmaster of Wells
Cathedral, for the form in which the tune appears.

KEN'S COFFEE-POT (p. 208).

CHAPTER XXVIII.

" Music's ethereal fire was given
    Not to dissolve our clay,
  But draw Promethean beams from Heaven,
    And purge the dross away."

J. H. Newman.

" Child-like though the voices be
    And untunable the parts,
  Thou wilt own the minstrelsy,
    If it flow from child-like hearts."

John Keble.

THE life of Ken presents an almost, if not altogether, unique
instance of a man who, while continually writing poetry, probably from early manhood to the very close of life, reserved all
that he had written, the three Hymns for Morning, Evening,
and Midnight excepted, for posthumous publication. The fact
seems to me singularly suggestive. If I understand his
character rightly, he was one of those who find, in writing
verse, what Keble in his *Prælectiones* calls the *vis medica* of the
poetic art.[1] He wrote to relieve his mind from emotions, which
otherwise would have been too strong for him, from thoughts,
for which other men might have found utterance in sermons or
controversial treatises. It lay, in the nature of the case, that
he, his gifts being what they were, should be wanting in the
sublime self-confidence which led Dante to class himself with
the Five, who were the greatest of whom he knew in the world
of letters, or Milton to believe that he could write something
which the world "would not willingly let die." He shrank, if
I mistake not, from the ordeal of publicity, lest, as he may have
counted, in his hours of introspection, the chances of an author's
fate, he should be unduly elated by praise, or overmuch de-

[1] *Præl.*, i. p. 12.

Q 2

pressed by censure, according as the wind of criticism blew
from the west or east. And so he wrote on and on, and
apparently told no one how he was employed. He could
not reconcile himself, however, to the thought of consign-
ing what he wrote altogether to oblivion. He would not
bury his one talent in the earth because it was only one. His
verses might soothe others, as they had soothed him. They
might, at any rate, help a future generation to understand what
he himself had been. They would be the best return he could
make to the friend and protector to whom he had been indebted
for a home.

It would be idle, after this interval of time, to claim for Ken,
on the strength of the poems thus posthumously published,
any conspicuous niche in the Temple of Fame, any place on
the higher slopes of Parnassus. In the matter of poetical
reputation it is true that, in the long run, *Securus judicat orbis
terrarum*, and that we cannot hope to reverse its judgments. In
his epics he was but a weak follower of Cowley ;[1] in his devotional lyrics he was but a weak follower of Herbert, and perhaps
of Quarles and Crashaw. At the most we can only say that he
has as good a right to be remembered as some of those whose
lives Johnson wrote, as some of those also who have found a
resting-place in the Poets' Corner of the Abbey of Westminster. But, for the reasons which I have stated above, his
poems have a merit of which his biographers have not taken
adequate account. They speak of his verse, it seems to me,
in tones of undue disparagement. To Bowles, from whom, as
himself taking his place among the minor poets of England, we
might have expected a more intelligent sympathy, his *Edmund*
seems full of "discordant imagery," full of "vulgarity of
language," and "wretched execution," "far below Blackmore."
Even his devotional poems only serve to "dissipate the illu-
sion" that might have been formed from his Morning and

---

[1] Here and there I find traces of Milton, whose *Paradise Lost* and *Regained*
were in Ken's library, as in the description of Mammon's crown, "with oriental
diamonds bright, and various gems" (ii. 104), and of the spears which "were
tall Norwegian masts" (ii. 27). One can scarcely read too the narrative
of the Creation and the Fall (*Hymnotheo*, B. xi.) or the debates of demons in
Edmund, without feeling that Ken is treading (*longissimo intervallo*, alas!) in the
steps of the *Paradise Lost*.

Evening Hymns, and are "not clear of that worst and most nauseous style" which "uses the language of human passions in speaking of divine and spiritual objects." He gives a fairer judgment, perhaps, when he says that these faults were mainly owing to his following " a false and artificial model," and that, had he looked to Milton, and not to Cowley, as his master, he would possibly have " preserved ten stanzas out of every thousand," that would have been worth preserving (Bowles, ii. 290—300). Anderdon, in like manner, though he quotes with admiration many passages from the *Dedications* and *Anodynes*, and other devout poems, gives it as his judgment that " it would have been well for his poetic fame, if his epic *Edmund* had been consigned to a like fate with its hero, and drowned in the depths of the sea "[1] (p. 204). Miss Strickland thinks, (presumably having read the epic in such haste as not to notice the repeated allusions in it to Wells, which indicate a later date) that it "bears the unmistakeable marks of a young, in-experienced writer," that it is a " mere collection of boyish exercises," that it has " nothing local or historical," that there is but one good passage in it, *i.e.* that beginning with

"Give me the priest these graces shall possess."

Of the poems on the Festivals she cites two, as having an " innocent pretty quaintness," and she thinks it probable, and in this I agree with her, that both Charles and John Wesley may have been largely indebted to Ken's four volumes.[2]

My own experience in this matter has been very different from that of my predecessors. When I first read the poems, and it was not till 1884 that I chanced to come across them, after I had already begun collecting materials for a fresh biography, I felt that, while I could not recognise him as, in any sense, a master poet, I had lighted on what was a perfect treasure-trove, a mine hitherto scarcely worked, of materials which were, partly consciously, partly unconsciously, of an autobiographical character. I found here and there many

---

[1] Anderdon seems to forget that Edmund, though thrown by fiends into the sea, was after all not drowned, but caught up in Philydor's " chariot of celestial mould."—[C. J. P.]

[2] *Lives of Seven Bishops*, pp. 238, 240, 318.

passages sufficiently pointed and epigrammatic to have come from the pen of Cowley or of Dryden. I found also the utterance, in not a few instances, of Ken's convictions on the leading theological and political questions of his time, so that one could best arrive at a knowledge of those convictions, as I now propose to do, by examining the poems, rather than by treating of them in a separate chapter. Some of the first class I have already quoted from Ken's *Hymnotheo* in Chapters II. and V. I purpose now to select some passages of the other types and begin with *Edmund*. The hero of the poem is Edmund, the East Anglian prince—

"The Christ-like Hero, Martyr, Saint, and King."

His story is told from Edmund's early youth at Nuremberg, to his death at the hands of the Danes. Councils of demons plot his destruction, and he is defended by angelic hosts. He aims at making his kingdom of Anglia a model polity in Church and State, and therefore calls his counsellors together, some of whom try to lead him astray from the right path, while he is supported by the true and wise of heart. Alfred, hearing of his wise government, goes to learn from him how to rule. Edmund visits Wells, and falls in love with the saintly Hilda, whom he ultimately marries. I content myself with this briefest outline of the plot of the epic, and do not attempt to follow the story through its somewhat intricate windings.

As shewing the period in Ken's life which the poem represents, I begin with a passage which shows, beyond the shadow of a doubt, that it was not written, as previous biographers have thought, either in his earlier years, or during the voyage to Tangier, but certainly, after his appointment to his Bishopric, probably, after his deprivation. Edmund has had a vision of his future bride, and seeks to know where she is to be found, and this is the answer—

> "'Tis Theodorodunum, near whose Wells
>   Edmund's best friend and God's dear Fav'rite dwells;
>   The city by proud Mendippe Hills surveyed,
>   Its treasure, shelter, pasture, and its shade;
>   In ancient time Arviragus there reign'd,
>   Against the Roman force his Crown maintain'd;

That Town Arimathean Joseph bless'd,
Before he was of Avalon possess'd.
There first the Sun of Righteousness arose,
For saving Truth the Island to dispose;
The City, for refreshing Springs renown'd,
Which fertilise the neighbouring Country round;
Heaven in that Type would to all Albion shew,
That living Waters thence should overflow:
King Ina there a goodly Temple rear'd,
To the bless'd Andrew's name, which he rever'd." [1]

(II., p. 215.)

It will be admitted, I think, that this was not likely to
have been written while Ken was at Oxford or Winchester, or
before his affections were bound up with the fair City of Fountains, of which he was the spiritual pastor. It is not probable
that either the troubles or the activities of his short six years'
episcopate, before his deprivation, would have allowed leisure
for the composition of an epic in thirteen books, and containing, roughly, some eleven thousand lines. I take the poem
therefore, so far as it reflects Ken's thoughts on matters ecclesiastical or political, as representing those of his matured age.
Here, then, is his view of Democracy :—

"The People, giddy and repining, rave,
What they would have, they know not, and yet crave.
Precipitous usurping Force to crown,
Precipitous next day to pull it down.
Lies are by them infallibly believ'd,
They are contented only when deceiv'd.
Their leaders they revile, they all distrust;
Servile, ungrateful, envious, and unjust."

(II., p. 8.)

Here is the picture of an ideal Court, as contrasted with
what Ken had seen under Charles and James :—

"All with the Priest to Temple daily went,
Morning and Evening Off'ring to present:

---

[1] Theodorodunum was one of the old names of Wells, and appears in Leland.
It implied the existence of a mythical British prince, Theodoros. Avalon is, of
course, Glastonbury. The Cathedral Church of Wells was founded by Ina, and
dedicated to St. Andrew. An earlier name, Tethiscine, or Tydeston, also appears
in old chronicles.—Cassan, *Lives of Bishops,* i. p. 20.

No Oath, no Word blasphemous or impure,
No Lust, no Drunkard Edmund could endure ;
No Vice, no Lye, Chastisement could evade,
Virtue with liberal Reward was paid :
No Gaming he permitted in his Court,
But yet indulg'd them all innocuous Sport." [1]

(II., p. 47.)

And here are his views on free education and the maintenance of the poor ; not without interest, as anticipating some
modern ideals of the application of Christian principles to the
organization of labour and the relief of poverty, and including,
we may note in passing, Greenwich and Chelsea Hospitals, the
foundation of which he lived to witness, the former in 1694, the
latter in 1690.   It will be remembered that he had tried, when
he was at Wells, to turn one of those ideals into a reality, and
had failed (i., p. 251) :—

" In all Great Towns he Granaries ordained,
    That in bad Years the Poor might be maintained :
    Built Schools, and able Masters there endow'd,
    That to learn *Gratis* Poor might be allow'd : [2]
    Built some where Mathematick Skill was taught,
    And Youth was up to Naval Knowlege brought ;
    On great Resorts he Libraries bestowed,
    Himself he Learning's liberal Patron shewed,
        *   *   *   *   *
    He Hospitals was careful to erect,
    And for their Regulations Laws project,
    For Infants, Ideots, Lunaticks and Blind,
    Sick, Aged, Lame was Competence assign'd.
    Soldiers and Seamen who had spent their Heats,
    Had, by his Care, agreeable Retreats ;

[1] What these were we learn from the passage quoted in page 239.

[2] In laying stress on this point Ken was but following the continuous teaching
of the Church.   The inscription of the monastery at Salzburg, " *Discere si cupias,
gratis quod quæris habebis,*" is typical of the mediæval Church (*D. C. A.*, art.
" Schools ").   That at Sherborne, on the portrait of Edward VI., represents the
feeling of the Reformers, " *Gymnasium hic pueris statuit, gratumque Minervæ ; Ut
gratis discant.*"   The foundation of the numerous Charity Schools in the earlier
years of the eighteenth century indicates that of Ken's contemporaries and
fellow-workers.

No sturdy Beggars in the Land could lurk,
But were in proper Houses forced to work."

(II., pp. 49, 50.)

What he had seen of military life at the Hague and in Tangier among Kirke's "Lambs," and of naval life on his voyage in Lord Dartmouth's ship, had led him to an ideal in that region also :—

"A Priest was to each Regiment assign'd,
All were to hear the daily Prayers enjoyn'd,
All taught that Soldiers best grim Death defy,
Who go to Field the best prepar'd to die :
No Soldier durst his Captain disobey,
No Captain robb'd his Soldiers of their Pay :
Well pay'd themselves, their Quarters they defray'd,
And Towns a gain of quart'ring Soldiers made."

(II., p. 251.)

In the picture of the life of sailors we may, perhaps, find some reminiscences of James's naval administration both as Duke of York and King, as well as of Ken's own work under Lord Dartmouth (pp. 163—165). Of all the departments of the State that of the Admiralty was conspicuous at that time as almost a solitary instance of efficiency and incorruption :—

"He, to enlarge his Navy, made new Docks,
New Men of War were always on the Stocks :
To Mariners he lib'ral Wages gave,
Who for their King inhabited the Wave.
*   *   *   *   *

His Royal Fleet secured the Anglian shores,
His Arsenals were full of Naval Stores ;
Planks, Anchors, Cables, Timber, Tar and Masts,
And spreading Sails to gather kindly Blasts.
Strict Rules he made Impiety to scare,
No Seaman unchastis'd an Oath could swear ;
A Priest read daily Prayers to every Crew,
Taught them their Vow baptismal to renew ;
That they who run the Dangers of the Deep,
Their Souls at peace with God should always keep."

(II., pp. 53, 54.)

Even foreign policy and diplomacy—and he had seen more

of both than most bishops of his time—presented to Ken, aided, perhaps, by his recollections of Walton's *Life of Sir Henry Wotton*, an ideal aspect :—

> " Th' Ambassadors in his due Praise conspir'd,
>   Edmund by all their Monarchs grew admir'd :
>   All, in their Treaties, on his Word rely'd,
>   Who never in each other could confide.
>   For Mutual Safety, Peace, Defence, and Aid,
>   He with his Neighbours firm Alliance made.
>   When an Ally sunk under lawless Might,
>   By his kind Succour he retriev'd his Right :
>   He of all Monarchs gained the sole Renown,
>   To be styl'd Patron of the injured Crown."

(II., p. 54.)

And here, at somewhat greater length, is the picture of the ideal king himself :—

> " He sits without a Partner on his Throne,
>   Will always Counsel take, yet reigns alone ;
>   What others singly know, his Soul combines ;
>   Science in him in Constellation shines.
>   For War, Peace, Leagues, Law, Counsel, Sea and Land,
>   He always is the Oracle at hand ;
>   To his Word he is unalterably true,
>   Though he his own Sincerity should rue :
>   Kings sacred Honour more than Int'rest eye,
>   Had rather lose a Town than tell a Lie.
>   His Counsel open is, his Heart is clos'd,[1]
>   His Thoughts, when needful only, are expos'd :
>   Great as he is, he sweet Reproof can bear,
>   But Flatterers his Detestation are.
>   His Carriage is obliging, gentle, mild,
>   He treats each loyal subject as a Child ;
>   Their Interest he never will forsake,
>   Or 'gainst the Country, a Court Party make :
>   Of Vertue he has firm Foundations laid ;
>   To Avenues of Vice fix'd Barrocade (*sic*) ;
>   Studious of Peace, he yet for War provides ;[2]

---

[1] We recognise, at once, the *Viso sciolto, pensieri stretti*, of Wotton's maxim in his letter prefixed to Milton's *Comus*, ed. 1645.

[2] Obviously a paraphrase of *Si vis pacem, para bellum*.

Princes treat best with sabres by their sides;
Ambitious still he is that all his Time
People should feel no War, commit no Crime;
War, which for Remedy prescribes a Woe,
And from Necessity, not Choice, should flow.

No Hours the King in Idleness e'er lost,
The Publick and his Pray'rs his Time exhaust;
In Intervals his Mind he will unbend,
And these in Royal Recreation spend;
His Hawks he oft at Game Aerial flew;
His Hounds would oft the generous Stag pursue,
Sometimes a flying Hern or running Buck,
He with his right-aimed Shaft or Javelin struck:
Divertisements most manly he most priz'd,
And all that were effeminate despis'd.

God's Book lies always next to Edmund's heart;
That teaches him of Empire the true Art;
That makes the King and Saint in him unite,
That gives him both Humility and Hight,
In his heroick Soul that reconcil'd
The Just and Merciful, severe and mild;
Frugal and Lib'ral, Affable and Great,
Glorious and Modest, th' Awful and the Sweet,
The Patient and the Brave, the Friend and King,
Of Love and Fear the never-failing Spring,
He in Attempts is bold, in Council wise,
Assiduous to compleat an Enterprise;
Not rash, yet expeditious in Affairs;
Concentring in himself the publick Cares;
Anglia by him o'er Albion rears its Head,
And has a Resurrection from the Dead."

(II., pp. 65—67.)

It will be admitted that few portraits of a patriot king—certainly not Bolingbroke's—present a nobler ideal of monarchy. It would be natural to pass at once from the picture of a perfect State to that of a perfect Church, but I pause, as I read the poem, to give an extract of an almost pathetic autobiographical interest, in which we find traces of Ken's poetical aspirations, perhaps also of his dreams of poetical fame in a near or distant future.

Alfred, as I have said above, hearing of Edmund's greatness, determines to visit him and learn by personal observation. Before he starts on his journey he visits Godwyn, a hermitsaint, who has his cell near Winchester, who thus utters his prophecy of William of Wykeham :—

> "Of Centuries when a full Lustre's past,
>   When Learning ready is to breathe its last,
>   God will in Winton a great Prelate raise,
>   Who shall recover it from its Decays.
>   As at the Cedar-bearing Liban's feet,
>   The Jor and Dan in Christal Jordan meet;
>   Whence the full Stream, which both the Fountains drains,
>   Sheds kindly Moisture o'er Judæan plains;
>   Thus from the two Wicchamick Springs shall rise,
>   Diffusive Streams the Church to fertilize;
>   *Kenneo* in them both Retreats shall find,
>   Best suited to his unaspiring Mind;
>   He, rais'd on high, will rather down be thrown,
>   Than conscientious Loyalty disown,
>   His Solitude with Songs he'll intersperse,
>   He'll you and Edmund celebrate in verse."

(II., p. 69.)

This, again, it will be noticed, is decisive as to the date of the poem as being completed subsequent to Ken's deprivation.

I pass on now to the ecclesiastical side of Ken's thoughts.

He represents Edmund as resolving on a reform of the Church, which he finds in a corrupt and fallen state. He is helped in his efforts by Bishop Humbert—

> "They both agree,
>   A Synod the Restorative must be."

(II., p. 201.)

And a Synod is accordingly called at Bury. Humbert presides, with Lucio and Justo, the representatives of sound doctrine, as his coadjutors.[1] Edmund states his wishes as to reform, and the debate opens. Romano, as his name indicates, represents the Romish controversialist; Proteo, the school of an Erastian Indifferentism. Edmund begins by pointing, as Ken did in his

---

[1] We may, perhaps, conjecture that Humbert stands for Juxon, Justo for Sheldon, and Lucio for Morley, or that the three represent respectively, Sancroft, Hooper, and Ken's idealised self.—[C. J. P.]

will, to the primitive Church, the Church of the undivided East
and West, as the pattern to be followed :—

> "Mind not what Rome, what Greece has added new,
> But eye th' Original, which Jesus drew.
> *   *   *   *
> Good Shepherds to their Flocks true patterns give,
> How Sheep should pray, believe, repent and live."
>
> (II., p. 208.)

Humbert pleads his age and infirmities, and says but little.
Then Lucio rises. He finds in the Twelve and the Seventy
of the Gospel story the pattern of Church government :—

> "And the Distinction Jesus first ordain'd,
> The Church in Priest and Bishop still maintain'd."

And then gives a brief outline of the history of the Church of
the Apostles. He is followed by Justo, who expounds the
pattern of the " Ideal Church : "—

> "'Tis to that Church God's Promises are made,
> No Counterfeit those Blessings can invade ;
> That Church is One, and will no Schisms endure ;
> Is holy, from notorious scandals pure,
> Is Catholick, for Doctrine, Time and Place,
> Receives all faithful Souls in her embrace ;
> The Apostolick Truth has still retained,
> With all succeeding Heresies unstained ;
> She'll militant and visible appear,
> Though God alone can number the Sincere ;
> She'll last till all her ghostly War shall cease,
> And she Triumphant gains eternal Peace.
> She'll no one spurious Fundamental own,
> She'll make no bold Encroachments on the Throne."
>
> (II., p. 213.)

Romano rises and reproduces the stock arguments of the
Papal controversialists of the time :—

> "Is holy Church to Anglia now confined ?
> Does Anglia see when all the World is blind ?
> Shall we new Dictates on this Church obtrude,
> And the great Western Patriarch thus exclude ?

We Saxons have derived our power from Rome; [1]
Can we her Power thus to oblivion doom?"
(II., p. 216.)

Lucio replies, as Ken himself would have done, had he taken part in the controversy :—

"It is no Schism from Errors to abstain,
No Schism to be what Jesus' laws ordain;
It is no Innovation to restore,
And make God's Spouse as beauteous as before;
The older Error is, it is the worse;
Continuation may provoke a Curse:
If the dark Age obscur'd our Fathers' Sight,
Must their Sons shut their Eyes against the Light?"
(II., p. 217.)

He dwells on the earlier missionary work of the English Church :—

"Our Willibrod first Faith to Frisia brought,
Our Boniface the Truth to Germans taught;
We have converted Realms as well as Rome,
Yet no Dominion o'er those Realms assume.
          *   *   *   *
Fraternal Love to Rome we gladly show,
But no Subjection to that Crozier owe:
We, who of Rome a grateful Sense retain,
Her Usurpations justly may disdain."
(II., p. 218.)

Next in order, Proteo appears as the advocate of Latitudinarianism :—
"The Head of them
Who, Skepticks, all religious Truth contemn."
(II., p. 219.)

It will be allowed, I think, that Ken allows Proteo to state his case very fairly, in the very accents, almost, of Dryden's *Religio Laici* :—

"If Right and Wrong we in Opinions own,
Sure God for their Opinions will damn none;

---

1 The reader will note that Ken adopts the Shakespearian pronunciation, as in "there's room enough in Rome." Comp. the rhymes "great" and "sweet" in p. 239.

Soft Charity in Jesus is most priz'd,
'Tis that, not Faith, which Christians canoniz'd."
   *   *   *   *

" If we should Tests on fickle Minds impose,
We the Breach widen we pretend to close."
   *   *   *   *

" God in Variety takes most Delight."
   *   *   *   *

" God's Spouse knows what will please her Lover best,
And in a various-coloured Robe is drest."
   *   *   *   *

" One narrow Path a wand'ring Soul may miss ;
God's Goodness opens numerous Ways to Bliss."
   *   *   *   *

          (II., p. 220.)

His comprehensiveness, however—and this was probably the lesson Ken had learnt from the Latitudinarians of his time—runs sooner or later into pure and simple Erastianism in doctrine as well as polity, and Proteo[1] is but a " state cameleon :"—

" We by Experience learn that all Restraints
Make numerous Hypocrites but rarely Saints ;
Yet God's Anointed *Proteo's* Faith shall sway ;
'Tis mortal error Kings to disobey."

          (II., p. 221.)

Proteo is answered by Lucio :—

" Errors into unnumbered Mazes run,
Truth, like the Godhead, always is but One.
Variety in Error God abhors,
Against high Heaven it makes perpetual Wars ;
From the broad Way God every soul deters ;
And shews the Narrow, where none ever errs."

He states the limits of Church fellowship :—

" We with all Churches in Communion join,
As far as they to Fontal Truth incline ;
Nothing can us of Charity bereave,
We pray for those whose Pray'rs we justly leave."

          (II., pp. 222—3.)

---

[1] Is Proteo meant for Tillotson ? (See p. 79.)

Finally, the Synod decides on accepting the Nicene Creed and the first Six General Councils as the standard of doctrine, in words which remind us of Ken's will :—

> "In them they own'd true Catholick Consent,
> Ere East from West deplorably was rent."
>
> (II., p. 224.)

They adopt canons for the special government of the Anglican Church. The Bible, interpreted by Catholic tradition,[1] is the basis of the Church's teaching. The claims of Rome are rejected :—

> "If any Church must the chief Honour share,
> It is not Peter's, but bless'd Jesus' chair ; "
>
> (II., p. 225.)

i.e. the Mother Church of Jerusalem.

They assert the communion of the laity, as well as clergy, in both kinds, and reject transubstantiation, "purgatory tales," and undue veneration to images. They will not dogmatise on pre-destination—

> "but agree
> That both God's Grace and human Will were free."

They assert that " Jesus dyed for all." They—

> "Censur'd no Church for disagreeing Rite,
> Lov'd Lamps of any Fashion with true Light."
>
> (II., p. 227.)

Prayers are to be said in a "tongue understanded of the people." "Stations and paschal fasts" are to be restored as helps to discipline. Festivals are—

> "For Annual Catechisms to weaker Brains."
>
> (II., p. 228.)

The penitential discipline of the Church is to be revived and enforced.[2] Convents should be retained, but bishops should have power to apply their surplus wealth to " pious uses." No

---

[1] He is careful, however, to qualify the statement : "Tradition, when derived from God alone," for " God only souls infallibly can guide," thus taking up a position like that of Hales and Chillingworth.—[C. J. P.]

[2] The reader will recollect one example of this during Ken's episcopate (i. 250).

priests are to be, as such, " exempted from the civil Rod." The marriage of the clergy is to be permitted. Solitary masses, " reliques canonis'd," and indulgences are forbidden, as also the use of " lustration water" and other—

"Customs from Pagans borrowed, or from Jew."

Finally, when all this is settled, Humbert reminds them that above all the clergy must be examples to the flock, for—

"Our best Arguments are holy Lives,"

(II., p. 234.)

and draws a picture of what a priest should be, in which we may recognise, in part, the ideal at which Ken consciously aimed all his life long, in part also, an unconscious portrait of his own character and life :—[1]

> " Give me the Priest these Graces shall possess;
>   Of an Ambassador the just Address,
>   A Father's Tenderness, a Shepherd's Care,
>   A Leader's Courage, which the Cross can bear,
>   A Ruler's Arm, a Watchman's wakeful Eye,
>   A Pilot's Skill the Helm in Storms to ply,
>   A Fisher's Patience and a Lab'rer's Toil,
>   A Guide's Dexterity to disembroil,
>   A Prophet's Inspiration from Above,
>   A Teacher's Knowledge, and a Saviour's Love.
>   Give me the Priest, a Light upon a Hill,
>   Whose Rays his whole Circumference can fill;
>   In God's own Word, and sacred Learning vers'd,
>   Deep in the Study of the Heart immers'd,
>   Who in such Souls can the Disease descry,
>   And wisely fit Restoratives apply.
>   *   *   *   *

The ideal of a bishop's character is naturally that of a priest on a higher level, and, as it were, transfigured :—

> " Bishops are Priests sublim'd, are Angels stiled,
>   And they should live, like Angels, undefil'd;
>   In an enlighten'd Love should spend their Days,
>   In pure Intention, Joy, Obedience, Praise;

---

[1] A like self-portraiture, also, of course, in the form of an ideal character, is found in *Hymnotheo* (iii. pp. 56, 57), which I have not space to quote.

Should here on Earth be Guardians to the Fold,
And God, by Contemplation still behold.
High Priests had, on the Plate fix'd on their Breast,
For a Memorial, the Tribes' Names imprest ;
Thus every Bishop on his Breast should grave
The Names of those whom he is charg'd to save,
That he may lead and warn them Day and Night,
And in his Prayers their ghostly Wants recite ;
That he may ever lodge them near his Heart,
And in their Sorrows bear Paternal Part.
We, the more Spirits we from Dross refine,
In higher Thrones and brighter Rays shall shine."

*　　　*　　　*　　　*

(II., p. 231—3.)

I would fain go on quoting, but the narrowing limits of space
warn me that I must refrain. One passage, however, in the
Hymnarium, p. 131 (in the same volume with *Edmund,* but with
a separate pagination), calls for notice, as showing how fully
Ken shared in the wider hope for the heathen, which in the
seventeenth century began to be asserted, as by Chillingworth,
Barrow, and other Anglican divines, so also by the Jesuit
theologians on the one side, by Milton, Barclay, and Penn on
the other : [1]—

"Thought," *i.e.* man's faculty of spiritual apprehension, is
personified as led by Lazarus through the unseen world :—

"Thought, then by *Lazarus* o'er Hades led,
　　The Region of the happy Dead,
　　Saw Infants numberless, who, pure
From wilful Sin, seem'd to die immature ;
　　Yet ripe for Heaven, lodg'd safe above
　　From Ill, which might deflour their Love :
Thought in the outward Court of Hades bless'd,
Saw numerous Souls, cloth'd in a dusky Vest.
'These are,' said *Lazarus,* 'of the *Gentile* Race,
　　Trophies of Universal Grace.' "[2]

And then Lazarus leads the pilgrim to Socrates, as the great

---

[1] See the present writer's *Spirits in Prison,* ch. vi., " On the Salvation of the
Heathen."

[2] Compare *Hymnotheo,* p. 160, " God's Love to human Race is unconfined."

representative instance of heathen wisdom and righteousness, and hears his story :—

> " 'Know,' Socrates reply'd,
> 'I for the one true God a Martyr dy'd;
> I knew great God by native Light,
> And Conscience told me what was right;
>   *   * . *   *
> My soul with *Miserere* left my Clay,
> And, as I rov'd to find the happy Way,
> An Angel brought me to the Judgment Seat;
> And, prostrate at God's Feet,
> Taught me the Virtue of the promis'd Seed,
>   With humble Confidence, to plead;
> No Gentiles to this Region ever came
> But Pardon gained by that and by no other Name.' "
>   (*Hymnarium*, pp. 131, 132.)

"Thought" finds in this the explanation of the promise to the penitent robber, who—

> " As he breath'd his last,
> Or, as to Paradise he pass'd,
> By some good Angel catechis'd,
> E'er he reached Bliss, all saving Truth compris'd."

And then Socrates continues :—

> " God, when Himself to Israel he reveal'd,
> Our Reprobation never seal'd;
> We hymn God's Goodness, who decreed
> A lighter yoke for us than Abram's Seed;
> *   *   :   *
> The more enlighten'd Souls more happy are;
> We have of Bliss a just, though lesser, Share,
> And the Philanthropy Divine
> More in our Bliss than their's we judge to shine;
> Since we the Grace that we obtain,
> By Super-effluence uncovenanted gain."
>   (*Hymnarium*, p. 133.)

And so "Thought" passes on from height to height, and Gabriel takes the place of Lazarus, and leads him where the Church Militant stands with the Angel at the Gate. Romano and Sectario find it hard to enter in, and have to wait a while, but

the true sons of the Church Catholick in Britain find a prompt
admission, and the pilgrim and his guide mount, like Dante and
Beatrice, "in one minute" ten million miles to the solar beam,
and the "forty thousand leagues of a star's diurnal way" are
traversed by them "in one Pulse, as Sages say."   But as yet,
they see not all :—

> " The Glories of this upper World,
> Till the Great Day, will never be unfurl'd,
> But Saints, who beatifick Vision gain,
>   Will see all Wonders plain,
> From the first Sphere, which all the Globe contains,
> Down to the least of all the sandy Grains."
>
> *Hymn.,* ii., p. 139.

I ask myself as I read this, whether Ken, who was, it will be
remembered, an Italian scholar, was not in all this consciously
following in the steps of the pilgrims of the *Commedia*, thinking,
it may be, that Lazarus, the Lazarus of the Parable, was a better
guide than Virgil, and rejoicing that a clearer vision had been
given to him of the state of unbaptized children, and of the
heathen who knew not God as revealed in Christ, than had been
given to the Florentine.[1] Here we have some better thing than
the " sighs of a sorrow without pain," or the longings of those who
" without hope live ever in desire."   The poem from which I
quote is the last and fullest in the *Hymnarium*. It seems to me
the completest utterance of Ken's faith, his *Theodikæa*, by which
he sought to " vindicate the ways of God to man."

I must quote yet a few more passages which seem to me to
bear on Ken's life and character. This, which follows, is also in
the *Hymnarium*, and its subject is *Eternity*. As he meditates
on that attribute he finds it more and more incomprehensible.
It is something more than "infinite duration," for it excludes
"succession," and "Eternity admits no Past." It is "one fix'd
Eternal Standing Now." As he contemplates it, he remembers
the old legend of the Monk and the Bird :—

> "I thought on the Recluse, perplex'd,
>   As he at Matines sang the Text,

---

[1] In Ken's "There is no hope in Hell " we have a distinct echo of *Inf.* iii. 9.

That one short Day in Godhead's Eyes,
A thousand Years would equalize;
Till a wing'd Envoy from the Airy Sphere
Was sent by Heaven, the Mystery to clear.

" The Bird by his harmonious Note,
Allur'd him to a Wood remote;
Three Centuries her song he heard,
Which not three Hours to him appear'd,
While God to his dim-sighted doubtful Thought,
Duration boundless, unsuccessive, taught."[1]

Hymn., ii., p. 10.

I cannot pass from this survey of some, at least, of Ken's poems, without noticing the more strictly biographical element in the *Dedications.* He seems to have wished to transmit to posterity, through that channel, his estimate of the character of the two men to whom he felt most indebted, and whom he most delighted to honour. He dedicates his first volume to his friend and protector, Lord Weymouth. He compares his own retirement to that of Gregory of Nazianzum, and he writes at least fourteen years after he had entered on the' life of con-

[1] Of the many books in which the story is found, I incline to look to the work of Nieremberg, *On the Difference between Things Temporal and Eternal,* which has met us as a favourite with James II. (i. 263), as that to which Ken was indebted. That work is found among his books at Longleat, and another by the same author, *De Adoratione,* among those at Wells. The story appears in Caxton's compilation from the *Legenda Aurea* of Jacobus de Voragine, the *Gesta Romanorum,* &c., based upon De Vigny's French translation of the former work, but is not, I am informed, in the original. Cornelius à Lapide reproduces it in his note on 2 Pet. iii. 8, and adds that the story had been investigated, and that its scene was a monastery between Alost and Brussels. Matthias Faber (*Sermon* II. p. 755, ed., 1859) quotes it from the *Speculum Morale* of Vincentius Bellov, a Dominican friar of the thirteenth century. T. Crofton Croker, in the *Amulet* for 1827, gives it as taken down from the lips of an old peasant woman in Ireland, and as quoted in an Italian devotional book, *Prato Fiorito,* from the *Speculum Exemplorum* of Henricus, a writer of the fifteenth century. It has been reproduced by Tholuck in his *Stunden der Andacht,* p. 462, 5th ed.; in Kenelm Digby's *Broad Stone of Honour*: *Tancredus,* p. 177; by Longfellow in his *Golden Legend,* and by Trench in his *Justin Martyr and other Poems.* I am indebted to C. J. P. and other correspondents for the statements that I have thus brought together, but I have not had the opportunity of verifying all the references. The underlying thought is identical with that of the Seven Sleepers of Ephesus, which fascinated Gibbon (Ch. xxxiii. *ad fin.*), which Mahomet introduced in the Koran (Sura. xviii.), and to which Gregory of Tours (*de Gloriá Martyrum,* l. c. 95) gave currency in Europe.

stant suffering of which his letters bear so many traces. In one respect, he says, his lot is happier than that of Gregory :—

> "When I, my Lord, crush'd by prevailing Might,
> No Cottage had where to direct my Flight;
> Kind Heav'n me with a Friend Illustrious blest,
> Who gives me Shelter, Affluence, and Rest;
> In this alone I Gregory outdo,
> That I much happier Refuge have in you;
> Where to my Closet I to Hymn retire,
> On this side Heav'n have nothing to desire.
>
>   *   *   *   *
>
> I the small dol'rous Remnant of my Days,
> Devote to hymn my great Redeemer's Praise ;
> I, nearer as I draw towards Heavenly Rest,
> The more I love th' Employment of the blest.
> In that Employment while my Hours I spend,
> This Prayer I offer for my Noble Friend,
> Whose shades benign to sacred Songs invite,
> Who to those Songs may claim Paternal Right :
> Rich as He is in all good Works below,
> May He in Heav'nly Treasure overflow ! "
>
>   (*I. Dedication, ad fin.*)

So in like manner he dedicates his *Hymnarium* to the friend whom he had virtually chosen as his successor. He, in his age and retirement, stands to Hooper in the same relation that Valerius, Bishop of Hippo, did to Augustine. He had grieved as he saw his flock wandering on the dark mountain of error; and then, in a line which was musical to his ear with one of the compound words in which he most delighted,

> "Heaven, my Lord, super-effluently kind,[1]
> In you, sent a Successor to my Mind ;
> In you all Austine's virtues are supply'd,
> Too bright for your Humility to hide.
> I on a load presum'd I could not bear,
> Happy presumption which enforc'd my Pray'r !
> Since Heav'n thence took occasion you to rear,
> You, who irradiate all the sacred Sphere;
> You, in whose Care I feel as full Repose,
> As old Valerius when he Austine chose.

                    [1] I. 283; ii. 92, 132, 247.

Accept, my Lord, the Products of that Ease
You gave, when you accepted of my Keys;
O may the Flock a grateful Sense retain,
Of Blessings, which they in your Conduct gain;
I in my Requiem Hymn God's Love will sing,
For shelt'ring them in your paternal Wing."

(*Dedication*, p. v.)

And at the close of the volume there is what Ken calls a *Ritornello*—one notes in passing the familiarity which this indicates with the forms of Italian poetry, as confirming the conjecture I have ventured on above (p. 248)—in which, with an almost childlike simplicity, he pours forth his admiration of a learning which he venerated as far wider than his own:

"Song, silent at the Closet Door attend,
Of my sweet-temper'd, venerable Friend;
You'll him the sacred Volume reading find,
Submissively to search his Maker's Mind;
The Glosses of bold Criticks to expose,
And the full Force of the bless'd Tongue disclose;
Or by his Pray'rs hard Places to unfold,
Or to extract from Mud rabbinick Gold;
Or he the rich Chaldæan Treasure drains,
Or Wealth of Zabian, and the Syrian Plains;
Or he digs deep in the Arabian Mine,
For Ore, which he expends on Writ Divine;
Or he from Latian and the Grecian shores,
Himself with sacred Erudition stores;
Or he is on his Past'ral Care intent,
To guide his Sheep, and Strayings to prevent;
Or he, consulted, gives Responses clear,
Which move the Church his Wisdom to revere;
Or, if his Mind he for awhile unbends,
He Minutes in his youthful Study spends,
Some philosophick Treatise to peruse,
Or on Depths Mathematical to muse;
Or, to range o'er the Modern Tongues, to view
What they improve, or steal, or boast of new.[1]

---

[1] The subjects of Hooper's chief works are sufficiently suggestive of the range of his attainments: (1) *A Discourse concerning Lent*, giving an elaborate history of its origin and observance; (2) *The Church of England free from the Imputation of Popery*; (3) A Latin treatise, *De Valentinianorum Hæresi*; (4) *An Enquiry into*

Stay, Song, till leisure Moments you descry,
Then bow to his judicious candid Eye."

One cannot help feeling, as one reads this tribute at the close of Ken's life to the higher wisdom of his friends, how "earthly happier" his own lot might have been, had he, on that memorable night at Lambeth (p. 43), been not "almost, but altogether," persuaded to follow his friend's example, and to take the oaths which, the next morning, he resolved not to take. Did some feeling of regret come over him, as the shadows lengthened, that he had taken a course which had brought so much suffering on himself and others, and had all but involved the Church which he loved so dearly, in the misery of a perpetuated schism? Or did he satisfy himself, as such a man might well do, with the thought that he had then acted as his conscience prompted him; that if he had been in any way biassed, it was by the attraction of what seemed to him the "doctrine of the cross;" that, as it was, privation, suffering, pain had entered into the discipline of his life, and had brought him to the haven where he would be? We ask these questions, and feel that we cannot answer them. It is enough for us to know, as these latest utterances tell us, that he could, at last, pour forth his swan-song as a *Nunc dimittis.* Now, at last, he could say, after the storms and troubles of his life, that all was well; that it was given to him to depart in peace, with brighter hopes for the flock, for which he would gladly have laid down his life, and for the Church, which he had served not less faithfully, if less wisely, than his friend.

I proceed to give a few of the short epigrammatic lines of which I have spoken as found, not rarely, in Ken's poems.

(1.) Dipsychus,[1] the double-minded man :—

" He acts the Hermaphrodite of Good and Ill,
But God detests his double Heart and Will ;
He lives two men, and yet but one he dies."

(II., p. 116.)

Ancient Weights and Measures; (5) A treatise on *Jacob's Blessing* (Gen. xlix.), in the Hebrew and Arabic texts ; besides many sermons. He had read with Pococke, the great Orientalist.—Cassan, *Lives of Bishops of Bath and Wells,* ii. p. 168.

[1] See James I., 8.

(2.) The Palace of Error :—

> "There half learn'd Clubs fallacious volumes vend,
> And Critics spoil the Authors they amend.
> *   *   *   *
> False Prophets here false pleasing Things presage,
> And wrest th' Apocalypse to fool the age."

> "The rising Side in Church, in State, they take,
> Which, when it sinks, the Vermin all forsake."
>
> (II., pp. 118, 119.)

(3.) Vertumno, the Trimmer and Erastian :—

> "He t' all Religions opens the wide Gate,
> Damns none but those who enter at the Strait."
>
> (II., p. 119.)

(4.) Counsels :—

> "To keep all Men your Friends yet trust but few."
>
> (II., p. 153.)

(5.) The World :—

> "You short-liv'd, little, despicable Thing,
> You that have nothing certain but your Sting."
>
> (II., p. 140.)

(6.) Late Repentance :—

> "His youthful Heat and Strength for Sin engage;
> God has the *Caput Mortuum* of his age."
>
> (II., p. 138.)

(7.) Apparent Failure :—

> "Short of my Aim I infinitely fall ;
> I love Thee, Lord, I love, and that is all."
>
> (II., p. 166.)

(8.) Youthful Piety :—

> "Few years will wash away unwilful Taints ;
> Religious Children soon grow aged Saints."
>
> (III., p. 128.)

(9.) Callousness in Vice :—

> "As petrifying Fountain, by degrees
> Into a solid Stone soft Willows freeze,
> In sensual Pleasures thus my Soul immers'd
> Turn'd Marble."
>
> (III., p. 120.)

(10.) The Pure in Heart :—

"Whom no one fashionable Vice can taint,
Who in a Sodom can continue Saint."

(III., p. 57.)

(11.) Prayer and Praise :—

"Pray'r often errs ; Praise is that Grace alone
Which true Infallibility may own."

(III., p. 145.)

(12.) The Misery of Sin :—

"To grieve Thy Love is ante-dated Hell."

(III., p. 369.)

(13.) Confession :—

"Confessions private at their Chairs are made,
Which they to Souls command not, but persuade."

(III., p. 75.)

I have reserved to the last a passage which seems to me infinitely pathetic in its autobiographic interest. Ken paints in Edmund his ideal of manhood. In Edmund's bride, Hilda (not the saint of Whitby), he paints his ideal of womanhood. The picture is a somewhat full one, and I must content myself with a few of the more striking features of it :—

"No vain Expense she on herself bestow'd,
A Spirit frugal, and yet gen'rous, show'd.

* * * *

The Poor had an allotted lib'ral share,
In all that she with Decency could spare ;
Her Speech was uncensorious and restrain'd,
All that she spoke a pleas'd Attention gain'd.

* * * *

Her usual Dress was comely, never gay,
No new vain Fashion could her Judgment sway.

* * * *

She could no Praise, no Flatt'ry ever bear ;
She seem'd to have ne'er known that she was fair.

* * * *

Meek in Command, of Conversation sweet,
Free from harsh Words, Disdain, Pride, peevish Heat ;
In well-chose Friendships constant and sincere,
And pitiful, when forc'd to be severe.

* * * *

Women and Virgins she to serve her chose,
Whom best she could to Discipline dispose ;
These by Example, more than Force she train'd,
And proper Works for every one ordain'd ;
At work she charm'd them with her sweet Converse,
Which she with pleasant things would intersperse.

    *   *   *   *

And when she any naked Wretches spy'd,
Out of her Ward-robe she their Wants supply'd.
Schools she built for her Sex, and Laws ordain'd,
That they to Work and Virtue might be train'd ;
Large Hospitals she built, and there would spend
Choice Hours, the Sick with Sweetness to attend ;
With tender Heart she Jesus' Brethren fed,
Could bear the Stench of a Poor Man's sick Bed ;

    *   *   *   *

She Visits in Disguise to Prisons made,
And by a Hand unknown their Debts were paid ;
Early she rose ; her dressing was in haste,
Would at her Toylet but few Minutes waste.

    *   *   *   *

God was her constant Sovereign, dearest Care,
Her Closet fum'd with th' Incense of her Prayer ;
Three Times a Day she would for Prayer retire,
Daily frequented twice the public Choir ;
Her Library was with her Bible fill'd,
And with good Books which Piety instill'd ;

    *   *   *   *

And oft spent piously diverting Hours,
As Jesus midst the Lillies, midst her Flowers :
The Fasts and Feasts of Holy Church she kept,
And oft in secret for the Kingdom wept ;
She each Lord's Day on the immortal Bread
With sacred Hunger at the Altar fed ;
She liv'd God's Constant Lover, hating ill,
Conform both to his Image and his Will."

                                    (II., pp. 273—275.)

I agree with Anderdon (p. 183) in thinking it impossible to
compare this description with that given of Lady Margaret Maynard in Ken's *Funeral Sermon*, without feeling that the one is
the idealised expansion of the other. And on this supposition we

have to think of the old man in the later years of his life—I have proved that *Edmund* belongs to that period—as going back in memory to those early years that now lay nearly half a century behind him, and still dwelling on the vision of the beauty of holiness, which had then been granted to him. Different as the two men were in power and character, there was this in common to both Ken and Dante, that each cherished, all his life long, the recollection of an idealising devotion, suggested by the presence of one in whom all that he most reverenced and loved was free from every touch of baseness. He found his Beatrice in the Lady Margaret, the Monica or Proba, as he calls her, of Little Easton. He had, for not a few years, guided her spiritual life, and in doing so, had found that she was in reality guiding him in the paths of purity and peace. In the hours of weariness and pain, in the epic in which he hoped that he should live to a future generation, he enshrined her memory with a loving and loyal tenderness, which, to those who enter into the heart as well as brain of a poet, more than redeems his work from its occasional prosaic heaviness. I feel, as I read the words in which he tries to set forth her true likeness, that I understand Ken better than I have done before, and find him, in the end as in the beginning of his life, more loveable and human. If there was in his experience the bitterness which the heart knew for itself, there was also the joy with which a stranger doth not intermeddle.[1]

[1] Of the *Anodynes* I have spoken sufficiently in Chapter xxvi. The other poems, the series of *Psyche or Magdalum, Sion or Philothea, Urania or The Spouse's Garden,* call for a passing notice as being possibly, I think, an idealised picture of the life of the Sisterhood at Naish, especially in the loving care for the souls of penitents. On this supposition we may trace a half-conscious portraiture of Ken himself in the character of Gratian as the spiritual director of the sisterhood (see p. 169). The poems on *Church Festivals* may, perhaps, have suggested Keble's *Christian Year.* Could Ken have known that they had done so, he would, I believe, have rejoiced that his own work had been superseded by a poet with greater gifts, and have been content, in his lowliness, to say, " He must increase, but I must decrease."

CHAPTER XXIX

ESTIMATES, CONTEMPORARY AND LATER.

> " I have been honour'd and obey'd,
> I have met scorn and slight,
> And my heart loves earth's sober shade
> More than her laughing light."
>
> *J. H. Newman.*

DURING the greater part of Ken's career it might almost seem as if he were exposed to the "woe" of those of whom all men speak well. There must have been something singularly winning and loveable in one who gained the affection of so many men and women of all sorts and conditions. His school and college friendships with Turner, and Thynne, and Hooper, and Fitzwilliam, last through life. Morley and Walton look on him with almost paternal fondness. In his first parish he becomes the confidential friend and adviser of a lady of rank and cultivated excellence. Lady Margaret Maynard's friend, Lady Warwick, records from time to time in glowing terms the impression made on her by his sermons. A Winchester poet writes to him on his appointment to his bishopric in terms of devout admiration.[1] He attracts the respect of Charles and James, even of William and of Bentinck. Mary does all she can to postpone, to the last moment, the deprivation which could not be averted. Anne takes the first opportunity to show her reverence for him by offering to re-instate him, and when he refuses, gives him a pension for the remainder of his life.

---

[1] Thomas Fletcher, of New College, an under-master of Winchester School. He may be identical with a Prebendary of Wells of that name, appointed in 1696. I quote from Bowles (ii. 282) a few words in which Ken is described as " gliding through these peaceful glades," "like some calm ghost." The phrase seems to me singularly suggestive.

His praises are sung and his friendship courted by the most
eminent laymen of the time, by John Evelyn and Robert
Nelson and Henry Dodwell, by Lord Dartmouth and Lord
Weymouth. In the last-named instance the attachment stood
the crucial test of a twenty years' trial of the relation
between guest and host, and remained unbroken to the end.
Men and women look to him for spiritual comfort in their
hours of sorrow, as in the instances of the Student Penitent,
and the tragedy of Statfold, and the two "Ladies of Naish."
Everywhere he is spoken of as the "good Bishop." In the
more public portion of his life, crowds of all classes flock to
his sermons at Whitehall and St. Martin's. He is a welcome
guest, as at Longleat, so also at Leweston, and Shottesbrook,
and Poulshot, and Salisbury, and Winchester. As in the case
of Lewis Southcombe, he inspires in men much younger than
himself the most fervent devotion. He becomes, through his
Manual and his Hymns, as in the case of Ambrose Bonwicke,
who read the former and sang the latter daily, the spiritual
guide of young devout souls, who, even though they did not
know him personally,[1] thought of him as the "seraphic prelate." He is taken, in the crisis of the history of the Church
and Nation, into the counsels of Sancroft and his brother
Bishops, of Lord Clarendon and others, like-minded with himself. Even Roman Catholics, as in the instance of the critic
who attacked his Bath sermon, acknowledge that he had "the
parts of an Orator, and would have been an Evangelical one
too, had he but been trained in the bosom of the true Church."
A higher tribute from the same quarter comes, during his life-
time, from the pen of John Dryden in his paraphrase of
Chaucer's portrait of the "poore Persone of a Towne."[2] Most

---

[1] Mayor, *Life of Ambrose Bonwicke*, pp. 10, 59, 67. The young man records
with reverent interest what he has heard of Ken's burial.

[2] I follow Anderdon, Miss Strickland, and the writer in the *Quarterly Review*
(lxxxix. 306), in accepting the lines as intended for Ken. Dryden represents his
ideal priest as sixty years old, as a Non-juror, as a writer of hymns, and those
three elements meet in Ken, and do not meet in any of his noticeable contemporaries. The only point on the other side is that in which the poet speaks of
his priest as not "deprived," but that admits of the very natural explanation
that deprivation by Act of Parliament was, from Dryden's standpoint, a nullity,
and that therefore Ken's leaving Wells, and not formally asserting his claims

readers will, if I mistake not, thank mo for quoting the poem somewhat fully.

> " A parish priest was of the pilgrim train,
> An awful, reverend, and religious man ;
> His eyes diffused a venerable grace,
> And charity itself was in his face ;
> Rich was his soul, though his attire was poor, ⎫
> (As God had clothed his own Ambassador, ⎬
> For such, on earth, his blest Redeemer bore). ⎭
> Of sixty years he seem'd, and well might last
> To sixty more, but that he liv'd too fast ;
> Refined himself to soul, to curb the sense,
> And made almost a sin of abstinence.
> Yet had his aspect nothing of severe ;
> But such a face as promis'd him sincere.
> Nothing reserv'd, or sullen was to see, ⎫
> But sweet regards and pleasing sanctity ; ⎬
> Mild was his accent, and his accents free. ⎭
> With eloquence innate his tongue was arm'd ;
> Tho' harsh the precept, yet the preacher charm'd ;
> For, letting down the golden chain on high,
> He drew his audience upward to the sky ;
> And oft, with holy Hymns, he charm'd their ears
> (A music more melodious than the spheres);
> For David left him, when he went to rest,
> His lyre ; and after him, he sang the best.
> He bore his great Commission in his look ;
> But sweetly temper'd awe, and soften'd all he spoke.
> He preach'd the joys of Heaven and pains of Hell, ⎫
> And warn'd the sinner with becoming zeal ; ⎬
> But on eternal Mercy lov'd to dwell. ⎭
> He taught the Gospel rather than the Law,
> And forc'd himself to drive, but lov'd to draw.
>
>   *   *   *   *
>
> Wide was his parish, not contracted close
> In streets, but here and there a straggling house ;

against his successor, was practically a voluntary act. The likeness was at all events soon recognised. Dryden's poem was published in 1700, and in 1711 it was quoted as describing Ken, in the Preface to the *Expostulatoria,* published with his name. A friend (C. J. P.) suggests that Dryden's lines are, as a whole, more applicable to Kettlewell than to Ken, but Kettlewell did not write hymns.

Yet still he was at hand, without request,
To serve the rich, to succour the distress'd,
Tempting on foot, alone, without affright,
The dangers of a dark, tempestuous night.[1]

    *   *   *

The proud he tamed, the penitent he cheer'd,
Nor to rebuke the rich offender fear'd.[2]
His preaching much, but more his practice wrought,
A living sermon of the truths he taught.

    *   *   *   *

The prelate for his holy life he priz'd,
The worldly pomp of prelacy despis'd.
His Saviour came not with a gaudy show,
Nor was His kingdom of the world below;
Patience in want, and poverty of mind,
These marks of Church and Churchmen he designed,
And living, taught, and dying, left behind.

    *   *   *   *

Such was the Saint who shone with every grace,
Reflecting, Moses-like, his Maker's face.
God saw His image lively was express'd,
And his own work, as in Creation, bless'd.
  The Tempter saw him with invidious eye,
And, as on Job, demanded leave to try.
He took the time when Richard was deposed,
And high and low with happy Harry closed;
This prince, though great in arms, the priest withstood,
Near though he was, yet not the next in blood.
Had Richard unconstrain'd resign'd his throne, ⎫
A King can give no more than is his own,   ⎬
The title stood entail'd, had Richard had a son. ⎭
  Conquest, an odious word, was laid aside,
Where all submitted, none the battle tried.

    *   *   *   *

He join'd not in their choice, because he knew
Worse might, and often did, from change ensue;
Much to himself he thought, but little spoke;

---

[1] Dryden, paraphrasing Chaucer, had, of course, to describe the life of a parish priest and not of a deprived Bishop; but it is, I think, probable that he reported a tradition of what Ken's work had been at Little Easton, Brightstone, Woodhay, or St. John in the Soke.

[2] We remember Charles II.'s " I must go and hear little Ken tell me of my faults."

And, undeprived, his benefice forsook.
Now, through the land his cure of souls he stretch'd,
And, like a primitive Apostle, preach'd;
Still cheerful, ever constant to his call,
By many followed, lov'd by most, admired by all.

* * * *

With what he begged his brethren he reliev'd,[1]
And gave the charities himself receiv'd,
Gave while he taught, and edified the more
Because he shew'd by proof 'twas easy to be poor.

* * * *

It was not, of course, to be expected that a man of Ken's
character and in his position should altogether escape the censures of unsympathising critics. Pepys, from the height of his
superior knowledge, thought of him as "nothing of a natural
philosopher," and his sermons, though fine, were "all of forced
meat" and wanting in substance. Others spoke of him as
inclined to Rome, and looked on his celibacy and asceticism
with suspicion. The tongue of slander, as we have seen,
attacked him with "immodest insinuations" in his own cathedral city. The *via media*, the lonely way, the *parte per se stesso*
which he took, exposed him to the attacks of extremists on
either side. Even Dodwell for a time thought him "fluctuating." The Jacobites of Bristol spoke of him with scorn as the
"poor gentleman" whose strange fancies were doing irremedi-
able mischief to their cause, and Hickes talked of his "wheed-
ling" ways. And, on the other side, the violent Whigs
attacked him, as in the *Modest Enquiry*, as skilled chiefly in
"persuading silly old women to tell down their dust." The
most systematic depreciation came, however, as we have seen,
from the pen of Burnet, between whom and Ken there seems
to have been a feeling of mutual repulsion, and with the single
exception of his acknowledging that he spoke by the death-
bed of Charles II. "as a man inspired," he seems never to lose
an opportunity of a fling at him.[2]

In striking contrast with these disparaging estimates we have
that of Ken's friend, Dr. Fitzwilliam, in a letter to Lady

---

[1] See Ken's action on behalf of the Non-juring clergy (p. 96).
[2] See i. pp. 179, 180, 185 n.; ii. pp. 66, 136.

Rachel Russell (1689).[1] "The Bishop of Bath," he says, "though his conscience may be *tender*, hath this *tenderness* without weakness; his head, if I know anything by him,[2] or can judge anything of him, being as full of clear light as his heart is of devout heat."

In the year of Ken's death (1711), his memory received a tribute of another kind. The Rev. Joseph Perkins, who filled the post of Latin Poet Laureate to the Queen, published an elegy in both Latin and English. I quote from the English version a few passages which connect themselves with some of the facts of Ken's life.

> "Turner and Kenn London affords no room;
> These noble guests both to my lodgings come."[3]

Of Monmonth's rebellion he writes—

> "An hundred criminals in prison lye,
> By Æacus[4] condemnèd all to die,
> But Ken, renownèd Ken, their pardon sought,
> And life and safety to the captive brought."

Of the Princess Anne at Bath—

> "When to the Baths her Royal Highness came,[5]
> Kenn made the Abbey Church resound his fame."

Of the Trial of the Seven Bishops—

> "When, from the Tower freed, brave Kenn returns,
> In every street a blazing bonfire burns."

[1] The letter is not printed in Lady Rachel's correspondence, but is found among the Fitzwilliam MSS. in the Bodleian Library.

[2] The reader will note the use of the preposition in its old sense as in the A.V. of 1 Cor. iv. 4.

[3] Perkins lived at Woodmansterne, in Surrey; but, perhaps, the word "lodgings" implies London. I am unable to fix the date when the two friends visited Perkins, but the fact is interesting as showing that the poet wrote of Ken from personal knowledge.

[4] Jeffreys.

[5] Anderdon (p. 379) states that the fact that Ken's voice was heard throughout the Abbey was communicated to him as a tradition in the family of his informant, the possessor of the original note from the Princess Anne to Turner, Bishop of Ely. See i. 271.

Of his lowliness—

" Whilst other Prelates ride in brave carosse,
On foot this humble-minded Prelate goes."[1]

The fact above referred to, that Dryden's poem was published in the edition of the *Expostulatoria* in 1711, as describing Ken, may be again noticed as an expression of the feeling of reverence, which was, as it were, waiting for his death to utter itself, as also were the republication of the *Royal Sufferer* (whether the book be genuine or spurious), under the title of the *Crown of Glory* in 1625, the twelve editions of the *Winchester Manual* between 1711 and 1799, the *New Year's Gift*, with the three hymns, published in 1712, the republication, from time to time, of the *Practice of Divine Love*, and the *Prayers for those at the Bath*. Hawkins's edition of three of his sermons and his *Life* prefixed to it in 1711, probably did something, imperfect as the latter was, to make his name familiar to a later generation, but I have not found any mention, in the literature of the eighteenth century, of the four volumes of Poems which he published in 1721. Hawkins himself speaks of them as " containing the full beams of Ken's God-enamoured soul," and this may fairly be looked on as expressing a generally received opinion of the character of the poet. A like estimate is implied in the epithets which meet us incidentally here and there, and which speak of him as the *Spiritualis Drexelius et Seraphicus*[2] of the English Church, or as a *Doctor Seraphicus, Angelicus*. The eighteenth century, however, was not favourable to the study of the representative divines of the Anglo-Catholic School of theology, and though Ken is mentioned respectfully in the Biographical Dictionaries (Kippis's and others) there is no trace of any effort to learn more about him than was to be found in Hawkins's meagre narrative, or Salmon's *Lives of the Bishops* (1733). His fame was waning, and seemed on the way to pass into the dim region of shadowy

[1] The lines probably refer to the reign of James II. and to Ken's visits to London, perhaps to the time of the trial of the Seven Bishops.
[2] Ballard MSS., Bodl., vol. 41, *ad fin.* in Anderdon, p. 117. Drexelius, author of the *Heliotropium*, was a Jesuit preacher of Augsburg, famous in his day (d. 1638) as a writer of devotional books. The *Heliotropium* has been recently republished.

forms, of whose names we speak with honour, but of whom also we often know little beyond the names. Even the use of the Morning and Evening Hymns, which became common in the latter part of the period, did not do much to make his name more widely known, seeing that they were often printed in Tate and Brady's *Supplement* and other hymn-books without it. Towards the close of the eighteenth century, however, an anonymous pamphlet, *An Address to the Archbishop of Canterbury, &c., &c., by a Country Clergyman*, London, 1791 (quoted by Round, *Preface*, p. ix.) shows that the older, more enthusiastic feeling had not quite died out. The writer speaks of Beveridge and other bishops :—

" But there is one of that venerable order, whose memory, above all others, I shall ever love and cherish to my latest breath : Hail, immortal Ken, guide of my youthful steps !¹ Thy bounty never ceased to feed the poor, nor thy tongue to instruct the ignorant. Thy presence, or thy spirit, continually pervaded all parts of thy extensive diocese. It illuminated her churches and darted comfort through the cheerless gloom of her prisons. . . . . Hail, gentle, blessed spirit, for thy sake may the mitre ever flourish ! "

One would fain know more of one who thus took his place among those who handed on the traditional veneration of their fathers for the name of Ken to a later age,

Et, quasi cursores, vitai lampada tradunt,

and if any reader can throw light upon the authorship of the pamphlet, I shall welcome the information.

It is significant that Ken begins to emerge from this obscurity about the time when the school of the Stuart divines began to attract more notice than before, at the hands of students both of English literature and theology. Among the former Southey takes a fairly prominent place. In his *Omniana* he gives some anecdotes of Ken's life (see i. 3, 23). In his *Common Place Book* (iv. p. 346), he furnishes a short account of the four volumes of Poems, and is, so far as I know, the first writer since their publication who seems to have read them with any intelligent

---

¹ One conjectures that the writer may have been a Wykehamist, and was thinking of the *Manual*.

interest. He notes the poem *On the Nativity*,[1] in particular the couplet—

> "The Virgin Mother, near the Manger plac'd,
> In her soft Arms the boundless Babe embrac'd,"

as "full of Catholic passion," thinks that Parnell imitated, in his *Hermit*, Ken's description of Sophronio in his *Edmund* (ii. p. 76), and applies to his poems in general Maggi's lines,[2]

> *" Belle d'affetti più che di pensieri."*

There also it was true of the author—

> *" Più che gl' ingegni alteri*
> *Ama i cuori devoti, e nè suoi canti*
> *Val per esser Poeta essere amante."*

Bowles's *Life*, with all its imperfections, is, at least, welcome as a proof that men were beginning (1830) to think of Ken as one of whom they would be glad to know more. How far he was drawn to his subject by Southey's influence I am unable to say. Nothing can be warmer in reverent admiration than the tone in which he speaks of Ken throughout, with the one exception of the judgment which he passes on his poems (p. 232).

On the side of the students of Anglican theology, in this as in other things, Alexander Knox was the precursor of the Oxford school, and I quote from his writings some thoughtful criticisms.

(1.) Ken's Hymns.

"A comparison of the hymns of Doddridge, Watts, Ken, and Wesley would show that Doddridge rises above Watts from having caught the spirit of Ken ; and Wesley is deep and interior from having added to the Chrysostomian piety of Ken the experimental part of St. Augustine. Watts is a pure Calvinist ; Ken is as pure

---

[1] The poem is, perhaps, the finest of the *Hymns Evangelical* of the first vol. of Ken's Poems. It appears in the volume published by Pickering in 1868 under the title of Ken's *Christian Year*, as for the 2nd Sunday after Christmas. One may, perhaps, trace here and there reminiscences of Milton's *Ode on the Nativity*.

[2] Carlo Maria Maggi, an Italian poet, b. 1630, d. 1699.

a Chrysostomian. Doddridge is induced to blend both, and the effect is valuable and interesting; Wesley advances this union."[1]

(2.) Ken's *Edmund.*

" Pray read some gnomic verses extracted from Bishop Ken; as they occur in a very long, and sometimes dull, epic of the good Bishop's, they may hitherto have escaped your notice ; to me they seem not merely the description, but the effluence of a very mature state of Christianity."[2]

And generally—

" I ought to have named Bishop Ken, than whom none approach nearer the primeval warmth of soul." [3]

And again—

" The characters to which I refer have been Spiritualists rather than Theologists. . . . . I must not multiply names ; yet I cannot but specify Herbert, Taylor, and Ken; each of these excellent persons (as well as Doddridge and Leighton, with the whole happy class who have been like-minded) pursued religion not merely on account of the evils which it averts, but for the sake of the good, even the present good, which it confers ; they felt the force of that admirable saying of St. Augustine, *Fecisti nos ad te, et inquietum est cor nostrum donec requiescat in te.* . . . (Cont. i. 1). While corporeally on earth, they lived mentally in eternity. The more attentively I examine and compare these almost transparent characters, the more deeply I am satisfied that Christian piety is in them an anticipatory Paradise."[4]

Those who, consciously or unconsciously, followed in Knox's footsteps, and became the leaders in the Oxford Catholic revival, could hardly fail to be attracted even by the little that was then known of the life and character of Ken. It was, as the event showed, precisely the type of character with which they were most in sympathy, the ideal which they aimed at

[1] *Remains,* iii. p. 226.
[2] *Thirty Years' Correspondence with Bishop Jebb,* ii. p. 260.
[3] *Remains,* iii. p. 109.
[4] *Remains,* iii. pp. 434—35. The last sentence is but a paraphrase of some lines in Ken's *Hymnotheo,* Works, iii. p. 256 :—
" The Saints below, the Bless'd above,
Are only happy in their love.
Ah! how shall I Thy Goodness know,
Thence to begin my Heaven below."
[C. J. P.]

reproducing. I have shown in my *Life of Dante* how powerfully the revival of the study of the representative poet of Mediæval Catholicism affected the Oxford movement. As I pass from Dante to Ken I am struck with the fact that his name also is intimately associated with it; one representing its scholarly and historic side, the chain which connected it with the great history of Latin Christendom, the other presenting to us the more direct descent from the Anglo-Catholicism of the seventeenth century, and the type of a devout asceticism.

The earliest indication of the influence which Ken's memory was thus exercising is found in an unpublished letter from John Keble, to his friend and brother Fellow, C. J. Plumer.[1] He writes from Fairford, July 19th, 1825—

"I will tell it you, if you will promise to keep it secret to yourself. Tom[2] and I have a notion of editing some of Bishop Ken's remains, one or two sermons, and some letters, and little tracts, which would make one small volume, and some choice bits of his poetry, which would make another; but one or two of the tracts are very scarce, and I dare say I should have to come to the British Museum for them."

The letter suggests some questions of interest. What letters did Keble then know of? What tracts did he recognise as Ken's? Did they include the *Expostulatoria*, the *Royal Sufferer*, the *Letter to Tenison*? All this we are left, however, to guess.

Keble's plan, at all events, was not realised, and the work of publishing Ken's prose works and letters was left to the Rev. J. T. Round, a former Fellow of Balliol, in 1838.[3] Of the merits and demerits of this work I have spoken in the Preface.

[1] Communicated by the Rev. J. R. Bloxam.
[2] John Keble's brother.
[3] It is significant that a review of Round's volume appeared in the first number of the *British Critic* that came out under Newman's editorship (No. xlvii., 1838). Cardinal Newman does not remember who wrote it. Internal evidence leads me to conjecture W. J. Copeland, who was then a leading member of the Oxford school. It displays a much more full and intimate acquaintance with Ken's life and works than we find in Round, and is written throughout in a strain of devout admiration. Notably he maintains the genuineness of the *Letter to Tenison*, and thinks it possible that the *Expostulatoria* may have been the outcome of strong feeling in Ken's youthful days. He has studied the Poems carefully and protests against the "flippancy" with which Bowles

In 1836, however, there had been a significant proof of the impression made by Ken's character on the chief of the triumvirate who were recognised as the leaders of the Oxford movement. In that year (the Tract bears the date of the Feast of St. John Baptist, June 25) John Henry Newman published No. 75 of the *Tracts of the Times*.[1] In many respects it is among the most remarkable of the whole series. The writer had become impressed with the " excellence and beauty " of the services of the Breviary. He avowedly wrote to claim "whatever was good and true " in those devotions " for the Church Catholic in opposition to the Romish Church." The latter "has appropriated treasure which was as much ours as theirs." To compile selections from them, or services after the same plan, not in Latin, but in the vernacular, and to recommend them for private use, was from this point of view "an act of re-appropriation." The Tract proceeds accordingly, after a short historical account of the Breviary, to give a series of services, after the same pattern. Of these one is for August 6th, the Festival of the Transfiguration ; the second, for August 10th, as that of St. Laurence ; and the last, for March 21st, as Bishop Ken's day, the anniversary *i.e.* of his burial.[2] He practically took upon himself to canonise the Bishop, and to commend him to the commemoration of devout Christians, justifying himself

had spoken of them. To him Ken seems " as literally and entirely to illustrate the Scripture characteristics of a Christian Bishop as any one of whom we know, very nearly to exemplify the theory of the Church of England ; to have felt and developed its Catholic principles, and Catholic spirit."

[1] I am authorised by Cardinal Newman to name him as the author. He says in his *Apologia* (p. 154) that it " frightened his friends."

[2] Ken died on March 19th, and was buried on the 21st. Was Cardinal Newman led to choose the latter day by the fact that it was already dedicated to St. Benedict?—(C. J. P.) Another more mysterious service is a commemoration of Sunday, June 21, 1801. It fills fifty pages, gives forms for three Nocturns, Lauds, Prime, Third, Sixth and Ninth Hours, and includes the *Te Deum* and the Athanasian creed, and many Psalms and hymns. The lessons are chiefly taken from the warfare of David against the Philistines, spiritualized as an allegory of the Christian's conflict with the world, and from the call of the first four Apostles. The reader is left to guess what the service commemorates. The year 1801 was that of Cardinal Newman's birth, but his birthday was February 21st. Was the service a self-reminder of the life to which that year called him, when it witnessed his baptism into the Church of Christ ? The Breviary, which, at this time, seems to have determined the current of his thoughts, was Froude's dying gift. (*Apol.*, p. 154).

in doing so at the time, as of course he could not now justify himself, on the ground that general testimony, as when it is said of the people in our Lord's time, " *omnes habebant Joannem sicut prophetam,*" was a sufficient ground for recognising the saintliness of his character. The service is one of singular beauty, and though too long to be reproduced in its entirety, deserves a fairly full analysis.

(1.) After the usual versicles, " O Lord, open Thou my lips," &c., we have as an " Invitatory " prefixed to Psalm xcv., the words—

" O come, let us worship the Lord, the King of Confessors."

This is followed by two hymns for alternative use, one from the poem for *St. Matthias,* the other from that for *St. John the Evangelist* in the *Christian Year.*

Nocturn I.

After Antiphons from Psalm i., ii., iii., we have a Verse and Response—

" The Lord loved him and adorned him,
  And clothed him with a robe of glory."

Lesson I. is from 1 Timothy iii. 1—6, and is followed by—

Verse and Response I.—" *Well done, thou good and faithful Servant, thou hast been faithful over a few things, I will make thee ruler over many things.*

" Lord, thou deliveredst unto me five talents, behold, I have gained beside them five talents more."

Lesson II. is from Titus i. 7—11—

Verse and Response II.—" *Let thy Thummim and thy Urim be with Thy holy one, whom thou didst prove at Massah, and with whom Thou didst strive at the waters of Meribah; they shall put incense before Thee, and whole burnt sacrifice upon Thine altar.*

" Bless, Lord, his substance, and accept the work of his hands; smite through the loins of them that rise against him, and of them that hate him, that they rise not again."

Lesson III. is from Titus ii. 1—8, followed by—

Verse and Response III.—" *Let the Saints be joyful with glory, let them rejoice in their bed, let the praises of God be in their mouths and a two-edged sword in their hands : to bind their kings in chains, and their nobles with links of iron.*

"That they may be avenged of them, as it is written, Such honour have all His saints."

NOCTURN II.

Antiphons from Psalms iv., v., viii.—

Verse and Response IV.—" The Lord hath chosen Him as a priest unto Himself.

"To sacrifice to Him the offering of praise."

Lesson IV. relates the story of Ken's life in the time of his chaplaincy at the Hague, giving the Zulestein episode, as told by Hawkins, without the names.

Verse and Response V.—" Princes have persecuted me without a cause, but my heart standeth in awe of Thy word.

"I will speak of Thy testimonies also, even before kings, and will not be ashamed."

Lesson V. continues the life, reporting the Nell Gwyn anecdote, and Ken's ministrations at the death of Charles II.

Verse and Response VI.—" Many shall be purified, and made white and tried ; and many of them that sleep in the dust of the earth shall awake.

"And they that be wise shall shine as the brightness of the firmament ; and they that turn many to righteousness as the stars for ever and ever."

Lesson VI. goes on with the life, recording the petition of the seven Bishops, and Ken's deprivation and death in 1710 (✠✠), with the comment :—

"Thus he gave to Cæsar the things that be Cæsar's, and to God the things that be God's. He was as meek, gentle, and affectionate in his bearing as he was bold in the cause of the Gospel ; and he took his troubles cheerfully and lightly. He possessed, in an especial way, that most excellent gift of charity. Once when four thousand pounds fell to his See, he gave great part of it to the French Protestants then under persecution ; and when he was deprived, all his means, after the sale of his goods at his palace and elsewhere, was not more than seven hundred pounds. When State interests interfered with the prosperity of the Church in Scotland, he said[1] he conceived great hopes that God would have mercy on the English branch of it, if she did but compassionate and support her sister ;

<hr>

[1] See Letter xxx., p. 49.

and he bore testimony shortly before his death, saying that he died in the Holy Catholic and Apostolic Faith, professed by the whole Church before the disunion of East and West. Such was he then, a burning and shining light, bringing back primitive times.

"But Thou, O Lord, have mercy upon us."

Verse and Response VII.—"*I said I have laboured in vain, I have spent my strength for nought and in vain; yet surely my judgment is with the Lord, and my work with my God.*

"He hath made my mouth like a sharp sword; in the shadow of His hand hath He hid me."

NOCTURN III.

Antiphons from Psalms xv., xxi., xxiv.

Verse and Response VII.—"*The key of David will I lay upon his shoulder.*

"He shall open and none shall shut; he shall shut and none shall open."

Lesson VII., Luke xxii. 25—30.

This is followed by a passage from Jeremy Taylor, on the joy of the saints in heaven.

Verse and Response VIII.—"*Whosoever shall confess Me before men, him shall the Son of Man also confess before the Angels of God.*

"To him that overcometh will I grant to sit with Me on My throne."

Lessons VIII. and IX., are, as before, from Jeremy Taylor.

Verse and Response IX.—"*In the sight of the unwise they seemed to die, and their departure is taken for misery, but they are in peace.*

"Though they be punished in the sight of men, yet is their hope full of immortality."

After Lesson IX. the service ends with the *Te Deum.*

It is difficult to throw ourselves into the state of mind of which these services were the outcome. One thinks that the writer must now look back on them as part of a fevered dream, in which he half-pictured himself as the restorer of a Church that was sinking into a Latitudinarian Protestantism, to the earlier catholicity of which he found a representative in Ken. One asks how and when he thought they would be used. Did he contemplate a community like that of Little Gidding, in which they should be used as supplementing the offices of the Prayer-book?[1] Anyhow, this special service has, if I mis-

[1] I am informed by Cardinal Newman that the service was never used.

take not, a special psychological interest, both in the singular appropriateness of the Lessons, Antiphons, and Responses, as bearing on Ken's character, and as showing how strong a fascination that character then had for the great leader of the Anglo-Catholic revival. It is hardly an overstrained inference to believe that, with that half-conscious aspiration which rises in the minds of most men, when they contemplate a life in which they recognise the embodiment of their own ideal, the John Henry Newman of those days sought to be the Ken of the nineteenth century, striving to lead the Church of England, and, through her, other Christian communities, to the doctrine and the worship of that undivided Church of the East and West, after which Ken yearned even to his dying hour (p. 209). If I am right in my conjecture as to the mysterious service as for Sunday, June 21, 1801, that hypothesis attains almost the position of a certainty. That year was, for him at least, much to be remembered, for it witnessed both the natural and the new birth into the Anglican branch of Christ's Church, of him who, as he then dreamt, was called to be as the *vox clamantis in deserto*,[2] possibly also its restorer to a fuller life and mightier power as a witness of the Truth.

A poem in the *Lyra Apostolica* (cxiii.) shows that Ken was scarcely less prominent in the thoughts of another poet-prophet of the Oxford school, Isaac Williams. The angel of the Church is seen mourning " with earth-bent brow forlorn," grieving less for the attacks of enemies from without than for the lukewarmness of those within, for the " something left behind : "—

> " The unshackled high resolve, the holier aim,
>   Single-eyed faith in loyalty resign'd,
>   And heart-deep prayers of earlier years ;
>   And since that popular billow o'er thee past,
>   Which thine own Ken from out the vineyard cast,
>   Now, e'en far more
>   Than then of yore,
>   An altered mien thy holy aspect wears."

[1] These words form the motto inscribed on a label attached to the rude cross which appears in the right hand of St. John Baptist, forming the frontispiece to the *Library of the Fathers*. On the rock at St. John's foot is "Advent, 1836." —[H. W. P.] One more passage from the *Apologia* (p. 273) may be cited as suggestive. " Our position," he writes in 1841, " is diverging from that of Ken," as though that had hitherto been the parallel case by which he had been guided.

A sonnet in the *Cathedral* of the same author (p. 58) is worth reproducing, both for its own beauty, and as indicating the same reverential devotion.

KEN.

" Ye holy gates, open your calm repose,
  Between him and the world your barriers close ;
  Nought hath he but his lyre and sacred key,
  Which the world gave not, nor can take away.
  One of that Seven against a King he stood ;
  The world was with him in his fortitude.
  One of that Five, he scorn'd her flattering breath,
  And firm in strength which wisdom cherisheth,
  Where Truth and Loyalty had mark'd the ground,
  Stood by that suffering King, allegiance-bound ;
  Then, as in him his Saviour stood reveal'd,
  The world in anger rose, against him steeled,
  And drove him from her—Open your repose,
  And, her and him between, your heavenly barriers close."[1]

*   *   *   *

I turn from these estimates to one from a very different quarter, yet belonging to the same period and tending to the same conclusion. I find in Lord Beaconsfield's *Correspondence with his Sister*, 1886, p. 119, the following—

"Feb. 1839. I met a M. Rion[2] who . . . . spoke English, and is the most astonishing litterateur I ever encountered. He says that

---

[1] A striking passage from Bishop Moberly's *Sermons on the Beatitudes* (p. 5) may find a place here. His text is, " Blessed are the meek, for they shall inherit the earth." He draws a contrast between Marlborough and Ken, sketches the fame of the former, and then says of the latter, " He was poor, evil spoken of, and watched with jealousy, even in his works of charity. . . . . And yet, if any man should attempt to gauge the influence, the real, lasting influence of these two men, the real, essential, enduring power, the true weight on man, on his liberty, on his heart, on his prospects, on his real self, which, think you, has most truly inherited this earth in power, the author of the Morning and Evening Hymns or the conqueror of Blenheim ? he whose simple words and few, not in themselves particularly able or particularly beautiful, whose simple words make, and have made, and, no doubt, will make sweet Christian music in the hearts of millions who have never heard his name ; or he whose station, ability, and success blazed before the world's eyes for a few years, and, their effects swept away after a time, then disappeared absolutely and for ever."

[2] I conjecture that A. F. Rio, author of *De la Poésie Chrétienne*, is meant. It is interesting to note, in connexion with the poem which follows, that the meeting took place at one of Monckton Milnes's breakfasts.—[C. J. P.]

Bishop Ken was the Fenelon of England, and that the Oxford Tracts are a mere revival of his works.   It is the Non-jurors again."[1]

A tribute of another kind comes in the form of some lines by Lord Houghton, then R. M. Milnes, on Ken's grave at Frome. I am unable to fix the date, beyond the fact that it was obviously prior to the work done in Ken's honour at Frome in 1844.

> "Let other thoughts, where'er I roam,
>   Ne'er from my memory cancel
> The coffin-fashioned tomb at Frome,
>   That lies behind the chancel :
> A basket-work where bars are bent,
>   Iron in place of ozier,
> And shapes above that represent
>   A mitre and a crozier.
>
> "These signs of him that slumbers there
>   The dignity betoken ;
> These iron bars a heart declare
>   Hard bent, but never broken ;
> This form portrays how souls like his,
>   Their pride and passion quelling,
> Preferred, to earth's high palaces,
>   This calm and narrow dwelling.
>
> "There ,with the churchyard's common dust,
>   He lov'd his own to mingle ;
> The faith in which he placed his trust
>   Was nothing rare or single.
> Yet lay he to the sacred wall
>   As close as he was able ;
> The blessed crumbs might almost fall
>   Upon him from God's table.
>
> "Who was this father of the Church,
>   So secret in his glory ?
> In vain might antiquarians search
>   For record of his story ;

---

[1] The writer of a life of Nicholas Pavillon, Bishop of Alet (1869), suggests also, as I have shown (i. 258), an interesting parallel between that prelate and Ken.

But preciously tradition keeps
The fame of holy men ;
So there the Christian smiles or weeps
For love of Bishop Ken.

" A name his country once forsook,
But now with joy inherits,
Confessor in the Church's book
And martyr in the Spirit's !
That dared with royal power to cope,
In peaceful faith persisting,
A braver Becket—who could hope
To conquer unresisting.

With this we may compare a short poem by Bowles in his *Life
of Ken* (ii., p. 263)—

"The Grave of Ken.

" On yonder heap of earth forlorn,
  Where Ken his place of burial chose,
Peacefully shine, O Sabbath morn !
  And eve, with gentlest hush, repose.

" To him is rear'd no marble tomb,
  Within the dim cathedral fane,
But some faint flowers of summer bloom,
  And silent falls the winter's rain.

" No village monumental stone
  Records a verse, a date, a name ;
What boots it ?   When thy task is done,
  CHRISTIAN, how vain the sound of Fame !

" Oh, far more grateful to thy God,
  The voices of poor children rise,
Who hasten o'er the dewy sod,
  ' To pay their morning sacrifice.'

" And can we listen to their Hymn,
  Heard, haply, when the Evening knell
Sounds, where the village tower is dim,
  As if to bid the world farewell,

" Without a thought, that from the dust
  The morn shall wake the sleeping clay,
And bid the faithful and the just,
  Up spring to heaven's eternal day ? "

Lovers of the more elegant forms of lapidary Latinity will, I
believe, thank me for bringing before them two inscriptions by
the late Rev. Francis Kilvert, of Bath.[1]

"THOMAS KEN

" DIVINO QUODAM CHARITATIS ARDORE INSTINCTUS,
EANDEM DUCEM SIBI
TOTIUS VITÆ DEGENDÆ
PROPOSUIT :
HAC VELVT CYNOSVRA VSVS,
DVM MVNVS APOSTOLICVM EXERCERET,
VT PASTOR OVICVLAS, VT GALLINA PVLLOS,
VT MATER TENELLOS,
SIC CLERVM POPVLVMQUE SVVM,
MITI NEC MINVS FIRMO
IMPERIO, REGEBAT,
EODEM DVCTV,
QVVM, PRÆTER JVS FASQUE,
REX DEMENS
ECCLESIÆ REBVS SE INTROMISISSET,
MALVIT CVM PAVCIS PATIENDO RESISTERE
QVAM CVM MVLTIS
INIQVO IMPERIO MOREM GERERE.
CONTRA,
QVVM REX IDEM,
A SVIS DESERTVS,
INJVRIOSE A SOLIO PATERNO PVLSVS ESSET,
CVM PAVCIS MALEBAT
OFFICIO BONISQVE CEDERE
QVAM CVM MVLTIS,
FIDEM REGI DEBITAM DATAMQVE,
AD ALIENVM DOMINVM TRANSFERENDO, FALLERE.
DENIQVE, HOC DVCE,
BONORVM CÆLESTIVM FIRMISSIMA SPE CONCEPTA,
IN FIDE ECCLESIÆ NONDVM DIVISÆ,
VITAM INOPEM,
DOMVS MVNIFICÆ SVBSIDIIS,
LÆTE PLACIDEQVE TOLERATAM
VERIS ET ÆTERNIS OPIBVS
COMMVTAVIT.

---

[1] Published in his *Pinacotheræ Historicæ Specimen.*

KENNI CUBICULO APUD LONGLEAT
IN COMIT. WILT. INSCRIBENDUM

CVBICVLVM HOC,
DOMICILIVM SENECTUTIS SVÆ,
PER ANNOS PROPE XX HABVIT
THOMAS KEN,
EPISCOPVS BATHON. ET WELLEN. DEPRIVATVS,
QVEM, INIQVITATE TEMPORVM SEDE DEPVLSVM,
DOMVS ISTHÆC,
EXEMPLO, CONSILIO, SOLATIO EJVS
ADJVTA,
VELVT ANGELVM EX IMPROVISO RECEPTVM,
EXPERTA EST,
CVJVSQVE BEATAM MEMORIAM,
ADHVC VIRENTEM,
GRATISSIMA RECORDATIONE
PROSEQVITVR.''

A tribute of singular and almost reverential warmth comes from the pen of the great Whig historian.[1]

The historian is describing Charles II.'s death.

"Thomas Ken, Bishop of Bath and Wells, then tried his powers of persuasion. He was a man of parts and learning, of quick sensibility and stainless virtue. His elaborate works have long been forgotten, but his Morning and Evening Hymns are still repeated daily in thousands of dwellings."[2]

Elsewhere he speaks of him as—

"Both in intellectual and moral qualities ranking highest among the Non-juring Prelates."[3]

And again—

"Ken quietly retired from the venerable palace of Wells. He had done, he said, with strife, and should henceforth vent his feelings, not in disputes, but in hymns. His charities to the unhappy of all persuasions, especially to the followers of Monmouth and the persecuted Huguenots, had been so large that his whole private fortune consisted of seven hundred pounds, and of a library which he could not persuade himself to sell. But Thomas Thynne, Viscount Weymouth, though not a Non-juror, did himself honour by offering to the most virtuous of the Non-jurors a tranquil and dig-

[1] Macaulay, *History of England.* [2] Chapter ii. [3] Chapter xix.

nified retirement in the princely mansion of Longleat. There Ken passed a happy and honoured old age, during which he never regretted the sacrifice he had made to what he thought his duty, and yet constantly became more and more indulgent to those whose views of duty differed from his."

Among the less direct results of what may be described as the revival of Ken's name and fame initiated by the leaders of the Oxford movement, we may note the more public tributes to his memory. For nearly a century and a half his own diocese had remained without any memorial but the iron grating at Frome, unaccompanied by a single word of inscription, as Lord Houghton has described it. In 1844 a committee was formed for the general restoration of the church of St. John Baptist at Frome, and in particular, for some special tribute to Ken. It numbered among its members the Rev. Charles Phillott (then Vicar of Frome), the Warden of New College, the Warden and Head Master of Winchester College, Mr. Justice Coleridge, the present Sir T. D. Acland, Bart., Mr. A. H. Dyke Acland, Mr. F. H. Dickenson, and others. The tomb was left undisturbed, but was enclosed and covered by a small stone coping, designed by Mr. Butterfield. A memorial window, given by Harriet, Marchioness of Bath, was placed in a chapel south of the chancel, of which the following is a description—

"In the upper part of the centre opening is a figure of our Lord, as the Good Shepherd, bearing the lamb upon His shoulders,—the text, 'Where I am, there shall also My servant be; if any man serve Me, him will My Father honour.' (S. John xii. 26.) On the one side, the subject is our Lord's charge to S. Peter, 'Lovest thou Me?—Feed my lambs.' (S. John xxi. 16.) On the other side, a group of angels, holding scrolls, upon which is written, 'Holy, holy, holy:' the text, 'Salvation to our God Which sitteth upon the throne, and unto the Lamb.' (Rev. vii. 10.) In the lower part of the centre opening, under 'the Good Shepherd,' is a kneeling figure of Bishop Ken, having his faldstool and book before him, and his mitre and staff lying by his side;—the likeness has been taken from the original portrait of the Bishop, at Longleat, and wrought with much care. The text accompanying this figure is 'The Lord will be a defence for the oppressed, even a refuge in due time of trouble: for Thou, Lord, hast never failed them that seek Thee.' (Psalm ix. 9, 10.) The other subjects are, 'The Feast,' illustrative of the

Bishop's benevolent custom of entertaining at his table a number of poor persons once a week. The text, 'They cannot recompense thee: for thou shalt be recompensed at the resurrection of the just.' (S. Luke xiv. 14.) Our Lord at the pool of Bethesda, surrounded by the sick and maimed. The text, 'O ye fountains, bless ye the Lord; praise Him and exalt Him above all for ever.' "

An inscription on a brass plate below has the heading—

"ALL GLORY BE TO GOD.
THOMAS KEN,
BORN AT LITTLE BERKHAMPSTEAD, IN THE COUNTY
OF HERTFORD,
1637;
CONSECRATED BISHOP OF THIS DIOCESE,
1684;[1]
IMPRISONED BY ONE KING,
1688;
AND DEPRIVED BY ANOTHER,
1689;
SUFFERING IN BOTH CASES FOR THE TESTIMONY
OF A GOOD CONSCIENCE,
DIED AT LONGLEAT, UNDER THE ROOF OF HIS FRIEND
THOMAS VISCOUNT WEYMOUTH,
MARCH 19TH, 1710,[1]
AND BY HIS OWN DESIRE WAS BURIED IN THE
ADJOINING CHURCH YARD.
MANY REVERING HIS MEMORY HAVE JOINED
TO PROTECT FROM INJURY THE GRAVE OF THIS
HOLY CONFESSOR, AND TO RESTORE
THIS CHANCEL
TO THE GLORY OF ALMIGHTY GOD.
WITH LIKE REVERENCE THIS MEMORIAL WINDOW
HAS BEEN SET UP BY
HARRIET, MARCHIONESS OF BATH.
MDCCCXLVIII.

In 1867 Taunton followed in the footsteps of Frome, and by the exertions of Mr. Arthur Kinglake and his personal friends a bust was placed in the Town Hall, side by side with those of other Somerset worthies, Locke, Blake and Pym. The inscription runs as follows—

[1] Date given according to the old reckoning. Ken was consecrated January 25, 168⅘. So 1710 stands for 17¹⁰⁄₁₁.

T 2

"THOMAS KEN

DESCENDED FROM AN ANCIENT SOMERSETSHIRE FAMILY,
BORN AT BERKHAMPSTEAD IN THE COUNTY OF HERTFORD 1637,
CONSECRATED BISHOP OF BATH AND WELLS 1684,[1]
IMPRISONED BY ONE KING, DEPRIVED BY ANOTHER,
IN LIFE BLAMELESS, OF DOCTRINE PURE,
THE JEWEL OF MITRED SAINTS,
AND A PATTERN TO ALL BELIEVERS.
DIED AT LONGLEAT 1711."

This is followed, first by eight lines from Dryden's panegyric beginning with—

"Rich was his soul, though his attire was poor,"

and secondly by Ken's Confession of Faith in his Will.

Lastly, in 1884, the Cathedral church of Ken's diocese took in hand a long-delayed duty. With the exception of the lines in the Latin epitaph to Kidder, which have been quoted in p. 63, there was no visible record there of the fact that he had ever been connected with it. Subscriptions were invited from those who honoured his memory and loved his hymns, and the appeal was not made in vain. A memorial window was placed in the north aisle of the choir, executed by Messrs. Lavers, Barraud and Westlake, of which the following is a description—

"The central panel of the memorial window contains a portrait figure of the Bishop in cope and mitre, holding a pastoral staff. Over the Bishop's head are the words 'All glory be to God,' which he was in the habit of writing as the superscription of every letter. The text below the figure, '*Et tu quaeris tibi grandia? Noli quaerere,*' ('And seekest thou great things for thyself? Seek them not' (Jer. xlv. 5), has been chosen as having been found written in Ken's own hand in two books that were in constant use by him. At the foot of the window runs the inscription, '*In piam memoriam viri sanctissimi, dilectissimi, Thomæ Ken, S.T.P., Olim Bathon. et Wellen. Episcopi. N.* 1637, *Ob.* 1711.' Below the central panel is the Bishop's coat of arms, those of the Kenn family, of Kenn Court, Somerset, impaled with the arms of the diocese. The motto, '*Pastor bonus dat animam pro ovibus*' ('The Good Shepherd giveth his life for the

1 See *note*, p. 279.

sheep,' John x. 11), is that which the Bishop chose for himself as embodying his ideal of the pastoral work of the episcopate. Above the central panel are three figures :—(1) St. Andrew as the patron saint of the diocese and Cathedral, with the words, '*Piscator hominum*' ('Fisher of Men.'—Matt. iv. 19). (2) David, as representing Ken's work as a hymn-writer, with the inscription, '*Egregius Psaltes Israel*' ('The sweet Psalmist of Israel.'—2 Sam. xxiii. 1). (3) Daniel, as the subject of one of Ken's most memorable sermons, in which he has unconsciously portrayed his own character, with the words, '*Vir desideriorum*' ('A man greatly beloved,' or 'A man of desires.' —Dan. ix. 23). The subjects in the side-panels have been chosen as representing some of the most characteristic features in Ken's life and work. (1) St. Paul teaching Timotheus, as answering to Ken's work in writing his 'Manual for Winchester Scholars' and his 'Exposition of the Church Catechism.' The two texts of this panel are '*Finis præcepti caritas*' ('The end of the Commandment is charity,' i. Tim. i. 5), and '*Prædica verbum*' ('Preach the Word,' ii. Tim. iv. 2). (2) Our Lord's Charge to St. Peter, with the words '*Diligis me ?*' ('Lovest thou me ?') '*Pasce agnos meos*' ('Feed my Lambs') from St. John xxi. 15. (3) St. Paul before Agrippa, as parallel to Ken's protest in the Council Chamber of James II. The two texts are '*A tenebris ad lucem*' ('From darkness to light,' Acts xxvi. 18), and '*Coram gentibus et regibus*' ('Before the Gentiles and Kings,' Acts ix. 15). (4) St. Peter in prison, as answering to Ken's imprisonment in the Tower. The two texts are '*Sequere me*' ('Follow me,' Acts xii. 8), and '*Et in carcerem*' ('Even to prison,' Luke xxii. 33). (5 and 6). The subjects of the two side panels at the foot of the window are intended to illustrate the Morning and Evening Hymns. On the left are men going forth to their work and their labour in the early dawn, singing the canticle, '*Benedicite, omnia opera,*' with the word '*Mane*' ('in the morning') below. On the right side is a priest with choir men and boys chanting their '*Nunc dimittis*' by the light of a lamp, with the word '*Vespere*' ('At evening "). The two words are taken from Psalm lv., 17.[1]

On June 29th, in 1885, in the bicentenary year of Ken's consecration, on the anniversary of the Trial of the Seven Bishops, a Commemorative Festival was held in the Cathedral, in connexion with the first appearance of the window just described, and a Sermon preached by the Right Rev. William Alexander, D.D., Bishop of Derry and Raphoe. Those who had

[1] The Latin texts are throughout taken from the Vulgate.

the privilege of hearing that sermon felt that it was worthy of the subject and the occasion, worthy also of the preacher's fame. I cannot close this series of estimates better than by printing it *in extenso*.

> "*My reward is with me, to give every man according as his work shall be.*"
> REV. xxii. 12.

Bishop Ken "died as he lived, a plain, humble man." He desired to be buried in the churchyard of the nearest parish within his diocese, Frome Selwood, under the east window of the chancel, just at sun-rising, without any manner of pomp or ceremony besides that of the Order for Burial in the Liturgy of the Church of England. Probably one reason of this desire was his characteristic dislike of funeral sermons. "Sin was seldom wanting in them," he said. To be preached over at a funeral seemed to his humility to be the addition of a pang to death.

In the case of one who has so long entered into his rest, the preacher's poor words of praise can scarcely offend the modesty of immortality. I shall, therefore, after (1) attempting to grasp the idea in the text, proceed (2) to apply it to the life-work of Thomas Ken.

The risen Lord speaks in the text of "the Reward" and "the Work." Let us fix our attention on these familiar words.

(1.) *Reward* (or *hire*)—for speaking to man, Scripture must, at all events Scripture *does*, speak "with the tongue of Man." The most dangerous errors have arisen from pressing metaphors too far. And so "reward," in its practical bearing upon men, must be viewed as an approximate term. It is not precisely so much wages for so much work. It is the idea of hire, paid for labour, transferred to the Divine payment, with the limitations implied by the feebleness of the labourer, and by the infinite freedom of the grace. And the truth conveyed by "reward" must be important. For the word is not dropped as if accidentally. It occurs again and again. Let him who is suspicious of it remember how it comes to us, as if it were swinging to and fro, three times over, on the chime of Christ's sweetest bells of promise—"shall receive a prophet's *reward*," "shall receive a righteous man's *reward*," "shall in no wise lose his *reward*." The importance of this idea of reward may be seen by its bearing on two aspects of the Christian life.

It fills up what otherwise might be a moral gap upon the moral side of the gospel. It is an effectual answer to one objection to Justification by Faith.

The circle has but one centre, salvation has but one Saviour.

Has man, then, nothing to do beyond a passive acceptance of this great truth ? We are not, indeed, hirelings who dare to bargain with a Father, who, after all, only "crowns his own gift in us." But He, in a sense, condescends to bargain with us. We do not work up to a life which we win, but on from a life which we receive. "Not grace from works, but works from grace." Yet the judgment is according to works, and the reward is proportionate. Every half hour is golden. God's wages are not paid at the end of every week, but they are always paid.

How necessary Reward is to Hope, one need scarcely show at length. Above the long bead-roll of worthies of Faith (of whom Ken was one) stands the eternal principle that "he that cometh to God must believe that he is;" *i.e.*, that he *exists*; and that "He *becomes* a rewarder of them that diligently seek Him."

The second word in the text to which I invite your attention is "*work*"—not "*works*."

This word, in the singular, is frequently used, as in the text, with very deep solemnity. It is the look back from the other side of life. The thinker's busy brain is stilled, and the worker's weary hands are folded. The man's journeys, business, pleasures, conversations, thoughts, deeds, have been. So far as these are concerned, the pilgrim of life has gone on "into the shadow vast, the silence that must last." All the multiplied outward acts; all the inner acts which co-exist in such countless numbers, and succeed each other with a rapidity which baffles analysis—all those doings which seem to us so varied, and which we alternately approve or condemn, are compressed into a tremendous unity.

When we are close to a cataract, we are dazed with the countless, bewildering succession of hurried movements. It is all variety; vastness, and rapidity of mutation,—myriads of lines of foam, and clouds of spray, and torn masses of ever-plunging waters. But leave the cataract, and some miles away, in clear weather, turn to look back. Far off, in the lustrous distance, you see one broad white unwavering ribbon or banner, nailed, as it were, to the steadfast rock of the mountain side. And so our myriad thoughts and doings, every day and night, are our *works*. But all the hurry and variety is lost in the retrospect from the awful distances of eternity. The countless things, whose very essence seems now to be their mutability and their multiplicity, stand out, as if they were entirely *one* under that summer sky, whose light never goes down—the one work which we have done, the one work which we have made ourselves, the one work which we are, the one work which *is*. Each man's *works* have shrunk into each man's *work*. The plural is almost an anachronism in the land from which we survey the place where our past lies. "My reward is with Me to give," ay, to pay it off, and give it out to the uttermost farthing—"according as His work *is*" (*not* "shall be"). For Christ thinks with the thought and uses the tense of God—that eternal unity of each man's existence—"his work" —O that eternal present!—"as his work *is*."

(2.) On this day of memories let me attempt to speak of the work of Ken. Gazing upon it from the remoteness of 174 years, we can examine it with an almost passionless impartiality.

Think first of his ministerial work.

As a Bishop the circumstances of his day neither required, nor permitted, the varied and minute activities which are exacted from a Prelate of the nineteenth century. But Ken was a true Bishop, as he had been a true Parish Priest. He was diligent in confirming, and in preaching round his Diocese. He took an interest in schools and charities which was unusual in his day. The picture which he himself has drawn was, unconsciously no doubt, painted from the life.

> "Give me the priest these graces shall possess:
> Of an ambassador the just address,
> A father's tenderness, a shepherd's care,
> A leader's courage which the cross can bear,
> A prophet's inspiration from above,
> A teacher's knowledge and a Saviour's love;
> Give me the priest, a light upon a hill,
> Whose rays his whole circumference can fill,
> Who is all that he would have others be,
> From wilful sin, though not from frailty, free."

The lesson of toleration is one which was slowly learned in England as else-where. But Ken was the friend and instructor of the pious Nonconformist, Elizabeth Rowe, of whom it was said by Dr. Johnson that she and Isaac Watts are of those " to whom human eulogies are vain, whom I believe applauded by angels, and numbered with the just." "The Church of England," said the holy Bishop of Bath and Wells, " teaches me charity for those who differ from her."

As a preacher, Ken stood in the foremost rank. He possessed a power which has been granted to few of the great Anglican divines. His sweet face, musical voice, and thrilling earnestness, fairly enchanted the congregations who listened to him. In the great Abbey Church at Bath his ringing tones were heard from the pulpit to the west door. For an hour and a half on one occasion he poured forth a stream of alternate logic and passion, which even a Jesuit who was present could not altogether resist. Again and again, in Whitehall, when Ken preached in that singular Chapel[1] (where the frivolities of earth are richly painted upon walls now dedicated to the service of Heaven), multitudes burst in long before the previous service was ended. " Crowds of people not to be expressed," says a contemporary writer, "nor the wonderful eloquence of that admirable preacher." From that pulpit he once spoke in an hour of danger and of glory. When the Ahaz of England would have combined an altar of Damascus with one of higher origin and purer design, Dr. Ken appeared there as the Prophet of the English church, to plead for civil and religious liberty. Before that time he had boldly rebuked royal vice. "I must go and hear little Ken tell me of my faults," said Charles the Second with what for him may have been a melancholy smile. The monarch knew his man. He remembered why and when his Chaplain had said "Not for his kingdom."[2] Notes and diaries remain to show that addresses of Ken's in humbler churches were the occasion of penitential tears and holy resolutions, of full surrender of the heart to Christ. There can have been little truth in the criticism of envy or polemical acerbity that "his sermons were rather beautiful than instructive."[3]

As a Theologian, Ken produced no elaborate work. His one considerable book, *The Exposition of the Church Catechism*, is none of those monuments which surprise, almost appal us, by the mass of their learning ; by pages so overloaded with erudition that they are fain to spill their contents upon a margin, which, in turn, groans under the burden. But it is evident that Ken's knowledge was compacted and accessible. The grosser particles of his learning were fused and clarified by the fires of thought, of feeling, and of prayer. In this he stands

---

[1] The present Chapel at Whitehall is not, however, that in which Ken preached his sermons, but was then the Banqueting Hall of the Palace. The old Chapel, as well as that which James II. built for his own use, were destroyed in the great fire of January 2, 1698, which, in Evelyn's words, left " nothing but walls and ruins." The Banqueting Hall, however, escaped, and has been used as a Chapel since the time of George I. The painted ceiling, of which the sermon speaks, represents the Apotheosis of James I., by Rubens. (Wright's *London*, i. 363). I imagine that Ken, when he saw that ceiling, would have echoed Bishop Andrewes' prayer (*Prec. Priv.*, Day vii.) to be delivered, as "from the flattery of the people," so also "from the apotheosis of kings."—[E. H. P.]

[2] Ken had refused to allow Nell Gwyn to occupy his prebendal house at Winchester (i. 158).

[3] Bishop Burnet, in his *History of his Own Time.*

almost alone among our elder divines. But with Ken the dogma is simple and catholic, the devotion tender and ardent, and the dogma and the devotion are one. With most orthodox theologians dogma is like an armour, necessary indeed, but cumbrous; with Ken the armour becomes winged, and lifts him from the earth. No portion of his prose writings is more characteristic than that which relates to the Sacraments. Nowhere is his "Glory be to Thee, O Lord!" "All Glory be to Thee!" more fervent or more natural. For Ken, one Sacrament is that of regeneration. The other is accompanied, assisted, pervaded by a presence, whose reality is assured to faith, while its manner cannot be rationalised into an absolute definition. By loving contemporaries he was called "the seraphic Ken." But while his heart was rapt in the ardours of devotion before the altar, his grave and serious intellect was on its guard. His words were wise as well as burning—explained or modified, if misunderstood. If he never "evaporated" the Sacrament into a "metaphor," he never materialised the presence which he confessed. One gift was bestowed upon Ken in no ordinary measure—the gift of producing prayers which can really be used. If we measure the value of products by their rarity, then such prayers are the most precious of all products. They are not compositions. They are not rhapsodies. They are effusions. The press teems with Manuals of Devotion. But to-day they are, to-morrow are cast into the oven. Monarchs, senates, convocations, may order forms of prayer. They may get speeches to be spoken upward by people on their knees. But prayers which have the one condition of precability they can no more command than they can order a new Cologne Cathedral or a new epic poem. It has been remarked that the one form of State prayers which alone can have been largely influenced by Ken,[1] breathes more of the spirit of the Liturgy, and is more free from "the adulation and the malignity" which too often disgraced such productions, than any other of their time. Among all the prayers which have passed from an individual spirit into the sanctuary and into the closet, and which, like some mysterious vestment, fit every human soul in the attitude of supplication, few exceed those which are to be found in the extracts from the *Exposition*, which have been published separately under the title of *Approach to the Holy Altar*. Faith sighs prayers ; "the Spirit himself maketh intercession for us, with sighs that none may speak." Penitence weeps prayers ; "the Lord hath heard the voice of my weeping." Love looks prayers; "My prayer will I direct to Thee, and I will look up." There are such looks of love pictured in the heart of Him who is upon the Throne. Is it not recorded on an undying page, "Stephen looked up stead-fastly into heaven?" As far as those sighs, and tears, and looks have a grammar and a tongue, and can be written in a book, Ken has written them. He reminds us that to pray truly is to believe in God within and without, God within praying, God without hearing.

Such was the model which inspired Dryden's "Character of a good Parson." The first sketch was, of course, copied from Chaucer's Parish Priest, but Dryden's heart and imagination kindled as he looked upon Ken. Chaucer is always picturesque. He has that touch of genius which suggests much when it says little. But here the original is bettered by the imitation. The music of the

---

[1] The three Collects "for Repentance," "for the King," "for Peace and Unitie," issued by Archbishop Sancroft in October, 1688. The remark is from Macaulay's *History*. (See p. 32.)

cadences is lofty and varied. The masculine and sonorous verse perhaps just pauses on the line where eloquence, whose summits must always be clear, reluctantly refrains from passing into the sunlit mists of the highest poetry. But if, as has been said, there is "always prose in Dryden," it is glorified prose.

> "A Parish Priest was of the pilgrim train,
> An awful, reverent and religious man ;
> His eyes diffused a venerable grace,
> And charity itself was in his face.
> Yet had his aspect nothing of severe,
> But such a face as promised him sincere ;
> Nothing reserved or sullen was to see,
> But sweet regards and pleasing sanctity ;
> Mild was his accent and his action free.
> And oft with holy hymns he charmed their ears,
> A music more melodious than the spheres ;
> For David left him, when he went to rest,
> His lyre ; and after him he sang the best.
> He preached the joys of Heaven and pains of hell,
> And warned the sinner with becoming zeal,
> But on eternal mercy loved to dwell :
> He taught the Gospel, rather than the law,
> And forced himself to drive but loved to draw." [1]

(3.) Think again of Bishop Ken as a loyal Churchman. One or two lines from a monumental brass tell us in outline all which most concerns us—" Consecrated Bishop of the Diocese, 1685 ; imprisoned by one King, 1688 ; and deprived by another, 1689." His pure conscience would not trifle with an oath. He passed from his Palace to a scanty income, and a house which was offered to him by the love and veneration of friends. Longleat, in return, possesses something beyond its magnificence, beyond that which a friend of Bishop Ken called "the enchantment of that fairy land." "I can but give you," he whispered, in his last hours, "my all, myself, my poor heart, and my last blessing." [2] Over all the stately pile, and through all the glorious woods, there abides a quiet memory, a beauty not of spring or summer. A saint said for twenty years, "peace be to this house"—and his peace has rested upon it.

Natural tendencies might well have led Ken to inaugurate or assist a formidable schism. His reading and the spirit of his devotion would have inclined him to side with those who desired to restore ancient usages. His intimate friends were without the slightest disposition to submit to Rome. But they longed for a closer approximation to some features of the ancient Liturgies ; for a more primitive rule of life ; for more of mystery, of elevation, of beauty in worship. Ken's dislike to latitudinarian prelates might well be intensified as he thought of the occupants of Lambeth and Wells. One so venerated as himself would have been the idol of the separatists. And no man is a popular preacher with impunity. It is hard to find, hard even to conceive, an orator without ambition. Every orator must have, in some degree, a nervous excitability of temperament, a

---

[1] See p. 260.

[2] I do not find the "whispered" words in any narrative of Ken's death, but they embody the feelings expressed in the *Dedication*, quoted in p. 250. See *Note*, p. 205.—[E. H. P.]

sympathetic emotion, a passion and a capacity (as the first of living orators has said), for "giving back to his hearers in rain what he has received from them in mist." Ken could never have forgotten the anxiety and enthusiasm of England on June 29th, 193 years ago. On this day thousands were praying that the miracle in the portion of Scripture for the epistle for St. Peter's day might be repeated; that "the iron gate might open to them of its own accord." The shout of ten thousand voices, which seemed "to crack" the very beams of Westminster Hall, when the foreman came in with his memorable "Not Guilty," must often have sounded in his ears. He well knew what followed. He had heard the storm of cheers, the sobs of joy; he had seen the vast crowds upon their knees, imploring his blessing and that of the Primate. Letters and eye-witnesses had told him of the rapidity with which the news had spread through England; of the cathedral peals and village bells set ringing by the hurricane of joy; and of the seven Bishops to whom men attributed the preservation of the Protestant Religion and of the Church of England. His own name stood foremost. Modern Bishops can scarcely be a picturesque body of men. The life that seems so quiet, the load of little accumulated cares, does not much appeal to general sympathy. The days may darken round the lonely man; but the world does not suspect the pathos of it. The heart-strings may snap; but they make no noise in breaking. Ken, with Wesley's impatience, out upon a theological campaign, might have rent the Church of England in sunder. With himself and his friends he would have carried away from the National Establishment the acorn in which lay folded the Church Revival. By his voluntary and canonical cession of his See to the pious and orthodox Bishop Hooper, and by his expressed determination to receive the Holy Communion from the hand of his successor, the fear of a formidable division was averted, and the long line of Bishops has gone on without solution of continuity to its present beloved Chief Pastor. This great success was not achieved by Ken without self-restraint and self-crucifixion. By the extreme men on both sides he was distrusted and even maligned. By one party it was whispered that he might have Roman predilections or be concerned in mysterious political conspiracies. By his own side he was sometimes accused of the deadliest of deadly sins in theological coteries, reasonable moderation. An episcopal correspondent wrote to him, not without cruelty, that the line which he adopted in presenting to livings in his Diocese "gave great advantage to those who were so severe as to say that there was something else than conscience at the bottom." Ken replied with pathetic dignity, "I perceive that, after we have been sufficiently ridiculed, the last mortal stab designed to be given to us is to expose us to the world, for men of no conscience—and if God is pleased to permit it, His most holy will be done; though what that particular portion of corrupt nature is that lies at the bottom, and which we gratify in losing all we have, will be hard to determine." [1] His recommendations after some years to lay friends to attend the services of the National Church were sneered at by some of the extreme non-jurors as time-serving encouragements to "occasional conformity and amphibious devotions."

Ridicule, as Ken himself indicates, was not wanting. "Giving up rank and fortune for a Utopia." Utopia! To him Heaven was the one thing that had solidity. "The city that hath *the* foundations." Ah! still, as in the Russian poet's song of initiation, there are two voices as the neophyte pledges his troth.

[1] See p. 47.

"Fool!" hisses from below, while "Saint!" is heard overhead, and dies away in the starlit distance.

Let us for a few moments consider Ken as a Christian poet.

The agonies of disease apparently incapacitated him for some years from severe studies. Much of his sacred verse was composed (to use his own words) as an "anodyne and alleviative of pain." Of the four volumes of his poetical works not a little could doubtless be spared. We would gladly exchange much of the "cumbrous narrative ;" of the "languid lyric ;" of the clumsy machinery of the epic of *Edmund*—for one or two of the golden and glorious sermons to add to those which alone have been preserved. Yet any one who will read the volumes with tender reverence will be rewarded with lovely surprises.

The heroic couplets occasionally remind us that we are between the richness of Dryden and the compression of Pope. The shorter measures not seldom assume a sweet and simple stateliness, and are rounded into a self-contained completeness.

> "Love gains of boundless love the care,
> By the sweet violence of prayer." [1]

> "The wings of the all-gracious Dove
> Shed soft sweet penitential love." [2]

> "O realm of undisturb'd repose,
> Thrones unassaultable by woes ;
> O robes unspottable and bright,
>   Day void of night." [3]

We are reminded for a moment of the cadence of Keble, and of Keble at his best.

Bishop Ken, indeed, may well have offered such a prayer as that which is expressed with beautiful simplicity by a living poet.

> "O primal Love ! who grantest wings
> And voices to the woodland birds,
> Grant me the power of saying things
> Too simple and too sweet for words."

Outside the psalter, no lines have ever been so familiar to English Christians as Ken's Morning and Evening Hymn.

Other hymns have been more mystical, more impassioned, more imaginative— have perhaps contained profounder thoughts in their depth, have certainly exhibited richer colouring upon their surface. But none are so suitable to the homely pathos and majesty of the English Liturgy ; none are so adapted to the character which the English Church has aimed at forming, the sweet reserve, the quiet thoroughness, the penitence which is continuous without being unhopeful. They are lines which the child may repeat without the painful sense that they are beyond him, and the man without the contemptuous sense that they are below him. They appeal to the man in the child, and the child in the man. They are at once a form of devotion, a rule of life, a breath of prayer, a sigh of aspiration. They are the utterances of a heart which has no contempt for earth, but which is

---

[1] *Works,* iv. 77.   [2] *Works,* iii. 139.   [3] *Works,* i. 516.

at home among the angels. When we listen to them or repeat them with congenial spirit, in whatever climate we may be, the roses of the English dawn, and the gold of the English sunset are in our sky. No church may be near us, no copse or lawn within a thousand miles—but there are two sounds which they always suggest—the roll of the organ and the music of the thrush.

Such stands "the work" of Ken before us on this day. Such is it as suggested to us by the memorial window. How feebly it is now described, and with what imperfect knowledge, the preacher keenly feels. His deficiencies will be supplied by one who will bring to the task full knowledge, and the congenial inspiration of a poet.

"Such his work is;" may its spirit more and more pass into our Bishop and clergy. A bishop and pastor unsurpassed; a preacher of Christ unrivalled in that touch of the magic of grace, that witchery of Heaven, that "light and sweetness" of God which is called unction; a theologian of the true English type, who brings us the purest silver of antiquity stamped with the honest hall-mark of the English Reformation; a churchman, to whom the National Church was so dear that he subordinated all private feelings and preferences to the "peace of Jerusalem;" a poet, who if he has written much upon the sand has at least engraven some lines upon the rock, from which they have passed to the hearts and lips of millions in each successive generation. And if we venture to speak of reward—though his own meek soul, if he had ever ventured to pray, "Remember me, O my God," would have added, "and spare me according to the greatness of Thy mercy." He had his reward even here. Once again, the meek man, pushed forth from his home, "possesses the earth" with the spirit at once of a child and of a king. "He is both dead and buried, and his sepulchre is with us to this day." The iron grating, strangely ribbed, with mitre and pastoral staff, abides over his dust at Frome. "He is not ascended into the heavens." His spirit is in the land where (according to his own strange, but lovely fancy), one disembodied soul may be moulding itself for a habitation of the ruby, and another for a tabernacle of the pearl.[1] It longs (according to the inscription, written by himself for his own tomb) for "a perfect consummation of bliss both in body and soul at the great Day;" a longing which he has described with something of the spiritual beauty of that favourite of Gordon—"The Dream of Gerontius." In that land he is. His is the sweet life, the life of purity, for which he trained himself, "bearing himself full maidenly," from Winchester, until the day came to seal his body, with its self-invested shroud, in the coffin; ("they are virgins; these are they which follow the Lamb, whithersoever he goeth,")—the life of Music, where that "inarticulate poetry" of earth which he loved so well, becomes yet more rapturous and more soothing, the life of song, where no sweet bird is dumb in all the depths of the forest glades of the paradise of God; above all the life in that Presence without which for such as Ken, Heaven would be unheavened; the life with Jesus.

Still, as in successive readings of Scripture with the Church we draw near to the end of the vision of which the Apostle says in his simple, stately way, "I, John, saw these things, and heard them;" still, as the colours of the Apocalypse melt in enchanted distance, and the storm of music dies into something faint and low, as the breathing of our hearts,—still, as we feel that the sights of heaven are displaced for the seer by the lights and shadows of the Grecian hills, and the

---

[1] *Edmund*, B. vi.

songs like many waters, by the break of the wave upon the rocks ; still we hear a voice. It is like the voice—it *is* the voice—to which we listen in the Gospels. Still as gravely and severely sweet,—still with the same imperious oracular tenderness,—still claiming all from us, and promising all to us. It speaks with such awe as never master to workmen ; with such trembling pathetic tenderness as never mother to children, whom she has trusted for half an hour without her, to diffuse her loving influence over every moment of her absence. " Behold, I come quickly, and my reward is with Me." Yes! for He Himself is the reward of His saints—"to each according as his work *is.*"

APPENDIX I.

KEN PORTRAITS.

I can scarcely hope that the facts which I have brought together under this head are at all exhaustive. It is probable, I think, that here and there throughout the country there may be portraits of Ken in private houses of which I know nothing. I shall be grateful for any further information which may tell me of the existence of such pictures or of the history connected with them.

I. I am able to enumerate at least ten portraits in oils: (1) in the Palace at Wells; (2) at Longleat; (3) in the Refectory at Winchester; (4) in the Warden's Lodge at Winchester; (5) in the Hall of New College, Oxford; (6) in the Warden's Lodge at New College; (7) at Oriel College; (8) in the National Portrait Gallery; (9) one mentioned by Anderdon (p. 333) as in his possession; (10) one in the possession of the Rev. J. W. Wickham, of Horsington Rectory, Somerset. I am not aware that any one of these has been identified as the work of any well-known painter. All that I can learn of (1) is that it is believed to have been left by Bishop Ken, of Bath and Wells, to some one at Salisbury. I conjecture that it may represent a Waltonian tradition, possibly may have belonged to Ken's nephew, Izaak Walton, jun., Canon of Salisbury. Such of the portraits as I have seen agree in representing something of the feebleness of age; the eyes are lustrous, but the cheeks are flabby and the lips pendulous, and seem to have been painted, like the portrait engraved by Vertue as a frontispiece to Ken's poems, in the later years of his life. Many have, more or less, the same style of workmanship, as though they had been copied from the same original. (10) gives the face with a younger and more cheerful look; (8) and (9) agree in representing Ken as in one of six medallions (portraits of the Bishops of the Petition) round a central portrait of Sancroft.

II. The engraved portraits of Ken may be divided into two groups:—

A. Those published to commemorate the trial of the Seven Bishops. Of these I print a list from the catalogue of the Sutherland Collection (London, 1837, i. pp. 70, 71) in the Bodleian Library, given by Anderdon (p. 438) :—

"THE SEVEN BISHOPS.

"Sheets.

"Seven ovals, with ornaments. Engraven by R. White, and sold by R. White.

"A similar print. Engraven by J. Drepentier.

"Another ; with vignettes below. Dutch and French inscription. A. Haelwig, scul.

"Another ; with Moses and David. Allegories. M. vander Guest, scul. Sold by T. Bowles.

"Another. The Portraits in Mez. ; the ornaments etched. R. Robins *fecit et ex.*

"The Seven Candlesticks. Small ovals of the Bishops and their Counsel. The Royal arms, emblematical devices, &c. With letterpress, ' Primitive Christianity restored in England.' S. Gribelin.

"Folio.

"Seven ovals, with ornaments. Engraven and sold by J. Sturt.

"Seven ovals. ' *Immobile Saxum.*'

"The same. (Proof before ' *Immobile Saxum.*')

"Seven ovals, with ornaments. A mitre above.

"A similar print. R. White, scul. Printed for Bassett and Fox. Small.

"The Seven Candlesticks. Small ovals, with ornaments and emblematical devices. S. Gribelin, *in. et scul.* 1688. Sold by T. Jeffries.

"The same. (Proof before Gribelin's name.)

"Mez. Seven ovals ; and a vignette of the Tower, &c. Dutch verses. P. Schenck, *fecit et ex.*

"Quarto.

"Seven ovals ; with a View of their going to the Tower. Dutch.

"Two ovals ; with a View of the same. In a border. German.

"Going to the Tower. Dutch and French inscription. A. Schoonebreeck *ex.*"

To these I have to add an engraving of the Seven Bishops, by Loggan, from which Anderdon says (p. 806) that the portrait prefixed to his "Life of Ken " has been taken. This and such others of the engravings as I have seen, agree, as might be expected, in giving Ken's face as it was at the time of the trial, when he was fifty-one.

B. Separate engravings. Here also I am indebted to Anderdon (p. 806) for the list which he gives from the catalogue of the Sutherland Collection (i. pp. 571, 572):—

"Octagon, in a pen-flourish. By J. Dundas, Epsom, Surrey. Octavo.

"Æt. 73. With arms. G. Vertue. Octavo.

" A similar print, the portrait rather smaller. By the same. Octavo.

" Oval. The same on a tablet below. Octavo. The same, *proof*, without letters.

" Oval, in a frame. Proof, without letters. Octavo.

" From a shop bill. From J. Dunbar, a vender of gowns and cassocks. Octavo.

" A book plate. G. Adcock, scul. Published by Seeley. Octavo.

" With arms. J. Basire, scul. Sold by Hazard. Duodecimo.

" Oval. G. Vertue, scul. Duodecimo.

" Oval. Proof, before letters. Duodecimo.

" Oval,—facing the reverse way."

Most of the above were published as frontispieces to one or other of Ken's works. That which I have chosen as a frontispiece to Vol. I. has been reproduced from the engraving by Vertue in the Print Room of the British Museum. It seemed to me that the choice of that portrait by the editor of Ken's poems, who was Ken's great-nephew, might be fairly taken as evidence that it was looked on by the family as more satisfactory than the others. The portrait in Bowles' *Life* is given as from a drawing in the possession of Sir R. C. Hoare, Bart. It purports to be taken from the Longleat portrait, but it represents, as it seems to me, the face of a much younger man.

III. A list of the medals which give Ken's head, with those of his companion Bishops, will be found in page 9 of this volume ; they are too small to be of much service in the identification of his features.

APPENDIX II.

—◆—

KEN'S BOOKS.

I have, from time to time, in the course of these volumes (i. pp. 94, 95, 192, 259), called attention to some of the books which were in Ken's possession, and have drawn inferences from them, more or less suggestive,—I am bound to add also, more or less precarious —as to the nature of his studies. I enter now on a further examination of the catalogues of those books, as they are found at Longleat, in our cathedral library at Wells, and in that at Bath. I wish I could impart to my readers something of the interest which I have felt in taking down volumes of the second group, connecting them, as I did so, with some special crisis in Ken's life, with his travels, with the part he took in the religion and politics of his time, with personal friendships,[1] and the like. I ask myself, " Where, and when, and why, did he buy this book ? What influence did it have upon his mind ? How far can we trace that influence in his writings or his works ? "[2] Even for those who feel no special interest in Ken, something will, I imagine, be gained for a fuller estimate of the divines of the Restoration period, by giving what no one has ever, to my knowledge, before attempted to give—materials for judging of the range of studies of one of them, who possessed a wider culture and a higher standard of saintliness than most others. Of Walton's Library I have spoken in i. 18.

The omissions of the list are, to begin with, more or less suggestive. Shakespeare is not there, nor any other of the Elizabethan or Stuart dramatists, nor Spenser, nor Bunyan, nor Dryden, nor

---

[1] I note Goodman's *Penitent Pardoned*, a red morocco volume, with "Mary Kemeys, her book," as a singularly touching instance of what I mean. I take it to have been a gift or legacy (ii., p. 169).

[2] My limits of space compel me to omit some books of minor importance, and the dates and places of publication.

Cowley. The German Reformers, Luther, Melancthon and their fellows; the English Reformers, Tyndale, Cranmer, Ridley, Latimer, Parker, and the others, with whom the Parker Society has made this generation familiar; these are, as I have said (i. 94), simply conspicuous by their absence. So also are the Puritan Divines, Baxter, Manton, Howe, Calamy, and Owen, and even most of those of the Anglo-Catholic school, Bramhall, and Bancroft, and Bull, and Andrewes' Sermons and Pearson. The great interpreters of Scripture, Roman Catholic and Protestant—Maldonatus, and Estius, and Cornelius à Lapide, Hammond, and Grotius and the other writers collected in the *Critici Sacri*—found no place on his shelves, though the latter are represented by Poole's *Synopsis Criticorum*. It may, I think, be inferred from this that Ken, acting perhaps on grounds of personal edification, deliberately excluded from his studies the whole region of lighter literature, and that he had a positive distaste for controversial reading. In the absence of any indication of a taste for the exegetical study of Scripture, after the methods which we employ in the study of other books, such as we find in the Commentators I have named, I note a marked parallelism with the line of study traceable in some of the leading minds of the Oxford School, notably in Newman and Keble, Dr. Pusey presenting, of course, in his *Minor Prophets* and *Daniel*, a marked exception. I pass on to special groups of books.

I. GREEK CLASSICS.—Here again we miss what we should certainly have expected to find. Neither Homer, nor Herodotus, nor Demosthenes, nor Æschylus is found there. With these exceptions, the range is tolerably wide. I find Aristophanes, and Sophocles, and Euripides, and Thucydides, Isocrates, and Theophrastus, and Epictetus, and Sappho, and Lucian, and Longinus, and Aratus, and Dioscorides, and Dionysius of Halicarnassus. As a matter of convenience, I close the list with Hellenistic writers who are not commonly counted as classics — Josephus, Philo, and the Pseudo-Aristeas.

II. LATIN CLASSICS.—Here, reflecting the dominant taste of the time in school and college training, the list, and in some cases the number of editions of the same author, indicate that these, rather than those of Greece, were Ken's favourite authors. Thus we have thirteen different copies of Horace (see i. 16, 198), ten of Livy and of Ovid, and six of Tacitus, Virgil, Valerius Maximus, and Sallust; while the authors represented by single copies are Juvenal, Claudian, Cicero, Catullus, Petronius, Justin, Lucan, Statius, Martial, Terence, Plautus, and Pliny's *Epistolæ*.

III. HEBREW AND ARABIC.—It was somewhat of a surprise to me

to meet with so many volumes indicating a range of studies of which I had found no traces in Ken's writings, and which are not mentioned by any of his contemporaries. The list, it will be seen, if it does not give proof of a standard of scholarship in these matters equal to that of his friend Hooper (see i. 90; ii. 251), shows that he was, at least, able to appreciate him. It includes the *Mischna* in Hebrew, Bythner's *Lyra Prophetica*, some of Buxtorf's works, the *Lexicons* of Cocceius and Pagninus, a grammar by Levi, Kircher's and another Concordance. In Arabic, I find Pocock's edition of Abulpharagius, Eutychius, Golius's *Lexicon*, Erpenius's *Grammar*, and *Historia Saracenorum*. An edition of Ephraem indicates some knowledge of Syriac. A general interest in Oriental matters is shown by books like Ockley's *Introductio Linguarum Orientalium*, Maundrell's *From Aleppo to Jerusalem*, Prideaux's *Life of Mahomet*, Buxtorf's *Church History of Ethiopia*.[1]

IV. GREEK FATHERS.—These, as might be expected with one whose ideal was that of the undivided Church of the East and West, are well represented. Athanasius, Athenagoras, Barnabas, Clement of Alexandria, Cyril of Jerusalem, the *Historia, Præparatio,* and *Demonstratio* of Eusebius; Epiphanius, Justin Martyr, Theodoret, Theophilus of Antioch, Gregory of Nazianzum, Gregory of Nyssa, Origen, Dionysius the Areopagite, form a sufficiently copious list, though one misses Chrysostom. A small Porphyrius, *De Abstinentiâ*, seems to indicate a wish to include the ascetic mystic side of Neo-Platonism within the range of study. A *Rituale Græcorum* may well close the list.

V. LATIN FATHERS.—I content myself with familiar names: Ambrose, Augustine, Bernard, Jerome, Gregory, *De Curâ Pastorali,* Hilary of Tours, Lactantius, Tertullian, Isidore of Seville, Vincent of Lerins, Optatus, Minucius Felix. A *Corpus Juris Canonici* and *Boëthius* may, perhaps, be named under this head.

VI. THE SCHOOLMEN.—These are represented by the *Sententiæ* of Lombard and the *Summa* of Aquinas.

VII. ROMAN CATHOLIC THEOLOGY.—The prominence of the works that come under this section in all the three divisions of Ken's library is, perhaps, its most striking feature. If I held a brief, as the *Advocatus Diaboli*, against his canonisation as an Anglican Saint, it would not be difficult to make out a *primâ-facie* case for the theory that he was a 'Jesuit in disguise.' I need not say to those who have read these volumes that I do not hold that theory, but the fact that he

---

[1] I surmise that Ken's mind may have been turned in this direction by his sympathy with Frampton, who had been chaplain at Aleppo for many years, as well as with Hooper. (See p. 27.)

loved to gather and read such books as those of which I give the titles, accounts, in some measure, for the suspicions which led men to look on him, till the crisis of 1686—88 forced him to take up a definite position, as more or less "Popishly inclined." (See i., 276.) It will be noticed, however, that very few of the volumes in the somewhat long list that follows are of the directly controversial type. Of that class I find only De Cressy's *Exomologesis* (see i., 25), and Maimbourg's (see i., 127), *Method for Uniting Protestants*, and an anonymous *Moyens sûrs pour la Conversion de tous les Hérétiques.* Authoritative statements of the doctrine of the Roman Church are represented by the *Catechismus* of the Council of Trent and Bossuet's *Doctrinæ Christianæ Expositio ;* the Moral Theology of that Church by Cabassutius, by a *Manuale Confessariorum*, and by the books which he presented to the library of Winchester Cathedral when he was made Bishop (see i., 192). What seems to have attracted him much more, as it afterwards attracted John Henry Newman, was the stately ritual of that Church, so rich in the profusion of its materials, and often in the poetry of its symbolism ; and so we have Bona's work on *Liturgies*, the Roman *Missal* and *Breviary*, and *Horæ Diurnæ*, Mabillon's *Liturgia Gallica*, and the *Rituale Romanum*. Far outnumbering even these are the devotional books of the ascetic and mystic types, which include (I give the names without any definite order, and I reserve the Spanish and other books in the Bath Library for a separate paragraph), *Flores* from the works of Luis de Granada, the *Passio* of S. Felicitas, S. Brigitta's *Prayers*, Francis de Sales on the *Devout Life* and on the *Love of God*, the *Life of Ignatius Loyola*, the complete *Opera* of Thomas à Kempis, Bishop Fisher's *Precationes*, the *Ærumnæ Christi* and *Praxis Vivæ Fidei* of Thomas à Jesu, the *De Deo Inserviendo* of Alphonso of Madrid, the *Tears of Mary Magdalen*, the Roman *Martyrologium*, the *Mariæ Virginis Officium*, Nierem- berg's *Difference between Things Temporal and Eternal* (see i., 263), his *Vita Divina* and *de Adoratione*, Rossignol's *Disciplina Christianæ Perfectionis*, the *Life of St. Teresa*, the *Life and Glory of the Blessed Virgin*, Bellarmine's *De Gemitu Columbæ*, Horstius' *Paradisus Animæ*,[1] Joan's *De Sequendo ductu Divinæ Providentiæ*, the *Manual of the Arch-Confraternity of the Passion of St. Francis*, and the *Circulus Aureus*, a manual of devotions for the Christian seasons, and the *Arte della Perfezione Christiana*, and Molinos' *Spiritual Guide* (see i., 117).

The remarkable collection of Spanish books left to Bath Abbey

---

[1] Cardinal Manning classes this book with Dante's *Paradiso*, as the nearest approximation in human language to the beatific vision. (See my Translation of Dante, ii., 455).

deserves a separate treatment. Of these some have been already mentioned, but I repeat the titles for the sake of completeness.

1. Luis de Granada (see i., 259). *Doctrina Christiana.*
2. —— *Primera Parte de la Introduccion de la Fé.*
3. Palafox de Mendoza. *Eccelencias de S. Petro.* A full treatise on the prerogatives of the Pope.
4. —— *Historia Real Sagrada.* A commentary on the history of Samuel, Saul, and David, dealing with the duties of kings and subjects.
5. —— *Luz á los Vivos y Escarmientos en los Muertes* (Light for the Living and Warnings from the Dead). Notes on visions of the souls in Purgatory which had been given to Francis of the Most Holy Sacrament. The Bishop omits the names of the souls in Purgatory out of respect for the feelings of their relations.
6. *Vida di Juan de Palafox.* Life of the Bishop, by Antonio Gonzales di Rosande, now in the thirteenth vol. of his collected works.
7. Juan de Avila. *Vida e Obras.* Life and works of the great preacher, commonly known as the Apostle of Andalusia (see i., 259).
8. Fr. Juan de la Cruz. *Obras* (Works) (see i., 259). Lately translated into English (2 vols., 1864).
9. —— *Sermones Solennes de España.* Possibly by the same writer, but possibly also by a Dominican friar of the same name, who wrote a *Directorium Conscientiæ.* There is a French Translation by M. le Père Maillard, S.J., 1864.
10. Garcia di Mello. *Mystica Ciudad de Dios.* Of the author of this book I can learn nothing.
11. Antonio di Molina. *Exercicios Espirituales.* A devotional book written for the lay-brothers of the Carthusian Order.
12. Quevedo Villegas. *Politica di Dios y Govierno di Christo.* A book for the instruction of princes. The writer was a Knight of the Order of Santiago (St. James of Spain).
13. Juan de Palafox. *El Pastor di Nochebuena* (The Shepherd of Christmas Night). The vision of a shepherd who falls asleep on the evening of Christmas Day and has visions of the Christian life which take the form of an allegory, after the manner of the *Pilgrim's Progress.*[1]

One small group of books deserves a separate notice as indicating the interest which Ken took in the Port-Royalist Controversy. It consists of the works of Jansenius, Nicole's *Instructions Théologiques*, St. Cyran's *Lettres Chrétiennes*, and the *Statuts Synodaux du Diocèse d'Alet* (see i., 258), and, disguised under the title of the *Mystery of Iniquity*, an English translation of the *Lettres Provinciales.* Labadie's *Recueil de Maximes Chrétiennes* stands, for reasons given in the note, apart by itself.[2]

[1] I am indebted for most of the information given as to these books to Cardinal Manning, who, though not a Spanish scholar himself, kindly obtained it for me from a friend who is, and to the Rev. H. W. Pereira.

[2] Labadie seems to have been a man of the De Lamennais type, enthusiastic and changeable. His Jesuit opponents, followed by Bayle, accused him of

VIII. Foreign Protestant Divines.—The list includes the *Corpus Confessionum,* the *Acta* of the Synod of Dort, the Westminster Assembly's *Catechism,* the *Liturgia Tigurina* (Zurich), Antonio de Dominis' (the forerunner of the old Catholic movement) *De Republicâ Ecclesiæ,* Dallæus' (Daillé) *De Usu Patrum,* Calvin's *Opera,* the *Institutiones* of Turretin (a Genevan divine ; see i.), Grotius' *De Veritate* and *De Imperio,* Wollebius' *Compendium Theologiæ,* and Jurieu, *Vraie Système de l'Eglise,* and Outram, *De Sacrificiis.*

IX. English Divines.—Of Ken's own school I find Andrewe's *Devotions,* Cosin's *Scholastic History* and *Transubstantiation ;* Scandret's *Sacrifice the Divine Sacrifice ;* Heylyn, *On the Creed ;* Field, *Of the Church ;* Pearson, *Vindiciæ Ignatianæ* (but not *On the Creed*); Sanderson's *Sermons ;* Sancroft's *Fur Prædestinatus ;* Thorndike's *Just Weights and Measures ;* R. Boyle, *Considerations on Holy Scripture ;* Kettlewell's *Measure of Obedience ;* C. Leslie's *Discourses,* and Forbes's *Considerationes Modestæ,* and Jeremy Taylor's *Life of Christ.* Among those which can hardly be thus classed, I note Mede's *Works,* Spencer's *De Legibus Hebræorum,* Johnson's *Julian the Apostate ;* Kidder, *On the Pentateuch.* A passing interest in the Quaker controversy, arising, probably, out of Ken's relations with Penn, is shown by his having Barclay's *Apology* and Keith's *Deism of Quakers,* and his *Answer* to Barclay. Dodwell, *On the Soul's Immortality,* has been already spoken of (p. 128). *Julian* is balanced by Hickes' *Jovian.* Three of Burnet's works found a place on his shelves, the *Vindication of the Revolution,* the *Rights of Princes,* the *Deaths of the Primitive Persecutors,* as did Sherlock's *Case of Resistance* and the *Sermons* of E. Young, who had preached at his consecration. The tone of anxiety and fear which pervades his letters and his poems as he looks forward to the free-thinking of the next generation as the child of the Erastian Latitudinarianism of his own, finds an explanation in the fact that he had read the *De Religione Gentilium* and the *De Veritate* of Lord Herbert of Cherbury, George Herbert's brother ; Hobbes, *On Human Nature ;* and Toland's *Christianity not Mysterious.* Gassendi's *Philosophia Epicurea* and Vanini's *Amphitheatrum Divinæ Providentiæ* [1] may have led him to a forecast of a

uniting high pretensions to spiritual perfection with the grossest impurity ; but the former were not over-scrupulous, as we see in the cases of Molinos and Pavillon (i., 117), in bringing such charges against their adversaries, and Bayle was only too ready to repeat any stories that had the merit of indecency.

[1] As Vanini's work is but little known, it may be well to give a brief account of it. The *Amphitheatrum* was published in 1615, with the warm approval of the censor who acted for the Archbishop of Lyons. It was after the pattern of

wave of unbelief passing over Europe, threatening old faiths and old institutions, and having its ultimate outcome—if anything in this world of ours can be called ultimate—in Voltaire, and the Encyclopædists, and the French Revolution.

X. ENGLISH AND FOREIGN LITERATURE, SCIENCE, &c.—What I have already said will have prepared the reader for a singularly narrow range of study in the lighter regions of English literature. I find hardly anything beyond Milton's *Paradise Lost* and *Paradise Regained*, and his *Defensio.* Crashaw, Herbert, Donne, and Sandys contribute their respective poems. So, of works which represent the scholarship of Europe, I find only the *Adagia* and *Epistolæ* of Erasmus, translations of Casaubon's *Credulity and Incredulity*, and Puffendorf's *Religion and Civil Society*, Vigerus' *De Idiotismis*, Grotius' *De Veritate* and *Votum pro pace Ecclesiæ*, Vossius' *De Sibyllinis Oraculis*, and Campanella's *De Monarchiâ Hispanicâ.* Of studies in the region of science, notably in that of medicine, to which he was perhaps led by his own sufferings, we have traces in the *Systema Cosmicum* of Galileo, Ray's *Wisdom of God in Creation*, Fournier's *Geographica Orbis Notitia*, Drelincourt's *De Febribus*, the *Opuscula* of Galen, Fioravante's *Il Reggimento della Pesta*, a treatise *On Coffee and Chocolate*, an anonymous *Entretien sur les Sciences*, and some odd volumes of the *Bibliothèque Universelle* and the *Journal des Sçavans.*

XI. HISTORY.—The range of reading here is not a very wide one, but for the subjects in which Ken was chiefly interested in connexion with his epic of *Edmund*, and with ecclesiastical history in general, it was, I take it, for his time, sufficiently thorough. In the former region I find Spelman's *Vita Ælfredi*, the *Chronicles* of Speed, Holinshed and Froissart, the *Historiæ Anglicanæ Scriptores Veteres*, Ussher's *Britannicæ Ecclesiæ Antiquitates*, Bede's *Historia Ecclesi-*

Gibbon's celebrated chapter (ch. xv.) on Christianity. It purported to be a Defence of Natural Religion and Christianity against Atheists and Epicureans. But the defence was ironical, and the drift of the book was to destroy and not to build up. This was followed up by *Dialogues* of the same type in 1616. Here also there was the mask of a defender of orthodoxy, and three doctors of the University of Paris affirmed that it contained nothing contrary to the Catholic faith, even though it ended with a quotation from Tasso's *Aminta* that "all time was lost but that spent in love," the love of which he spoke being that of the freest license. After this he threw off the mask, and the scandals of his life and his open impiety became notorious, and in February, 1619, he was condemned to the stake by the Parliament of Toulouse. I take my facts from a *Biographical Dictionary* of 1798, which gives Durand's *Vie et Sentimens de Vanini* (Rotterdam, 1727) as its authority. The history presents a painful parallel to that of Giordano Bruno, and may, perhaps, admit of a like *Apologia.*

astica, Sheringham's *De Anglorum Gentis Origine*, and Buchanan's *Rerum Scoticarum Historia.* In the latter I note Dupin's *Bibliothèque des Auteurs Ecclésiastiques*, Fleury's *Histoire Ecclésiastique* (only vol. ii.), the *Histoire des Empereurs*, and *Mémoires Ecclésiastiques* by "D. T." (I conjecture De Tillemont, d. 1698), Davila's *Guerres Civiles de France*, and Moni's *Histoire des Nations du Levant.*

This closes my examination of the books which entered so largely into Ken's life, which, of all his possessions, were the only treasure from which he could not bear to separate himself, and which he left on his death to the friend and to the institutions which were dearest to his heart. The task which I have undertaken in examining the contents of three catalogues, only one of which was alphabetically arranged, has involved a considerable amount of labour. I think it will be admitted that the results are not altogether uninteresting or unprofitable.

NOTE.—*The Sherborne Proclamation* (p. 25).—I seize on a spare corner to state a fact that bears upon this question, and which comes to my knowledge too late for insertion in its proper place. I find in a collection of *State Tracts* published in 1692 by R. Baldwin, "In Defence of the auspicious and happy Revolution," the proclamation known by this title, in company with documents, every one of which is authentic. Up to that date, four years after its publication, it had not been repudiated. Is there any evidence that it was treated by any one as spurious till S_peke claimed the credit of its authorship?

INDEX.

Abjuration, Q. Elizabeth's Statute on, i., 153, 154
Abjuration Oaths, ii., 126 (n), 150 (n)
Abjuration and Attainder Acts of William III., ii., 105, 150-1
Addison, Lancelot, i., 47 (n), 162
Admiralty, efficiency of, under James II., i., 127; ii., 237
Albuquerque, ii., 106
Alexandrian Codex, the, i., 66
Allibone, John, squib by, i., 46 (n)
Amasia, Archbishop of, Papal Nuncio, i., 267, 277
"Amphibious Devotions," ii., 137, 287
Anne, the Princess, i., 136, 205, 230 (n), 271, 289; ii., 26, 119, 257, 262
"Anodynes." Ken's poems so styled, ii., 199, 200, 226, 233
Antony, S. of Padua, i., 114
Arthurian Legends, i., 200
Ashmole, Elias, i., 15
Asparagus, i., 256, 286 (n)
Attainder Acts of James II., i., 213, 217 (n)
of William III., ii., 105, 150-1
Attendance at parish churches questioned by Non-jurors, ii., 126 (n)
Augustine, S., and Valerius, ii., 132, 134, 250

Bacon, Lord, i., 105
Baltimore, Lord, i., 241, 295
Bampton, i., 123, 124
Barillon, i., 186
Barlow, Bishop of Lincoln, i., 46 (n), 310
Barrow, Dr. J. S., Bishop of St. Asaph, i., 43, 124
Bath, Ken's sermon at, i., 275; ii., 284
Bathurst, Ralph, i., 48 (n), 52, 54 (n), 180, 200, 201, 215, 227 (n)
his will, i., 201 (n)
Beacham, John, Ken's nephew, i., 171; ii., 206

Beaconsfield, Lord, his novel, *Lothair*, i., 186
Bedsteads at Winchester, i., 36 (n)
Bentinck, i., 136, 137, 141, 145, 147 (n), 148, 152; ii., 23 (n), 29, 34, 106, 257
Berkhampstead, i., 3, and n.
Beveridge, Bishop, ii., 51, and n.
Bishop, Ken's ideal, ii., 245
Blagge, Margaret (Mrs. Godolphin), i., 76, 130, 142 and n., 304; ii., 150
Bohun, Edm., ii., 94
Borromeo, S. Carlo, i., 113, 117
Boscobel, i., 187
Bossuet, i., 108; ii., 152 (n)
Bourdaloue, i., 108
Bowles, W. L., ii., 227, 232-3, 265, 267 (n)
Boyle, Robert, i., 50, 52. 107
Bradley, Thomas, ii., 102 (n)
Bramston, Sir John, i., 73
Breda, declaration of, by Charles II., ii., 57, 126
the Peace of, i., 134
Brent, Sir Nathaniel, i., 40
Brokesby (Non-juror), ii., 192, 195 (n)
Browne, Sir Thomas, ii., 222
Bruno, S., i., 110
Bubwith, Bishop, i., 193
Bull, Bishop, ii., 152, and n.
Burgess, Cornelius, i., 198
Burnet, Bishop, i., 107, 108, 109, 111, 112, 116, 127 (n), 131, 137, 140, 152 (n), 179, 183, 184 (n), 185 (n), 189 (n), 223, 261 (n), 263; ii., 2, 20, 22, 34, 35, 38 (n), 41, 44, 46, 48, 49 (n), 53 (n), 261, 284
Busby, Dr. Richard, i., 50, 202; ii., 38 (n)

Cante, Matthew, singular account of, i., 91 (n)
Cartwright, Bishop of Chester, i., 267 and n., 281 (n), 285, 297 (n), 300, 301, 310 (n); ii., 3

Catharine of Braganza, i., 67, 107 (n), 161, 200, 210
Chalkhill, Ion, father of Ken's mother, i., 2, 3
    John, Fellow of Winchester College, i., 12 (n), 20, 33 (n), 138 (n)
Chaplains, naval, their status in 1684, i., 164
Charity schools in London, i., 251 (n)
Charles I., i., 9, 29, 74 (n), 162
Charles II., i., 74 (n)
    court life under, i., 21, 63, 76, 98, 182-3.
    undergraduate life at Oxford on his restoration, i., 47
    his secret treaty with Louis XIV., i., 128
    history of that treaty, i., 128 (n)
    his proposed palace at Winchester, i., 158
    conduct about Tangier, i., 162
    his sayings about Ken, i., 159, 171, 178, 183 ; ii., 260 (n), 284
    Johnson's estimate of, i., 178 (n)
    last days and death, i., 183 seq.
    rumour of his having been poisoned, i., 198, 213
    his burial, i., 191
Chartreuse, the Grande, i., 110
Cheney, Thomas, i., 203 and n.
Cherry, Mr., ii., 57, 59, 194
Cheynell, Thomas, i., 40, 41 (n)
Chillingworth, W., i., 15, 40, 41, 65, 67, 84, 152 (n); ii., 31
"Circum," to go, i., 36, 99
Clarendon, Lord, i., 125-7, 300; ii., 2, 18, 39 (n), 51
Clarke, Edward, Fellow of New College, Oxford, i.. 45
Clement of Alexandria, his story of St. John, i., 60, 63
Cloberry, Sir John, i., 194 (n)
Clutterbuck, Alderman, i., 124
    Dr., ib.
Coffee, i., 253 ; ii., 208
Coles. Gilbert. i., 122, 124
Collier (Non-juror), ii., 192
Compton, Bishop of London, i., 128, 140, 145, 146, 149, 152, 153, 180. 183, 268, 285, 301, 312 (n) ; ii., 8, 10
"Conditional Immortality," ii., 76 (n), 128 (n)
Coney, Prebendary, ii., 131 (n)
Consecration feasts, expenses at, i., 130 (n), 191
Copeland, W. J., ii., 267 (n)
Cotton, i., 15, 107
Court life of Charles II., i., 21, 63, 76
Cowley, Abm., i., 15, 33 ; ii., 232, 233, 234
    his Davideis, i., 18, 64, 96

Cranmer, Archbishop, i., 15 (n)
    George, i., 23
Crashaw, Richard, ii., 232
Cressy, Mr. and Mrs., ii., 197, 198 (n)
Crewe, Bishop of Durham, i., 52, 180, 183, 207, 267 (n), 268, 310 ; ii., 227
Creyghton, Robert, Bishop of Bath and Wells, i., 130 (n), 131. 199
    Robert, Precentor of Wells, i., 202 and n.; ii., 138 (n)
    Mrs. Frideswide, i., 214, 215
Croft, Herbert, Bishop of Hereford, i., 310
Cromwell, Thomas, Deanery of Wells assigned to, i., 199
Cross, doctrine of the, ii., 102, 252
Cutler, Sir Thomas, i., 225, 265
Cyprian, St., i.. 245 ; ii., 42 (n)
Cyprus, i., 90 (n); ii., 184, 185, 207 (n)

D'Adda. Count Fe dinand. See "Amasia"
Daniel, Ken's Lent sermon on, i., 205, 206, 209, 265
Dartmouth, Lord, i., 162, 163, 168, 170 (n) ; ii., 15, 258
Davenport. Christopher alias "Francis à Sanctâ Clarâ," i., 25 (n), 67, 68, 105, 266
De Cressy. Hugh, i., 25 (n), 105 (n), 108, 275 (n) ; ii., 198 (n)
De Rancé, ii., 105, 118
De Sales, S. Francis, i., 111 (n), 117, 265 (n)
De Witt, the brothers, murder of, i., 134 ; ii., 1, 66
Dodwell, Henry, ii., 41, 42, 53 (n). 58, 69, 76 (n). 109, 110 (n), 113, 128, 142 (n), 191, 192, 193, 194, 198 (n), 258, 261
Donne, Dr., i., 15, 18. 19, 20, 33, 171
Drayton, author of the Polyolbion, i., 75
Drexe ius, ii., 263 (n)
Dryden, John, i., 202 ; ii., 234, 259
    his Absalom and Achithophel, i., 211 ; ii., 128 (n)
    his Religio Laici, ii.. 242. 285
Duppa, Bishop, i., 72, 74 and n., 171
Duras, Louis, i., 187 (n)

Earle, Bishop of Worcester, i., 130 (n), 191
Edmund. Ken's poem, i., 18, 22, 60, 62 (n). 69 (n), 80 (n), 95, 98 (n), 112, 117, 119, 169, 200 ; ii., 232, 233 and n., 234, 254, 255, 265, 267, 287, 289
Elizabeth's (Q.) Statute on Abjuration, i., 153, 154

Evelyn, John, i., 15, 37 (n), 46 (n), 51, 52, 54 (n), 72 (n), 107 (n), 129, 130, 155, 194 (n), 201, 269, 288, 301 (n), 395 (n) ; ii., 2, 26, 30, 31. 33, 51, 157, 258
    his description of Charles II.'s last hours, i., 182-3
    of Charles's burial, i., 191
Exclusion Bill, The, i., 137, 156, 195, 204, 208, 210, 240, 295 ; ii., 33
" *Expostulatoria*," question as to Ken's authorship of, i., 55 *seq.*, 119, 249, 284 (n) ; ii., 115, 259, 263, 267 and n.
" Exsurgat " money, i., 39 (n)

Fairfax, Thomas, Lord, i., 40
Fell, Dr. John, Bishop of Oxford, i., 49, 50, 84, 191
Fenwick, Sir John, ii., 101 (n), 103 and n.
Ferdinand, Count d'Adda. *See* " Amasia "
Ferguson, the Plotter, i., 212 and n., 216 (n) ; ii., 25 and n.
Ferrar, Nicholas, i., 19, 31 and n., 73
Feversham, Lord, i., 187 and n., 216, 225, 265, 266 ; ii., 7
Finch, Heneage, i., 312 ; ii., 8 (n)
Fitz-Patrick, Colonel, his "conversion," i., 148 and n., 149 (n)
Fitzwilliam, Dr. John, i., 51 and n., 73, 78, 88, 128, 159, 160, 174, 282 ; ii., 40, 45, 103, 257, 261
Fletcher of Saltoun, i., 212
    Thomas, ii., 257
Florence, i., 114
Fowler, Edward, Bishop of Gloucester, ii., 51
Frampton, Dr. Robert, Bishop of Gloucester, i., 16 (n), 57, 243 (n), 253 (n), 262, 301 ; ii., 27 (n), 46 (n), 50, 53 (n), 69, 80, 103, 120, 121 (n), 126 (n), 142 (n), 152 and n., 191
Francis à Sanctâ Clarâ. *See* " Davenport "

Gates, Sir John, i., 198, 215 (n)
Geneva, state of, i., 111
Gibbons, Dr. Orlando, i., 52
Gidding, Little, i., 19, 31 (n). 73
    The brotherhood at, i., 110 ; ii.. 27
Godfrey, Sir Edmundbury, i., 213, 305
Godolphin, Lord, i., 75 ; ii., 101 (n)
    Mrs. Margaret, i., 76, 130, 142 and n.
Grahme, Colonel James, i., 128, 142, 173 (n) ; ii., 157
Gregory Nazianzen, S., i., 245
Grey of Warke, Lord, i., 212, 214, 217

Grigge, Mrs, i., 50 (n) ; ii., 52, 53
    Rev. Thomas, ii., 53 (n)
Grove, Rector of St. Andrew's Undershaft, i., 301
Gunning, Peter, Bishop, i., 6 (n), 31 (n), 43, 72, 73, 304
Gwynn, Nell, i., 158, 177, 178, 189 ; ii., 270

Hales, Sir Edward, i., 15, 263, 297 ; ii., 26
Hall, Bishop, i., 18, 33, 37 (n), 54 (n), 171
Hammond, Dr. Henry, i., 15, 42, 50, 84
Harbin, Mr., ii., 54, 107 and n., 108, 111, 181, 183, 184, 202
Harmar, John, i., 66
Harris, Dr. John, Warden of Winchester College, i., 30, 32, 34 (n)
Hart Hall, Oxford, i., 19, 42 and n., 51 (n)
Harvey, Dr. William, i., 40
Hawkins, Dr. William, i., 121
    William, Ken's great-nephew and biographer, i., 10, 12, 56, 57, 58, 93, 144 (n), 224, 250, 251, 293 ; ii., 201, 202, 227, 263
    Heathen husband's inscription to his wife, at Lyons, i., 109
Henry, Matthew, i., 47
    Philip, i., 47, 202
Herbert, George, i., 16, 18, 21, 22, 33, 45, 73, 98, 99
    Influence of his works on Bishop Ken, i., 21, 22, 81, 253 (n) ; ii., 232
Hickes, Dr. George, i., 226, 227, 229 (n) ; ii., 87, 108, 109 (n), 120, 135, 142, 192, 261
    John, i., 226, 229 (n), 254 (n)
Hobbes of Malmesbury, i., 200
Holt, Chancellor of Wells, i., 202, 215
Homer, i., 62
Hooker, Richard, i., 22, 23, 33, 198, 292
Hooper, Bishop, i., 50, 90 and n., 129, 140, 141 and n., 142, 147 (n), 150 (n), 178, 179, 202, 218, 231 (n), 301, 305, 310 ; ii., 43, 109, 110, 127, 131, 132, 133, 139, 140, 149 *seq.*, 191, 202, 250, 257, 287
Huddleston, John, S.J., i., 128, 187, 279
    his account of Charles II.'s last moments, i., 188 ; ii., 12 (n)
Huguenots, The, i., 109 and n., 239 *seq.*, 247 and n. ; ii., 270, 277
Huse (or House), i., 194 and n.
Hutchinson, Colonel, i., 98
    Lucy, i., 76

Hyde, Anne, i., 125, 175, 207 (n), 208

Hymnotheo, i., 5, 17, 35, 60, 61, 62, 64, 69, 80, 91, 93 (n), 95, 98, 115 (n), 202 (n), 253; ii., 157, 159, 174, 200, 226, 232, 234, 245, 246

Ichabod, i., 56, 57, 58, 258, 284 (n)
Icon Basilike, i., 74 (n), 264
Ignatius, S., i., 231 (n)
Imitatio Christi, The, i., 131, 259
Inglesant, John. See "Shorthouse."
" Ion," as a Christian name, i., 2 (n), 13 (n)
Ireland, James II.'s policy towards, i., 268
Irenæus, S., i., 109
Italian and Spanish books, Bishop Ken's, i., 94, 251, 263 (n)

Jacobite formulary, ii., 59
" Jam lucis orto sidere," i., 34 (n); ii., 218, 224
James II. marries Mary Beatrice of Modena, i., 132, 135
    resists his brother's pressure to adopt a mock conformity, i., 128
    first address to his Council on succeeding to the throne, i., 204
    his coronation, i., 207, 208 and n.
    his first Declaration of Indulgence, i, 57, 65, 241, 271
    ditto for Scotland, i., 268
    his second Declaration, i., 293
    touches for the Evil, i., 277, 281 (n)
    goes to hear Penn after attending Mass, i., 281 (n)
    his Order in Council for the public reading of his Declaration in churches, &c., i., 297
    his rumoured transfer of Ireland to Louis XIV., ii., 40, 49 (n)
    respect for Ken, ii., 257
    his death, ii., 104
Jeffreys, Judge, i., 225 and n., 226, 227, 242, 266, 268, 310, 312, 314, 315; ii., 2, 14 (n), 27
    his last days; ii., 27 (n)
John, St., traditions respecting, i., 17, 60, 62
Jones, Mr., ii., 52 (n), 71 (n), 124 (n), 125 (n)
Juan de Avila, i., 259
Juan de la Cruz, i., 259

Keble, Rev. John, i., 236 (n)

Kemeys, The Misses, of Nuish Court, i., 5 (n), 256 (n), 259 (n); ii., 57, 58 (n), 127 and n., 136, 137 (n), 138 (n), 139 (n), 142, 144, 167 *seq.*, 172, 175 (n), 186, 187 (n), 191, 215, 256 (n), 258
Kemeys, Sir Charles, ii., 172
KEN, BISHOP, his descent, i., 1
    founder of the house, i., 1 (n)
    place and date of his birth, i., 3, 9
    influence of his sister, i., 5, 7, 8
    his home in Izaak Walton's house, i., 8
    "Kenna," in *The Complete Angler*, i., 7 and n.
    genealogies of his family, i., 9, 10, 11, 12
    his love of nature, i., 16, 17
    habits of observation, i., 17
    influenced by George Herbert, i., 21. 22
    by Hooker, i., 22
    rule of life adopted by Ken and his fellows, i., 26, 27
    admitted a scholar at Winchester College, i., 29
    elected to New College, Oxford, i., 33
    admitted to New College, Oxford, i., 43
    friendship with Francis Turner, i., 31
    life at Winchester, i., 33, 38, 97
    life at Oxford, i., 39
    his habit of distributing alms during his Oxford life, i., 52
    member of a Musical Society at Oxford, i., 53
    whether he was the author of *Expostulatoria*, i., 55
    his *Hymnotheo*, i., 5, 16, 35, 60, 61, 91, 95, 98, &c.
    appointed to Little Easton, i., 69
    to Winchester, i., 82
    resigns Easton, i., 82
    Chaplain to Bishop Morley, i., 84
    undertakes the charge of St. John's in the Soke, i., 86
    Rector of Brightstone, i., 87
    Prebendary of Winchester, i., 89
    Rector of Woodhay, i., 90
    writes the *Manual of Prayers* for Winchester scholars, i., 91, 95, 96, 97, &c.
    alleged miraculous cure, i., 91 (n)
    ascetic life at Winchester, i., 92
    love and practice of music, i., 92, 122, 202 (n)
    literary tastes and studies, i., 93, 94

KEN, BISHOP, his *Exposition of the Church Catechism*, i., 81, 231, 276
his love of children, i., 97 and n.
attached importance to personal intercourse as an element of spiritual life, i., 100
Meditations on the Holy Eucharist, i., 101
republished by Bishop Moberly, i., 104
makes alterations in the *Manual*, i., 101
goes abroad, i., 105 *seq.*
visits Milan, Venice, Rome, i., 107, 113, 114, 115
becomes acquainted with the French, Italian, and Spanish languages and literature, i., 121
his use of the prayer "R.I.P.," i., 123, 124
becomes popular as a preacher, i., 125
Chaplain to the Princess Mary, i., 125
at the Hague, i., 125, 138
life at the Hague, i., 139 *seq.*
takes a text from Jeremiah as the "watchword of his life," i., 139
resigns his Chaplaincy to Queen Mary in consequence of the Zulestein affair, i., 144
interests himself in: 1. The Union of Protestants. 2. The Conversion of Colonel Fitz-Patrick, i., 145 *seq.*
his letter to Bishop Compton, i. 146
his letter to Archbishop Sancroft, i., 148
his letter to Lord Maynard on the death of Lady Maynard, i., 157
his bold faithfulness, i., 158
Nell Gwynn, i., 158, 159
sails with Lord Dartmouth as Chaplain of the Fleet, i., 164
at Tangier, i , 167, 177
life at sea, i., 168
Burnet's description of him, i., 179
consecrated Bishop of Bath and Wells, i., 180
declines to give the usual consecration dinner, i., 191
a letter to Lord Dartmouth, i., 193
his episcopal seal and motto, i., 193, 209
life at Wells, i., 195 *seq.*
his Lent Sermon at Whitehall, 1685, i., 205, 265

KEN, BISHOP, his Lent Sermon at Whitehall, 1687, i., 269
ministers to prisoners at Wells, Taunton, and Bridgewater, i., 226
his address to the Privy Council, i., 226
letters to Viscount Weymouth, i., 224, 254 ; ii., 13
writes *The Practice of Divine Love*, i., 230, 237 ; ii., 263
makes alterations therein, i., 236, 277
his *Hymnarium*, i., 178, 231 (n) ; ii., 132 (n), 246, 247
his teaching on "The Holy Catholic Church," i., 232
on "The Communion of Saints," i., 233
devotions on the 2nd Commandment, i., 234
thoughts on the Lord's Day, i., 234
thoughts on the 4th Commandment, i., 235
thoughts on Holy Baptism, i., 235
makes alterations in his phraseology respecting the Eucharist, i., 236
Directions for Prayer for the Diocese of Bath and Wells, i., 237
exhortation to prayers for the king, i., 237
issues prayers for the visitors to Bath, i., 238
encyclical letter to the Clergy "in behalf of the French Protestants," i , 239
Whitehall Sermon for the Refugees, i., 242
his munificence, i., 243 ; ii., 57
pastoral for Lent, i., 244, 245
"Articles of Visitation and Inquiry," i., 248
his sympathy with the poor, i., 251, 252
and with others, i., 256 and n. ; ii., 96, 276
purposes to set up a workhouse at Wells, i., 251
probably a total abstainer, i., 93, 253
his adherence to the cause of James II., i., 261
his personal attachment to the king, i., 261, 264
his Sermon at St. Martin's-in-the-Fields, i., 270
his success as an Expounder and Catechist, i., 271 and n.

KEN, BISHOP, attractive character of
    his Whitehall and other Ser-
    mons, i., 54, 242, 265, 288 ; ii.,
    284
    his Sermon at Bath, i., 275 ; ii.,
    258
    animadversions   thereon   by
    "F. J. R.," i., 275 seq.
    literary history of his three
    hymns, ii., 210 seq.
    his fondness for coffee, i., 253 ;
    ii., 208
    suspended from the exercise of his
    office, ii., 46
    deprived, ii., 51
    his deliverance from the storm of
    1703. ii., 133
    his opinion of latitudinarianism,
    ii., 139
    purposes to resume Communion in
    the Cathedral at Wells, ii.,
    195
    his view of democracy, ii. 235
    his estimate of Lord Weymouth,
    ii., 249
    compares his retirement with that
    of S. Gregory Nazianzen, ii.,
    249, 250
    his ideal Priest, ii., 248
    „   Bishop, ii., 248
    his picture of an ideal court, ii.,
    235
    of an ideal king, ii., 238
    his Theodikœa, ii., 247
    increasing illness and suffering,
    ii., 199
    his poems entitled Anodynes, ii.,
    199, 200, 226, 233
    writes an epitaph for himself, ii.,
    203
    not inscribed on his tomb, i., 124 ;
    ii., 203
    puts on his own shroud, ii. 202
    his end at Longleat, ii., 202
    his burial, ii., 204
    his will, ii., 206
    service for commemorating him
    in "Tracts for the Times," ii.,
    268
    effects of his influence contrasted
    with that of Marlborough, ii.,
    273 and n.
    poetical tributes to him by R.
    M. Milnes (Lord Houghton),
    and W. L. Bowles, i., 274,
    275
    portraits of, ii., 291
    notices of his books, ii., 294
Kettlewell, John, i , 128, 129, 159 ; ii.,
    45, 58, 101, 102, 121 and n., 124,
    126, 158, 159, 198

Kettlewell, Mrs., ii., 102 (n)
Kidder, Bishop, i., 203, 253: ii., 51, 52,
    53, 57 (n), 60, 61, 130, 131 (n),
    134 (n), 136, 137 (n), 138 (n), 191,
    203
    his epitaph in Wells Cathedral,
    ii., 63
Kinaston's hoax, i., 66
King, Bishop, i., 15
    Mr., i., 229 (n), 254 and n., 255
    and n. ; ii., 107
Kirke, Colonel Percy, i., 167, 168, 169,
    225 ; ii., 20, 237
    his "Lambs," i., 225 ; ii., 237
Knox, Alexander, ii., 265

Lachrymæ Ecclesiarum, i., 56
Lake, Bishop, i., 140, 145, 303, 307
Lamplugh, Bishop of Exeter, i., 54 (n) ;
    ii., 8, 17 (n)
Landor, W. S., i., 107
Langley, Sir Roger, ii., 6, 7 (n)
"Latitudinarian Traditour, A," ii.,
    133, 134 (n), 135
Latitudinarianism, i., 65
    Ken's description of, ii., 139, 243
La Trappe, ii., 105, 118
Laud, Archbishop, i., 9, 41, 48, 65,
    67, 106
Lauderdale, i., 261 (n)
Lazarus, i., 253 ; ii., 246, 248
Legge, Colonel, i., 162
Leighton, Archbishop, i., 130 and n.,
    131 (n), 147 (n)
    Sir Elisha, i., 130
Lent, Ken's description of its proper
    observance, i., 205
Lenten Pastoral, Ken's, i., 244-5
L'Estrange, Sir Roger, i., 194 and n.
Levinz, Baptist, i., 202, 203
Leweston, i., 254 ; ii., 57, 172, 258
Lisle, Alice, i., 226, 229 (n)
Lloyd, Bishop of St. Asaph, i., 66. 140,
    145, 180, 274, 301, 303, 312 ; ii., 2,
    103, 120, 140, 142 (n), 144 (n), 149,
    191
    Nicholas, Fellow of Wadham Col-
    lege, Oxford, i., 66
Locke, John, i., 60 and n., 107, 108 (n);
    ii., 53 (n)
Longleat, i., 50, 211, 228, 229 (n), 254,
    263 (n), 286; ii., 44, 46 (n), 54 (n), 58,
    59
    view of, ii., 56
Longueville, Viscountess, i., 97 (n)
Louis XIV. of France, i., 108 (n), 118,
    128, 133, 135, 162, 240, 295 ; ii.,
    14, 19, 40, 93, 106
Lucaris, Cyril, i., 65
Luis de Granada, i., 259

Macaulay, Lord, i., 260 (n); ii., 82, 83, 86
" Maids of Taunton, the," i., 213
Malmhé, Mr., ii., 138 (n)
Manual for Winchester Scholars, i., 22, 36, 91 95, 96, 97, 122, 125, 261; ii., 215, 218, 219, 263
Marshall, George, made Warden of New College, Oxford, i., 45, 53
Mary of Modena, i., 132, 135
Mary, the Princess, i., 9, 136, 150 (n), 177, 264 ; ii., 34, 35, 257
    her remarks on Bishops Ken and Frampton, ii., 55 (n)
Mary, Queen of Scots, ii., 182, 183
    Register of the commission by which she was tried, ii., 183, *seq.*
Maynard, Lord and Lady, i., 70, 71, 74, 76, 87, 128. 155, 156, 268, 285, 286 (n) ; ii., 255, 256
    their household, i., 110
    portrait of Lady Maynard, i., 77
Medals commemorating the acquittal of the seven bishops, ii., 9
Meggot, Dean. i., 158, 177, 266
Melfort. ii., 104, 110, 111 (n)
Memorial rings. *See* " Rings "
Mews, Bishop Peter, i., 177, 178, 199, 210 (n), 216 and n., 217 (n), 225, 253, 255 (n), 301 ; ii., 18, 27 (n)
Milan, Sunday-school in the cathedral, i., 113
Milton, i., 21, 63, 64, 96, 166 and n.; ii., 232, 233
Molinos, Michael, i., 117 and n., 118
Monk and the bird, legend of the, i., 263 (n) ; ii., 248
Monmouth, the Duke of, 159, 183, 209 *seq.*, 229 (n)
    his letter to the university of Cambridge, i., 48 (n), 210
    his declaration, ii., 25 (n)
    his cowardice, i., 217
    dealings of divines with him before his execution, i., 218 *seq.*
    his execution, i., 228
    popular disbelief of his death, i., 224, 225 (n)
More, Mrs. Hannah, i., 230 (n)
Morley, Bishop, i., 8 (n), 15, 42, 51 (n), 82, 83, 84, 85, 88, 89, 121, 126, 127, 128, 129, 130, 131, 137, 140, 155, 156, 164, 171, 174, 191, 253, 262, 282 (n), 298 ; ii., 257
    his austere habits, i., 175
    his munificence, i., 175
    his death, i., 174, 175
    his will, i., 176
Morley, Francis, nephew of the Bishop, i., 192, 194 and n.

Morning and Evening Hymns, earliest recorded use of, i., 99 (n)
Mossom, Dr., i., 7 (n), 72, 73, 74
Motto chosen by Bishop Ken, i., 209
Musical society at Oxford, i., 52, 165, 229 (n)

Nag's Head Tavern, i., 130 (n)
Naish Court. *See* " Kemeys "
Nantes, the edict of, i., 239
    Revocation of, i., 240, 295
Naseby, battle of, i., 40
Naval chaplains, their status in 1684, i., 164
    life, ii., 237
Nelson, Robert, i., 15, 251 (n); ii., 45, 58, 61, 152 (n), 192, 193, 194, 195, 198 (n), 225, 258
New College not among the contributors to the royal treasury, i., 39 (n)
Newman, J. H., xii. (n) ; i., 120 ; ii., 268, 295, 297
Nicæa, Council of, i., 246
Nicholas, Dr. John, i., 31, 43, 122, 124
Nieremberg, i., 117, 263 and n.; ii., 116, 249 (n)
" Non-compounders," ii., 120 (n)
Non-jurors, i., 226 ; ii., 32, 38 (n), 45, 47, 52 (n), 54 (u), 56, 95, 142, 261 (n)
Non-resistance, the doctrine of, 159, 224, 298 ; ii., 40, 49 (n). *See* also " Passive Obedience "
Nowell, Dean, i., 18, 33
Oath, episcopal, i., 193
" Occasional conformity," i., 207 (n) ; ii., 131, 137, 287
Oley, Barnabas, i., 73, 81
Overall's convocation book, ii., 44
Owen, John, Puritan Vice-Chancellor of Oxford, i., 48, 49 (n), 66
Oxford University under Puritan rule, i., 39 *seq.*, 67
    at the restoration, i., 53, 59

Palace, the episcopal, at Wells, i., 196
Parental influence, i., 1, 3, 4
Parker, Samuel, Bishop of Oxford, 177, 297 (n), 310
Pasquinade, 118 (n)
" Passive Obedience," i., 39, 159, 224 ; ii., 39, 40, 48, 49 (n), 102
" Patriarch Jeremias," the, i., 65 White, i., 44
Patrick, Bishop, i., 54 (n) 300, 301 ; ii. 51

Pavillon, Nicholas, i., 110 (n), 180 (n), 258, 259 (n), 288
Pechell, Dr., i., 163 ; ii., 15 (n)
Penderell family, i., 187
"Pennyless Porch," i., 193
Pepys, Samuel, i., 129, 161, 163, 164 seq. ; ii., 261
Perkins, Joseph, Latin Poet Laureate, i., 217 (n), 225 and n., 275 (n), 301 (n) ; ii., 262
Peterborough, Lord, i., 161
Peters, Hugh, i., 46
Petre, Father, i., 263, 277, 290, 311 (n); ii., 19 (n), 27
Petty, William, i., 51, 52
"Philistinism," i., 26, 27 (n), 32
Phillips, Colonel, ii., 57
"Philotheus," i., 31, 34 (n), 36, 98, 99 ; ii., 218 and n.
Pierce (or Piers), Bishop, i., 199
Pink, Dr. Robert, Warden of New College, Oxford, i., 43, 44, 72
Pollexfen, ii., 8 (n)
Poulett, Lord, married one of the Kens, i., 2, 10, 12
"Pretender, The," ii., 59, 151 (n)
Priest, the Model, Ken's picture of, ii., 245
Prowse, Mrs. (daughter of Bishop Hooper), ii., 131
Prynne, William, author of Histrio-mastix, i , 40
Pullen, Josiah, i., 51 (n)
Puritan Visitation of Oxford University, i., 40

Quarles, ii., 232

"Rabbi" Smith, ii., 179
Reading sermons, i., 48 (n), 201, 210
Refugees, French. See "Huguenots."
"Requiescat in Pace," i., 122, 124 ; ii., 104, 105, 106
Restoration, social and religious "down-grade" of the, i., 53, 59, 97, 98
Reynolds, Puritan Vice-Chancellor of Oxford, i., 41 and n.
"Ridding, Mr. and Mrs.," ii., 71
Rings, Memorial, i., 20, 171, 176
Robber, The Penitent, ii., 247
Rome, i., 116
   social and moral condition of, ib.
   nepotism and venality of, ib.
Rosmini, i., 58
Rous, Francis, chief "Trier of Preachers," i., 41
Routh, Dr. M. J., ii., 151
Rowe, Elizabeth, i., 52 (n) ; ii., 172, 284

"Royal Sufferer, The," i., 226 (n), 264, 316 (n) ; ii., 31, 115 seq., 120, 263
Rupert, Prince, i., 39, 46, 161
Russell, Lady Rachel, i., 51 (n), 76, 78, 128, 159, 160, 174 ; ii., 40
   William, Lord, i., 159, 211 ; ii., 49 (n)
Ruvigny, i., 241 and n.
Rye House Plot, The, i., 159, 165, 211

St. Cyran, i., 259
Sancroft, Archbishop, i., 175, 180, 183, 204, 207 (n). 242, 243, 248 (n), 268, 285, 288, 292, 298, 299, 300, 302, 308, 311, 312, 313 ; ii., 12, 16, 19, 22 and n., 27 (n), 36, 39, 50, 180, 258, 285 (n)
Sanderson, Bishop, i., 15, 24, 41, 42, 84
Sandys, Edwin, Archdeacon of Wells, i., 23 (n), 203 (n); ii., 57
Savile, Sir Henry, i., 32
Sawyer, Sir Robert, i., 90 (n), 312 and n., 313 ; ii., 8 (n)
School-life at Winchester, i., 35, 36 (n)
Seal, Ken's Episcopal, i., 193
Sedgmoor, i., 215, 217, 225
"Seekers, The," i., 47 (n)
Seven Bishops, petition of the, i., 287 ; ii., 270
   trial of ditto, ii., 1 seq.
   acquittal of, ii., 7
Shakespeare, i., 105
Sharp, Dean of Norwich (afterwards Archbishop of York), i., 268; ii., 195
Sheldon, Archbishop, i., 15, 16, 40, 41, 42, 298 (n)
   his costly banquets, i., 130 (n)
Sherborne Proclamation, The, ii., 24, 25 (n), 301
Sherlock, Richard, Chaplain of New College, Oxford, i., 43
   William, Dean of St. Paul's, i., 300, 301, 309 ; ii., 44
Shorthouse, Mr., author of John Inglesant, i., 6, 25 and n., 26 and n., 63 (n), 67, 73, 117 (n)
Sidney, Hon. Algernon, i., 142, 159, 211
   Hon. Henry, i., 142, 147 (n), 152, 153, 154, 155, 208 and n., 309 ; ii., 8
   references to his diary, i., 143, 144, 145, 148, 154
   Sir Philip, i., 142, 147 (n)
Skinner, Bishop of Oxford, i., 37 (n), 54 and n.
Smith, Dr. Thomas, i., 282 ; ii., 102, 168, 179 seq., 191

Socrates, ii., 246, 247
Soke, St. John in the, i., 86 (n), 91 (n), 176, 179, 229 (n)
Somers, John, afterwards Lord, i., 312; ii., 5, 8 (n)
Somersetshire peasantry, heathen ignorance of, i., 230 and n.
Southcombe, Lewis, ii., 258
Southey, Robert, ii., 264
Speke, Hugh, ii., 25 (n), 27 (n)
Spenser, Edmund, i., 2, 61, 64
Spinckes, Nathaniel, ii., 101
Spirits, Discussion on, between Pepys and Ken, i., 165 *seq.*
Sprat, Thos., Bishop of Rochester, i., 52, 180, 268, 297 (n), 310; ii., 3, 14
Stamp, Mr., ii., 137 (n), 147 (n), 148
Stillingfleet, Edward, Bishop of Worcester, i., 16 (n), 288, 300, 301
Storm of Nov. 26th, 1703, ii., 129, 130
Stringer, Dr., Warden of New College, Oxford, i., 33, 44, 45
"Student Penitent, The," ii., 155, 258
"Super-effluence," i., 283; ii., 92, 247
"Super-effluently," ii., 132, 250
Sylvius, Sir Gabriel, i., 137 (n), 142, 143; ii., 157

Talleyrand, i., 28
Tangier, the garrison at, i., 162
   social condition of, i., 167
Taylor, John, the "Water Poet," ii., 217
"Te lucis ante terminum, ii., 218, 224"
Tenison, Archbishop, i., 143, 219, 223, 251 (n), 264, 270, 300, 301, 305; ii., 79, 86, 101 (n), 106 (n), 117, 129 (n)
   Ken s letter to, i., 135 (n), 264; ii., 86, 267
Test Acts, i., 133
Texts written on the flyleaves of Ken's Grotius and Greek Testament, i., 139 and n.
Thorndike, Herbert, i., 57, 73
Thurcross (or Thruscross), Dr. Timothy, i., 6 (n), 72 and n., 73
Thynne, Sir Frederick, i., 229 (n)
   Mr. Henry, i., 254 (n); ii., 172
   Mrs. Henry, i., 254; ii., 57, 172, 258
   Thos., i., 227
   Mr. Thos., afterwards Viscount Weymouth, i., 50, 229 (n); ii., 257
Tillotson, Archbishop, i., 147 (n), 300; ii., 39, 44, 49 (n), 51, 53, 61, 79, 243 (n)
"Traditour," ii., 138

Trelawney, Sir Jonathan (Bishop of Bristol, Exeter, and Winchester), i., 36 (n), 142, 274, 306; ii., 150
Turner, Francis, Bishop of Ely, i., 31, 37 (n), 43 (n), 50 (n), 51, 72, 106, 128, 155, 179, 180, 183, 207, 208, 218, 224 (n), 265, 270, 300, 304, 308, 316; ii., 18, 40, 53 (n), 55 (n), 56, 71, 83, 103, 107, 126 (n), 148, 198 (n), 257

Universalism, i., 111
Ussher, Archbishop, i., 15

Venice, i., 113, 114
"Virtuosi," the Society at Oxford, i., 52, 200
"Vizo sciolto," &c., i., 21; ii., 238

Wagstaffe, Thos., non-juror suffragan Bishop, ii., 101, 102 (n), 120, 192
Wallis, Dr., i., 51
Walters, Lucy, i., 209, 210 (n)
Walton, Izaak, i., 2, 5, 7, 8, 11, 12, 13, 14, 17, 18, 19, 20, 23, 24, 33, 37 (n), 46, 52, 61, 73, 83, 98, 107, 121, 164, 203 (n), 292; ii., 257
   his death, i., 170
   epitaph, i., 170
   Dr. Izaak, junior, i., 92, 107, 116, (n), 121, 171 (n); ii., 23 (n), 38 (n), 52, 53, 206, 207, 208
"Warming-pan Story, The," ii., 2
Warwick, Lady, i., 77, 78 (n), 88, 156; ii., 61, 257
Watson, Thos., Bishop of St. David's, i., 310; ii., 19, 20 (n)
Well, St. Andrew's, at Wells, i., 197
Wells, Episcopal Palace at, view of, i., 196
Wentworth, Lady H., i., 211, 218, 223
Wesleys, the, i., 310; ii., 225, 233
Weymouth, Viscount, i., 228, 229 (n), 251 (n); ii., 38 (n), 55, 58, 151, 249, 258
White, Bishop of Peterborough, i., 297, 300, 304; ii., 101, 103
White, "The Patriarch," i., 44
Whiteare, Benjn., i., 180 (n)
Whitehall Sermons, i., 209, 242, 265, 269, 288
Whiting, last abbot of Glastonbury, i., 199
Wilkins, Bishop of Chester, i., 51, 52
William of Orange, i., 133, 208 (n), 212 (n); ii., 21, 257
   marries the Princess Mary, i., 136
   his "Petruchio" policy, i., 140; ii., 36
   his death, ii., 105

William of Wykeham, i., 35
Williams, James, Sacrist of Wells Cathedral, i., 215
Woodward, Dr., Warden of New College, Oxford, i., 53
Workhouse, Ken's proposal to set one up at Wells, i., 251
Wotton, Sir Henry, i., 15, 16, 20, 21, 25, 98, 105, 171
Wren, Sir Christopher, i., 51, 52
Wroth, Sir Henry, i., 142
    Jane, i., 142, 144

York, the Duchess of, i., 175
    her death, i., 127 (n)
Young, Arthur, i., 109
Young, Edward, Dean of Salisbury, i., 31
    Edward, junior, author of "Night Thoughts," i., 95, 180

Zulestein, Count, i., 55, 136, 144, 145; ii., 21, 23 (n), 270
    Madame, 147 (n)

THE END.

PRINTED BY J. S. VIRTUE AND CO., LIMITED, CITY ROAD, LONDON.

By the same Author.

Two Vols., medium 8vo, price 21s. each.

THE COMMEDIA AND CANZONIERE
OF DANTE ALIGHIERI.

A NEW TRANSLATION.

With Biographical Introduction, and Notes Critical and Historical.

VOLUME I.—Life. *Hell, Purgatory.*

VOLUME II.—*Paradise, Minor Poems.* Studies : The Genesis and Growth of the Commedia. Estimates of Dante. Dante as an Observer and Traveller. Portraits of Dante, &c.

OPINIONS OF THE PRESS.

The Saturday Review says:—" The Dean of Wells may be congratulated upon the completion of his labour of love. . . . . In the English rendering of the *Paradiso*, as well as in the notes to that portion of the poem, the Dean's profound and intimate acquaintance with the theology of the Middle Ages has given him a great advantage over other translators and commentators. . . . . For Students of Dante, the 'Studies' will be found most valuable and interesting. A large quantity of material has been collected and arranged as it only could have been by one thoroughly conversant with his subject, and giving his best abilities and affections to the accomplishment of his work."

The Westminster Review says:—" A work of a very high order indeed . . . . we may safely prophesy that this noble work will hold the field."

The Spectator says:—" No book about Dante has been published in England that will stand comparison with Dean Plumptre's. He deserves the gratitude of all true lovers of good literature for writing it. We have nothing further to say of it except that, take it for all in all, the only fitting epithet we can find for it is ' noble ; ' and that we do most heartily wish it all the success which it richly deserves."

The Record says:—" Conceived in the lofty and generous spirit of a true scholar. Nowhere will the cultivated English Christian find so much help as this work will give him in understanding and enjoying the message of Dante to men. The second volume deepens the impression made by the first. The parts interlace as well as complete each other; the volumes are two, the book is one. The Dean 'stands on his achievement.' It is no unworthy pedestal."

The Academy says:—" The whole work is a monument of many years' devoted study; it is illustrated throughout by an unusual range of reading and culture in other fields of literature ; and it is accompanied by a most copious and valuable index of subjects and names."

The Bishop of Ripon, in the *Contemporary Review*, says :—" Dean Plumptre is entitled to the gratitude of all Dante students. He has given us notes full of sympathy and knowledge and to these he has prefixed a biography of Dante which is cultured and graceful."

The Scotsman says:—" The completion of Dean Plumptre's important work is worthy of its commencement. He has shown a literary tact and accuracy of feeling which are reflected in every page of his version. The notes alone would give importance and value to the volumes. As a whole, the translation is very close and accurate, and stands in the front rank."

The Churchman (New York) says:—" The Dean of Wells has enriched the English language and English literature with a translation of Dante, which, we do not doubt, will probably efface all other English translations. We do not hesitate to say, that never before have English readers been able fully to realise the beauty as well as the grandeur, the charm as well as the thrilling fascination, of this ' divine poem.' "

Literarisches und Central-blatt (Leipsic) says:—" We do not hesitate to give to the second volume in fullest measure the praise which we gave to the first. The beautiful work. which has gained many friends on this side of the Channel, is published with a beauty of outward form which rivals the excellence of its contents."

THE TRAGEDIES OF ÆSCHYLOS.

A New Translation, with a Biographical Essay.

And an Appendix of Rhymed Choruses. Crown 8vo, price 7s. 6d.

"Dean Plumptre pits himself with more and abler rivals than when he essayed Sophocles; but here, too, he will be found to hold his own."—*Contemporary Review.*

THE TRAGEDIES OF SOPHOCLES.

A New Translation, with a Biographical Essay.

And an Appendix of Rhymed Choruses. Crown 8vo, price 7s. 6d.

"Sophocles has certainly never before had an English dress half as simple and graceful, half so free from the disguise of artificial ornament or rhetorical ambition."—*Spectator.*

THINGS NEW AND OLD.

A Volume of Poems. Small Crown 8vo, price 6s.

"The last volume, 'Things New and Old,' is quite worthy of Dr. Plumptre's reputation. 'Chalfont St. Giles,' a letter from Elwood, Milton's friend, describing his intercourse with the blind old man, is a piece of true poetry. The Buddhist poems have great sweetness and power. 'In Memoriam' is a section of the volume which pays tribute to Maurice, Stanley, and other friends."—*London Quarterly Review.*

LAZARUS, AND OTHER POEMS.

Fourth Edition. Small Crown 8vo, price 6s.

CONTENTS.—Thoughts of a Galatian Convert—Jesus Barabbas—Gomer—The House of the Rechabites—Three Cups of Cold Water—Vie de Jésus—Rizpah—The Song of Deborah—The Earliest Christian Hymn—Hymns for School or College, &c.—Notes.

"Polished and often beautiful verse. . . . A scholar's reading of the religion of the times, clothed in the rhythm and music of a poetical mind."—*Spectator.*

"Rich in the results of modern culture. . . . The outpouring of an earnest and affectionate mind."—*Guardian.*

MASTER AND SCHOLAR,

AND OTHER POEMS.

New Edition. With Notes. Small Crown 8vo, price 6s.

CONTENTS.—Master and Scholar—Augustine, *In Memoriam Adeodati*—Evil Merodach—The Queen of the South—Miriam of Magdala—Demodocos—Claudia and Pudens—The River—"And there was no more Sea"—An Old Story—Eumenides—A Plaster Cast from Pompeii—The Last Words of Socrates—A Voice from Oxford—Mozart's Zauberflöte—Not Without Witness—Gilboa—Translations.

"Worthy to be put on the same shelf with Heber and Keble."—*Westminster Review.*

"The exceedingly able article in the *Contemporary Review* for 1866, by the same author, on 'Friar Bacon,' should be read as a commentary and introduction to this poem ('Master and Scholar'). With exquisite delicacy the writer pours forth once more the pitiful wail of poor Eloisa's broken heart over the idol of her passion, . . . and weaves the traditions of the Magdalen into a charming poem."—*British Quarterly Review.*

MOVEMENTS IN RELIGIOUS THOUGHT.

CAMBRIDGE UNIVERSITY SERMONS.

I. ROMANISM.   II. PROTESTANTISM.   III. AGNOSTICISM.

Small 8vo, price 3s. 6d.

"Thoughtful lectures, conceived in a very large spirit, and set off by that sort of scholarship which adds so much of literary effect and vividness to the discussions of the religious thinker. The last lecture is one fuller of insight into the sources and roots of Agnosticism than any we have read for many years from a clergyman of our National Church."—*Spectator.*

CHRIST AND CHRISTENDOM.

THE BOYLE LECTURES FOR A.D. 1866. Demy 8vo, price 7s. 6d.

CONTENTS.—1. Cravings after Union, and Lives of Jesus. 2. Sources for the Life of Christ. 3. The Training of the King. 4. The Names of Christ. 5. The Miracles of Christ. 6. The Work and Teaching of Christ. 7. The Ministerial Work of Christ. 8. The Resurrection.

APPENDIX.—A. Attempts at Union since the Reformation. B. Recent Lives of Jesus. C. The Apocryphal Gospels in their relation to Theology and Art. D. The Relation of the Two Epistles of St. Peter to the Gospel according to St. Mark. E. The Relation of the Epistle of St. James to the Gospel according to St. Matthew. F. The Asiatic Epistles of St. Paul and the Gospel according to St. John. G. The History of the Infancy. H. The Influence of Apollinarianism on Modern Theology. I. The Personality of Evil.

"It is long since the Church of England produced two more noble works of controversy than these ('Christ and Christendom' and Liddon's 'Bampton Lectures'), more likely, by the blessing of God, to influence public opinion."—*Contemporary Review.*
"The Boyle Lectures for 1866 will stand not unworthily by the side of those produced by Professor Plumptre's most eminent predecessors. In them he displays with ease, force, and constant readiness, all the resources of a ripe scholar, a keen critic, and an eloquent writer."—*Athenæum.*

BIBLICAL STUDIES.

Post 8vo, price 5s.

CONTENTS.

OLD TESTAMENT.—1. The Lord of Saboath. 2. The most High God. 3. Shiloh—Immanuel—The Lord our Righteousness. 4. The Tree of Life. 5. Caleb, the Son of Jephunneh. 6. The Revolt of Absalom. 7. The Earthquake in the Days of Uzziah. 8. The Psalms of the Sons of Korah. 9. The Authorship of the Book of Job. 10. The Old Age of Isaiah. 11. Three Generations of Jewish Patriotism. 12. The Babylonian Captivity. 13. The Last of the Prophets.

NEW TESTAMENT.—1. The Prophets of the New Testament. 2. Stephen, the Proto-Martyr. 3. Manaen. 4. Simon of Cyrene. 5. St. Paul and the Sisterhood at Philippi. 6. Aquila and Priscilla. 7. The Old Age of St. Peter.

"We have seen few books which will serve more efficiently to give life and body to ordinary people's conception of biblical characters, events, and narratives."—*Literary Churchman.*
"Mr. Plumptre has gone into the byways of sacred history, and has studied them profoundly, ... so that the whole life of its greatest characters and the course and meaning of the divine drama become more luminous in his hands."—*Contemporary Review.*

THEOLOGY AND LIFE.

Small 8vo, price 3s. 6d.

CONTENTS.—1. The Ministry of Great Cities. 2. The Consecration of the Priesthood. 3. Anathema from Christ. 4. Aiming at Completeness. 5. Kicking against the Pricks. 6. The Prophets of the New Testament. 7 Music in Worship and in Life. 8. Our Life in Heaven. 9. The Life of Moses. 10. The Theology of the Book of Proverbs. 11. The Social Ethics of the Book of Proverbs. 12. Dangers Past and Present. 13. The Education of the Clergy. 14. Self-Knowledge dependent on Obedience. 15. The Ordinary and the Marvellous in the Religious Life. 16. The Dangers of the Religious Temperament. 17. The Confessions of King Solomon. 18. Things New and Old. 19. The Shepherds who Feed Themselves. 20. Other Men's Labours. 21. Justification by Faith, and its First Preacher.

APPENDIX.—The Authorship of the Book of Job.

"Vigorous in thought and unconventional in manner, faithful, earnest, and sound in the faith. . . . At once scholarly, instructive, and practical.' —*British Quarterly Review.*

"It is long since we have read a volume of sermons which maintain so high a level of thought, feeling, and expression."—*Theological Review.*

"Earnest, clear, eloquent, . . . adhering to the old formulæ."—*Spectator.*

SUNDAY.   *11*

8vo, price 3d.

"A learned, comprehensive, and singularly candid and valuable treatise."—*Scotsman.*

CONFESSION AND ABSOLUTION.

Price 1s.

THE LAW OF DEVELOPMENT IN THEOLOGY,

AND

RESPICE, ASPICE, PROSPICE.

Two SERMONS. Price 6d.

WELLS CATHEDRAL AND ITS DEANS.

With a Ground Plan of the Cathedral. Demy, sewed, price 1s.

www.ingramcontent.com/pod-product-compliance
Lightning Source LLC
Chambersburg PA
CBHW060512030726
47498CB00004B/919